IN THE
COAL MINE
SHADOWS

IN THE
COAL MINE
SHADOWS

SARAH MARTIN BYRD

Sarah Martin Byrd

AMBASSADOR INTERNATIONAL
GREENVILLE, SOUTH CAROLINA & BELFAST, NORTHERN IRELAND

www.ambassador-international.com

In the Coal Mine Shadows

ISBN: 978-1-62020-631-7
eISBN: 978-1-62020-635-5

All Scripture quotations, unless indicated otherwise, are taken from the King James Version. Public Domain.

Cover Design and Page Layout by Hannah Nichols
eBook Conversion by Anna Riebe Raats

AMBASSADOR INTERNATIONAL
Emerald House
411 University Ridge, Suite B14
Greenville, SC 29601, USA
www.ambassador-international.com

AMBASSADOR BOOKS
The Mount
2 Woodstock Link
Belfast, BT6 8DD, Northern Ireland, UK
www.ambassadormedia.co.uk

The colophon is a trademark of Ambassador

There are so many people who stand by me as I strive to create my stories. First and foremost I dedicate this work to my Lord and Savior, Jesus. Without His guidance I can do nothing. Thank you to my family who stands by me, even though sometimes they don't understand my madness. Thanks to my publishing company Ambassador International, and all the team there. A special thank you to my friend, Jo Martin who many years ago did the first edit on "In the Coal Mine Shadows" and saw its potential. And especially I want to thank my readers for cheering me on, encouraging me to "hurry" and get another book out. Without you my work is but ink on paper. Thank you for breathing life into my stories.

—Sarah

NOTE FROM THE AUTHOR

Over three hundred years ago, coal miners in the colonial village of Midlothian, Virginia, south of Richmond, Virginia, labored in one of the most hazardous work environments men could ever encounter. Crawling on their bellies in damp, rat-infested pits, choking on poisonous gas, they successfully produced the first commercially mined coal in what was to become these United States.

Disasters often embrace these tunnels to hell. Silently, like a lover in the night, toxic air sneaks into the innards of those who dare to venture into the core of the earth. The plight of a miner, some buried alive, struck a chord of empathy and horror deep within me. What would befall the women and children left behind? Who would provide? Families surviving on weekly wages were left homeless after their loved ones had vanished into the bottomless pits.

After visiting the Beckley, West Virginia Exhibition Coal Mine, I knew I had to explore the struggles of a coal mining family. Therefore a plot was born.

In the Coal Mine Shadows is the saga of one such family, the Blackwells. Beckley, West Virginia, provides the landscape of a realistic, early 1900s mining town where place and circumstance push the characters to their fates.

The disaster that hit the fictional Blackwell family only hints at what coal miners all over the world have experienced firsthand.

From the first piece of coal mined out of Midlothian to the last piece that will ever be touched by human hands, I dedicate this novel to every single man, woman, and child who has suffered or died for the cold, dark coal.

—Sarah Martin Byrd

SHADOWS

Out the window, I gaze at the full-moon night
Wind-rustled branches
Cast eerie shadows that
Dance and sway on the ground
It is such a mystical show for my imaginative mind

Bright, sunny day with soft pillow clouds
Standing with my back to the warm, orange glow
I look to the ground
I see myself
But not perfectly
Only an image, a dark silhouette, a shadow

And now another day, another time
Many nights of dancing with scarred images have passed
Memories of bright days
With summertime shadows have dimmed, the waltz has ended

Now old and tired
All I see are hints of memories past . . . Ghost Shadows
I've had them hidden for so long, but now
I'm too weak to fend them off
They're much stronger than
My foggy mind

Troubled soul, please set my Spirit free
It's time for the shadows to become truth
So my weary soul can be put to rest
The battle is finished
The shadows have won.

PREFACE

HAVE YOU EVER DONE A deed so horrible that you never got over it? Oh yes, you know you have, maybe no one but you and the good Lord know about it, but you've done it. In the early hours of morning, you wake in a cold sweat, heart pounding, breaths coming short as you remember the moment you did the unthinkable, the act that would dominate your every waking moment and penetrate your peaceful sleep with demons who laugh and mock you.

My name is Mary Margaret Blackwell Paddington, but everyone just calls me Mame. I was named after my mother, Mary, a mother I would come to detest with every fiber of my being. A woman I believed to be a heartless monarch who drove me to the devastating act that left my life in the shadows, forever shying away, hiding with my deep, dark secret. My sin, a transgression I thought was hidden, a sin I prayed I would silently cradle inside my heart and carry to my grave.

This is my story. It's not for the weak. It's true, it's ugly, and it's me. Hopefully you will glean something positive from my struggles and not make the same mistakes I did. For nothing is ever hidden . . . all things are seen . . . all things are heard.

But if you fail to keep your word, then you will have sinned against
the Lord, and you may be sure that your sin will find you out.

—Numbers 32:23

CHAPTER ONE

BECKLEY, WEST VIRGINIA

1912

THE MOUNTAINS ARE MERCILESS, THE bread of life not coming easy for those men who crawl beneath the mounds, nor for the women and children who anxiously wait day to day to see the coal-blackened face of their husband, father, or son arrive home safely. For those who survive the depths and pull themselves back to the sunlight day after day are a rare breed . . . a clan to be reckoned with . . . a people with exceptional grit, a coal miner.

A day of darkness and of gloominess, a day of clouds and of thick darkness, as the morning spread upon the mountains: a great people and a strong: there hath not been ever the like, neither shall be any more after it, even to the years of many generations.

~ Joel 2:2

A loud, piercing cry broke the silence of the cool spring morning as Mary Margaret Blackwell entered the world on May 1, 1912. She was the fourth child of the Blackwells' soon-to-be seven, as well as the only girl.

"Boys, come in and meet your baby sister."

Henry Blackwell motioned to his sons. Hank, James, and Jared peeped around the doorframe, stealing a glance at their mother, Mary, who lay with the new baby in her arms. They shyly tiptoed into the dimly lit bedroom, mere babes themselves at six, four, and three years old.

"Come closer, don't be afraid. Your new sister won't bite," Mary said ever so softly to her sons.

"Sister? Yuck. I want another brother—take it back."

As usual, Hank, the oldest of the Blackwell children, was the spokesperson for the trio. He bravely stepped forward, leaned over his mama's arm, and looked at the bundled up package. The other two boys followed suit. All three puckered up their faces as if they had just bitten into a persimmon before the frost tamed the bitterness.

"What's its name?" Hank asked. "And why is it so wrinkled up?"

"Hank, don't call your baby sister an *it*. Her name is Mary Margaret. Don't you know newborn babies are always wrinkled?" Mary said.

"Mary Margaret? *Mary*, that's your name, Mama, and *Margaret*? Where did that come from? Sounds too girlie to me," Hank protested.

"Your papa and I named her Mary after me, and Margaret is a strong name, full of character. It means beautiful, like a rare pearl."

The boys shuffled their feet, anxious to get back outside and into the mischief that always seemed to follow them.

Standing on tiptoe, young Jared leaned toward the baby and kissed her on the cheek. "I like her, Mama. She's soft."

"Yes, she is, Jared, and you are her big brother. You're not the baby anymore."

"That's okay, Mama. I don't want to be a baby. I want to be big and strong like Papa."

James eased forward and took Mary Margaret's little hand in his own small one. With a wide grin, his face shown with pride.

"Okay, boys, enough visiting for today, outside with you. Let's let Mama and Mary Margaret get some rest," Henry said.

Hank turned toward the door. "Mary Margaret—yuck."

James quickly let go of his baby sister's hand and mimicked his older brother, "Mary Margaret—yuck."

Jared stayed silent.

Outside, Hank sat down on the flat river rock that served as the front porch step. He pondered a while, picking up a pebble and then tossed it out into the dirt yard. James and Jared stood by quietly.

Hank finally broke the silence. "Mary Margaret. That name just won't do. I ain't calling no sister of mine Mary Margaret."

"Me neither," James and Jared chimed in at the same time.

After a long discussion the boys made their way back into the house and were soon standing beside their mother's bed.

"Mama, Mary Margaret just won't do for our sister's name. It don't rightly suit her. She'll grow up all prissy and mushy with that pearly name. We got something better to call her. Me and James and Jared will be calling our sister *Mame*," Hank said with all the authority a six-year-old could muster.

Having spoken their piece, the trio stomped out, finalizing their decision, without waiting for their mama's response. For days Mary resisted the pet name, but she soon found herself calling the baby girl Mame like everyone else. And so, the life of Mame Blackwell began.

Mame's family lived in a modest home nestled against the shadows of the Appalachia Mountains. Its walls were insulated with pages from the *Beckley Miner's Gazette*. The house was packed with people, beds, food, a coal burning heater, and laughter that always filled the small space with smiles and love. When Henry was home and all the Blackwells were nestled inside their quaint little house, worries of a life of coal mining were forgotten.

In the evenings they tried not to think about Papa leaving for the pits, but it was hard not to when his coal-dusted boots sat by the door mocking them, laughing at their vulnerability and lack of hope for a better life.

If one could see inside the walls of that house and read the words of the Gazette, they would know the truth. Henry Blackwell and every coal miner like him lived a life of back-breaking, deadly labor. Page after page would tell the stories of death and despair, truths laced with sonnets of heartache and hardships for those digging in the ground as well as the ones left at home to worry.

Each ticking moment of every day, Mary waited anxiously for the front door to open. The children felt the strain too, how could they not, knowing some of their friends were now fatherless. Day after day the fear was there, scratching at the door like a coonhound clawing at the base of a tree, trying its best to get to its prey.

There was a satisfied feeling, a lightness when Mame's papa got home. A feeling of relief, knowing she'd have her papa one more day.

At the sound of the door opening, young Mame ran and wrapped her arms around her papa's knees. "Papa, you're home! Will you toss me up in the air?"

"Sure, pumpkin. Just give me a minute. I need to clean up a bit."

Mame never forgot the look of her papa when he came home from the mine. Simply said, he was black. From forehead to fingertips, his skin was tainted with the color of coal. Even his teeth were stained. Only the whites of his eyes shone ghostly against his blackened face.

Mary was always waiting, wet washcloth in hand, when Henry stepped through the door.

"Here, Henry, wipe your face."

After Henry cleaned up, he'd call for his children to come gather around the kitchen table. With Mame snuggled in his lap, he'd open up the pages of the Blackwell Family Bible and read aloud for a short while. After he finished, he always led his children in a song or two.

Mame sang loudly in her papa's ear: *Go tell it on the mountain, over the hills and everywhere, go tell it on the mountain that Jesus Christ is born.* Her brothers got tired of singing the Christmas song all year long and complained, but Mame didn't care, and her papa didn't either because he loved to see the smile on his little girl's face when she was singing.

Those were the good times, the moments to remember.

Mary's concern for her husband's safety grew more urgent every day. As evening approached the children would find her gazing out the kitchen window toward the mine, anxiously waiting the return of the only love she had ever known, her childhood sweetheart.

Nothing good could be said about what was happening in the small mining town of Beckley, West Virginia. It seemed every few days, word came of another daddy dying from lack of oxygen, or a father's head split open by a felled support beam.

Like the pages of *The Beckley Gazette,* those miners were shrouded in darkness. Useless pages, useless lives. It's hard for a man crawling around on his belly like a snake to have any self-worth. Miners were treated no better than a discarded scrap of newsprint filling the space between two walls. The only difference between man and paper was that newsprint helped to keep the cold out, and the men dug coal to help keep the warm in, both white covered in black.

The entire town knew the owners of the coal mines were heartless, having sold their souls to the almighty dollar. Greed can entrap a man. Make him lose his good sense and reasoning. It was as if they tossed men down in those pits like they were nothing more than useless pieces of nasty trash. Those rich mine owners would be thinking a mite different if they were sending their own sons down in the cold, dark earth.

Yes, a man's value, not what's in his pocketbook, but what's in his heart, means a lot more than any riches. That kind of self-worth is hard to grasp while he's crawling around on a cold, dirt-sodden floor with a wooden bird cage dangling over his shoulder. Miners never give names to the doomed fowl because most of the birds, like some of the miners, don't last long in the pits. It's hard to give a name to something you know is going to die.

In a matter of seconds, the invisible attacker can wrap its bony fingers around your neck, smothering you in its deadly grasp. Hour after hour, day after day, a miner's head is always moving, back and forth, back and forth: from the bird to the vein, back and forth, back and forth, bird, vein, bird, vein. A steel pick in one hand, the Word of the Lord tucked in his breast pocket close to his heart. Knowing there would be no time for reading, but feeling its comfort anyway.

While Henry worked as bondsman to the coal, Mary, like all the other women in Beckley, stayed home raising babies and taking ever-loving care of her family. Life at Mame's house was hard, just like it was for all the families who made their living by climbing down into the core of the Appalachian Mountains.

Yes, times were tough, but living it every day made it seem natural, just a way of life. When you're poor, you don't know any better than to think you're wealthy. And, who's to say what rich is, anyway?

That winter of 1919 would go down in the record books as being the coldest in the history of West Virginia.

"Mame, I need you to go down in the cellar and bring up a sack of sweet potatoes. They'll go good with them squirrels your brothers killed this morning."

"Yes, Mama." Young Mame could almost taste the red spuds, dripping with butter and honey. Ready to do as she was told, Mame turned to go out to the root cellar. "You need anything else, Mama?"

"No, just the potatoes."

Mame was too young to know what being proud of someone meant, but she was old enough to know that her mama always kept the house warm and her children's bellies full.

If Mary hadn't tilled that rocky soil, growing fruits and vegetables to can and dry, the Blackwells would surely have starved. Word of mouth spread rumors that some fancy ship named *The Titanic* had sunk and that World War I had just ended; all while in Beckley, West Virginia, families were treading in their own waters just to stay afloat.

Unlike that luxury liner, the Blackwells would prevail. Henry had been able to hang onto one hundred acres of Blackwell land that had been in his family since the early 1800s. The landscape was hilly, so rocky you could hardly find a place to drop a seed, but Mary fared well with her garden of pole beans, summer squash, tomatoes, potatoes, okra, and rhubarb. The white potatoes that grew around the cobblestone were as knobby as Great-Grandma Blackwell's arthritic knuckles. Them taters might have looked tainted, but they sure were good fried up with some wild ramps.

At times the mine at Beckley would shut down for days because of dangerous levels of toxic gas, but Mame and her family seemed to manage, bellies full, house warm. Money wasn't coming in, but Mame and her brothers were thankful to have their papa home. They'd all sit around the kitchen table listening to Mama and Papa tell stories about when they first met and courted and such.

Two more brothers had been born to Mary and Henry since Mame's birth: Timothy and Thomas. Mame had two-year-old Thomas sitting on her knee, trying to keep him quiet so she could hear the stories.

"Mama, tell us about you and Papa growing up together," Mame said.

"Surely you don't want to hear that story again."

"Yes, we do, Mama," Jared said. "Please?"

"Very well then. Your papa and I met ten years before we were married. I was eight and he was twelve. Everyone always said I was born already grown up. I never had time to be a child since my own mama died when I was younger than you, Mame.

"Daddy moved us to Beckley from Pulaski so he could work in the coal mine when I was five and my sister Connie was seven. Mother died of a ruptured appendix, or so the town doctor said. It was hard times, and I missed my mother so much I thought my heart would never hold any more love for anybody. It just hurts too badly when you lose someone you love so much.

"Your papa and I were inseparable. His mama, Mother Blackwell, would invite my older sister, my daddy, and me here to the farm for Sunday dinner. We played tag, hide and seek, fished, caught lightning bugs, and dreamed for hours on end while the grown-ups sat on the porch sharing their own wants and worries."

Mary reached over and took hold of Henry's hand. "Your papa helped fill the void in my life, made my heart feel whole again, and put the brokenness back together."

Mame watched the hands of her mama and papa joined. Their love made Mame's own heart feel full. Satisfied. Blessed.

Blushing to a crimson red, Mary gently slipped her hand from Henry's and continued.

"Maybe that's why we were always together, he was and will forever be my soul mate, my rock, my love."

As Mame listened to her mama, she shifted Thomas around and nestled him up onto her shoulder, hoping he'd drift off to sleep and not interrupt her mama's rememberings.

"In 1904, Connie married and moved to Roanoke. Your papa and I married a year later on May 6, 1905, and moved here into this very house. Back then it was nothing more than a little shack used to house tools and an occasional sick animal. Here on this very property, we began our wonderful journey through life.

"The day after our wedding, my daddy moved back to Pulaski where his brother needed help on his hog farm."

Smiling at Henry, Mary continued, "Daddy said he'd miss me, but he'd rather work in stinking hog droppings than crawl around on his belly for the rest of his life. I can hear him now as he walked away on that bright spring day. *Being a coal miner might pay the mining shack rent, but the suffering and risks just ain't worth it. I've seen enough birds die.*

"I have never blamed Daddy for leaving Beckley," Mary finished.

Mame watched as the whole family sat absorbed in their own thoughts. All of them wishing Papa could escape the coal mine too. A cold chill rushed over Mame. She snuggled the now-sleeping Thomas ever so closely to herself and tried to erase the image of her papa down in the ground, digging toward hell for a bit of coal.

Some had a choice, a different trade, but not Henry. He was born a coal miner right here on this land, and he reckoned he'd die here. Coal mining was his life. His own papa was a miner, and his daddy's pa before him. Coal had a way of wrapping its ebony fingers around you, pulling you in, then squeezing the life right out of you. There was no escape.

One more little one was born to Henry and Mary. They christened him William Wilson Blackwell, naming him after their president, Woodrow Wilson.

Another boy, Mame thought. She had prayed for a little sister, but Mame just figured God didn't have time to hear the requests of a girl from the hills of West Virginia.

Months turned into years, and bit by bit Henry improved the small shanty the nine Blackwells shared. It was obvious that Henry and Mary had an everlasting kind of love. Mame couldn't remember her parents saying a harsh word to each other. They somehow always found something to laugh about, even that year the coal mine was shut down due to extremely high levels of toxic gas. The mine owners would not have shut down then, but the government was becoming more cautious and was implementing new safety rules and regulations.

No one in the family seemed to notice that Mary was very careful to ration the food, always preparing just enough to fill everyone up. Each morning during that worrisome year, Henry set out on foot to find odd jobs. Some days he'd come back with fifty cents or maybe a dollar, but on others he'd be empty handed.

Mame watched as her mother saved every single scrap of food, even the tater peelings, throwing them into a crock to save for soup.

"Mame, don't you tell your brothers what's in this soup, you hear?"

"No, Mama, I won't."

She never told her brothers or papa about the potato skin soup, or about the time she saw her mama skinning what looked to be a fat o'possum. She didn't tell, but she also didn't eat the fatty stew. The boys were none the wiser. They were full and satisfied, so all was well.

Yes, times were hard, but Mame reckoned God did hear her prayers, because He always provided, one way or the other.

Henry went back to work as soon as the mines opened back up in 1922. During that same dreaded year, Mame lost her Grandpa Thomas. Henry's pa died from something the doctors called "black lung."

Henry Blackwell was fully aware of how dangerous the mines were, but where else could a man work in this town and make decent money to support his family?

Many times Mame heard her papa repeat, "A man's just got to do what he's got to do. Sometimes there just ain't no choice."

Mame was aware of the dangers lurking in the mines. Explosions, falling timbers, poisonous gas, and now a demon sickness called black lung. She never forgot the hacking coughs of Grandpa Thomas as he drew his last hoarse breath. Mame knew she would always remember the red blood stains on her grandpa's coal black lips.

The day Thomas Blackwell's body was carried to the hilltop gravesite, Mame looked up at the dark clouds rolling across the crest of the Appalachian Mountains. Suddenly a bolt of lightning nipped the top of one of the highest peaks, and sparks flew. A dark feeling of dread seeped into Mame's belly. Then the haunting clouds dipped closer to the ground, threatening to consume the mourners. The clouds cast an eerie shadow on the entire group, a shadow that would get even darker in the weeks ahead. A shadow that would become a companion no one invited or wanted to keep around.

In a mining town, death was dreaded but soon accepted. There was no time to mourn and little room in the day for grieving. Habits are born from the routines of life.

Most days started out the same for Mame and her brothers. Get up, do chores, eat breakfast, go to school. Their one-room school house was separated into sections by the grade you were in. Mame looked across several rows of seats and saw her oldest brother Hank. He was leaning in close to his sweetheart, Olivia, twirling the tresses of her golden hair.

"Mr. Blackwell, are you having trouble keeping your hands to yourself?" Ms. Caldwell asked.

Mame watched as the teacher, Miss Caldwell walked toward the love birds. "I said, Mr. Blackwell, are you having a problem keeping your hands to yourself?"

Hank sat in a love-struck trance, barely able to pull his fingers from Olivia's hair. "No, ma'am, I mean, yes, ma'am. I know how to keep my hands to myself. I just don't rightly want to."

"Hank Blackwell, until you can learn some respect for me and especially this young lady by not pawing her in public, I think it would be appropriate for you to open your literature book and read aloud a few stanzas of Shakespeare's *Romeo and Juliet*. Start on the first page and I will tell you when we've heard enough."

Mame was not surprised or embarrassed by her oldest brother's actions. She was used to this sort of thing happening. Hank had been trying to woo Olivia since before he knew what love was. Hank had never had eyes for anyone but Olivia. Mame could tell Olivia liked Hank as much as he liked her, but of course it is a lady's prerogative to play hard to get.

Hank had been reading for almost thirty minutes. Mame's head drooped, bored of listening to her brother butcher the sonnets of Shakespeare. Suddenly a loud rumble shook the school house floor, bringing Mame and everyone else in the classroom stumbling to their feet. The sound was like the thunder she'd heard at her grandfather's funeral, except louder, a mightier, growling groan that rattled the glass windows so hard two shattered. The sound vibrated, echoing off the weather-boarded walls of the school room. There was an eerie sense about the sound, as if it had erupted from the core of hell, an explosion, an outburst of evil from the innards of the mountain. It was exactly one month since Mame's grandfather had been laid to rest.

Mame heard the book Hank was reading hit the floor. Then she heard his words of dread. "The mine, there's been an explosion at the mine."

Mame was ten years old.

Chaos and complete confusion marked the next several days in the small mining town. Life was a blur as Mame watched her mama paw at the ground around what once was the opening to the mine. Mary's fingers were as raw as a slab of skinned out beef. Her clothes were torn and would never again look anything but the color of coal dust. Eyes sunken, dark, and downcast, Mary looked barely alive.

Tears streamed down Mame's own face, leaving a white streak through the grit and grim. Her heart broke for her mama, who kept screaming for her lost husband, calling his name over and over again.

"Henry . . . Henry, answer me, Henry! Come up out of there. We've got supper to fix, and William is in need of some sourwood to chew on since he's teething. Henry, where are you? I need you! Henry . . . Henry . . . ."

Minutes turned into hours, hours into days. The first three days that followed the explosion were a blur as smoke, dust, and fumes surrounded the mourners. People moved around with sorrow-glazed eyes, seeming to have no destination in mind, just moving to keep busy. Cries and screams echoed through Mame's head as another body was dragged out of the deep, dark hole and identified. Justin Bell, Marshall Tucker, Otto Bryant . . . Silas Butcher . . .

Mary barely left the entrance of the mine, desperately waiting for some sign of Henry, a shoe, a button, his pocket Bible . . . his body. Every time another man was pulled from the pit, Mary was there, bucket of water and cloth in hand. She'd wipe the coal dust from each man's face. Even when she saw it wasn't her Henry, she'd continue to wipe the miner's face clean of any remnant of the dark earth. She labored tirelessly to rid the men of the hellish color of coal. As the body of each departed soul rose from the ground, Mary's hopes would rise with it, only to be squelched after the first wipe of the rag.

Mame watched and deep down inside her own self, she knew her mother would never get to shed her papa's face of the dreaded coat of black. Her mama would never again get to look into the eyes of her beloved Henry or hold his rough, callused hand. Even at Mame's young age, she had the gift of knowing. Knowing when something was finished, knowing when it was time to stop praying, knowing her papa was gone forever . . . knowing there would be no more tosses into the air . . . no more nothing . . . he was dead.

Papa had said the mine owners swore that the mines were safe, that there was no more gas, that there was no danger. But the owners were wrong, fatally and eternally wrong. After three days of digging, the death count was up to seventy-three.

On the fourth day of searching, the rescue crew knew they had done all they could do. Any spark of hope was extinguished when another ear-shattering explosion rumbled from the depths of the mine.

Mame stood with her mama and brothers by the entrance to the closed tomb when the foremen boarded up the hole. Three men were never found, dead or alive, and Henry Blackwell was one of them. The other two were Manuel Blackburn and Curt Luffman. A man's name should be spoken and not forgotten when he's dead. Standing in the filth and rubble, Mame vowed to never forget . . . to hold close and remember each and every touch of her papa's hand and hide away in her heart every word spoken from his mouth.

Out of the corner of her eye, Mame saw her mama, then her brothers. They were all a mess of dirt, skin, bones, and tears. A feeling of hopelessness pulled at her innards as she longed to see her papa just one more time. But there would be no more one more times. Change was coming; nothing would ever be the same.

"What now, Mama? What are we going to do without Papa?"

"Hush up, Jared. Stop that whining. We'll do what we've always done. We'll get up every morning, put our feet on the floor, and we'll go to work. You hear me, boy? Do you all hear me? Do you?"

Mame listened to her mama and knew by her voice and the look in her eyes that she must have gone a little mad that day. In the years to come, Mame realized it more and more.

Life in Beckley would never be the same. Over one hundred coal miners and twelve rescue workers had lost their lives. Wives were left alone, unsure of their futures. Little children would grow up not remembering their daddies. Those fatherless children were cheated out of seeing the true character of their fathers for themselves. Everything they knew of their daddies would be hearsay and sad memories.

Mary Blackwell was one of those women. She was left to provide for her own fatherless children: Hank (sixteen), James (fourteen), Jared (thirteen), Mame (ten), Timothy (eight), Thomas (five), and little William (who was not quite one).

During the next few weeks of endless funerals, Beckley was filled with grief and despair. Widows and children walked the streets alive and breathing, but inside they were gored out, empty. The Blackwells watched as wagon after wagon left Beckley with boxes filled with all the dashed hopes and dreams of young women who had lost everything. With no one to support them, most were traveling to faraway territories to live with relatives, though some were headed for cities like Charleston and Roanoke, where a woman could find a job in a factory or employment as a domestic servant.

Mary Blackwell never once considered moving. As she stood on her front porch watching wagons piled high with useless belongings disappear to the unknown day after day, she vowed never to leave. Beckley was where she and Henry grew up, fell in love, and started their family. She owned the land that Henry's father had left them. Somehow she would live off the land. She had heard rumors of farmers raising burley tobacco in nearby Bluefield; maybe she would try the new crop herself. After all, tobacco couldn't be any harder to farm than a row of beans. Could it?

After the mine explosion, Mame soon realized that being born the only girl in the Blackwell family would bring her hardships like she never would have ever imagined. How she missed the days of being tossed into the air by Papa.

Echoes of the old hymn riveted through her head . . . *Go tell it on the mountain.* Now the only thing to tell was horror stories, tales of death and dark, smothering mining pits.

God, where are you?

Over the next several months, ten-year-old Mame became woman of the house while her mother set off to explore the possibilities of growing this new crop called burley tobacco.

Mame fed and tended to her youngest brother, William, while her mama had all her other brothers out clearing fields. Mama even had little Timothy and Thomas dragging brush.

"Mama, you're being too hard on the little ones. Can't we all just rest for one day? Look at little Thomas; he's not much more than a baby. Please, Mama, can't we sit and rest for just a little while?" Mame pleaded.

"Rest? There is no rest for those of us who don't know where our next meal will come from. Do you think I enjoy seeing my children's fingers bleeding from grubbing stumps? Do you think I want you in *my* kitchen? The place where I should be cooking your papa's supper?"

Afraid of this stranger in front of her, Mame shrank back. Mama's face was red, and her voice sounded strange, almost foreign. Who was this person? Not the same mama who once sat at the kitchen table telling funny stories and holding Papa's hand!

"We all have to do our part if we are going to survive. Do you hear me, girl? DO YOU HEAR ME?"

Mame was backed up against the stove, trying her best to escape the wrath of her mama. "Yes, ma'am, I hear you."

"We must survive, and you don't do that by dreaming the day away. Get to work! You've got hungry brothers coming in from the fields soon."

Survive. That was exactly what Mary dedicated every waking moment to doing. Even if Henry had deserted her, she still had his children to provide for. Many were the days when Mary Blackwell wanted to give up, but she never gave in to self-pity or let herself dwell on the memories. Dead was dead, and gone was gone.

Mary became a very hard and cold person, a vessel of skin and bones, an empty shell. Something had snapped in her as she walked away from the stench of death at the mine that last day. Blood pumped through her veins, her heart still beat, her flesh was yet warm, but her passion for life died with Henry. What drove her now was an instinct to survive, a will to succeed, to beat the odds, to overcome the unseen.

To hell with these hills of coal that reek of gas, with this mountain that eats people alive. Mary vowed her children would never have to delve beneath the earth for their existence. The once laughing, smiling

Mary became a sad, work-driven tyrant. It was as if she had died right along with Henry Blackwell, and maybe she had, because all that was left was a body with no heart.

Mary's once youthful and caring face became tired and drawn. She never spoke of her husband and forbade the children to do so. It was as if she were angry with Henry for leaving her alone. She felt wrestled down with all the pain and heartache the mountains had laid upon her.

CHAPTER TWO

Having the understanding darkened, being alienated from the life of God
through the ignorance that is in them, because of the blindness of their heart.

~ Ephesians 4:18

THE YEAR FOLLOWING HENRY'S DEATH presented a constant flow of problems for the Blackwells. One of the hardest parts for the children was realizing they had not only lost their papa but also their mama. She'd drawn right up into herself. Sure she was still the hard-working woman she'd always been. But, Mary's mind was not on the usual domestic chores of a housewife. There was always food on the table, but the meals did not come from Mary's loving hands but from Mame's. Mary was more concerned about clearing land than cooking and washing, and all she ever talked about was growing tobacco. Never more did any of them receive a loving pat on the head or peck on the cheek. Her once-coddled children were now nothing more than a group of farm hands.

By the time spring sprouted green, Henry had been gone for nearly a year. Mary had driven Mame and her brothers to the point of exhaustion. The boys had cleared half a dozen acres of rocky soil, and Mame had kept everyone fed, clean, and clothed. Now it was time to plant.

Early on a frosty March morning, Mary packed a few supplies in her saddlebags and headed down to Bluefield. In her right pants pocket was ninety-two dollars, folded over and bound with twine into a tight, thick wad. She could feel its weight on her thigh, but she reached into her pocket just to touch it, to feel it and make sure it was still there anyway. Ninety-two dollars, her and Henry's life's savings. At that moment, she could almost feel Henry's breath on her cheek when he leaned in to kiss her goodnight. Most of that money would be spent that day on tiny black specks of gold called burley tobacco seed. The future of the Blackwell family depended upon nothing more than a thimble full of seeds.

Before daylight Mary rode away, leaving six of her seven children staring after her as she faded into the morning fog. Only little William was left to sleep away the darkness. The rest of the Blackwells had chores, and they knew they better have them done before Mama returned.

By the time Mary arrived at the Feed and Seed store in Bluefield, the afternoon sun was beginning to drop in the western sky. Mary was weary, but she had only one thing in mind: to purchase the priceless seed that would either make her future or be her ruin.

Mary started her thirty-mile journey back to Beckley without so much as a look in the window of the mercantile. There was no time to think about fashioning a pretty dress for herself, and no reason to since Henry was no longer there to look at her. She didn't give buying material for Mame a new dress a second thought either. She hadn't even noticed that Mame had outgrown her everyday dress and had started wearing her brothers' hand-me-down britches and shirts.

Mary hadn't noticed because though she had seen her children, she had not really looked at them. She gave no notice to their hurts, wants, or needs. The only way Mary knew her offspring was around was by the amount of work getting done. To Mary Blackwell, Henry's brood had become nothing more than a workforce, a small army of ants whose only purpose was to keep the queen happy.

Mary returned late in the night. After bedding down the horse, she made her way toward the house. Not used to riding as far as Bluefield and back in one day, every muscle in Mary's body ached as though someone was wringing her skin out like a washcloth.

A lone lantern shone in the window, reflecting the image of one young son. Mary stopped and stared. At thirteen, Jared was looking more and more like his papa every day. For just a minute Mary let herself feel the joy of her years with Henry. For one split second, it felt as if her husband was on the other side of that door, willing her to open it. Reality wedged its way back into Mary's mind when she crossed the threshold and found no husband there, only Jared.

"Hey, Mama. I couldn't sleep until I knew you were home safe."

Mary collapsed onto a chair at the table. She sat motionless for the longest time and then reached into her right front pocket. This time there was no wad of dollars, only a small burlap sack. She eased the drawstrings apart and looked inside at the dots, each not much bigger than a grain of black pepper. Then she stood and went to the cupboard. Reaching high, she pulled down a cup and carried it back to the table. She took the sack and poured the seeds ever so slowly into the cup, being careful not to let even one single seed fall to the plank floor.

"Jared, this is our future." Mary peered into the cup. "I never thought that someday I would hold all hope for tomorrow in a small tea cup."

She held the cup toward her son. "Look, Jared, these seeds are so black they sparkle like onyx chipped straight out of the mountain. Our lives depend on these few grains. They are our only hope, our salvation, and our last chance. I know it's the truth because your papa told me so."

Mary lifted her gaze from the cup to somewhere beyond Jared, seeming to look through him to address the nothingness of thin air. "I know you're right, Henry, this is our one and only chance at survival."

If Jared noticed that Mary had called him by his papa's name, he didn't say so. Maybe he thought his mama was just tired. Mary sat and stared at those magical little beads until her eyes grew heavy. She bundled the seeds back into the sack and laid her head down on her arms; she sat there the rest of the night dozing, head on the table, hand covering the burlap sack.

In the days to come, that bundle would become the Blackwells' master, the driving force that would hopefully see them through to better days.

Jared sat watching his mother sleep for a while before he got up and laid a worn blanket over her shoulders. Jared loved his mama very much, even though she did drive him and his siblings too hard. He knew looking so much like his papa made him special to her. Sometimes he found her staring at him with a hint of a smile on her face. Those were rare times, happy memory times, times to cherish, times that were few and far between.

Over the next several days Mary, and her boys planted the tiny seeds in seed beds the tobacco farmers called plant beds. The earth had been prepared in advance under detailed instruction from

Mary. Days passed and the specks of black sprouted, climbing their way toward the sun. At night Mary, her older sons, and Mame took turns keeping small fires burning all around the seed beds to keep the young plants warm. Early mornings were cold in the mountains. Frost could cover and blacken the new growth way up into late spring.

Mame watched out the kitchen window as her brothers tore pieces of old clothes and blankets to make tents over the seedlings. For six weeks, they tended the plants every night, praying the cold spring air would not curl its icy fingers around the tender plants and choke the life out of them.

Night after night they stood vigil over the strange little sprouts. Hank took the first shift lighting the coal pits, James the second. Then Mame relieved him for a few hours. Jared's turn was next, but most of the time Mary was already up for the day and took his turn. Mary's partiality for Jared did not go unnoticed by anyone.

All her life Mary had heard the night was darkest just before dawn. As she walked around the beds of plants night after night, fanning the warmth under the makeshift tents, she not only saw that darkness, she felt it. She had never been more alone in her life. Thoughts of Henry buried alive in the cold dark earth suddenly smothered her. She struggled to get a deep breath.

Chills rippled up her spine as a shooting star fell to the ground not more than a hundred feet in front of her. Some people might call that a good omen. Mary thought it was just a shooting star. Schoolgirl dreams and wishing on a falling star were gone from her life. Her dreams were now rooted in the land with hard work and survival.

Finally the night vigils were over. All fear of the chilling mist had passed. Now all they had to do was wait until the plants grew big enough to transplant into the fresh-tilled soil. That day couldn't arrive soon enough for Mary. To get ready, the Blackwells dug hundreds of holes, one by one, with a heavy, wooden-handled mattock. It took two weeks, with everyone working every day from daylight to dark, to finish the transplanting. Finally six acres were in the ground.

Skeptical neighbors stood along the edge of the field and watched as the Blackwells took the delicate plants and dropped them into the rich mountain earth. What a blessing it would have been had those neighbors volunteered to help. But no help was forthcoming.

It was no easy feat dodging and moving the rocks from the granite hills. Mary stopped for a second and looked around. Mountains of stones were piled everywhere. It would be a miracle if the seedlings found enough dirt for their roots to latch into the rocky mountainside.

The long hot summer days were quickly approaching. Soon the seedlings were knee high to William. Time to walk each row, hoeing and spreading livestock manure beside each plant. The boys and their mother continued this cycle of hoeing, fertilizing, and pruning all summer. Every day, even on Sunday, no matter if it rained or if the sun blazed hot, they were in the fields.

Hank, James, and Jared got pretty restless doing nothing but work. The boys were fast approaching manhood. Even though Mary drove them hard, some days to the point of falling on their butts dirt tired, they knew their mother was working as hard as they were. Even though she drove them hard, they had formed a new respect for their mama.

Months passed, and harvest day arrived. It was time to start chopping down the tobacco stalks, stacking them in the fields like old-timey Indian teepees. After days of drying in the field, the tobacco started to turn a golden yellow. It was then time to hang it in the barn loft to finish the curing process.

As the last tobacco-laced stick was hung in the rafters that September day, there rang out an earsplitting yell, a mournful groan, a sound that could be heard for miles, echoing through the mountains and into every disbelieving neighbor's home. The sound came from Mary Blackwell as she fell to the ground. This was the first real emotion she had shown in almost two years. For the first time since Henry died, she felt as if she could breathe. The tight knot in her chest was beginning to unwind. She looked up at her family, spread across the now-empty rows like scarecrows. It was as if she were seeing her children for the first time in years.

They were no longer mere youngsters. Even little William, not quite three, helped Mame in the house. They had been fellow workers doing much more than seemed possible. All odds had been against them—a woman and a bunch of kids raising a tobacco crop? Never, the townspeople had predicted. There were even bets placed against them. No one imagined tobacco growing in the hills of West Virginia. But Mary had asked the right questions, done her homework, and taken the chance. She had bought the new burley seeds that were better suited to their cool climate. And it had worked. That wad of ninety-two dollars had turned into what Mary believed was a fine crop of tobacco, one that would soon be loaded into the wagon and ready to sell.

CHAPTER THREE

*He that goeth forth and weepeth, bearing precious seed, shall doubt-
less come again with rejoicing, bringing his sheaves with him.*

~ Psalm 126:6

THE TRIP TO THE TOBACCO market was long, over forty miles.
The hot sun beat down on Mary; sweat clouded her eyesight, making
her tense nerves even more on edge. It took Mary and Jared almost
two full days to get to Charleston. They stopped only during the
darkest part of the night, allowing themselves and the weary mules
time to rest. None of the Blackwell siblings were surprised to hear
their mother was taking their brother Jared with her. As usual, Mame
and her other brothers were left behind to do all the work and look
after the farm.

Mary pulled the mules to a halt as she topped a small mountain
range. Her first glimpse of Charleston, known as the city by the river,
left her astounded. She gazed out across what appeared to be acres
of one, two, three, four, and even five-story buildings lined up row
after row. Straight in front of her, jutting out a story above the tallest
building, was a church steeple. How ironic. Her gaze focused on the
glorified image.

These past couple of years, Mary hadn't thought much about God. Where had He been two years ago when Henry and all the others died? Where was He now? Mary knew the answer. She knew in her heart that God had always been with her. The Alpha and the Omega, from the beginning till the end, through the good and the bad. She just wasn't quite ready to open up that part of her heart that she had tucked Him away in. In all honesty, she was just plain-out mad at Him.

Maybe somehow that steeple was a sign from the Lord, an indication that things were about to change for the Blackwell family.

"Mama, have you ever seen anything like it? So many buildings, and the river, oh my goodness, look at the way it winds in and out all through the town."

Mary turned her gaze from the steeple to her son. "No, Jared, I have never seen the likes of a city this fine before, but if our dreams come true and we can make our living growing tobacco, we'll see this sight again and again. Giddy up, boys, let's go sell ourselves some tobacco."

When Mary pulled her wagon into town, a little yellow kitty sat right in the middle of the street. She had to pull the reins back quick, or the mules would surely have trampled it. Jared jumped off the wagon before it even stopped moving. He squatted down and started calling for the cat to come to him.

"Here kitty, here kitty, come here, pretty kitty."

The cat completely ignored Jared and ran up the street. Following it, Jared suddenly looked down to see that he was walking on a sidewalk made of boards.

"Hey, Mama. Isn't this fancy? In this fine city you don't even have to walk in the dirt."

At the sight of her excited son, Mary felt her heart strings pull tight, smothering the breath right out of her. Jared was her tender-hearted one. God never created a creature this boy would hurt. Not even the time a copperhead almost bit him. He'd had a hoe in his hand, but he just shooed the snake away. He wouldn't even kill a pesky housefly. So much like Henry.

Jared moved toward the cat, bringing Mary out of her precious memories. He caught up with the cat and sat on the weathered side-walk boards, stroking and talking gently to it. Mary hoped his gentle spirit wouldn't be his weakness. It seemed to her that only the tough survive, and sometimes not even the toughest made it.

"Let's go, Jared, you can play with the cat some other time. We've got business to take care of."

"Can I bring him with me, Mama?"

"No, son, I'm sure he's someone's pet. You don't want to take him away from his friends here, do you?"

Jared quickly answered, "No, Mama. I don't want someone to miss him like I miss Papa."

Neither spoke as Jared pulled himself back up on the wagon seat. Their thoughts were hundreds of feet beneath the ground.

Back on their way, Mary didn't have a clue which way to go to get to the market. She reined to a stop when she saw a man in an apron sweeping off the planked sidewalk.

"Hey, Mister, can you tell me how I might find my way to the tobacco buying market?"

The man stopped sweeping and leaned onto his broom. He eyeballed Mary and then glanced at Jared.

"Tobacco market? What you want to go there for? Don't you mean the farmers market? You got produce to sell?"

"No, sir, I need directions to the place where they buy cured tobacco by the pound."

The man scowled, and without so much as a grunt, he turned and went back inside his store.

Mary stopped three more times to ask for directions. At each encounter she was ignored and given the same ill-mannered treatment. Men stared at Mary as if she were crazy. None of them had ever done business with a woman, and they were not going to start now. Everyone knew it was bad luck to bring a woman in on a business deal.

Finally, after hours of driving the streets of Charleston, Mary found the right street. The rest of the day was spent pleading for someone to look at her dried tobacco and make her any kind of offer. No one was interested in dealing with a woman, especially not a stranger.

Jared started to panic. "What are we going to do, Mama? We've done all this work for nothing!"

The truth was almost too much for Jared's young mind to suffer through. It looked as if no one would help them and buy their tobacco. He hung his head.

Jared not only looked like his father, his ways were more like Henry's than any of the others. That was one reason Mary had brought him along with her. He reminded her so much of the husband she still loved with all her heart, the lifemate she would never see again.

Mary's mind raced with all the horrible thoughts from that dreaded day at the mine. She felt as if the weight of all those lives were upon her chest, smothering the life out of her too. What were they to do? Again the Blackwell's fate seemed out of her control.

For the first time since the explosion, Mary prayed.

Hobert Frost's eyes followed the frantic woman as she went from buyer to buyer, pleading for someone to please buy her tobacco. Hobert could see the desperation on her face and even worse on that of her young, pitiful-looking companion. The boy was half-grown and crying like a weaned baby.

Suddenly, a twinkle gleamed in Hobert's eye and a wide, toothy, tobacco-stained grin spread across his face. He casually strolled over to the woman's wagon and reached up and tapped her leg through her long skirt. The woman jumped at his touch. And after a look at him, she scooted over closer to her son.

"What do *you* want?" the woman asked.

"Not so fast there, little lady," Hobert said. "I hear you're wanting to sell this here load of tobacco."

After a moment's consideration, the woman answered him with a stout, "Yes, I do."

"I'll give you five cents a pound."

"Five cents? What did you say? Five cents?" Her shock was evident. "Everybody knows the going price is at least ten cents a pound, or better."

Hobert shrugged. "Take it or leave it, lady. I'm a busy man. I don't have time to waste."

About that time a crow flying overhead caught Mary's attention. She followed its path to the top of a building. When her gaze reverted back to the nasty looking man, a black line of tobacco spit had slipped out of the corner of his mouth and was about to drip off his chin. She shivered involuntarily. No one else in the busy buying yard had paid any attention to her. She closed her eyes. At least five cents a pound would get them through the winter. But then what? Nevertheless, five cents a pound in her pocket was better than hauling a wagonload of tobacco back home to rot.

All the pain and hardships of the past two years flooded Mary's mind. As hot tears scalded her eyes, she raised her head, preparing to accept the man's offer. Through the tears she blinked, trying to focus on the five-cent man. But another face took the place of that man's devilish image. She now looked upon the kindest face she had seen since Henry left for the mines that last morning.

The nicely-groomed older gentleman with the kind eyes was standing behind Hobert, and the look on his face told Mary that he had overheard the conversation. She watched as the gentleman dropped a hand on the shoulder of the bum and spun him around.

"What the—!" the man shouted. "What do you think you're doing, Paddington?"

"First of all, Hobert Frost, I'm giving you a chance to offer this lady a *fair* price, and second, if you don't, I'm giving you fair warning: you'd better get out of my sight. And be quick about it."

Hobert Frost glanced toward the tobacco-filled wagon, then at Jared and Mary.

"I've got a deal working here, Paddington. Leave us be."

"It sounds more like a steal than a deal. Now get out of here before I get really riled."

Hobert turned his back to the man he'd called Paddington and addressed Mary. "Little lady, you taking my offer?"

Before Mary could reply, Paddington spun Hobert around and punched him in the stomach, sending him sprawling to the ground.

"Get out of here, you sorry excuse for a decent man."

Hobert stood up, clutching his stomach. Leering at Mary and Jared before turning a scowl toward Paddington, Hobert turned and stumbled away.

"What'd you run him off for?" Jared hollered, showing more spunk than Mary had ever seen before. "He's the only one who's offered us anything!"

"Settle down now, son. I ran that man off because he is a swindler. Don't fret, I am willing to offer you a fair price for your crop, that is, if it's any 'count."

Paddington stepped to the back of the wagon, pulled the cover away, and lifted out a bunch of tobacco. He flipped it over, pulling the leaves apart and bringing the bundle up to his nose to sniff. Then he reached way down to the bottom of the pile, got another bunch, and went through the same routine. After a thorough examination, Paddington walked back to the front of the wagon.

"Where's your husband, ma'am?" Paddington asked, staring into Mary's face as if she were one of the most beautiful women he had ever laid eyes upon.

Mary frowned and studied him through narrowed eyes. With a spark of her former spirit and strength, she asked, "What does it matter where my husband is? Do you want to buy this tobacco or not?"

Paddington smiled in response. "Son, pull that wagon up the street to the first buyer's table, and we'll weigh it."

Jared picked up the reins and started to snap them against the horses back, but Mary put her hand over Jared's to stop him.

"Wait." She hesitated for a second, pushing a clump of stray hair out of her eyes. "My name is Mary Blackwell, and this is my son Jared."

"Pleased to meet you, Mrs. Blackwell. I am Theodore Paddington. Most people call me Paddy." Turning, he walked toward the buyer's table. Jared looked at his mama. "What do you want me to do?"

All of a sudden the heavy load behind them felt much lighter. "Let's go sell ourselves some tobacco."

"Mama—twenty cents a pound. Is that what he said, twenty cents? Will we be rich?"

Mary didn't answer, she just looked at Jared and smiled a true, heartfelt smile, a smile that started on the inside and showed all the way through to the outside. A smile that reminded Jared of the way Mama used to be, but could hardly remember.

CHAPTER FOUR

And the stars of heaven fell unto the earth . . .

~ Revelation 6:13a

MARY COULD NOT BELIEVE HER eyes as she counted the money. It was more than she had dreamed for—three hundred and sixty-two dollars. A peace came over her like she hadn't felt in years. But truthfully, she didn't know if the feeling came from the profits or from this interesting man called Paddy who had bought her crop. Her mind went in two directions at once. Yes, she was grateful to this man who had rescued her. Then her pride took over, and she was angry, not wanting anyone doing her any favors. Besides, she had earned this money, every single dollar. Maybe one day she'd give this Mr. Paddington more thought.

Thanks to the success they'd had and all the new thoughts that were going on in Mary's head, the two-day ride back to Beckley seemed much shorter on the return trip. To Mary this man called Paddy appeared to be rather wealthy, judging by the way he dressed and the five-story warehouse that sported his name across the front. Yes, this man could probably afford to buy anything he needed or wanted.

Mame was sitting on the front porch shelling peas when she caught sight of the wagon hauling Jared and Mama coming around the bend in the road. Jumping up, she spilled a whole apron-full of field peas onto the planks. But she didn't care. She could already see the smiles on Mama and Jared's faces. All must have gone well. Mama hadn't smiled like that since Papa's death, and it was a beautiful sight to see.

Not a month after the selling trip to Charleston, a letter was waiting for Mary inside the post office at the general store.

Paddington & Company

Dear Mrs. Blackwell,

It was a pleasure doing business with you. I'll be looking forward to working with you on next year's crop.

Sincerely,

Theodore Paddington

Paddy had never handwritten a letter to any of his clients, but he couldn't help himself in this case. Over the next several months, he wrote three similar notes to Mary. She filed them all away with some other important papers in the back of her leather-bound ledger. Out of sight, but not forgotten.

The year passed quickly. That first successful tobacco crop lightened Mary's serious mood a bit, but she was determined to raise even more tobacco the coming year.

By spring, Mary and the boys had cleared a few more acres, and the seed planting started all over again. Nights of fanning the warmth into the young sprouts didn't seem nearly as long as they had the year before.

One lonely night as Mary walked the rows of seedlings, another shooting star—just like last year—split the heavens, bursting into the night sky but never reaching the ground. She remembered last year and knew the shooting star had been a good omen, and now another one. Surely this year's crop would again be blessed. The lonesome nights weren't as smothering as they once were. Visions of Henry still floated through Mary's head, but now there was an occasional glimpse of the man from the tobacco market.

In no time the entire crop was turning a rich golden color as the sun radiated through its leaves. The stalks were cut and fashioned into the now-familiar teepees. Mary was anxious, looking forward to the day they would load the bundles onto the wagon and head back to Charleston. She and Jared again would travel to the big city.

When they topped the final rise before entering town, Mary saw the church steeple jutting up toward the clouds. It rose as a torch, welcoming them to the fair city. Paddy was there that second year, waiting for them just as he would for years to come.

Through the years a comfortable friendship evolved between Mary Blackwell and Theodore Paddington. Every year at Christmas the Blackwells received a box of goodies delivered right to their door—candies, heavy fruit cakes, and toys for Timothy, Thomas, and

William. By the third year Paddy had started delivering the presents himself. Arriving a few days before Christmas, Paddy would spend a couple of hours with Mary then be on his way back to Charleston to spend the holidays with his only child, a son named Clint. Nobody but Mame seemed to notice or even care when Mary took long walks with Paddy up into the mountains behind the house.

Mame often wondered if her mother would marry Paddington since he too was a widower. But whenever it was mentioned, her mother would stomp her foot and sharply answer . . . *never*.

"In my heart, I'll always be married to your papa. Dead or alive, he's still my husband."

CHAPTER FIVE

For unto which of the angels said he at any time, Thou art my Son,
this day have I begotten thee? And again, I will be to him a Father,
and he shall be to me a Son?

~ Hebrews 1:5

IT WAS THE FALL OF 1931 and Mame was getting ready to make her first trip to Charleston. She was nineteen years old and had never been farther than the outskirts of Beckley.

Her brothers Hank and James were both married and had built homes close to the homeplace. The tobacco farm was now a thriving business. Over the past eight years, the Blackwells had cleared more and more land and were farming close to thirty acres. Instead of one wagon traveling to Charleston, they had to use three. Even though they were doing well, Mary and the boys still spent their money wisely—no frills, just roofs over their heads, food on the table, and plenty of hard work. Even though The Great Depression was bearing down heavily on the people of West Virginia, the Blackwells just kept doing what they had always done: work. Tobacco prices were down, but it was still profitable enough to keep the farm and equipment maintained and left sufficient funds to keep food on their tables.

Many of the townspeople who had laughed at Mary for trying to grow tobacco were now making their own living the same way. No one snickered at Mary Blackwell; she was a well thought of and trusted mentor to most of the men in the area.

That fall of 1931, Mary took her entire family with her to market: Hank, James, and their wives, Olivia and Phoebe, as well as Jared, Mame, Timothy, Thomas, and even little William, who was now ten years old.

As they drove into Charleston that brisk afternoon, Mame had a romantic notion that her life just might change forever. She couldn't care less about the tobacco market. What she was in the "market" for was a well-to-do husband. And, of course, he must also be very handsome.

On the other hand Jared, at twenty-two, showed no interest in any of the local girls. He was always at Mary's heels. Nobody really knew if he was protecting her, or if she was looking out for him. Either way, the family doubted he would ever marry because he was such a mama's boy.

Mother and son were never far apart for any length of time. Neither one seemed to mind; their closeness just came natural. It was typical to everybody except Paddy, but he never complained about Jared. Paddy had talked seriously to Mary several times, trying to get her to agree to marry him and move to Charleston, but she'd hear nothing of it. Without her saying it, Paddy knew it wasn't Jared's fault that Mary wouldn't marry again. The boy couldn't help it if he looked just like his father, reminding Mary of Henry every time she looked at him.

Hank had told Paddy one day that Jared was the spitting image of their father, and Mary herself was always commenting on how much Jared acted like Henry.

"Too many memories. Henry is all around me. He's in the land, the farm, and especially in his children. No, I'll never marry again."

Paddy played Mary's words over and over in his mind. He felt he might be too old for courting anyway, much less taking on a new family, so he eventually accepted Mary's decision and resigned himself to enjoying all the time he could share with her.

When his wife Vergie had died suddenly in 1917 from the flu epidemic, Paddy had poured his anger and need for companionship into his business, increasing his worth and reputation far beyond his inheritance. Paddy had all he needed with a housekeeper, a nanny for his then small son, and their stately Victorian home. The simple routine of having a wife around had become a foggy, long ago memory.

CHAPTER SIX

He that worketh deceit shall not dwell within my house: he that telleth lies shall not tarry in my sight.

~ Psalm 101:7

THEODORE PADDINGTON RECOGNIZED MARY'S WAGON coming up the dusty street. She still drove the original wagon that brought her first load to Charleston. As always, the bittersweet feeling of happiness and guilt overwhelmed him. The truth lodged in his throat until he felt he would choke. It had been nine years since that fatal mine explosion rocked the tiny town of Beckley sending all of its townspeople into a tailspin toward the unknown.

Paddington wondered, for the thousandth time, what Mary would think if she knew he was one of the silent owners of that mine. Silent? Oh, yes. Keeping silent had been the death of all those men. If he'd just said no . . . He hadn't felt right about the engineers' conflicting opinions about gas in the mine. Those miners would still be alive if not for the greed of wanting more and more profit.

Added wealth for a few had been a death sentence for over one hundred men. What is the true worth of one man's life? One hundred, one thousand, one million dollars? Paddy shook his head sorrowfully. He knew there was no sum large enough to post for a man's life.

The first year Paddy bought Mary's tobacco, he had given her much more than it was worth. But that had been the least he could do. He felt responsible for the widow and her children. Mary and others in Beckley had put in back-breaking work in an attempt to keep their land and families together.

Paddy had acquired a list of every family who'd been traumatized by the accident and had anonymously made provisions. Omega Drum had her baby the day of the explosion. Some of the older women stayed with her for several weeks. Then when her money ran out and it seemed she had no hope, a wire came from Charleston and with it a bank draft for one hundred dollars. The money came every time Omega needed it. She never knew why, or from whom, but she was eternally grateful.

Paddy made these arrangements through the pastor at Mount Hope Baptist. The preacher man never asked questions, knowing the Lord always used people to make a way for those who believe. Look at poor old Job from the Bible. Most would have given up, but not Job. In the end he received far more than he'd had at the beginning of his misery. Why? Because he trusted in the way of the Lord.

Riding through town, Mame's eyes and ears were introduced to images and sounds she'd never seen or heard before. As far as she could see, stores with huge plate-glassed windows lined both sides of the street. The wagon stopped where Theodore Paddington waited.

"Hello, everyone. Hey, Mary. It's so good to see you." Paddy raised his arms and lifted Mary down from the wagon, kissing her gently on the cheek. "I'm so glad you could bring all your family this year. We'll get you settled in at my house after everyone has a chance to look around."

Across the road, Mame saw the general mercantile with its window display of dresses, shoes, and hats in styles Mame had never seen. She jumped off the wagon and ran across the street, and like a small child pressed her nose to the window pane, leaving an oily smudge.

"This stuff must cost a small fortune," Mame said out loud.

Mary watched her daughter and realized she wasn't a child any more. Right before her eyes, Mame had turned into a fully grown woman who was quite beautiful.

At that moment Mary knew she had neglected her only daughter. In her desperation to save their home and land, she had viewed Mary Margaret more like a sharecropper, farmhand, and kitchen maid than a daughter. Right then Mary decided to splurge and buy Mary Margaret one of those pretty dresses.

"Look, Jared! There's a hat with a feather on it, and it matches that red dress perfectly," Mame called out.

Reluctantly, Mame left the window a few moments later and followed her mother and brothers back across and up the street. They stopped in front of the biggest house Mame had ever seen.

Theodore Paddington turned and addressed the Blackwells. "Welcome to my home."

Again he leaned down and kissed Mary on the cheek.

Since her father died, Mame had never seen this kind of attention showered on her mother. The bitterness that had been building inside Mame for years suddenly surfaced. All those years of staying at the farm, rearing her younger brothers, tending to the house and all the chores—not once had her mother shown her any of the love and attention Mary herself was now getting and probably had been receiving for years from Theodore Paddington. Mame never once received even a simple thank you.

Mame slowly climbed six wide granite steps leading to the veranda where ferns were sitting in every corner and hanging from the rafters. There were also enough rockers sitting on the porch for ten cigar-smoking men to sit while sipping iced tea—or their more preferred shot of brandy.

Paddington opened the thick, dark green door with a key from a heavily loaded ring. Lace fluttered in the side glass windows. Mame let her fingers slide across the frilly material as she entered the mansion. The foyer was much darker than the brightness from outside. It took a minute for her eyes to adjust and then she found herself standing on a thick rug braided with many colors.

Paddington flipped a switch on the wall; light burst forth to illuminate the entire area. The shining globe on the ceiling was much brighter than any lantern Mame had ever used. Shiny topped tables were everywhere, and Mame had never seen so many flowers. Vases of sunflowers, joe-pye weed, and lavender butterfly branches sat on top of crocheted table covers. The dining room at her left glittered with a full table of crystal and china that was bordered in gold trim. Mame had never seen such riches, but she had read about such things in books at school.

To her right was the parlor, where more dark red and green fringed rugs lay. There was enough carved wooden furniture with padded seat cushions to seat a small Sunday school class. Several portraits of what must be Paddy's ancestors were on display—a woman (maybe his deceased wife?), a young boy, and several younger children, plus framed maps, probably plats of his extensive landholdings.

Mame looked around at all the finery and thought: *This is where I belong. I swear I will never go back to my old farm in Beckley. I am finished with being mama's service maid. This life is what I've been dreaming for since sitting on Papa's knee as a youngster. I belong here. I deserve this.*

A plan began to spin inside Mame's head. A web of thoughts formed, and then the answer appeared right in front of her, the perfect prey stood not six feet from her.

Clint Paddington, Theodore's son, had met Mary each year when she'd come to town to sell her crop, but he'd never laid eyes on this pretty young filly. Could she be Mary's daughter, the one she'd kept hidden away, the ugly duckling he'd seldom heard spoken of? Where were the warts? The unsightly hair and crossed eyes he'd envisioned?

Standing right here in front of him was that daughter, whose eyes of green were as pure and perfect as the morning sun. The clear orbs mirrored her soul and bore into Clint with a boldness that shook him to the core. Her golden hair fell from a loose bun pinned at the back of her head, framing her ivory-skinned face. Clint could almost feel the silken strands between his fingers. The floor-length, high-collared dress she wore could not conceal the fullness of her bosom, or the slight curve of her hips, not to mention the tiniest waist Clint had ever seen.

He was unaware of Mary Blackwell's steady gaze, taking in the mutual attraction between Clint and her only daughter. Her lips were pressed together in a straight line before she turned her attention back to Theodore Paddington.

CHAPTER SEVEN

But I say unto you, That whosoever looketh on a woman to lust after
her hath committed adultery with her already in his heart.

~ Matthew 5:28

WITH A DEVILISH SMILE, CLINT Paddington stepped toward Mary,
greeting her with a handshake.

"Has another year passed already, Mrs. Blackwell? It seems like
you were here only a few weeks ago with a crop to sell."

Mary looked up at the tall, well-groomed young man of about
thirty. There was a twinkle in his eye, a spark she'd never seen before,
and a look that only a pretty girl could put on a man's face.

Clint was always courteous and gentle-spirited like his father,
but now Mary could see something different about him; she saw a
bit of rogue in him. As he propped himself against the archway of the
parlor and crossed his long legs, Mary sensed a surge of electricity, a
current of raw human need flowing between Clint and her daughter.
Mary couldn't help but think of Henry.

Clint had not been too keen on women since his fianceé ran off with another man about two-and-a-half years earlier. Since then he'd guarded his heart and vowed never to let another woman get close enough to hurt him. He'd felt the sting of betrayal and would never put himself in a position to experience that kind of pain again.

Breaking the uncomfortable silence, Mary spoke. "Clint, this is my daughter, Mary Margaret."

"No, Ma, that's Mame," young William said with resolve. "You know Mary Margaret is her girlie name."

Clint laughed, a robust, hearty chuckle that shook his entire body. Composing himself, he approached the most beautiful woman he'd ever seen. "My pleasure meeting you, Miss Mary Margaret, or may I call you Miss Mame?"

With a low bow, Clint took Mame's hand in his. Ever so gently, he drew it to his lips and kissed the top of it.

Mame snatched her hand away from him with a quick jerk. Her heart raced like a wild pony bucking and pounding his hoofs into the rich mountain earth, trying to free himself from the shackles of captivity inside her chest. What was she so afraid of? Maybe the fact that this was the first kiss of any kind she had received since those adoring long ago pecks from her father.

Clint, being accustomed to charming women, was addled by her sudden reaction. He took a step back from Mame. Surely this magnificent woman couldn't be cold and heartless like his fianceé had turned out to be. What a waste of a fine woman that would be if she were.

Little did Clint Paddington know that he had just ignited a flame in Mame that life, heartache, or time would be unable to extinguish.

Mary broke the uncomfortable silence. "Paddy, do you mind if we get settled in? This trip gets harder and harder on me every year."

Hoping to separate the young people as soon as possible, Mary shooed her clan toward the stairs.

"I understand," Paddy said, stepping toward the kitchen. "Mrs. Gentry, can you come out here?"

"Well, looky there, it's Mrs. Blackwell. How you doing?"

Wiping her hands on the green apron tied around her waist, the housekeeper offered her hand to Mary. Jettie Gentry had cooked and cleaned for Paddy ever since before Virgie Paddington, Clint's mother, had died.

Pulling Jettie into a warm hug, Mary spoke, "I am doing good, Jettie. How is your family?"

"Oh, gracious me, they're doing just fine. Grand-young'uns everywhere and into everything, and I do mean everything. And, you can't ever fill them bellies up neither."

"Jettie, you've never met my daughter, Mary Margaret, or my two daughters-in-law, Olivia and Phoebe. I believe you know the older boys. These are my young sons, Thomas, Timothy, and little William." Mary motioned to each, and they shook Mrs. Gentry's hand.

"Ma, I am not little any more. I was ten last month." William turned and looked at Mame. "Tell them, Mame! Tell them how strong I am and how I help you all the time with heavy stuff."

Mame looked toward William. With her attention focused on Clint, she had barely noticed her little brother was even talking to her. Her heart pounded so loudly all she could hear was its beat. Mame walked over to William and tousled his curly red hair. She felt an easy tenderness for this boy, the child she had raised.

"Yes, William. You are a very big help. I couldn't do all the chores, gardening, and housework without you."

Beaming, William proudly walked away from the group to look out the window.

Paddy laughed, clearly delighted to have Mary and her children in his house. With a cheerful smile, he spoke to his housekeeper. "Mrs. Gentry, would you put the ladies upstairs as we discussed? Men, you can follow Clint out back to the guest house. I think you'll have plenty of room. After you've all rested, we'll have dinner."

The evening meal was like nothing Mame had ever seen or tasted. There was a rich, creamy chicken soup; bowls of vegetables, some of which she could not name; tiny round cabbages called Brussels sprouts; several baskets of bread placed along the table; and a half a dozen kinds of sweets. The strangest thing was an entire pig in the middle of the table, head and all.

"What is that? Yuck," the ten-year-old boy declared. "Mama, there's a pig on the table."

"William, mind your manners," his mother said.

"I'm not eating a hog's head. You can just forget it," William said, holding his hand over his mouth.

"Come, Master William. I've got something in the kitchen I think you'll like better," Mrs. Gentry said.

Taking his small hand, she led him toward the half door that separated the rooms.

The remaining time at the dinner table was peaceful, and appetites were satisfied by all the tasty food. The pig's head would probably have made Mame sick too—that is, if Clint hadn't been sitting beside her with his leg occasionally grazing hers and his scent reminding her of one of her favorite places, the pine grove near the farmhouse. His essence filled her senses. Then he was leaning closer . . . his breath so close it tickled her ear. These new feelings made Mame's head spin like a child's toy top, spinning, tumbling, and reeling out of control.

Dinner ended, and with it, Mame's torture. The hour was late. At the farm everyone would be going to bed, but not here, not in this mansion, not here with these rich folks.

"Why don't we retire to the study and have a nightcap?" Paddy suggested.

"It's getting late, Paddy," Mary replied. "We've had a long day."

"A little brandy and small talk will be such a pleasant ending to a very special day. It's wonderful having your entire family here. We're finally all together. Yes, it's a special day, a special day indeed."

Mary could see the longing in Paddy's eyes. He wanted so much more than she could ever offer him. There was no room in her heart. Even after all these years, it was still full of Henry. Every waking moment he was there; even her dreams were of him.

Mary hated to disappoint Paddy. "Maybe just a few minutes, and that brandy sounds good."

Turning to her family, Mary said, "You can all turn in if you want to, I'll be up in a few minutes. We all need to be fresh and alert for tomorrow's tobacco sale."

No one argued but instead headed upstairs. When Mame was halfway up, she sneaked a glance back over her shoulder. Clint was not pretending to sneak a look. His bold stare took Mame's breath away. Though his eyes spoke a language she was not yet familiar with, her instincts screamed surrender.

Mame lay awake for hours that night. Thoughts of things she'd never even dreamed of made their way into her head. Pretty dresses, silk scarves with matching gloves, red dresses, expensive rugs, fancy meals, and, the most important, the way Clint Paddington made her feel.

But lurking in the back of her mind was a picture of her mother and Paddy down stairs sipping wine together.

Mame finally went to sleep, but she was restless. All night she dreamed of trying on pretty dresses and of Clint taking them off.

CHAPTER EIGHT

Nevertheless, to avoid fornication, let every man have his own wife,
and let every woman have her own husband.

~ 1 Corinthians 7:2

MAME WOKE THE NEXT MORNING long after sunrise. At the farm she would have already cooked breakfast and had the dishes washed, but not today. This morning someone else was going to serve her. There would be no cooking or cleaning for her today. All Mame wanted to do was lie right where she was, inside the folds of the softest sheets she had ever lain on.

She watched the sun filter through tiny holes in the white eyelet curtains. Glancing above her head, she took in the matching canopy. Such elegance was foreign to Mame. The bedroom had been designed for a daughter that Theodore Paddington never had. Mame stretched and rolled from one side of the bed to the other, reveling in the fluffy softness of the big feather bed. She knew she was spoiled after this one night.

Images of her handmade half-bed at home came to mind, but she pushed the vision far back to the part of her mind where things she didn't want to remember stayed hidden . . . things like explosions and death. Since her papa had died, she'd filled that part of her brain with lots of hurts and worries.

The aroma of breakfast wafted upstairs, filling her nostrils but not her belly. Her stomach growled. Stretching, she rolled over on her stomach to linger in bed just a few minutes longer.

A soft noise drew Mame's attention toward the door. Who but Clint Paddington would be standing there, peeking through the crack where the door hadn't shut all the way?

"You going to get up today, Miss Mame?"

Mame felt embarrassed seeing Clint after the dreams she'd had of him that night.

"What are you doing there?" Mame pulled the covers up under her chin.

"Watching you. You look like a sassy, old mama cat all sprawled out, stretching in the morning sun."

"Well, as you can see, I am not a cat, nor was I sprawled out. I was simply trying to get out from under all these silly covers. And why does a person need a bed with a cover over it? It's not likely to rain inside the house."

Mame realized her nerves were making her ramble, so she shut up and just stared at Clint.

Mame wasn't afraid of him; actually she wanted him to stay, maybe even come closer. But she had to pretend to be a lady even if she didn't feel like one just now. She was enjoying the way he looked at her.

Stepping all the way inside the door, Clint leaned against the wardrobe. "You want to go riding with me today?"

"If you mean a buggy ride, I might. I don't ride horses."

"You don't ride?"

"No one ever had time to teach me."

"You don't ride horses?" Clint shook his head with a wry smile. "I thought you were a country girl. I'm sure I can find the time to give you a few lessons. Get yourself up and out of that bed now, daylight's a-burning. Breakfast has been cleaned up a good while, but we might find you a cold biscuit. By the way, there's a riding suit that should fit you in that armoire. Put it on. A dress ain't quite suitable for horse riding. It would be a shame if you got bucked off and all them skirt tails flew over your head."

Mame watched Clint slowly back out of the bedroom, pulling the door shut, never once taking his eyes off her face until the door was completely closed. She imagined his long legs sauntering down the hall, boots sinking deep into the thick ruby red carpets. He was clearly full of himself. She would just play it cool until she had time to completely figure him out.

Like a movie, Clint's mind re-ran the scene. Creamy mounds of flesh exposed at the top of Mame's thin, white-cotton nightgown. Manners hadn't mattered once he'd seen her door ajar. Instead, he'd taken liberty to peek. Maybe it was her youth and innocence that were so appealing. It was rare to find someone virtuous and naïve in a town as bustling as Charleston. But Mame wasn't from here; she was from the country. For a second Clint was sorry she wasn't one of the town girls. He'd really like to go visit with her tonight.

Oh, what the heck, Clint thought. *I'll have a little innocent fun with her anyway.* Clint's stride was confident as he bounded down the steps.

Mame slipped her feet over the side of the bed and felt a little twinge of guilt. Had Clint seen too much of her while standing in the doorway? Realizing that Clint seemed to like what he saw, she blushed hotly with sinful pride.

Intimacy was foreign to Mame, except for watching her brothers flirting with their wives. She knew there was something familiar yet physical between a man and a woman. Something happened during mating that bonded them together emotionally for life. Unlike the farm animals she had watched, humans were meant to have only one mate. If Mary Margaret Blackwell had her way, her life companion would be the man she had last cast her eyes upon.

CHAPTER NINE

*And if thine eye offend thee, pluck it out: it is better for thee to enter
into the kingdom of God with one eye, than having two eyes to be
cast into hell fire.*

~ Mark 9:47

OPENING THE ARMOIRE, MAME WONDERED whose clothes
these were. She touched the fabric of a jade green jacket. Hanging
beside the jacket was a pair of pants the same color.

Mame had never worn such fine trousers, just her brother's hand-
me-downs. She pulled the clothes off the hangers and slipped them
on. The breeches were snug across her bottom, while the waist gaped
loose. The jacket was a total misfit. Across the bosom, the buttons
didn't even come close to reaching the holes.

Mame turned from one side to the other looking at herself in the
mirror and wondering what to do.

She again reached into the cedar closet and separated each article
until she saw, hanging toward the back, what appeared to be a man's
white, button-up shirt. She snatched it out and pulled it on. The shirt
was as much too large as the riding jacket had been too small. Still,
she rolled up the sleeves and tied the tails around her tiny waist.

A glance in the full-length mirror showed what might have passed for a cowboy, save for the long, curly hair falling over Mame's shoulders and the tell-tale signs of womanhood beneath the pants and shirt.

Mame slipped on and laced her old shoes. She pulled her hair back, knotting it into the unfashionable bun that she usually wore. Then she took the cloth that was lying beside the water basin, wet it, and rubbed her face with it until her cheeks had a rosy glow. She had become accustomed to the freckles that speckled the bridge of her nose, proof of the long hot hours spent working in the sunshine, tending the vegetable garden and tobacco field.

Have mercy, how Mame hated working in tobacco. Gummy hands, hot sweat running down every crevice, and those fat, juicy green worms that loved to eat the tobacco leaves.

Mame knew her mama hated those things. Every inch they ate meant less weight and less money. It was William and Timothy's job in the summer to walk the rows and look for the slimy green creatures and squash them. Of course, they poked more than one in Mame's face to scare her. Those worms were nasty but not scary. A slimy worm was the least of Mame's worries. How to get away from a hellish farm life was her main concern.

All that hot, spiteful work could very well soon be over. Maybe her freckles would fade in time. Who ever saw a real genteel lady with freckles?

Mame sat down on the edge of the bed, her head filled with fantasies. *My days of working in the scalding sun are over. I will soon be the one waited on. No more dirt under my fingernails, no water buckets to carry, and no more pole beans to pick.*

Mame felt cheerful as she finished lacing up her shoes. She strutted out the door and down the hallway to the top of the steps. All was quiet; no one seemed to be around. Everybody was probably down at the tobacco market.

Where was Clint? Hadn't he been in a hurry to get going?

She grabbed the stair railing and sashayed downstairs, determined to maintain her dignity despite her odd fashion.

About the time Mame hit the bottom step, Clint came out of the kitchen. Looking up, his lower jaw dropped. All he could do was stand there and gawk at the transformation of the woman. There was no questioning the long shapely legs and roundness of her hips. The neckline of the oversized man's shirt that she wore was open enough for him to see ample cleavage. His insides churned.

Mame stepped down from the last stair and walked toward Clint, stopping only inches in front of him. She had no idea what she was doing to him, he knew, as she boldly stepped closer.

Reaching up, Clint pulled Mame's hair combs loose, freeing her mane. It tumbled down her back in a mass of curls. This time, she did not flinch at his touch. He grasped a curl between his fingers and felt the silky softness of it. It took all the willpower he could muster not to crush his lips to hers.

Instead he snapped. "Bind your hair back up and get yourself some breakfast."

Mame's heart pounded, her knees were weak, and a hot, sensation started burning low in her stomach and slowly working its way down into parts of herself she didn't even know she had.

As she took back the combs Clint thrust toward her, he said, "Hurry up. I'll be waiting outside at the barn."

Clint had no sooner slammed the front door than Mrs. Gentry appeared from the kitchen. "Would you like me to warm you up some breakfast, Miss Mame?"

Shaking distraction from her mind, Mame slowly turned toward the voice.

"No, no, thank you. Just coffee and maybe a sliver of that blueberry pie from last night if there's any left."

"Come right on in here to the kitchen, child, and I'll get that pie for you. You sure you don't want some red-eye gravy and a biscuit?"

"No, ma'am. Coffee and the pie will be plenty."

"Land sakes. Young ladies of today don't know what a man likes; he wants a woman with some meat on her bones, don't you know that, Miss Mame?"

Following Mrs. Gentry into the kitchen, Mame didn't answer the matronly maid; she hadn't really even heard what she'd said.

She readjusted the combs in her hair and then sat, drinking her coffee and slowly eating her pie. She was anxious to get out to Clint but knew she needed to make him wait. She took her own sweet time, then gave into her restlessness and left the table, heading toward the back door for the stables.

When she arrived, Clint pushed away from the stable wall and said, "Took you long enough. What'd you have to do, wait till the chicken laid you an egg?"

CHAPTER TEN

This I say then, Walk in the Spirit, and ye shall not fulfil the lust of the flesh.

~ Galatians 5:16

CLINT PICKED THE GENTLEST MARE they owned for Mame. He slowly and purposefully positioned his hands around Mame's tiny waist, amazed at her hourglass curves, and hoisted her up into the saddle. Then he gave her a few simple instructions before mounting his own black stallion. Mame's first attempt at riding went pleasurably well. Because she was concentrating on keeping her balance, the lesson helped take her mind off the obvious.

Soon they were on their way, trotting down the oak-lined drive called Paddington Avenue. They rode past larger homes onto a smaller side street made of river rock until the houses became sparse and the town was far behind them, no more than a dot on the landscape.

Reining their rides into an open pasture, Clint clicked to his horse, and it began to trot. Mame's followed suit and after almost an hour, Mame's unconditioned backside was feeling the effect of pounding against a hard saddle.

"Hey, Clint, how about we rest for a while?"

Reining his horse to a halt, he waited on her. "We're almost to Elk River. We'll stop there so the horses can have a drink."

Sure enough, before too long Mame heard the swift current. This had to be more than a gentle flowing stream. Then Mame saw the river. It flowed from behind a stand of trees at the top of the hill and cascaded about fifty feet downward, creating a breathtaking waterfall. Clint jumped off his horse and went directly over to Mame and lifted her down from her perch. Again, his hands lingered.

Mame's inner thighs and backside were so numb it felt like stinging bees were invading her flesh. She walked unsteadily, stomping her feet until the circulation was restored. Mame cared not that she looked like a duck waddling around. She was sore and more than a little irritated that Clint had made her ride so far for her first lesson.

She had to admit the view of the waterfall actually was worth the pain. She had seen smaller falls dropping off the mountaintops back home, but nothing this magnificent. The roaring strength of it was almost deafening.

Clint grabbed an old blanket from his saddle bag, and the two headed down toward the riverbank. The horses followed beside them, neighing and kicking up their heels, happy to be free of human weight and ready for a drink of cool water. Clint spread the blanket out on the ground and sank down onto it.

Mame sat arranging herself on the opposite side of the spread. Being this close to Clint, she was beginning to have that new yearning again deep inside her.

"How old are you, Mary Margaret?"

"How old are you, Clint Paddington?"

"Old enough to know better than to be out here alone with a pretty young thing like you."

With that, he stood up, pulled Mame to her feet, and started walking toward the waterfall. The closer they got, the thicker the spray was, wetting their skin. Moisture clung to them like sweat on a hard-working day. Mame wanted to pinch herself to make sure she wasn't back home in the tobacco field.

Then Clint disappeared as he sidestepped behind the wall of water. She followed him and saw the opening.

"How did you find this place?" Mame asked, thrilled.

"This has been my secret hideaway since I was a young boy. I come here to think, to plan, and in my younger days even to fool around with a pretty girl now and then. I soon found out most ladies don't appreciate being wooed in a damp, dark cave like this. So most of the time, I just come here alone to skinny dip."

Acting as if he were all alone, Clint started unbuckling his belt. Then he pulled his shirttail out of his britches, unbuttoned it and pulled it off. Mame's eyes bore into the broadest expanse of chest that she had ever seen. Living with all brothers had not prepared her for what she was about to see. His thick, dark chest hair trailed down his torso toward his waist. Mame watched as he then started unbuttoning his pants. She was so stunned she lost all her inhibitions and continued to stare.

"You'd better turn your head, little girl, unless you want an eyeful."

Mame didn't turn her head because an eyeful was exactly what she wanted to see.

She didn't flinch as he yanked off his boots. Turning, he then pulled his faded dungarees down over his narrow hips and off, giving her a full view of his backside.

When Clint turned to face her, the awkwardness of the situation made Mame's eyes trail from his lower body upward to his face. Boldly their eyes locked. Mame made the decision in a split second, a choice that would change her forever. She realized that if her life was going to be different, then she'd have to take control of her destiny. Her future stood right in front of her, and she couldn't miss this one-time opportunity, a chance she may never have again. She felt strong and knew she could be just as brazen as he. Suddenly, thoughts of sitting in her papa's lap flooded her mind. Bible verses flowed like a river through her head. *There are seven things that the Lord hates . . . a heart that devises wicked plans, feet that make haste to run to evil . . .*

Trembling, she shut down the noise in her head and slowly untied the knot at her waist and started unbuttoning the bulky material of her borrowed shirt. Each button felt as if it were on fire, scorching her fingers with unknown desire.

Clint shook his head, trying to clear it of this vision in front of him. Where had the innocent little kitten from this morning gone? For now, he was positive this was a fully grown tigress waiting to pounce on him.

"What are you doing, Mame?"

"I'm going skinny dipping with you. My brothers have always done it, but I was never allowed. Now no one is here to stop me."

"No, you're not, little lady. Put your clothes back on. You don't have any idea what you're getting yourself into."

Turning, Clint walked right through the falling water. In a second he had disappeared through the wet curtain and under the water's rippling surface.

Suddenly she was behind him, coming up through the water, molding her body to his.

CHAPTER ELEVEN

Be not deceived; God is not mocked: for whatsoever a man soweth,
that shall he also reap.

~ Galatians 6:7

"MAME? I'M SORRY—I THOUGHT BY the way you were acting—that you were experienced. I would never have taken you, had I known."

Clint felt unnerved. Who had taken whom? He should have stopped, he knew better, but he'd been too far-gone to quit.

"Get your clothes on," he said.

He grabbed his pants and dressed with his back to her. Mame took her time, drying off as best she could. She had to admit she too was a bit shaky. She couldn't believe what she'd let happen, even encouraged . . . and with an almost complete stranger. Those verses rattled through her head again, *a heart that devises wicked plans.* But she truly believed she'd done what had to be done to secure her future. Mame could only hope he'd be an honorable man and marry her. Surely that would satisfy God.

The ride back to town seemed to take twice as long, especially in damp clothes. Not one word was exchanged between Mame and Clint. Both were lost in thoughts of their own. The happenings of the past hour rolling over and over in their minds.

Clint felt about as low as a yellow-bellied sapsucker, and Mame—what must she think of him now?

What in the world have I done? I've taken the innocence of my father's best friend's daughter. I don't even know this girl.

Slowing his horse's pace, Clint let Mame go on ahead of him. He watched her lovely backside bounce up and down on the saddle.

What was she thinking . . . what is she thinking now? Does she even realize what just happened?

Mame's thoughts were running wild; she knew exactly what she had done, even though she hadn't planned on it happening so soon. Maybe she should have played a little harder to get. Oh well, regardless of the timing, she had just insured herself a place in the midst of the Paddington clan. No more Beckley. No more being a slave to back-breaking chores. No more tending to little brothers.

Reaching the stable yard first, Mame jumped from her horse before Clint had a chance to lift her down. Soon he was beside her. As he guided their horses into the barn, Clint reached out and took Mame's hand.

"Listen, I'm sorry if I hurt you. By the way you were acting, I had no idea you'd never been with a man."

Mame looked up at him and burst into counterfeit tears. She jerked her hand from his and ran toward the house. She flung open the back door to the kitchen and came face-to-face with her mother, Paddington, and both of her sisters-in-law. Dashing past them, Mame ran up the stairs into the room where she had spent the night. She threw herself sobbing on the bed. The act was so real she almost convinced herself she was distraught. But she knew her tears were not sorrowful, but drops of joy.

"What was that all about?" Paddy asked. Mary started to follow Mame upstairs.

"Leave her be," Clint said, standing just inside the back door. "Dad, Mrs. Blackwell—I need to speak with you alone."

Clint quickly walked to the library with Mary and Paddy trailing behind him.

"Is Mame hurt?" Mary asked.

"I don't think so," said Clint, "at least not physically."

"Well, what's wrong with her then?" Paddington asked. "This morning you said you'd be glad to show her around town. Where did you go?"

"Out to the waterfall, Dad."

"So what happened?" Paddington asked.

"Well, I decided to go for a swim, and then Mame did too. One thing led to another, and it . . . just . . . happened."

"This is my fault!" Mary exclaimed with a hand on her flushed cheek. "I should have spent more time with Mame these past years, I should have explained things to her. I thought I had more time. She's never even had a suitor!" With a stricken gaze at Paddington, she said, "We—must leave. I'm going up to the buyer's market and find the boys."

"Mary—hold on. I know Clint's sorry for what he's done. I can see the remorse on his face. In the morning it won't look as bad as it seems. You know how emotional young girls can be."

He approached Mary, but the look she gave him caused him to stop beside his roll top desk and absent-mindedly straighten some papers. "We can talk this through, figure it out," Paddy said soberly.

But Mary had seen the look in Mame and Clint's eyes. She knew exactly what they'd done and knew it would happen again. She needed to get her family back to the farm before she lost complete control of Mame and their way of life.

"We must leave immediately. We'll get rooms at the hotel until our business is finished. I'll be back shortly with everyone to gather our things."

Mary left the library and went out the front door. The slamming of the heavy portal riveted through Paddy's head like a door had been closed in his life forever.

Paddy sat heavily in his worn leather chair. His shoulders slumped as if he were aging before Clint's eyes.

"Clint, we've hurt them again. What am I going to do?"

Paddy took out his handkerchief and dabbed at his teary eyes. His mind was filled with memories of long ago. A great sadness came over him. It never occurred to Paddy to blame Clint; he had brought all these problems, past, present, and the future, on himself. Re-opening the mine all those years ago was the worst decision Theodore Paddington had ever made, and that choice would haunt him to the grave and probably beyond.

"For years I've carried this guilt. I am the one who kept silent. I could have voted no, and the mine would not have opened back up. I didn't know how dangerous it was. I took the word of my partners, the ones who should have known what they were doing. They were the experts in coal mining; I'm a tobacco man. But I should have pushed for more testing . . . waited longer for the gases to go away. That explosion killed Henry Blackwell, along with all those others, and there isn't a thing in the world I can do about it." Paddy's head dropped even lower. "Over the years, I've tried to make it up to all the families who lost their husbands and fathers. I've helped them all, especially the Blackwells. They're special to me." He raised his head to meet Clint's gaze. "Since that first meeting with Mary, I knew she was a woman of strength and character, a lady worth knowing and calling friend. We've grown to become more than just acquaintances. I have a deep respect for Mary, but now I have once again turned her and her family's lives upside-down."

Clint dropped a hand on his father's shoulder. "Dad, you didn't have anything to do with this. I did it, and I'll take responsibility for it."

With that, Clint went out the front door in search of Mary Blackwell. He didn't notice that Mame had sneaked down the stairs and was hiding behind the library door.

Mame watched as Clint left the house. In her head she replayed the conversation she had just overheard. Theodore Paddington was the cause of her father's death. He was the one responsible for her not having a father and a normal life for the last nine years. Not to mention the cause of her mother's unhappiness and heartache. Mame felt pain as she dug her nails into her clenched hands. She trembled, both inside and out. She shook all over, and sweat dotted her upper lip.

In a low murmur she repeated over and over, *He will pay . . . he will pay . . . he will pay. Theodore Paddington will pay. Some way, somehow, I'll make him suffer as we have.*

Mame stepped quietly from behind the door and tiptoed back up the stairs, all the while running her fingers over the polished mahogany wood of the banister. All around her were fine things . . . overhead a great chandelier . . . pictures and paintings on the walls . . . soft rugs beneath her feet. She could already feel their wealth seeping into her deprived life.

Before, all she had wanted was to hook Clint Paddington for a husband. But now she wanted *all* the Paddingtons had, including her revenge. Everything would never be enough to replace all the Blackwells had lost or . . . so freely given away.

CHAPTER TWELVE

*Is any sick among you? let him call for the elders of the church; and let
them pray over him, anointing him with oil in the name of the Lord.*

~ James 5:14

MARY BEGAN GATHERING UP HER family. They had been enjoying the day, wandering through the town, and planning a picnic.
Clint hurried after them, for once at a loss for words and confidence.
He nearly ran into Hank, who was coming in the opposite direction
on the sidewalk.

"Who do you think you are, taking advantage of my little sister?"
The oldest of the Blackwell boys, Hank stood nose to nose with Clint.

"If you haven't noticed, your sister isn't so little. I shouldn't have
let it happen, but it did. I'm sorry that I can't take my actions back."

Mary was quickly approaching the two. She could see the confrontation was about to get ugly. Phoebe and Olivia trailed behind her.

"Mrs. Blackwell, I'm so sorry."

"Well, sorry don't get it," Hank said as he drew back his fist and
threw a quick punch into Clint's lower abdomen.

Clint doubled over but didn't go to the ground. "Dang, I deserved
that," he mumbled. He coughed until he got his breath back.

"Stop it, Hank!" Mary said. "Let's get Mame and go. Fighting won't fix this."

"No, but it will make me feel a whole lot better."

Hank raised his fist again, this time aiming for Clint's nose, but Mary grabbed her son's hand, pulling it down and leading him away from Clint. Hank knew better than to disobey his mother.

The Blackwell clan was quiet as they walked down Second Street, up the hill, around to the right past First Street, then on to Main and back to the Paddington house. Clint followed, but not too closely.

Mary was in such a hurry to collect her things from Paddy's house that it never occurred to her to knock on the back door where she always entered. The elegance of the formal front entrance always unnerved her, making her feel too much like a guest, instead of a friend. Opening that back door, she immediately saw the unconscious body of Paddy lying on the kitchen floor.

"Oh!" Mary cried.

Clint pushed the others out of the way. "What is it? What's wrong?" Then his gaze fell to where his father lay crumpled on the floor. Theodore Paddington had battled a weak heart for years, and it looked as if that heart had taken all it could stand. Clint knelt beside him. "Dad. What's wrong? What happened?" He pressed a hand to his father's chest and issued orders over his shoulder. "Somebody get Doc Stuart. His office is down Main beside the drugstore. Hurry."

James turned and raced toward town. Mary did a quick assessment of the situation—no bleeding, no bones protruding, and he was still breathing—so all she knew to do was sit on the floor by his side, hold his hand, and quietly beg Paddy to wake up.

Clint paced back and forth on the polished wooden floor.

"What is taking Doc Stuart so long?" Clint said to no one in particular, just as the door opened to reveal James with the doctor.

Doc kneeled, doing a quick head to toe exam. Finally he clicked the clasp closed on his worn, black bag.

"I'm not going to lie to you, son. Your father is in bad shape. I believe he's had a severe heart attack. He's weak, very weak. The next couple of days will be critical. He will need constant care, twenty-four hours a day."

Clint inhaled and exhaled slowly. "I'll see to it, Doc," he said. "You just tell me what needs to be done."

His own heart pumped fast and hard knowing the cause of his father's illness was his own transgressions. Clint would care for his father himself, with the help of Mrs. Gentry. He knew she couldn't be here all the time, she had her own family to care for, but he'd make do. His father would want Mary to nurse him. But did Clint dare ask for the Blackwells' help?

"Shouldn't we get him into his bed?" Mary said, concern resounding in her shaky voice.

"Yes, gently now, and make him as comfortable as possible. That's about all we can do."

Hank, James, and Jared helped Clint carry Paddy to his room upstairs. Mary followed. Timothy, Thomas, and William waited out on the porch with Phoebe and Olivia.

Before Doc Stuart left, he wrote down a long list of instructions for Clint on his lined prescription pad. He tore off the page and handed it to him. Then, after a sympathetic pat on the shoulder, he turned to leave, saying, "Send for me if there is any change."

Mary and Clint were struggling with guilt. Mary felt she hadn't helped matters by rushing out on Paddy. She should have stayed to talk about what happened between their children instead of turning her back on her old friend. Clint felt certain Paddy's attack was entirely his fault from the shame of his actions.

Clint sat down on the bed beside his father, hanging his head. Mary looked at Paddy, who was ghostly white and lying so still. Was he in pain? She hadn't thought to ask the doctor because her own misery had tied a knot in her tongue. A gentle love and growing sadness for Paddy swept over her. He had been such a cherished friend these years since Henry died.

Mary pitied Clint yet despised him for what he had done so disrespectfully to Mame.

Mame came out of her borrowed room and lingered outside Paddy's bedroom door with her brothers.

You got what you deserved. But this bitter pill is much too easy for you. You can't die now. You need to suffer much longer. Struggle like my poor papa must have done. Buried alive, suffocating, choking on deadly fumes, trying to pull in that last bit of oxygen from the thin air . . . dying as he struggled to suck life into his lungs. Air—such a simple thing.

Mame felt bile rise up her throat. A sickly feeling overwhelmed her as she thought of her papa, what had happened this morning with Clint, and now Paddy's collapse. She began formulating a plan in her mind. It was a long shot, but it just might work.

She approached Clint, who was now sitting on the stairs with his head buried in his hands. She let her hands rest on his shoulders.

"I hope he's going to be all right." Clint didn't look up.

Mame's mother crossed her arms and caught Mame's attention. "Mame, gather your things. We'll be leaving shortly." Then as Clint turned toward her, she added, "Clint, we will stay at the hotel a couple of days until we see if Paddy's going to be all right."

Mame's hands fell from Clint's shoulders as he stood and stepped toward Mary. "Please don't leave, Mrs. Blackwell. Stay here in the house. I promise I will not go near your daughter again. I need your help caring for Dad."

Mary sighed deeply and looked at Mame. Too much had happened this day. Mary's head was full, and her heart was heavy. It was such a hard decision. Get Mame away from Clint, or stay and care for Paddy?

Mame stepped forward and took her mother's hand in hers. "Mama, it's okay, we really should stay and help. I'm all right."

Mary squeezed Mame's hand before releasing it to sink down on the nearby window seat. It was as if her steely determination and common sense could no longer lift her beyond her fatigue and this strange turn of events. This was supposed to be a friendly visit, a normal business trip after another long, hard season of farming. The tight rein she had kept on her family and her livelihood seemed to have vanished. Not only did she not know her daughter well enough, she could not, for the first time, understand what complications were coming into her own simple friendship with Paddy. Was it companionship only . . . or . . . love? And if it was, was it too late?

"I'll stay until Paddy's out of the woods," she said at last. "Mame, you will leave with the others in the morning."

Mame knelt beside the window seat and looked into her mother's eyes. "But, Mama, you need me here. You can't care for Mr. Paddington by yourself, especially with all the tobacco business you've still got to take care of. You heard the doctor say it would be an around-the-clock job. I'm staying, Mama. I want to help."

Mary didn't like it, but she knew the logical thing to do was let Mame stay since Olivia and Phoebe had to return to the farm with their children, and Mrs. Gentry couldn't spare them more of her time. Mary would just have to keep a keen eye on her and Clint.

Most of the family returned to Beckley the next day. Mary and Mame stayed, and along with Clint and Mrs. Gentry, they made Paddy's recovery their main priority. They barely left Paddy's side that first day, and by the second, they had established a smooth routine. Mary washed Paddy's face and shaved him in the mornings, remembering Henry with every stroke of the razor, but somehow Henry didn't seem quite as clear in her head as he once had.

Paddy tried to open his eyes late in the evening on the second day. By the third, he was moaning and thrashing around. Mary, Mame, and Clint took turns nursing him, and after three days of unconsciousness, Paddy finally made some mumbling sounds.

On the fourth day, Paddy opened his eyes. Later that same evening, he tried to speak, but his words were slurred. Apparently more than a heart attack had happened. Paddy could move only one side of his body.

"Jettie, please go fetch Doc Stuart," Clint said.

Doc Stuart came, confirmed the stroke, and gave a whole new list of do's and don'ts to Clint. The long days of Paddy's recuperation began. Clint learned from Doc Stuart how to bend and move his father's leg and arm to keep the muscles flexible. Day and night, through wet and soiled bedclothes, they ministered to Paddy.

Mame mostly watched the others, using the excuse that she needed to help Mrs. Gentry with the cooking and washing. She wasn't sure she could trust herself around Clint or his father. Not yet anyway, not until her anger subsided.

CHAPTER THIRTEEN

Watch and pray, that ye enter not into temptation: the spirit indeed
is willing, but the flesh is weak.

~ Matthew 26:41

ALMOST A WEEK HAD PASSED since Paddy's stroke. Mary and Clint tended Paddy as an uneasy silence fell among them all. Mary apparently didn't know what to say to Mame; the interlude with Clint was not mentioned by either, although Mame would not forget it anytime soon. As much as she wanted revenge on the Paddingtons, she longed to feel Clint's touch again. That day at the waterfall would be etched into her mind forever.

All week Clint had not so much as given her a second glance. No idle chit-chat, only to-the-point statements about Paddy's wants and needs.

Mary decided that she and Mame would leave in a few more days, to Mame's dismay. Paddy's condition was still serious but stable. The doctor said Paddy might never be able to walk again or use his left side. He would need a nurse around the clock to attend to his needs. Mary felt sure with the Paddington's wealth they could afford a full time caregiver. She admitted that she hated to leave Paddy, but the pull of the farm was far stronger than the tending of Paddy's needs.

The morning of their planned departure arrived, but a nurse still had not been found, to Mame's relief. At Paddy's bedside, she took her mother's arm and said, "I'll stay until Clint can find someone. I'm used to the routine of caring for Mr. Paddington. I've watched. I'm sure I can do everything you and Clint have done. I really don't mind."

Mary considered Mame's offer and reluctantly agreed since it seemed Clint was no threat. He had barely spoken to Mame this past week, and she did feel more at ease about leaving Paddy, knowing that Mame would be here to watch over him. Mary wished she could stay herself, but her business in Charleston was over. Besides, it was her duty to get back to the Blackwell farm. Her sons were more than capable of running things, but over the years that farm had become Mary's passion, her lover, and her only mate.

Most men would have thrown up their hands and run from such hard work and trying times. Mary's initial need to survive was now a desire to succeed, prosper, buy more land, and clear more fields. She had to get back to her farm, for her own peace of mind and in honor of Henry's memory. She'd left him alone far too long.

Mame imagined that it surprised Clint when she volunteered to stay. He probably assumed she would want to get as far away from him as possible after what he'd done to her. Little did he know that her scheme to hook him was working. Now all she had to do was wait on nature to continue her trickery. During that past week, she'd tried to entice Clint back into her arms, but he would have nothing to do with her. Perhaps that was her mother's doing, but her mother was about to be out of the way. Mame knew what she wanted, and she'd do whatever she had to do to get it. Time would bring them together. A man was just as weak as his own flesh.

CHAPTER FOURTEEN

Be sober, be vigilant; because your adversary the devil, as a roaring
lion, walketh about, seeking whom he may devour.

~ 1 Peter 5:8

MAME SILENTLY STEPPED OUT THE back door of the Paddington home and felt the coolness of the early fall night. The crocheted shawl she had wrapped around her shoulders did little to ward off the chill. Underneath the wrap she was clothed in only a lacy chemise that she had found in the dresser drawer in her temporary room at the Paddington Estate. It was exactly what she needed to accomplish what must be done tonight. She had settled Paddy in earlier but had checked him again to make sure he was resting before leaving. Slow, even breaths were coming from his room. All was well, so she made her way down the stairs.

Out the door and through the back alleys of the streets of Charleston, she made her way into town. On the family's way into the city, Mame had seen the tavern. She knew this was where Clint went at night to have a few drinks to unwind. He'd told her if she needed him, that's where he would be. Well, she needed him, and hopefully he wouldn't be able to resist her this time, dressed as she was.

Jack Marsh glanced up when he heard the tavern doors swing open. His eyes came to rest on a busty wench with a body that would make a dead man drool. Her long, golden hair dangled over the shawl that partially covered her bosom.

Mame stood statue still in the doorway of the saloon, trying to get her bearings, adjusting her eyes to the room full of men and cigar smoke. Her eyes scanned the area for any sign of Clint, but he was nowhere to be found. Where could he be? Fear rose from the pit of her stomach as she looked at the faces glaring at her. Strange men with scraggly beards, weather-beaten skin, and the smell of the place had the stench of unclean bodies and urine. Some of the men showed no emotion at all, while others leered at her, stalking her with wild looking eyes.

Mame knew what she had come for, but obviously Clint was not here. There was no one in this place that even remotely favored him. Surely this was not the tavern he patronized every night. There must be another saloon in town. These men here were not even remotely handsome; they were unsightly and unkempt, so unlike Clint.

As naïve as Mame was about matters of men and women, she knew the more times you lie with a man, the better chance you had of becoming with child. She had counted on her plan working tonight. She needed to seduce Clint. At his house he avoided her at every turn, only talking to her about the care of his father. She had to nudge him to his breaking point, just like at the waterfall. But her plan couldn't work without Clint.

With all those eyes on her, Mame began to feel a bit spooked. She took a deep breath and started backing out of the bar.

From the corner of her eye, Mame caught a glimpse of the man she'd later learn was Jack Marsh. What she saw brought dread and disgust into her soul. A long, jagged scar ran from his left brow down onto his eyelid, across the bridge of his nose to his right cheekbone.

The scar disfigured his nose, tilting it off center on his face. As their eyes met, Mame saw a glint of evil, a glimpse of something unknown to her. She backed toward the swinging doors, hoping to avoid this man at all cost. But little did she know that when Jack Marsh set his mind on having something, he always got it.

"Hey, baby, where're you going? Come on over here and let Big Jack buy you a drink."

Mame turned to run out the door but was stopped by an arm around her waist. Without even looking, she knew it was that awful scar-faced man. Before she knew what happened, he had dragged her back to his chair and pulled her onto his lap.

"Where'd you come from, honey? I ain't never seen you around here before."

The foul odor of tobacco and sour whiskey on this stranger's breath made Mame's eyes water. The harder she tried to pull away from him, the closer he drew her to himself. In a panic, Mame began to sling her arms and legs, trying her best to free herself from this repulsive man.

Mame pushed away from Scarface with all her strength, causing the chair they were on to flip over backward. The man's grip on her didn't loosen at all. Instead, Mame went tumbling over with him and landed on top of him.

"A dame with grit, that's what I like!"

His roars of laughter frightened her. There in that crowded saloon, the wicked Scarface rubbed his bearded cheek across her face before crushing her lips with his own rough, uneven ones. Then he rolled to his side, pulling her over with him. Mame's shawl fell away, exposing the scant chemise she wore to seduce Clint.

"Come on, baby. We got things to do."

A crowd of on-lookers formed a circle around them, urging the man on. Mame heard one holler, "Kiss her one time for me, Jack!" Another wailed, "She's a beaut!" None came to her rescue.

"Come on, little lady! Let's show 'em what they're going to be missing."

Horrified by his intentions, Mame found herself hoisted from the floor, still tight in Scarface's grip. In front of the other men present, he grabbed the front of Mame's chemise and ripped it away from her breasts. Mame gasped and tried to cover herself while shoving the beast away, but her struggles were fruitless. Her efforts were like an ant trying to push a bushel of taters.

When this rough stranger decided he'd put on a big enough show for the crowd, he threw Mame over his shoulder and carried her up the stairs to his rented room. The cheering from the men below drowned out her cries for help. A couple of the more decent drunks, if there was such a thing, might have thought about helping Mame, but in her despair she knew it looked like she was getting what she wanted. Why else would she have come to a tavern half-dressed?

In the endless darkness of the upstairs room, Mame squeezed her eyes shut and tried to imagine that she was with Clint while this man who had called himself "Big Jack" tore what was left of her clothing off. She knew there was no use screaming. No one was coming to her rescue.

Soon the deed was done, sealing Mame's bad decision. The weight of the man's heavy, sweaty body came down hard on top of her. Trying to breathe under the bulk of him, Mame lay very still until she was sure he had passed out.

Mame had to get out of that room and away from this horrible nightmare. She slowly pulled herself out from under Jack's huge frame and rolled off the bed. Gathering what was left of her shredded garments, she threw her shawl across her shoulders. Everything had happened so quickly. She had lost control right from the beginning. As sheltered as she'd always been, how could she have known there were men in the world like this one? In Mame's wildest dreams, she never would have thought this night could have turned into such a terrifying nightmare. She had no idea that the consequences of this night would follow her all her days, to the end of her life . . . and beyond.

Stumbling from the room, Mame realized her old, black shoes were still on her feet. They'd carried her into this hellish place, and now they'd take her home to Clint. She slipped out the door and found the back steps that she hoped would lead her out of this devil's lair.

Though scantly dressed, Mame welcomed the cold air that caressed her near naked skin. She forced her mind to focus only on returning to the Paddington estate. Mame could only hope this night would be worth the soul she surely must have lost. She would never put herself in another situation like this—never. All she could do now was pray that she had conceived a child with Clint and not that horrible man named Jack.

Once Mame reached the Paddington house, she crept inside and up the stairs to her room. Thankful Mrs. Gentry had filled the washbowl, Mame undressed and scrubbed herself from head to toe, trying desperately to scrub away the memories and stench of that horrible man. By the time she finished, her skin glowed red, but there would never be enough water to wash his memory off.

Thank goodness Mama had gone home and Clint wasn't around. No one would ever know what had happened that night . . . no one.

Mame looked down at herself and saw the beard burns on her breasts; she picked up the hand mirror at her washstand and studied her scuffed face. Her knees buckled, and she fell to the floor. Mame's entire body shook in tremors. She could feel the bile rising in her throat, so she pulled herself back up to the washstand. She threw up until there was nothing left to heave.

It took her a while before she could stand without holding onto something. Slipping on a borrowed robe, she made her way to the bathroom. There she ran a tub of scalding hot water because a pan bath would never get the nasty traces of Scarface from her pasty white skin. Easing into the water, she scrubbed and scoured her self time and time again. From head to toe, she rubbed and then soaked. She knew her skin would come clean, but she would never be able to scrub the stink of Big Jack from her mind. There would never be enough soap and water.

Knowing a thousand baths would not cure her of the guilt, Mame made her way back to the bedroom, glad no one was there to see her—only Paddy—and thank goodness, he was too sick to care what she looked like or what she had been doing. Again she picked up the hand mirror, and just as quickly she laid it back down on the dresser and turned it over—she didn't want to see herself. The image made her sick.

The damage was done. All Mame could do now was wait.

CHAPTER FIFTEEN

Wash me thoroughly from mine iniquity, and cleanse me from my sin.

~ Psalm 51:2

CLINT LAY UNDER THE OPEN sky watching the stars sparkle as the full moon rose over the vast horizon. He was reliving his encounter with Mame and his father's illness and wallowing in his guilt. It was entirely his fault. If he had kept his wits and not let himself get carried away with Mame, his father would be fine. Clint's foolishness, added to his father's raw guilt over causing the Blackwell family pain and hardship, had brought on his father's heart attack and stroke.

What next? Tomorrow when I get home, I'll try to find someone to stay with Dad and care for him so Mame can go back home to her family.

I still can't believe she's been willing to stay and help me after what I did to her.

Mame. There's just something different about her. She's not like any other woman I've known.

Just the thought of her made Clint's heart pound hard and fast in his chest. Visions of her made his head swirl in madness. What was this control she had over him?

Since his departed fiancée Victoria left, he'd been careful not to get too close to another woman.

Thoughts of trusting in someone for the rest of his life hadn't occurred to Clint since Victoria. He'd let himself fall head over heels in love with her. Why shouldn't he? He'd planned on spending the rest of his life with her. He'd be lying if he didn't say there was still an ache in his heart when he thought of her. But truth always comes out. She couldn't keep her true nature hidden forever. She'd found someone better, or so she'd thought, and out the door she'd run, never once looking back or saying she was sorry.

I'm just plain stupid. She fooled me in so many things. Love was not what she'd been looking for. Hopefully she's gotten all she ever hoped for, living up in New York with her lawyer husband.

Mame seems different, not flirty and silly or squeamish. She acts mature and knowledgeable for a girl her age. Nineteen is not that young, though. She should have known better than to tease a man like she did.

But how could I have assumed that she was anything but a virgin? Heck, I hardly knew her name, much less anything about her. But she was so beautiful coming up out of that water . . . drops glistening on the tip of her nose and other places . . .

Does a person ever really know another person? Do we really even know our true selves and our own limitations?

Pure and simple, I took advantage of Mame's innocence. I've got to get away from her. Even with Dad lying there close to death, it's been all I could do to keep my hands to myself. She probably hates me for taking from her what a husband should have. And God knows I'm not husband material. That's why I left the note in the kitchen telling her I'd be gone for a couple of days moving cattle. I just had to get away from her . . . I just had to.

Clint dozed in a fitful sleep. Rotating his body first one way then the other in his bedroll, he dreamed of serpents and poison apples.

Before daybreak he had eaten breakfast and was moving the Paddington herd to their farthest bottomland. The task took him a little longer than he had estimated. His mind wasn't on keeping the herd together, so more than one stray had to be hunted and rounded up. His thoughts were constantly on Mame. Clint's daydreaming could have cost him a few dozen head, but he kept them moving, hoping one didn't wander away.

Mame found the note on the kitchen table that morning. If only she'd seen it before trying to find him at the tavern! At least she had a few days to recover before his return.

She worried about Clint's return in between her chores and taking care of Paddy. She couldn't sleep well, reliving time and time again her visit to the tavern. She tried every position possible in that soft feather bed to find the mysterious relief of sleep, but that peace did not come, for she knew she deserved little comfort.

Mame could still smell the stench of Big Jack and feel his body on top of her. Each of the five nights since the tavern, she had awakened soaked in a cold sweat of dread and remorse. It was a good thing Paddy had kept all his wife's garments in that old armoire, because Mame needed the extra nightclothes.

Before the shame of the tavern, she'd never had nightmares. But now she woke herself screaming several times a night. She was going to have to come to terms with her demons. How could she stop the horrific dreams she'd been having? They were so real that she could smell the smoke-filled tavern and see the toothy grins of the men as they cheered Big Jack on. All she could do was beg the good Lord for mercy, even though she knew any mercy given to her was undeserved.

This fretting had to stop, she told herself sternly. After everything she'd been through, Mame wouldn't let that wicked man continue to violate her mind. She had to think about her future, or it all would have been for nothing. So she forced it into the outermost shadows of her mind, into that special hiding place that also held the horrors of what happened to her father: Buried alive. Smothering. Gasping for one more airless breath.

Nothing was simple anymore. Her youth was gone, but she still had her dreams.

Most of the tell-tale marks from Big Jack had faded from Mame's chest, but his beard burns were still on her face. Her skin looked as if she had washed hard with sandpaper. If only she could polish away what evidence remained—if not, excuses would have to do.

The moment she heard Clint's horse whinny, Mame hurried to the back door. She watched him dismount, tie up his horse, stretch, brush off the dust, and start for the door. She felt anxious. Would he notice her face?

It seemed the answer was no, as he looked away from her as he strode toward the door.

"How's Dad?" he asked upon entering the house, still not making eye contact.

"He's improving each day," Mame replied, eyes downcast. "You can even understand a few of his words now."

"After I check on him, I'll clean up and go into town to try and find someone to take care of him so you can go home. Thank you for watching over him. I'll be forever indebted to you."

That wouldn't do at all. Mame reached out and put a hand on Clint's arm before he could walk away. "Oh—no, Clint. You don't have to find anyone to stay with Paddy. He and I have become pretty attached these past few days, and I know Mother would feel better knowing I am here with him."

Clint faced her then, meeting her gaze with a furrowed brow. "But don't you want to go home and get away from me?"

Mame dropped her gaze to the floor. "Clint—I am very—ashamed of the way I acted. How could you have known I was anything but a common harlot? What happened wasn't your fault. It was mine."

Mame's cheeks burned as Clint looked at her. If he noticed her blotchy skin, perhaps he would think she had been in the sun for too long.

"I don't know what to do. Are you sure you want to stay?" When Mame looked up at him, he dropped his gaze to his dusty boots. "If you do stay, I promise I won't lay a hand on you. You have my word."

"Yes, I'm sure. I'll stay and help you with Paddy. Don't worry, I'm not afraid of you."

Mame was relieved and took his promise not to touch her to heart. She wasn't sure she'd ever want the touch of a man again, not after her experience with Scarface.

But she knew Clint was not Big Jack, and she also knew it was just a matter of time before fate drew her and Clint together again.

Clint, exhausted and tired of making decisions, headed toward the kitchen.

Mrs. Gentry started fretting over him the minute he walked through the door. Clint blamed his haggard face and lack of sleep on a noisy, old owl that had perched above his head in a white oak tree and hooted all night. But it was no creature of the night that had caused his distress. It was the lady from the waterfall who clouded his dreams. It would be very difficult for Clint to keep his promise and keep his hands to himself.

In the following weeks, Clint proved himself to be the gentleman he said he'd be. Mame attended to Paddy's daily needs. She read him the newspaper every morning, and every afternoon he asked her to read a chapter from David's psalms. It was as if the words from Paddington's worn family Bible leaped off the page and went straight into her heart, convicting her even more of her sin.

Mame memorized Psalm 51 and repeated it continuously to herself throughout the day:

> *Have Mercy upon me, O God, according to thy loving kindness: according unto the multitude of thy tender mercies blot out my transgressions.*
> *Wash me thoroughly from mine iniquity, and cleanse me from my sin.*
> *For I acknowledge my transgressions: and my sin is ever before me.*
> *Against thee, thee only, have I sinned, and done this evil in thy sight.*

Mame could only pray that God would forgive her as He had his servant David, for surely Mame's sin was no worse than David's.

Their routine continued daily: exercise, bend, and stretch Paddy's left leg and arm. He could now sit up in bed, and one could understand most of what he said, even though it was still slurred. Though he had not been able to stand alone, Doc Stuart was hopeful that he would walk again, given enough time and careful nursing.

Mame actually grew to enjoy her days with Paddy. She knew he was genuinely appreciative of her help. It became harder and harder to dislike this kind, fatherly gentleman. Always polite, he asked for things. He didn't order. Most invalids were bitter, but Paddy seemed to have accepted his hardships just as if he were deserving of them. Yes, Mame could see why her mother was drawn to this man.

Her own father never got the chance to grow old like Paddy. If he'd had the opportunity to live, Mame knew Henry Blackwell would have been a kind soul also, just like Paddy. But she told herself never to forget exactly who Theodore Paddington was and the part he played in her father's death.

Another Scripture flowed through Mame's mind, one from long ago, one that might have been taught to her in Sunday school or by her papa while sitting at the kitchen table. Mame picked up Paddy's Bible and thumbed through the book of Matthew until she found what she was looking for:

> For if ye forgive men their trespasses, your heavenly Father will also forgive you:
> But if ye forgive not men their trespasses, neither will your Father forgive your trespasses.

Maybe God had already taken His revenge on Paddy by striking him down with this illness. Was it time to forgive?

She'd have to give all these new feelings some extra thought.

A month had passed since Mary returned to their farm in Beckley. Paddy had improved so much that he could now be helped downstairs, where he would sit in his favorite chair in the library. That was where he was when Mary knocked on the front door. Mame opened it, knowing her mother was due to arrive, for she had wired ahead a few days earlier saying she would be coming to see how things were before winter weather set in.

Mary squeezed her daughter's arm and asked how she was. That was about as emotional as Mary had ever been with Mame since Henry's death, but Mame was used to it.

"I'm all right, Mother. How are you?"

"Pretty tired, but the trip wasn't too bad this time. With you not home, I've been doing all the housework and cooking, not to mention getting the fields turned for the winter, so it was really kind of nice to just sit and ride."

Mary took off her coat and hung it on the hall tree, and then continued. "Our new buggy rides much smoother than the old wagon, and thankfully it's a lot quieter than those loud, new automobiles I've seen around town."

Mame peeped out the curtain at the shiny buggy. "It looks nice."

Mary went on, "Thomas helps a little with the house chores, but he doesn't cotton to doing women's work. William thinks since he's ten, he should be doing men's work out in the fields and not going to school. Anyway, we really miss you, Mame."

Far away from their peskiness, Mame laughed and missed her little brothers too. She blushed at her mother's tender, uncommon words. *They missed her.* She felt awkward, not being used to her mother's tenderness. Had her mama changed, or had Mame?

Mame looked toward the library. She was a little worn out herself from her nursing responsibilities, for she had taken them seriously, and had become a real Florence Nightingale.

"How is Paddy?" Mary asked.

"Doc Stuart says he's recovering nicely. Paddy's really a good patient too and does everything I ask him, but 'round-the-clock' care for someone is tiresome, not only to the body, but the mind. I sleep on edge, waiting for him to call me, even though he very seldom does at night."

Mary's unusual show of affection had made Mame uneasy and a little more talkative than usual, and she continued. "Clint's a great help lifting Paddy. He's rigged up some pulleys. He fastened them to the ceiling over Paddy's bed, so he can hold on with his one good hand and maneuver in the bed. He's even learned to stand on his good leg and shift into the chair.

"The worst part is when Paddy needs help with the bathroom. At first, he had no control. It was like cleaning a two hundred pound baby. But now that he's getting better, he despises asking for help. He hates having us clean up after him. He's truly a prideful man." *And a good man . . . maybe Mother doesn't need to know about his part in the mine explosion. I'll have to give that more thought.* "Go in and see for yourself," Mame said aloud, pointing to the library.

Mother walked slowly into the library as if fearful of what she would find. The left side of Paddy's face was still drawn tautly, and his hand lay stiff and crooked in his lap, but he was out of the bed, sitting up and looking a hundred times better than he had the last time her mother had seen him.

"Paddy, you're getting better."

Mr. Paddington gave Mame's mother his new, slow, lopsided grin. Reaching for her, he almost toppled out of his chair.

"Whoa, there!" Mary rushed forward and grabbed him. "You had us all pretty worried."

Leaning down, she kissed him right smack dab on the lips, and Mame's jaw dropped. "You'd better be up and about by next fall. You know I don't sell my tobacco to anyone but you."

Times had changed, and Mame knew Mother could sell her tobacco to someone else, but truth be told, she'd just downright miss Paddy.

Watching the scene from the doorway, Mame was furious at her mother's show of affection toward Paddy. Just when Mame was beginning to feel at peace about him, Mother had to go and kiss him. Maybe she should tell her mama about Paddy and the explosion. Then Mother would feel stupid for coddling him all these years. How could she kiss *him*? If she only knew that he was the reason for all their loss. Mother should hate him; instead she was loving on him.

As Mame started to step into the room, she heard Jared come through the back door. He had taken the buggy around and unhitched the horses. Clint was with him, and they were both laughing with their arms thrown around each other like long-lost friends.

"You just wait until tonight, Jared. There's this little lady down at the tavern named Miss Lana, she is the prettiest thing—petite, dark eyes, long hair, she's real pleasing to the eye, you'll like her." He slapped Jared on the back, unaware of Mame's presence in the doorway. "I could use a pretty diversion myself," he added.

Apparently Mame's brothers had decided to let bygones be bygones, especially with Clint's daddy's illness and all. Mame's temper boiled.

"I believe we both deserve a night on the town, don't you, Jared?"

That's when Clint noticed Mame standing at the kitchen door with her hands on her hips.

Deserve? What did he deserve? I've been here night and day, nursing his father. If anyone, I am the deserving one.

The thought of Clint's eyes and big, strong hands on another woman enraged Mame. Especially now that she knew what she knew for certain.

There was no doubt. For almost a week, Mame had woken up each morning feeling queasy, and there was no sign of her monthly. It was time to put the next step of her plan into motion.

"Hey, Mame." Jared looked a little sheepish.

"Hello, Jared," Mame said, swallowing her temper. "How are you?"

"Just fine. Mother's been working us to death, but that's nothing new. What have you been doing? Living it up like a city girl?"

"City girl, my foot. I'm almost as tired as I was when I was on the farm, but you wouldn't know anything about that, playing around out in the fields all day like you do."

The light conversation between Mame and Jared seemed to take the hard edge off Mame. "Why don't you scoot off in here to the kitchen and find yourself a snack?" Then she looked at Clint, "Can you help me at the springhouse?"

The Paddingtons had had running water and an icebox in the house for years, which explained Clint's look of confusion by Mame's request for help in the unused springhouse. She knew she had to talk to Clint, now, in private, before he took off to the tavern with Jared and into the arms of another woman. Before this day was over, Mame would probably need another Bible lesson on lying.

When Clint hesitated, Mame grabbed his hand and drew him out the back door and into the cool evening air. Clint held on as she walked ahead of him, pulling him ever so quickly toward the damp springhouse. Once inside, Mame turned loose of Clint's hand, hung her head, and began to cry.

"What's wrong, Mame?"

She hesitated. "I'm . . . I'm just scared."

"Scared of what?"

She shook her head as if in disbelief. "I've been trying to ignore it, thinking it wasn't so, but facing my mother now made me realize it was real. I know she'll see it. I know she'll be able to tell."

Clint's brows came together. "What are you talking about, Mame?"

Mame lifted her damp gaze to his face. "The baby, Clint. The baby."

"What baby?"

"Our baby," she said, placing her hand over her stomach.

Clint reacted as if he'd been sucker-punched. "Oh—no. It can't be so. We were only together one time. How—do you know?"

"Believe me, I know. I just thought it was only fair for me to tell you." She lowered her gaze to his shoes. "I . . . I'll go back home with mother and have the child. You are not obligated to me in any way. I was as much to blame for what happened as you."

She glanced up to see Clint pull his fingers through his hair and rub his temples. His eyes were closed. "I've got to think. I've made such a mess of things." He opened his eyes and looked at Mame. "Another blow like this might kill my father!"

Clint stepped back outside and inhaled in the night air. He tilted his face up at the sky. Mame looked up as well. It was becoming dark, and that first star of the evening caught her eye as it must have caught his and calmed him.

He turned to Mame. "Mame, we have to get married . . . now—before anybody knows. I will not have my father think we have once again wronged the Blackwells."

Mame did not miss his use of *again*. The only way her plot could work any better would be if Clint loved her. In time, maybe that would come. If it didn't, so be it. She was getting everything she'd ever wanted: a spot in the Paddington family photo album and away from Beckley forever. Love was only a schoolgirl fantasy anyway.

Clint was speaking again. "To pull this off, we have to pretend we love each other and that we are happy." He grabbed her hands. "Can you do that, Mame? Will you do it?"

It was all Mame could do to keep from jumping up and down. "Clint, I don't know . . . marry you?" She pulled her hands away and pretended to consider the idea. "I don't really even know you."

"In time you will. Let's go down to the preacher's right now."

"Right now?" Mame said, trying her best to contain the grin that was about to crack her solemn face.

"Yes, so no one will think we only got married because of the baby." Clint took her hands in his again. "Please, Mame, nothing has to change. I'll still leave you alone, I promise, but I need take care of you and our baby. You'll have a good life—I know you will."

Clint's powerful words of commitment sounded good, but he looked as if someone's hands were laced around his neck, squeezing tighter and tighter. Mame squeezed her eyes shut. Her head was spinning. She had assumed this would be much harder, but she had not factored in Clint's devotion to his frail father and their family guilt.

She pulled her hands away and stepped back, not wanting to appear eager. "This is all happening too fast. Let me think until after supper. I'll meet you in the barn after everyone goes to bed."

Mame turned quickly and rushed through the yard toward the house, up the three back steps, joyfully skipping the middle one.

She needed to calm down and act normal. Everything had gone so smoothly, she didn't even need the Bible lesson, and she hadn't even had to lie.

While Mame helped get Paddy to supper, and all through the meal, her mind reeled. *Mrs. Mary Margaret Paddington.* She was so excited she couldn't eat.

Across the table sat Clint, and Mame was aware that he watched her and also ate very little. Mary and Jared devoted most of their attention to Paddy and so seemed unaware of the strain between Clint and Mame. When everyone had finished, Mame helped Mrs. Gentry carry the last of the dishes into the kitchen.

Mame knew that each night after cleaning up the kitchen, Mrs. Gentry rushed home to be with her own family. Even though her children were grown and on their own, she loved keeping her grandchildren and hated leaving her husband Amos alone at night.

"Why don't you go on home, Mrs. Gentry? I'll finish the dishes tonight. You had more mouths to feed than usual with Mama and Jared here. You must be tired."

"Are you sure, Miss Mame?"

"Yes, go on now."

Mrs. Gentry did not have to be told twice. With a word of thanks accompanied by one suspicious look at Mame, Mrs. Gentry quickly hurried from the Paddington kitchen to get home to her own family.

CHAPTER SIXTEEN

Unto the pure all things are pure: but unto them that are defiled and un-believing is nothing pure; but even their mind and conscience is defiled.

~ Titus 1:15

"JARED, WILL YOU HELP ME carry Dad up to bed? He looks pretty tired after all the visiting today," Clint said while Mame set to work in the kitchen.

With effort, Paddy softly said, "I am pretty worn out. Mary, will you sit with me . . . upstairs for a while?"

It took effort to understand all of Paddy's words as they slowly slid together, but Mary was relieved at how much his speaking had improved. At least now she could make out most of his sentences.

"Of course I will, Paddy. Come on, boys. Let's get him up to his room."

After settling Paddy under the covers, Clint and Jared left their parents alone. Mary sat holding Paddy's hand in the old rocker.

"Paddy, you're doing so well. I'll bet in a few weeks you'll be as good as new." Mary kept hold of his hand as they quietly talked.

"Mary, you and I both know . . . I'll never be the same. Be honest with me like you always are. Sugarcoating this . . . won't make me better. We're too good of friends not to be . . . straight up with each other."

115

Paddy took his hand from hers and reached up to touch her face. After almost nine years of knowing Mary, he knew not to confess his love for her. He knew she cared for him too, but Henry's ghost was always shadowing them. You'd think after all these years, she'd want to move on, but the few times he'd stolen a kiss, Paddy had felt the resistance, seen the cold look in her eye that said, *don't get too close.* And now, in the shape he was in, he'd never be able to be more than her special friend. Maybe it had all been for the best not getting any closer than they had. As least now they wouldn't be missing something they'd once shared.

Suddenly, a sickening wave of guilt washed over Paddy, consuming him with the need for forgiveness. He longed to confess to Mary his part in the mine explosion. He'd fought this feeling so many times. What good would be accomplished? It might relieve some of his guilt, but then he'd lose Mary forever. He wasn't ready for that. He'd take what little time he had with her. As always, he'd take what he could get.

With his father settled in with Mary, Clint turned to Jared. "Hey, how about we go out on the town another night? Something's come up and I can't go tonight."

"Aw, heck," Jared said.

"You can go down to the tavern alone if you want. Maybe one of the girls will catch your eye." Jared shrugged as if he wasn't sure that was a good idea. Clint continued. "Like I told you, Miss Lana's real nice to look at, real nice indeed."

Jared hung his head and grinned. His ears turned a bright red, and he kicked at some unseen object in the hallway. Clint could tell Jared could use some loosening up.

"Come on, Jared. I've got a bottle of real good whiskey out in the barn. That darned brandy Dad drinks tastes like something a girl would sip at an afternoon tea party." Clint slapped Jared on the back, and they headed for the barn.

Mame could hear hints of Clint and Jared's voices in the hall as she finished cleaning up the kitchen. She casually waved at them as they came through the kitchen and out the back door. Then she hurried upstairs. Outside Paddy's open door, she could hear voices, low and intimate.

There her mother sat, holding the man's hand. *If she only knew . . .* "Mother," Mame said, interrupting the conversation, "since you're here to look after Paddy, I'm going for a walk before it gets too dark. If you're in bed when I get back, I'll see you in the morning."

"Sure, Mame. Good night."

"Paddy, do you need anything before I leave?"

"No, Mame . . . not a thing." Looking toward Mary, Paddy said, "I've got everything I need . . . here in this room. See if my boy will . . . walk with you. You both could use a break . . . from watching after my old bones."

Mame smiled. "I'll see if he wants to."

Feeling lucky again, Mame collected her thick shawl from her room and left for the barn. Across the short field, she could see a lantern burning inside the barn. Clint was already there, waiting for her.

What a disappointment it was to find that Clint wasn't alone. Jared was there, and he and Clint were sitting on a couple of barrels and passing a bottle of whiskey between them. Mame stood in the doorway trying to decide whether to act angry or confused.

Clint saw her standing there and stood. "Jared's trying to get his courage up so he can go down to the tavern and have a little fun."

Jared stood then and handed the bottle to Clint. He swayed a little as he headed toward his sister to leave. If Jared had ever tasted alcohol before, Mame didn't know it. Clint, on the other hand, must have been a seasoned drinker, because Mame couldn't see any effect of his whiskey drinking in his speech or stance.

"See you later, Jared. Don't do anything I wouldn't," Clint called as he corked the whiskey and returned it to a wooden box tucked under some shelves.

Mame grabbed Jared's arm. "Don't you think you'd better just go in the house and go to bed?" It was obvious that the whiskey had gone straight to his head.

"Nah, it's time I started acting like a man, and a man's got to have a little fun." Wobbling, Jared pulled his arm away and disappeared into the darkness.

Mame chose one of the whiskey barrels and sat. The scent of dried hay and horse manure filled her senses, the smells of the barn overwhelming her almost as much as Clint's closeness. He always smelled like the outdoors, sort of a piney cleanness. For a long time they sat, neither speaking, each caught up in their own private thoughts.

Mame wondered if Clint felt as if his world was spinning like fruit from a tipped-over cart, the chapters of his life rolling this way and that way . . . all out of control. So much had happened—his father's sickness, then a baby on the way. She jumped when he reached over and touched her arm, startled out of her thoughts.

"Mame, you must be terrified. Have you thought about things? Will you marry me?"

She kept her gaze on the floor, squeezing her hands together in her lap. "We've known each other only a few short weeks, but if I don't marry you, my family's name will be ruined, and my child will be fatherless."

With that, Mame's eyes welled up with tears. True, honest, tears. She was not scared of what was happening. Things could not be going any better, but the truth was that she really didn't want to drag her family name through the mud.

In the midst of her triumph, a vision of Big Jack's scarred face returned to her mind.

No one must ever know I've been with anyone but Clint. My future depends on it.

Willing the grotesque vision from her mind, Mame looked up at Clint.

"Yes, I'll marry you if you'll have me. I know you must think I am awfully brazen—I don't know what came over me that day. I was consumed with feelings that I had no control over—it was as if I was possessed by someone other than myself . . . a demon, a harlot."

Clint chuckled at her words.

"Why are you laughing?" Mame frowned and wiped at her tears.

"I'm sorry. I'm really not laughing at you. I was just taken aback by that serious look on your face and all that talk of being possessed. You were possessed all right, but not by a demon. It was lust, pure and simple. It was the fire of passion that had been building in that maturing body of yours. A fire that fought to be extinguished."

Clint stopped talking and moved his hands to her shoulders, turning her to face him.

"What do you say, Mame? Do we go see the preacher?"

She trembled from feeling the touch of his hands on her, but she was determined to stay calm and seal this deal.

"I suppose I don't have any choice, do I?"

Boldly she leaned over and laid her head against his shoulder.

Clint drew her to her feet. Sliding his hands up and down her arms, he kissed her, first on the forehead, then on her nose, and finally very gently on her lips. Mame drew in a sharp, deep breath. Her heart was pounding so fast; just for a moment she forgot her clever scheming.

He surely was handsome. Again she noticed that little indentation in his chin and the dimple that marked only his right cheek. How could anyone have ever left him for someone else? Victoria was a very foolish lady. Or was she? Was there more to Clint Paddington than the surface revealed? After all, Mame barely knew him.

Clint smiled, released his grip, and blew out the lantern. He reached for Mame's hand and led her out of the barn toward the street, and on to Reverend Jones's house.

Mame played the part of the scared little puppy very well, but she was not afraid. In fact, she was more excited than she had ever been in her life. No, she didn't love Clint, how could she ever? After all he was a Paddington, so shouldn't he share in the blame for her papa's killing and all their grief? Then, that yearning deep inside made her wants overcome her confusion and anger.

Yes, this was turning out to be a brilliant plan. Or so Mame thought. The words of Sir Walter Scott reverberated throughout the chambers of Mame's mind: *Oh what a tangled web we weave, when first we practice to deceive.*

Mame shut down her memories of school day poets and cursed the day she'd ever read that verse.

Reverend Jones raised himself from the kitchen table, leaving his Bible open to 1 Kings, chapter 16. It was not unusual for someone to come calling at night. Sickness, childbearing, death . . . people needed him at all hours of the day and night. He wiped the pound cake crumbs from his mouth, took the last sip of warm milk, and then straightened his shirt collar as he ambled to the door to see what tonight would bring. He was glad he had not already changed into his bedclothes.

Recognizing his visitor, he said, "Well, Clint Paddington. Come, come on in." He motioned Clint and his companion into the small parlor. "How's your father? Not worse, I pray."

"No. No, he's fine."

Reverend Jones nodded toward the pretty, young lady at Clint's side. "Please, have a seat."

Reluctantly they sat side by side on the minister's floral patterned settee. They were both much too excited and nervous to sit down but accepted the reverend's invitation out of good manners.

"Reverend Jones, this is Mame—ah, Mary Margaret Blackwell— and I'm wondering if you will marry us?"

"Marry you? Why, Clint, I didn't even know you'd met someone." The reverend took pride in being the first in the community to know most of the comings and goings, so he was secretly disappointed—and a bit skeptical. He'd had plenty of practice with surprises though, and he was nobody's fool.

"Of course I will. Congratulations." He looked toward the comely Miss Mame, Mary Margaret Blackwell, and nodded. "We've got much planning to do. What date have you set for the special day?"

"Right now, Reverend," Clint said.

"Right now? Why—what do you mean, right now?"

Young folks are always in a hurry. Old people should be the ones in the hurry, since our time is running out. But no, young ones have to have what they want sooner than later. They will learn. Time is the teacher and controller of all things. Past. Present. And future.

"It is too late to go to the church and get musicians, much less witnesses, and your father—we couldn't bring him out in this night air."

"That's the whole point. Dad's not up to all the excitement of a wedding, so we decided it would be best if we just got married and then told everyone."

The old minister stood silent for a moment, scratching his day old beard. Then he looked toward Mame.

"Miss Blackwell, how old are you?"

Mame stalled a moment, seeming to ponder the question. "Nineteen, sir."

"Well, you're rightly old enough." The reverend sat down in the chair across from Mame and looked her square in the eye, making her feel very uncomfortable. "Do you want to marry Clint Paddington?"

Not prepared for personal questions but knowing she shouldn't be too hasty answering this one, Mame hesitated just for a few seconds. Then she looked directly at Reverend Jones and nodded her head *yes.* Things were definitely going her way.

"All right. Let me get my Bible and Maybelle to witness."

Reverend Jones marked the place he'd been studying in his Bible and flipped to Ephesians 5:22–24, feeling the need to read this passage. All the while the character he had previously been studying kept popping into his mind. *Jezebel.*

Following the reverend into the parlor, Maybelle straightened her skirt and patted her gray hair. She'd had to dress quickly for the unexpected occasion. She shook hands with the eager couple.

"Now, everyone, shall we begin? Clint, bring Mary Margaret over here by the front windows. Maybelle, you stand right there. Now, we're all in place."

Mame heard "dearly beloved" and tried to focus on the reverend's words, but she slipped away into her own thoughts.

"Wives, submit to your husbands."

I know Clint said he wouldn't touch me, but I'll fix that. I'll have him submitting to me before this night is over. I may not love him, but that doesn't mean I don't want him.

In less than an hour, Mame's future was sealed.

As Reverend Jones announced, "I now pronounce you man and wife," Mame thought her knees would buckle from relief.

She could not believe she was married. As if from a distance, she heard the minister say, "You may now kiss the bride."

Very gently Clint reached down and tilted up Mame's chin. Leaning down, he lightly touched his lips to hers. Just that slight contact with Clint made Mame become absorbed in heat. An overpowering sensation started low in her belly, flaming to a scorching fire, melting her to mush. They both stood frozen for what seemed like an eternity, the moment broken only by another intrusive knock on the reverend's front door.

Reverend Jones left the enthralled couple to answer it.

"Hello. What is it? May I help you with something?"

A young, unfamiliar boy stood at the door. He looked unkempt and skinny, not one of the reverend's regular congregation attendees.

"Doc Stuart said for you to come quick. A drunk down at the tavern done crossed Jack Marsh. Somebody said his name was Blackwell. Doc said that young man's a-going to die, don't look good for him, don't look good a-tall."

Overhearing the boy's message, Mame knew that drunk named Blackwell hurt in the tavern must be Jared. The realization that Jared was bad off snapped Mame out of her heated thoughts of Clint.

In a panic, Mame tugged at Clint's arm. "Come, Clint. Let's get to the doctor's office."

Outside, the cool air did little to clear her head and calm her body. What could have happened? The last thing Jared would ever do would be to fight with somebody.

The doctor's office was only a block down the street. As they approached the office door, Mame froze. There in front of her stood the man whose scarred face appeared in her nightmares. The deputy had Big Jack's hands cuffed behind him.

"Marsh, you better pray that young man survives, or you'll be locked up for good."

Marsh. The monster's name was Jack Marsh, and when his gaze scanned the crowd, it settled on Mame. She could see, even in his drunken state, that he recognized her.

"Hey, baby. Where have you been?" asked Marsh, completely ignoring his predicament.

The deputy grabbed Marsh's arm and pulled him back when he started moving toward Mame.

"I've missed you. Why did you leave me the other night?"

Mame looked around, as if trying to figure out who he was talking to.

"Shut your drunk mouth, fool. You wouldn't know your own mother if she slapped you in the face," said the deputy. He struggled to hold Jack back, away from Mame.

"Yeah, you're right, deputy, but my mother don't look like this wench."

Mame felt the muscles in Clint's arm tense up and looked down to see his clenched fist. If she hadn't been so frightened of Jack Marsh and fearful for her brother's life, she might have been pleased that Clint was willing to defend her virtue. Instead, she shrank back, still holding his arm but trying to hide behind him.

Taking Mame by the elbow, Clint quickly hurried her past Jack and into the doctor's office. Unconscious, Jared lay on the examining table, his face swollen, with blood oozing from his nose and mouth.

Overwhelmed at all that was happening—the baby, the wedding, Big Jack, and all this blood on her sweet brother—Mame felt the room spin. Darkness encompassed her as she crumpled to the floor.

"Mame!" It was a good thing Clint was standing close. He effortlessly caught her in his arms as she collapsed. He carried her to the only chair in the room, sat her down, and started fanning her with his hand as he called her name.

Doc Stuart looked up from working on Jared. "She'll be okay. Somebody get her a cold cloth."

"I'll get it," Reverend Jones said, eager to be of help. He wrung out a cloth and glanced at the couple in the small mirror that hung over the water basin.

Passing out. Rushed marriage. Yes, just as he'd suspected.

First Kings 16:31—*That he took to wife Jezebel, the daughter of Ethbaal, King of the Zidonians, and went and served Baal and worshipped him.*

Blessed Jesus, Reverend Jones thought, *the girl is with child, and a harlot, conceiving out of wedlock, she's no better than Jezebel.*

Mame slowly became aware of her surroundings. She felt the cool cloths pressed on her forehead, and someone was fanning her with a book. In the corner of her clouded mind, Mame could hear the doctor telling someone she had fainted after seeing her brother in this awful shape.

Blinking, Mame saw that Clint was squatting beside her, and she could feel him holding her hand. Someone had fetched her mother, and there Mary was, standing next to Jared.

"I'm sorry, Mrs. Blackwell," said Doc Stuart. "He's pretty beaten up. Quincy said all your boy did was walk past Marsh at the bar and brush against him. That's all it takes for a man like Marsh, who's always looking for a fight."

Quincy Sneed had been at the tavern and saw the whole thing. He had helped carry Jared to the doctor's office, and he was the one Mame had overheard talking to Reverend Jones, saying the doc didn't think the boy would make it.

"What exactly happened to my son?" Mary asked in a voice that meant business.

Young Quincy bobbed his head. "Well, lady, your boy there came into the tavern and headed to the bar. Just as he was passing Marsh, he staggered into him, made Marsh spill his shot of whiskey, and then it was on. Marsh grabbed him by the collar and slammed his head into the mahogany bar. Your lad didn't know what hit him. The sound of that boy's head poppin' open shut the crowd up. The sight of blood squirting out of his head just made Marsh go at him that much harder. He kept slamming his fists into this poor boy's face and stomach. Finally your boy just withered to the floor."

Everyone in the room listened to every word. Most women would have made Quincy stop his detailed explanation. Not Mother. It was as if all feeling had left her. She didn't flinch, or say a word.

Slowly she turned from Quincy and looked at Doc Stuart. "What can we do for him?"

Looking at his patient rather than the patient's mother, Doc said, "Just keep him quiet, and maybe if his broken ribs didn't puncture a lung, he might just make it. I'll bandage him and try to keep him out of as much pain as possible. He'll need to be kept knocked out. Continue dripping a little chloroform on that cloth over his nose at least every fifteen minutes."

Mary looked at Mame. "What happened to you?"

"I just passed out, Mama. You know, seeing Jared like that." Mame looked away from her mother.

The minister stepped up beside Mary and took her hand. "I'm Reverend Jones, Mrs. Blackwell. I'm sorry about all your trouble."

You never know what hardships to expect with young people, he thought. Aloud he said, "I believe your daughter has had too much excitement tonight, with getting married and all."

"What—getting married?" Mary asked, turning her astonished face to Mame and Clint.

"Not more than an hour ago, I married this young lady to Clint Paddington. I am glad to see someone finally won his heart."

Seeing the amazement on her mother's face, Mame rose from her slumped position in the chair and went to her. "Mother, I'm sorry I didn't tell you. It just happened so fast."

It was hard to tell whether her mother wanted to slap Clint or hug him. "Why didn't you tell me so I could have planned a wedding for my only daughter?"

"Mrs. Blackwell, I didn't want to put Father through the excitement of a big wedding." He put an arm around Mame. "I hope you understand."

After a moment's hesitation, Mother reached out to Mame and hugged her. Mame stiffened in this rare, awkward embrace. Then Mary held her at arm's length and, looked into her eyes, asking her right in front of Clint, "Was marrying Clint what you really wanted to do?"

Mame's mind was still tilting to and fro from all the drama of the night. Still, she nodded ever so slightly, as if to clear her head more than anything. Then, standing very tall and straight, she answered her mother with a note of confidence in her voice that she'd never felt before.

"Mother, I've never been so sure of anything in my life."

Mary's eyes appeared to dampen as she gazed at Mame and Clint. "I pray you two will be as happy as Henry and I were, and that you will be blessed with growing old together."

With that said, Mary went back to Jared's side and took his hand in hers. Her vigil had begun. Mame knew their mother would stay by her son until she knew he would be okay.

With his bandaged head, it was impossible to recognize Henry Blackwell's look-a-like. His eyes were so swollen they were mere slits. His nose must have been broken because it was crooked right, and his lips were split in several places. But it was Jared. Mary knew it. Their spirits were one, but now half of Mary's very being lay dying.

CHAPTER SEVENTEEN

And it shall come to pass afterward, that I will pour out my spirit
upon all flesh; and your sons and your daughters shall prophesy,
your old men shall dream dreams, your young men shall see visions.

~ Joel 2:28

NO ONE GOT MUCH SLEEP that night. Clint and Mame went back
to the house to check on Paddy. On the way, they decided not to tell
Paddy about their marriage. Not just yet anyway. They would wait
until Jared was out of the woods before they hit him with the news.
They would warn visitors, as well as Mary, not to tell.

Paddy was sitting up in his bed just as Mary had left him when
she'd got the bad news. "How is Jared? What happened?"

His trying to talk fast made it harder than ever to understand
his words.

Clint shook his head. "Old Jack Marsh beat him up pretty badly
down at the tavern. Doc don't know how bad he might be hurt. Time is
the only thing that will tell if he's injured bad on the inside." He stepped
closer and laid his hand on his father's shoulder. "Try and get some rest,
Dad. Mary's with Jared, and I'll go back to Doc's office to make sure
they're all right. Mame, will you stay here and look after Dad?"

"Of course, Clint. How long will you be gone?"

"I'll be staying close to Doc Stuart's office so I can check on Jared through the night."

It would be best if I don't stay in this house tonight, Clint thought. The light touch of Mame's lips after the wedding ceremony had been electric. It would be impossible to stay away from her, especially now that they were married.

He had promised Mame that things would stay the way they had been, that he wouldn't touch her. That would be one very hard promise to keep, but he wanted to redeem himself and be as honorable as Paddy had reared him to be. Yes, he'd do all he could to keep his word.

Mame watched Clint leave the house. This wasn't exactly the way she had envisioned her wedding night. She knew, even though Clint had promised not to touch her, that she could have persuaded him to be with her. They had a destiny that could not be denied. Whether or not love would ever come of their attraction, Mame really didn't know. In fact, she could not fully imagine ever loving a Paddington after what they had done to her father.

Mame looked in on Paddy one more time before she went to her room. It was close to one o'clock in the morning, and she was sad. Tired too. As she curled up on her bed, she thought of Jared and prayed he would be better by morning. She also thought of Clint and knew whatever his last name was, she already loved him.

Morning brought more bad news. Jared just lay, lifeless, not moving or making a sound. He was no better, probably worse. His head had begun to swell. He was not a pretty sight. It was heartrending to see.

After three nights and two days, Mary finally decided she needed some solid sleep. Still, she would not leave her son. She did agree to use a bed in an adjoining room at the doctor's office to rest for a few hours. When she finally closed her eyes and drifted to sleep, her mind conjured images of Henry and Jared's faces. They were so much alike, gentle and caring.

In a deep, troubled sleep, dreams came. Mary saw Henry just as if he were still living. He was walking toward her as if on a fluffy cloud, weightless. His hand extended toward her, coaxing her closer. When the tips of their fingers were almost touching, Henry turned and took the hand of someone else. It was Jared. Henry was holding Jared's hand, and Jared was no longer injured. There was no blood, no pain, and he was smiling the most precious, peaceful smile Mary had ever seen—or would ever see again.

Mary willed herself to wake up. Frantically she reached for both men in the darkness of her clouded night's dream. She was terrified that she was not going to be able to get to them. Her heart raced. Her pillow and bedclothes were damp from the cold sweat that covered her entire body.

Then a cool breeze swept through the room, and a chill came upon her, settling on her like the first frost of winter on the tobacco fields. Her dream was so real that she could even see the dimple in Jared's cheek as he smiled at her before he and Henry turned away. Father and son, side by side, never once did either of them look back as they slowly faded from Mary's sight.

"Wake up, Mary." Someone was shaking her shoulder. "Mary, Mary—Mary—you must wake up. Jared needs you."

The sound of Doc Stuart's voice broke through the many folds of her deep sleep. Mary quickly jumped up. She dashed through the door and into the other room where Jared lay. "How is he?"

One look revealed that Jared was not of this world. Doc Stuart had been wrong; Jared no longer needed her or anything else on this earth. He was now traveling through the clouds with his earthly father, getting ready to meet his Heavenly Father. Was it a dream she'd had, or had she been granted a special privilege, a time to bid a loved one a final farewell?

Mary stood near Jared long after the icy fingers of death had cooled his skin. Gently stroking his bandaged head, visions of days spent with her little boy at her heels, tugging on her coattail . . . laughing . . . hugging . . . now only tears. As the scalding drops flowed from her eyes, Mary felt colder than she'd ever been in her life, more frigid than the day Henry left her. She was shivering so badly her entire body shook from the force of her pain. No parent should ever have to witness their child's death.

"Mrs. Blackwell, let me take you home. You are exhausted," Doc Stuart said, sympathetically patting her on the back.

Mary didn't speak. She simply leaned over and kissed Jared's steel cold cheek. Then, turning away from her pain, she left the doctor's office unassisted. She neither needed nor wanted help getting home. She was Mary Blackwell. Long ago she learned not to need anything or anyone. Need only brought heartache.

Mary walked down the sidewalk knowing she had been given a precious gift, a bounty that would last her a lifetime: the remembrance of seeing Henry again and knowing that he was no longer alone in that deep, dark coal pit. Now he had Jared, and Jared had his papa. She vowed to never forget Henry and Jared's faces. Mary had never seen such peace. She was thankful for that gift but knew she would never experience that kind of calm on this earth. Especially not now, not after losing her precious son, Jared.

Morning was breaking the eastern sky as Mary entered Paddy's house. The heavens were alive with multi-colored layers of promising sunshine filtering through the light clouds. Mrs. Gentry had just arrived and was brewing a pot of coffee. Mary followed the smell toward the kitchen.

"Mrs. Mary, you're back! Is Mr. Jared better?"

"Yes, Mrs. Gentry, he's well."

Mary walked to the stove and poured herself a cup of the steaming coffee. She sat at the kitchen table with a faraway look in her eyes.

Mrs. Gentry felt Mary's troubles, so she left her alone with her worries. She sure was glad to hear the news that fine young man, Jared, was okay.

Mary sat quietly, her full cup of coffee now as cold as Jared's stiff fingers. Mame found her like this when she walked into the kitchen.

"Mother, did Jared wake up? Is he any better?"

Mary just sat, a troubled look on her face. Then she turned to Mame and spoke softly. "Jared's with your papa."

Mame's hand flew to her mouth stifling the gasp. "No, no. It can't be. It isn't fair! Why Jared?"

Wrapping her fist around a quart jar of sourwood honey, Mame slammed it against the pale yellow kitchen wall. Mary didn't flinch or say a word. Honey ran down the wallpaper onto the broken shards of glass, spreading across the floor, just like Jared's blood had spread across the doctor's office floor.

"I'm leaving today to take Jared back to Beckley," Mary said then. "I want him to be buried on the hill behind the house with Grandma and Grandpa Blackwell."

No! Jared can't be dead. This place is cursed. It's all Theodore Paddington's fault. If he had kept that mine closed years ago, my papa would still be alive. We would never have had to come to this awful town and depend on the Paddingtons for our livelihood. Jared would never have been in that tavern.

Deep in her heart, Mame knew it was just as much her fault as anyone's. Clint and Jared were supposed to have gone to the tavern together that night. But she had overheard them and didn't want Clint to go and be with another woman. She shouldn't have cared, but she did.

If she had only allowed Clint to go with Jared, then he could have protected her brother from that monster, Jack Marsh. But if Clint had gone with Jared, she wouldn't be married. Mame just couldn't think about this anymore. Jared's death was *not* her fault. It just wasn't. It was all because of the Paddington curse.

Mary rose slowly from the table, leaving her untouched coffee, and left the kitchen. Mame didn't know what to do but follow her up the stairs that led to Paddy's room. When Mary entered Paddy's room, she shut the door behind her, shutting Mame out of her grief. Mame heard nothing for a few moments. Then she heard her mother's sobbing, interspersed with Paddy's low murmurs as he tried his best to console her.

Mame leaned against the balcony railing, slumping to the floor.

You didn't even touch me or give me a comforting word, yet you've run to him.

Mame felt the hate she harbored against her mother well up inside. Most of the time she kept that feeling hidden, but now it erupted. *Why did you go to him? Why didn't you let me comfort you, Mother? It's his fault, and you don't even know it.* Mame slammed her fist against her leg, wanting to cry but too furious to feel the relief of tears.

With a tight knot in her throat, Mame stomped back down the stairs just as the front door swung open to reveal Clint. She had seen very little of him over the past three days. What little he'd slept must have been in the barn or guesthouse, since the bed in his room was empty both nights that she checked. His bedding was rumpled and some of his quilts seemed to be missing, so he must have bedded down somewhere. He certainly was fulfilling his promise of staying away from her. What a honeymoon this was.

"Clint. Oh, Clint—Jared died."

Rushing toward her husband, Mame threw herself into his arms.

His heart went out to her. Clint already knew about Jared. He'd gone to the doctor's office first thing before checking the cattle. He felt sick, guilty, and sad. He needed some sympathy himself, and in their mutually distraught condition, Mame was impossible for him to resist any longer.

Impulsively, Clint's lips crushed down upon Mame's, the force of it almost brutal. The urgency in both of them was intense. It was as if they had finally glimpsed their undeniable future. A future Jared would never have.

Their closeness was interrupted as Mrs. Gentry swung open the kitchen door to step into the foyer. Clint let go of Mame, pushing her away so fast she nearly lost her balance.

"Sorry, Mr. Clint," Mrs. Gentry said, awkwardly tying her apron and looking down, embarrassed by their public show of affection. "You want some coffee?"

"Yes, please, and pour Mame some too."

Mrs. Gentry was glad for her chance to exit. She was still under the impression that Jared had improved, for no one had yet told her the final outcome of the deadly tavern brawl. Knowing of Jack Marsh's meanness though, she would not be surprised to hear the worst any day. Mrs. Mary had been in a daze, staring into space with her coffee getting cold, and now Clint and Miss Mame hanging onto each other like that, and with Mr. Paddington still not completely well.

Judging from what Mrs. Gentry had seen, there would be no peace and quiet around this house any day soon. All she knew for sure was that there were three meals to be cooked again today, and she'd do her best to give these families something they could count on. Food might not cure everything, but it sure did help matters a whole heap.

Clint tensely turned back toward Mame when he heard the kitchen door close behind Mrs. Gentry.

"Mame, I'm sorry. I don't know what came over me; the sorrowful look on your face just carried me away. It won't happen again. You know, Jared—was a kind, gentle boy—and I am just as sorry as I can be about all this."

Standing so close to Mame, Clint was saying the right words but feeling nothing but the call of her womanliness. Even as the last syllable left his mouth, his lips sought hers again, softly this time.

Mame was so engrossed in the feelings Clint provoked in her that she didn't hear Mother as she quietly came down from Paddy's room and stood behind them.

"Mame," her mother said, sniffling from her crying spell but smiling faintly. "I'm so very glad you two have found happiness. Cherish it always. Make every moment together a memory of love, friendship, and passion. We never know how long we have."

Mary saw the expressions that Clint and Mame shared. She wasn't quite sure it was true love, but attraction was something they could build upon. Mary could only be glad for a little brightness amid all this sorrow.

CHAPTER EIGHTEEN

O wretched man that I am! Who shall deliver me from the body of
this death?

~ Romans 7:24

RELUCTANTLY, CLINT AGREED TO HAVE Mrs. Gentry stay more hours with his father during the week he would be gone to Beckley with Mary and Mame to bury Jared. Clint's loyalties were torn, but his new bride and mother-in-law needed him by their side as they lay to rest their cherished loved one.

Mrs. Gentry was tremendously saddened by the news that the nice young man Jared had died and was of course willing to rearrange her schedule, making plans for her Amos to join her for his meals.

Mary insisted they leave right away. They would drive straight through the night and arrive in Beckley late the next night. She had wired the bad news ahead to her other sons so they could be as prepared as possible when she brought Jared home.

Mame was going back to Beckley much sooner than she'd have liked, but it would be only for a short time. Now that she was married to Clint, she might eventually find her rightful place in Charleston. Beckley held too much grief, sadness, and hard work for her.

Mame hung her head and rested her forehead in the crook of her arm as Clint's wagon jostled down the dusty road. Three graves would now be on the hill, graves of Grandpa Thomas, Grandma Jane, and now Jared. She thought of her papa and the fact that he'd never had a decent burial up on the hill with the other family. The cold dark pit of the coal mine had swallowed him up and robbed him of a decent resting place. *Bloody mountain, bloody coal mine.*

Silence prevailed on the journey home south through the mountains of West Virginia.

Choosing to drive alone, Mary's wagon carried the freshly built pine box they'd bought from the undertaker in town; Mary told Clint and Mame to lead the way. She was lost in her grief over Jared. She wanted to be left alone with her memories.

"Mame, why don't you put your head on my shoulder? Better yet, I'll get you a blanket out of the back to use as a cushion," Clint said.

Pulling back on the reins, Clint brought their buggy to a halt, jumped down, and got the quilt, making Mame a makeshift pillow of sorts. She was unaccustomed to such tenderness and felt tears well up.

Mary was pleased to see Clint minding her daughter's needs. After another hour, she pulled up beside their wagon. She noticed the dark circles under Mame's eyes and how tired she looked, but she didn't comment. She knew she didn't look any better. Never had she seen Mame this exhausted, but none of them had slept much lately. Even when Mame jumped from the wagon and threw up in the brown ragweed along the side of the road that morning after their simple roadside breakfast of cornmeal mush, Mary had left her alone. She'd let Clint tend to Mame, watching as he wet a cloth and swabbed her brow. Her husband should take care of her now. Mary felt a tug of guilt knowing just like her, Mame had been taking care of herself for years.

That guilt weighed heavy on Mary's heart, for she knew she'd not done much tending to anyone since Henry died, not even her own self. It wasn't that she didn't care . . . it's just that she had felt empty.

On their way to Beckley and the Blackwell home, it was too dark for Mame to see the familiar landmarks, so she counted the turns off the bumpy main road until they reached their farm. Clint jumped off the buggy, placed one lantern aside Mary's wagon near the burlap-covered pine casket, and lit a second lantern to carry as the three weary travelers waded through thick piles of fallen leaves. The light cast harsh, unwelcoming shadows against the front porch floor. It was as if a group of giants were coming to visit.

The entire Blackwell family had gathered at Mary's house and appeared to be fast asleep, so the three entered as quietly as possible. Mame lumbered into the house, feeling a thousand years old, and went straight to her old room. She never thought she'd welcome the sight of it again.

Unlike her guest room in Charleston, there was nothing luxurious about it. But whether she wanted to admit it or not, these familiar quarters were comforting tonight. She unlaced her shoes and kicked them off before collapsing on her bed, still dressed.

The next thing she knew, it was late morning and her sister-in-law Olivia was shaking her shoulder.

"Wake up, Mame. I just heard the news. You're married."

Slowly Mame sat up and rubbed her sleep-filled eyes. Fighting off a wave of nausea, she swallowed the bile that rose in her throat.

"Yes, Olivia, on the same night that Jared was beaten. It wasn't the wedding night I'd dreamed of."

Less than three months had passed since Mame had left this room. So much had happened. She had seen the big city. Slept under a canopied bed. Made love at a waterfall. Found out who was responsible for her father's death, and gotten married. And then, there was that devil Jack Marsh. Just the thought of him almost made her retch worse, so she swallowed again. At least she would never have to see him again. The deputy told Clint that Marsh would probably hang for beating Jared to death. The sickening taste of bile rose again as memories of Jared's beaten face flashed through her mind. She had to cover her mouth. He was gone. She'd never see her sweet-mannered little brother's freckled face again.

If there is any justice in this world, Jack Marsh will burn in hell.

Mame slipped on her shoes and followed Olivia into the kitchen, wondering on her way where Clint had slept. Her youngest brother William ran to her and threw his arms tightly about her waist.

"Mame, I missed you. You're not going to leave again, are you?" He looked up at her hopefully.

"Will, I'll only be here for a few days, and then I've got to go back to my new home in Charleston with my husband, Clint."

Mame hugged Will tight. A sharp pang of guilt hit her pretty hard in the gut. She felt tenderly toward him. Will was an easy child, and she had abandoned him. She couldn't think about that right now. Some things just couldn't be helped. Her mother should be the one feeling the guilt for not taking care of Will herself, not Mame.

Speaking of Clint, where was he?

That question was soon answered when he and her brothers Hank and James walked through the kitchen door, their pants legs and boots covered in dirt. Since early dawn the men had taken turns digging Jared's grave up on the hill.

Will tugged at Mame's dress, ignoring the men.

"What do you mean, your new home? *This* is your home, Mame."

Mame crouched down on one knee and looked Will straight in the eye. "I will miss you too, little man, but you can come to Charleston and stay with me any time you want to."

"It won't be the same," Will said, tears welling up in his big, green eyes. "I have to help Mama with the chores when you are gone, and I don't like it. Why can't you just stay here so everything can be just like it used to be?"

Little did William know that nothing would ever be like it once was. Someone still had to tell him about Jared. The world they once knew had changed forever. Mame and Jared would both be gone.

Mame knew Will would need their mother Mary even more than ever. Mame closed her eyes, hurting for Will. She knew, now that Jared was gone, that her mother had a tender spot for only one other person . . . Theodore Paddington.

CHAPTER NINETEEN

*Judge not, and ye shall not be judged: condemn not, and ye shall not
be condemned: forgive and ye shall be forgiven.*

~ Luke 6:37

NEWS OF MAME AND CLINT'S marriage traveled fast throughout the family. Even though they grieved Jared's passing, they felt a good measure of joy. Hank's wife Olivia and James's wife Phoebe were both giggling back and forth over the thought of little sister Mame and her new husband.

"Mame, why don't you come out on the back porch with us? We've got something to ask you," Phoebe said.

Mame knew what they wanted to ask, and she had to tell them the truth. She followed her sisters-in-law through the all-too-familiar kitchen and stepped out the back door onto the bare plank porch.

"Tell us everything, Mame. Don't leave out a thing." Phoebe and Olivia babbled at the same time.

They sounded like mother hens squawking, trying to gather up their lost chicks.

"I don't have anything to tell. We had just said 'I do' when we found out Jared had been hurt, and there hasn't been a chance for us to be alone since."

"Well, I suppose you haven't, but it's not like a man to let anything get in the way of his desires," Olivia said knowingly.

Olivia and Phoebe looked at each other, clearly disappointed that she didn't have stories to tell them. Of course, Mame had her own private memories, secrets that would make them hide their blushing faces. She hoped that soon she would have new stories, but she certainly didn't plan on sharing them.

That same afternoon, a crowd of townspeople gathered up on the hill with the Blackwells to lay Jared's body six feet under the cold West Virginia sod. Jared was now in a deep sleep, a rest that would last for all eternity. Twenty-two years to walk this earth was all that had been allotted to him. As the wooden box was lowered into the deep, dark hole, Mame silently affirmed her guiltlessness. It was not her fault that Jack Marsh beat up Jared. It was Theodore Paddington's fault, every bit of it.

Hot tears burned Mame's cheeks, leaving behind a trail of misery as they fell on her black coat. She wasn't sure if her feelings of despair came from sadness or anger—probably a combination of both.

She felt a touch. Looking through the haze of wetness, she saw Will's head leaning against her arm. He was almost up to her shoulder in height. The way he was growing, he'd soon be as tall as James, who stood close to six feet, much taller than either Timothy or Thomas.

Will whispered. "Mame, what will Jared do in heaven? Will he have to raise tobacco?"

Mame really didn't know how to answer, so she said, "I think first of all he'll go find Papa, or Papa will find him, and then I believe they'll go fishing or something fun like that."

"It's going to be too sad around here without Jared, especially with you gone too. I think I'd rather go fishing with Jared and Papa. What was Papa like, Mame? I don't remember him."

Mame patted his head. "We'll talk about it later. We need to listen to the preacher now."

But Mame didn't listen. She tuned out Preacher Houston's words. They were just too depressing. Looking around, she saw hardly a dry eye. Even her grown brothers were crying. But not Mother Mary. No, she stood tall and straight, a frown chiseled hard as stone on her face. Mame knew she was hurting, but why did she have to act so coldhearted?

Poor Will. He just might be better off fishing with Jared and Papa.

Clint held Mame's arm throughout the short graveside service and then led her down the hill when it was over. They would rest in Beckley through tomorrow and leave for Charleston the next morning. That meant two nights with Clint, in the same room, in the same bed. There was no way around it. Otherwise, how would she explain not sleeping in the same room with her own husband? After all, they were newlyweds.

Everyone at the Blackwell house turned in early that night. It had been a long few days. Traveling back to Beckley with Jared's corpse had taken its toll on Mary and Mame, as had the dreadful wait for the rest of the family. Everyone loved Jared so much. They couldn't imagine their days ahead without him. Especially Mary, when he was always in her shadow.

Clint excused himself as the family filed in different directions to their rooms. James and Hank had already taken their families back to their homes. Mame looked at Clint, a question in her eyes.

"I'll be back in a little while; I've got to get some fresh air."

Clint leaned down and brushed Mame's lips with his to keep up the illusion of being a loving husband. Mame watched with a forlorn expression as he slipped on his jacket and headed out into the moon-lit night.

Mame lay in bed wide awake for what seemed like hours as she waited for Clint. Where could he be? He'd have to come to bed sooner or later, or they would both look like fools. Finally, when Mame had almost given up, the doorknob turned, and Clint slipped through the door. He tiptoed in, trying not to wake her, not knowing that she had never gone to sleep.

Mame listened as Clint sat in the chair next to the window and wearily pulled off his boots. Then he leaned the chair back against the wall, and before long Mame heard the heavy breathing from his exhausted sleep. He had been up all last night driving the wagon and then helping with the gravesite.

It was just as well. It wouldn't seem right to be with Clint in the bed she grew up in, especially with Mother, Timothy, Thomas, and William in the bedrooms all around her.

Mame woke up early the next morning when a wave of nausea overcame her. She swallowed several times before hurrying to the washbasin. She barely made it as the vomit came forth. Eyes closed and head bent over the bowl, Mame was overwhelmed with self-pity. Sick, alone, and her brother dead . . . she had to get out of this cursed place.

She washed her face, rinsed her teeth, and dressed slowly in hopes of fending off more nausea. Mame wished this morning sickness would end soon. She prayed no one had heard her throwing up. Sighing, she noted the empty chair where Clint had slept last night. Sitting where he had been, she let the chair hold her since Clint would not.

By now, she should be about two-and-a-half months with child. Mame could not remember her sisters-in-law showing any sign of expecting until they were four or five months along, but her flat stomach already had a distinct roundness to it. As she touched the mound, a vision of Jack Marsh flashed through her memory. Mame hastily pushed Marsh out of her mind, for not only did the tavern memories threaten to make her sick again, they added to the horror of Marsh's hand in her brother's death.

Distraction was becoming an art with Mame. She jumped up and checked out her window to look for Clint. No sign of him, but up the hill she could see her mother at the new grave. Jared . . . Mame could not let herself think about him yet. Her stomach issued another rumble, so she held her breath, then swallowed until the threat of sickness mercifully passed. Her life was spinning out of control, and she didn't know what to do about it.

Where was Clint? Probably helping her brothers with the chores. Mame thought a good biscuit with molasses might ease her stomach, and later a long bath would feel excellent.

She glanced at her black funeral dress draped over the back of a chair. She hoped she never had to wear the thing again. Even the sight of it depressed her. She went over to her cedar chest and started rummaging through some clothes until she found the flannel, yellow dress. This would be a good traveling frock for their trip back to Charleston. She smoothed out the wrinkles, looked in the wardrobe for her boots. Before going through the door to face another day in Beckley, she ran her hand over Clint's jacket that he'd thrown over the end of the bed, the place where he didn't sleep last night.

It was only a short ride on horseback before Clint reached the New River that ran through the eastern part of the Blackwell bottoms.

He needed this time to think and cool off. Clint dove one more time into the icy water before getting out. Shivering, he shook himself like a wet dog trying to rid himself of all the water he could before he put his clothes back on. He still wore his suit pants from the funeral since the women hadn't had time to wash the clothes he'd muddied while digging the dreaded grave. The bright sun warmed his skin but did nothing to lift his somber mood, nor did it help ease his sore muscles that ached from sleeping all night in the chair. The freezing water was probably not the best antidote for stowed up joints. But that wasn't the worst of it. The alluring memory of Mame as she lay sleeping in the moonlight tortured him. He was barely able to pull himself away from the perfect vision, and it took all the willpower he could muster not to crawl between the sheets and lie with her.

The covers had been pushed down below her waist. Though her nightshirt was modest, it didn't hide the rise and fall of her breasts while she slept, nor did the fancy crochet work on the pillowcase compete with the beauty of her hair fanned out on the pillows.

Why did she have this effect on him? Why wouldn't she? Clint's thoughts went to the waterfall. He would never forget her boldness and the sure way she took control. How could he have known she was so innocent?

And since then, just the thought of her made him want much more than the few stolen kisses they'd shared.

So, here he was, literally up the creek without a paddle, swimming in the river in mid-October. It was worth it though. The water had cooled the fire in his loins. He must be losing his sanity. Crazy was something that Mame Blackwell was teaching him awfully well. He just couldn't get her off his mind. She was overpowering, weaving in and out of his every thought. Yes, he surely must be losing his good sense. Or, Mame must be a love conjuring witch, one who'd cast her enchantment spell over him. But there were no potions, no magical fairy dust, just two people who were destined or doomed to be together. Time would tell.

Both sisters-in-law returned to Mary's house while Mame was dressing. Olivia came with her two babies, and Phoebe had her little one riding high on her hip with another one soon on the way. They were full of questions about Clint.

"Okay, Mame. Tell us everything. Is he gentle? Does he whisper sonnets of love in your ear?" Olivia asked all starry-eyed.

Before Mame could think of a way to get rid of her nosy sisters-in-law, baby Ike, who was barely walking, made a strange noise before throwing up all over his shoes. So she could tend to Ike, Olivia handed little Emma to Mame.

Mame had never been as thankful in her life to see vomit. It made her only slightly nauseous. She was grateful that Ike's little mishap had taken the spotlight off her. Phoebe quickly took Aaron home, not wanting him to catch the bug from Ike. For now, Mame had dodged another unwanted interrogation into her private life. Not that there was anything to tell.

The rest of the day was pleasantly peaceful on the surface. Most of the closest neighbors and townspeople had heard about Jared. A slow trickle of different faces and hands bearing food came through the door all day.

Whispers back and forth between the townsfolk brought back memories of when they had all laughed at Mary when she'd first planted the tiny black seeds. Now they didn't laugh, but they were prying into her business.

Why did they need to know why Jared had been in a tavern? Truth be told, every one of these God-fearing Baptists sitting in her gathering room had probably had a shot of whiskey some time or another in their life, if for nothing more than to warm their gut in the wintertime.

Finally, Mary had heard enough. She walked out of the sitting room that held a dozen or so of Beckley's supposed finest citizens. She went straight into the kitchen, noting the two pies old Mrs. Connor had sent by her boy. The sweet smell of cinnamon and nutmeg couldn't sugarcoat these people's whispers concerning her family.

Mary could hear their voices rumbling in her head: What was that boy doing in a tavern? Why'd she bury him so quickly? If she hadn't babied him all his life, he would have known how to fight like a man.

They could all go straight to hell.

What were they doing here now, gloating and offering shallow condolences? Where had they been all those long years she struggled to raise enough tobacco to survive? Oh yes, she well remembered all their hushed whispers that first year after Henry died as they stood back and watched. Some called her the crazy woman. But she had proven them wrong. She didn't need them then, and she didn't need them now.

Out the kitchen door and up the hill she went, past the apple orchard to Jared's grave where she could re-live the haunting memories of his beaten face and think of Henry and that shadowed entrance to the coal mine . . . that pit to hell where he lay.

It was late morning before Clint showed back up at the house. Then he busied himself helping with chores, mostly just looking for anything to do to keep his hands and mind busy. Nobody was in the mood to do much work. Thoughts of Jared weighed heavy on each family member's heart.

Clint fed and tended the livestock so Hank and James could socialize with the company, but still the day passed slowly. There just wasn't enough busy work to keep Clint's mind off Mame.

The day finally ended, but Clint stayed away from Mame's bedroom until he thought she'd be sound asleep. He slipped into her room and settled himself into the woven-bottom straight-back chair as best he could. Sleep eluded him, but he must have drifted off some time during the night because he woke long before daylight with a kinked neck and memories of the dream he'd had.

The lingering moon shoot streams of light through the window. Clint couldn't help but stare at Mame in the moonlight. She was so beautiful. He couldn't resist the urge to touch her cheek. He breathed in a trace of her honeysuckle fragrance. Moving closer to the sleeping angel, he pushed the golden strands of hair from her face. The coolness of the evening had raised chill bumps on Mame's arms. Clint reached to cover her with the quilt; he couldn't resist brushing a fingertip across her rosy cheek. Mame shivered, knowing she'd been touched, and her eyes flew open.

Clint threw both his hands in the air as if caught red-handed stealing chickens. Mame was drowsy and snuggled deeper under the quilts for warmth. For a long time, they didn't move or make a sound. They just stared at each other. Then both started to speak at the same time.

"I'm sorry, Mame. You are just so innocent-looking when you sleep. So beautiful."

Mame had a look about her that was different from any other woman he'd ever seen. It wasn't just her golden hair that was highlighted with streaks of copper. It was her green eyes. They looked deep inside you, holding you, pulling you in deeper and deeper. He reached out to touch her again, caressing her narrow chin between his thumb and forefinger. Other people might have seen flaws when they looked at Mame, but not Clint. Pure and simple, Mame was a natural beauty.

"You could have come to bed these last two nights," Mame told him. "I don't bite, you know."

"But I can't be that close to you. You have no idea what you do to me, and I promised I would not touch you, remember?"

Mame raised up on one elbow. "Who asked you to promise me that? We are married now, Clint. It may not be because we are madly in love, but because of our situation, we are together. Why not make the best of it?" Mame reached over and laid her hand on his leg.

The look in Mame's eyes confirmed that she didn't want him to leave her alone. Mame's desirability surpassed that of any tavern girl Clint had ever known. Compared to Mame, Victoria's blood ran as cold as the river he'd bathed in yesterday. In fact, he needed to visit that river again, right now.

He shut his eyes and made himself stop thinking for just a minute. Then he shook his head, as if to rid himself of the fantasy in which he was living. He couldn't bed her now. Someone would surely be beating on the door any minute to call them out. Clint made up his mind that this was not the time or the place. He also knew that Mame was going to be completely worth the wait.

Scowling, Clint stood up from the edge of the bed, walked over to the chair, and sank slowly into it. He rubbed his closed eyes and scratched his unshaven chin.

"Get your things together. We leave for home this morning."

Mame slipped out of bed, slightly trembling and queasy, but this time it wasn't all due to morning sickness. The cold floor on her bare feet made her shiver. Actually, she was quivering all over, and it wasn't completely because of the cold.

While watching her out of the corner of his eye, Clint pulled on his boots. Mame threw the covers back and made her way to the basin and poured water from the flowered pitcher into it. She splashed her face and then looked at herself in the wall mirror that hung over the basin. Then she picked up her brush and yanked it again and again through her long mane. Sparks flew like fireworks from her golden tresses. Then, as if she were alone, she laid the brush down, crossed her arms in front of her, and gathered her nightshirt up and over her head. She stood nude and still for a moment, then went to her dresser, opened the drawer, and picked a chemise. With deliberation, she stepped into it and pulled it up over her hips, then put her arms through the armholes. She slowly reached down and started lacing up the front.

Clint sat hypnotized. Mame had been fully naked under her sleep shirt. Again he witnessed a vision of pure loveliness. Creamy skin spread over rounded hips, a deliciously full bosom, and he couldn't help but notice the slight roundness of her belly that had not been there a few months ago at the falls. The mound was not unattractive. It only made her look more sensual and womanly.

Before he could comment on her lovely nakedness, a loud rap sounded at the door, followed by Will's voice. "Mame, are you going to sleep all day? Mama says you're leaving this morning. May I come in?"

"Ah . . . just a minute, Will. I'm dressing. I'll be out soon."

Mame quickly pulled her dress up over the scanty chemise, covering her lush body from Clint's watchful eyes. She acted calm, but her insides were like the fluttering of a hummingbird's wings. Where did this boldness come from? And where was it leading her? When it came to being around Clint, Mame felt no modesty or shame.

"Come on, Clint. Hurry. They're waiting for us."

Breathless, Mame dragged her bag from under the bed and threw the rest of her things inside. How could one bag hold a lifetime? As she looked down at the old lace-up shoes on her feet, Mame vowed that they'd be the first things to go when she started her new life in Charleston. Those shoes had walked too many miles of bad memories.

Clint snapped out of the trance that Mame had him in and finished lacing his boots. He picked up her bag and followed Mame out the door, not quite ready to face the entire Blackwell family.

"Everyone wanted to come and see you off. With winter coming soon, I don't know when we'll all be together again."

Mary reached out and touched Mame's shoulder. This small sign of affection was a huge step for Mary, and it didn't go unnoticed by Mame. Before she could stop them, a couple of tears slipped down her cheeks. No, there was no time now for these kind of emotions, Mame had a new life to start. She wiped her cheek with the back of her hand and took her place at the table.

During breakfast, they all laughed and talked about Mame and Clint's future. They were glad for the happy conversation, for the shadow of Jared's grave up on the hill threatened to edge its way down the mountain and consume them at any minute. After the brief social, Clint loaded Mame's bag into the wagon.

Mame had gathered all her belongings into that one peddler's sack. She didn't want souvenirs to remind her of this life. In fact, she never intended to come back to Beckley or step foot on Blackwell land again. Never.

"Mame, you take care of yourself, and Clint, keep a watchful eye on Paddy and Mame for me, will you?" Mary said.

"Of course I will, Mrs. Blackwell. We'll see you in the spring, and maybe Father will be well enough by then to make the trip with us to visit you." Clint knew that was wishful thinking, but his words seemed to lighten the mood.

Mame stepped off the front porch and turned to study the family. Her older brothers wouldn't miss her. They had their own families now, and Timothy and Thomas were almost grown. Though she knew they would miss her, they both thought they were all grown up and couldn't show any childish emotions. But Mame could see their feelings in their eyes.

Then there was Will. A tight lump rose in her throat. Elephant tears rolled down his cheeks. Mame couldn't help it and started to sob herself. Everything inside her heart just came into her mind. Death, marriage, and babies—she needed a release, and the tears were it. She hurried across the porch and wrapped her arms around Will.

"Don't cry, Will. I promise you can come see me anytime you want to. You've got to be Mama's brave helper now."

Mame took Will's hand and led him to Mary's side. She placed his clammy little paw inside Mary's hand. Then she leaned in toward her mama's ear and whispered, "Mama, he needs you. Get to know him, let him inside your heart. He's more like Papa and Jared than any of us."

Mame could only hope Mary would love Will and give him the comfort he needed.

Mame did not hug Mary or say good-bye. She simply turned and walked away.

It was late morning by the time Clint and Mame were on their way back to Charleston. Mame was quiet for miles, alone in her own thoughts.

"Mame, are you okay?" Clint suddenly asked. "I'm sorry for taking you away from Beckley. I wish our lives could have started out differently. Hopefully we'll make the most of our rocky start and learn to be happy with one another."

Mame listened to Clint, noticing he didn't say maybe they could learn to love one another. Yes, she was a little sad, but mainly she was anxious to get her new life started.

"I'm fine. It was hard leaving Will. He's my main worry. But it's Mother's duty to make sure he'll be okay."

Shaking her head as if to clear her mind of all thoughts, Mame started a constant flow of light conversation centered on general matters like the weather and how they wished the railroad ran between Beckley and Charleston so they wouldn't have to endure driving the rig this long trip home. Before they arrived in Charleston, they were both wishing their time alone would never end.

It was almost sundown when Clint pulled the wagon over for the night near a small stream under a grove of short scrub pines.

"These pine needles will make us a good, soft bed, or you can sleep in the wagon if you want to."

Did Mame hear right? Did Clint say "make *us* a soft bed"?

Clint didn't wait for her answer. He jumped down from the wagon and began to set up camp. In no time at all, he had a nice fire smoldering and a pot of stew Olivia had sent simmering over the hot coals. Each preoccupied, they ate very little. Both were recalling that very morning in Mame's room.

After swallowing a few bites of stew, Mame excused herself to go down to the stream to wash up before turning in for the night. She took her time splashing the cold mountain water onto her face. Those few minutes alone cleared her head; she knew exactly what she needed to do.

When she got back to the pines, Clint had made one bed on top of the pine needles and another one in the back of the wagon.

"I thought you might be more comfortable in the wagon," Clint said to Mame as he lay down on top of the bedroll that he'd spread out on the ground.

The evening's coolness sent a shiver through Mame, making her shake. Clint mistook her shaking for nervousness.

"I'm not going to bother you. Don't be afraid."

Clint was sounding a whole lot surer of his self-control than Mame liked. Rather than answer him, she crawled up into the wagon, but not without noticing the disappointment that flickered across Clint's face.

She was out of his sight for only a few minutes before she reappeared, climbing out of the back of the wagon. She had wrapped herself up in the very quilt that had covered her that morning.

Mame wasn't sure how the quilt had ended up on her bed and then in the wagon. She recognized it as a family heirloom that had been given to Mary by Henry's mother on their wedding day. It usually lay neatly folded in the bottom of Mary's cedar wardrobe. Mame knew her mother must have given it to her.

She was shocked at Mary's kind and thoughtful act of love. But, she had no time for thoughts of sentimentality and quickly pushed thoughts of her mother out of her mind.

Mame scooted down from the wagon and walked slowly toward Clint. As she came forward, one side of the quilt dropped from her shoulder, revealing nothing but soft, creamy white skin.

Mame wore not one stitch under that family quilt.

Clint's gaze never left Mame, and she couldn't help it when the corners of her mouth lifted just a little. It took her forever to reach him. Almost three months had passed since they'd lain together. Even with her boldness, Clint seemed hesitant, as if he believed Mame was naïve. After all, she had been a virgin when he took her at the falls.

"Mame, do you have any idea what you are doing to me? I can't take your teasing much longer. You're driving me insane."

Paying no attention to Clint's words, Mame let the blanket fall completely to the ground. Unashamed, she revealed her voluptuous young body to her husband in the shadows of twilight. Oblivious to her shivering, she knelt and playfully lifted the rough blanket Clint had thrown over himself. Then she slipped in beside his expectant body.

They soon lost all sensation of the cold evening air, of the looming pines, and of themselves off the side of this lonesome road upon the soft pine needle bed, beside the red and white quilt. In the day's softly fading light, they were any set of star-struck lovers of any place, of any time.

Their fated union could no longer be denied.

The moon hung over them like a glowing lantern. Mame snuggled up against Clint. Their breathing was deep and harmonious. Neither spoke as Clint pulled Mame's wedding quilt over them and tucked it in around her.

Clint wanted to say something, but sometimes silence was far more effective than words. He couldn't speak words of love to her. Maybe love was what he felt, but he would need more time to be sure that it was not lust alone. He'd had one-sided love before. Victoria had been so prim and proper, he'd not had the raging desire he was experiencing with Mame. He was just plain confused. He raised himself on one elbow, gently leaned down, and kissed Mame on the lips. Electric shocks again sprang to life inside him, but he refused to act like a silly school boy who had just received his first kiss.

"Good night, Mame," Clint said as he snuggled and protectively laid his arm over her.

Lying there on the ground next to Mame in their soft bed made from nature, Clint slept the soundest he may have ever slept.

For a long while, Mame lay awake. Her mind was alive with thoughts and feelings she could not explain. Why was she so uninhibited when it came to Clint? Was this her revenge against him and his father for what had happened to her papa? Or was it something more?

Mame knew down deep that her need for revenge had diminished considerably. All those Bible verses about forgiveness must have sunk in to her subconscious. When she looked at Clint, she felt no malice. What she saw was a beautifully formed man. God had graced him with a gracious spirit and his sightly physique. His smiles were like a precious gift from heaven.

She could feel the muscled hardness of his entire body as he lay close to her. He also showed signs of caring and compassion, which most men did not seem to have. But to say she was falling head over heels in love with Clint Paddington might be a little too farfetched.

She had needed him in order to get out of Beckley, and now that she had accomplished that, she could either try to hate Clint and make his life and Paddy's intolerable, or she could let the terrible deeds of the past rest and make the best of her future with him. The words of God's disciple Luke rang loud and clear in Mame's head:

Forgive, and ye shall be forgiven.

Everything was just too new to Mame, especially love. She'd bide her time and enjoy the life she may not have deserved, but she sure felt like she had earned it.

Tired of thinking, Mame rolled over onto her side and snuggled her backside up against Clint. They seemed to fit together perfectly.

CHAPTER TWENTY

Children's children are the crown of old men; and the glory of children are their fathers.

~ Proverbs 17:6

BY THE TIME CLINT AND Mame arrived in Charleston, each knew more about the other than ever before, and the trip back seemed much shorter than the dreary ride home for Jared's funeral. All day during their travel, conversation flowed easily between them, though neither spoke of their lovemaking the night before.

Clint and Mame pulled into Charleston as the sun was setting low. He brought the wagon around to the back of the Paddington house, jumped down, and briskly moved to the other side of the wagon. There he took Mame by the waist and lifted her off in one strong, confident motion. She giggled in delight.

"Mame, I can't believe you'd never been out of Beckley until you came to Charleston."

"Well, Clint, nothing much has ever happened in my short life. Hard work and raising brothers have been about it."

"All that's getting ready to change. As soon as we can leave Dad, I'll take you to see Roanoke and Huntington. They're both beautiful towns."

They entered the kitchen door, both smiling and laughing. Mrs. Gentry was a little taken aback when they came in. How different they seemed from before. But after all, they were married now. *Maybe I judged her wrongly*, the cook thought as she looked at Clint's face and saw true happiness shining in his eyes.

"Mrs. Gentry, how is Dad?"

But before she could decide how to answer, Clint was through the door and headed for the stairs. Taking them two at a time, he reached the top and turned toward his father's room. There was Theodore Paddington, sitting in his favorite chair beside his bed. When he saw Clint, the uneven grin etched his face. Clint hurried to him and hugged him while asking how he was.

"I'm doing well, son. How are you and Mame, and . . . what about Mary?"

"Mame and I are fine. But Mary . . . well, she's a very strong woman who's in tremendous pain. But she'll make it. Loss is nothing new to Mary.

"I'm sorry we had to spring the wedding news on you so fast before we left. I wanted to have more time to explain it to you, but things were so hurried when Jared died. Mary was in such a rush to get him back to Beckley."

Clint recounted the highlights of their sad and difficult time during the funeral as best he could, for he knew his father would have been in Beckley to support Mary if he'd been able.

Paddy sat still, listening to his son thoughtfully as he rushed on. At last, Clint seemed to look to him for approval. That's when Paddy saw a sparkle in his son's eyes that hadn't been there before.

After recapping the burial of Jared, Clint grew solemn.

Paddy shook his head at another senseless tragedy. "I appreciate your efforts on behalf of our family."

Paddy thought about his deceased wife, Vergie. She'd been gone for so long now. She'd be proud of how honest and loyal her only child had turned out.

"Let's look toward the future, son. I wish you and Mame the very best. She has been very kind to me, and if she makes you as happy as I think she will, you have my blessing. I hope your years together are many and that your love for each other rewards me with many loud and playful grandchildren."

The prospect of grandchildren made Paddy quite happy. He deeply hoped that Mame was everything she appeared to be, as something about her made him feel a little uneasy. It was almost as if she knew things about him that were supposed to be hidden. His secrets.

From the way Mary had described her late husband's features, he caught a glimpse of how Henry Blackwell must have looked as he gazed upon Mame's face. The past sometimes smothered him. How often, and especially now, he wished he could turn back time and bring back the lives of those men who were lost in that mine so many years ago.

Some way, if he ever got back on his feet, Paddy would go to Mary and tell her the truth. He had resolved that he just couldn't live with his guilt anymore, nor did he want to die carrying all the lies with him to the grave.

CHAPTER TWENTY-ONE

And there appeared a great wonder in heaven; a woman clothed
with the sun, and the moon under her feet, and upon her head a
crown of twelve stars: And she being with child cried, travailing in
birth, and pained to be delivered.

~ Revelation 12:1–2

OVER THE NEXT FEW MONTHS, life at the Paddington house
went very smoothly. Soon after Clint and Mame's arrival back in
Charleston, it was obvious that Mame was with child. No one ques-
tioned the size of her stomach, even though she should be about only
three months' pregnant. In reality, she was closer to six months along.
She and Clint both knew why, but they too were a little concerned
about her size. With each day, she grew rounder and rounder.

Winter came, bringing more snow than usual. Mame and Clint
didn't mind. They snuggled up in front of the fire, talking and dreaming. Sometimes Paddy would sit with them, but usually he stayed in
his room, sitting, staring out the window. Everyone knew he was
pining for Mary.

Christmas was simple at the Paddington house that year. Even
though grief hung over them like a shroud, Clint and Mame managed
to find a quiet joy just being with each other.

Hardly a word had come from Beckley these past three months, only a couple of brief letters to Paddy asking about his condition. Will and Mame kept in touch, but as far as Paddy knew, Mame had not received one word from her mother. Paddy knew Mary was grieving for Jared, and maybe she felt guilty for the way she'd treated Mame. He couldn't for the life of him understand the distance between those two. Women—who could figure them out?

Easter morning 1932 brought warmth to Charleston, even though on the highest peaks of the Appalachian Mountains one could still see a cap of snow. As Mame and Clint set out for church that morning, a flock of wild geese flew over their heads.

"Ten, eleven, twelve . . . look, there comes another bunch. I'll bet there are thirty or forty in all, don't you think so, Clint?"

Clint looked over at the woman he'd grown to cherish. Her eyes were sparkling. She looked like a little girl on Christmas morning, except for her huge midsection.

"They're headed back up to Canada since it's warmed up. You'll see lots more. They always come this way. I think they follow the mountain range for direction."

Pulling up in front of the church, Clint fixed the brake handle and brought their brand new 1932 Ford Coupe to a halt.

"How's that for a ride, Mrs. Paddington?"

Mame looked around the church courtyard. Theirs was not the only motorized vehicle, though there were lots more carriages than cars.

"It certainly beats the buggy, but I'm still not convinced it won't blow up and kill us. All this noise and smoke—it just makes me nervous."

Laughing, Clint opened the door, scooted around the front fender, opened Mame's door, and extended his hand to her. Stepping out of the Ford, Mame's mind leaped back through the years. A poor girl from Beckley, West Virginia . . . a coalminer's daughter who would never have expected to have anything but a plain house and a tired back . . . coming to church in a fancy new car. An overwhelming sense of guilt passed through her.

She swayed.

"What's wrong, Mame? Are you feeling ill?" Clint held her steady.

For a moment, Mame couldn't speak. She closed her eyes and leaned against the car door. A flash of Jack Marsh's face came to her mind. She'd done a good job of keeping thoughts of him out of her head, but now all she could think about as she laid her hand on the hard mound of protruding belly was the ugliness of that night, the pain he'd put her through, then the realization of what she'd done.

Oh please, God. She looked up at the happy churchgoers in their Easter finery ascending the steps. *Don't let this baby be his.* Yet she knew it would be. That would be her punishment. For the rest of her life, she would have to look at Jack Marsh's child.

Patting her sweat-covered brow with her kerchief, Mame tried to calm herself. She shut her eyes and willed Marsh to leave her be.

"Let's go inside. I think I just got too hot."

"Are you sure you don't want to go home?"

"No, I'll be fine, just a dizzy spell."

Walking toward the church, Mame stared up at the same steeple Jared had looked at on his first trip to Charleston. He'd pointed it out to them as they approached the city on Mame's first trip to the river town. Another wave of guilt ripped through Mame as she pictured Jared's smile. His battered face would be etched on the canvas of her mind forever.

Not my fault. Not my fault. It was Mother's coddling that made him so weak. It was not my fault.

Once inside the church, Clint led Mame to the Paddington pew, the place they always sat, right side, fifth row from the back. Mame was glad for the seat because she didn't think she could stand another minute. She was sure her legs would give way soon if she didn't sit.

About halfway through the sermon, Mame's head started swimming again and she felt sure she was going to smother to death. She'd heard the crucifixion story many times, but today as the preacher so vividly painted a picture of spikes driven into Jesus' hands, and His head a bloody, mauled mess from all the beatings, all she could see was the face of her brother lying on the doctor's table after Marsh's cruel whipping.

Mame could listen no longer. Without saying a word, she stood up and stepped around the corner of the pew and ran for the door as fast as her bulkiness would allow. Outside, she gasped for the fresh, clean air to fill her lungs; all the blood was choking her.

Clint was right behind her. Taking her arm, he led her to the coupe.

"Mame, are you all right? What happened?"

"I'll be fine, just couldn't catch my breath. I had to stand up."

Mame could not voice her visions of Jared. If she spoke what she was feeling out loud, it would make it more real and too hard to shut out. No, she was finished. No more thoughts of death, guilt, or Jesus' sacrifice.

"Take me home, please. I just need to lie down for a little while."

Clint stayed close to Mame as time passed. The newlyweds continued to find any excuse to go to their room alone. About the first of May, Mame felt too huge to even climb the stairs to their room. Clint had never truly seen anyone pregnant up close, but he was sure Mame's once perfectly flat tummy was surely going to burst wide open. After all, it did resemble a ripe watermelon.

In actuality, she was almost at the end of her eighth month.

Paddy's health had progressed nicely through the winter. He could now get around with only the support of a cane. Maybe by the time the baby arrived, they'd drive the new car to Beckley. Surely Mame would want to show her mother the baby, and Paddy longed to see Mary. Clint knew when he looked at Mame that she could not possibly go another month before delivering their baby. And he was exactly right.

Mame sat at the kitchen table. It was early; Mrs. Gentry had not yet arrived to start breakfast. Easing out of bed while it was still dark, Mame tried not to wake Clint. At her size, that was no easy feat. She trudged downstairs and put the coffee on the stove, but before the water could boil, a contraction hit her. Down low in her abdomen, a sharp pain cut through her, taking her breath away. That one lasted only a minute, but for the next hour the pain was continuous, Mame couldn't tell when one contraction started or another one ended. By the time Mrs. Gentry arrived, she found Mame sitting at the table, clutching her extended belly, grimacing, her face wet with sweat, and the coffee pot boiling, sputtering hot drops of coffee all over the stovetop.

"What's wrong, Miss Mame?" Mrs. Gentry asked. "That pot's a-boiling away."

She rushed toward the stove and grabbed a dishrag to take hold of the coffee pot handle and move it off the red-hot burner. She turned around to scold Mame but saw the pain on her face and then the puddle of bloody fluid underneath her chair.

Pain ripped through Mame. She tried to stay calm. It wasn't quite time for the baby yet. It should be at least another three more weeks by her calculations and her doctor's, according to her one visit to Doc Stuart's at Clint's insistence.

All of a sudden, Mame felt an uncontrollable urge to push.

"Mrs. Gentry, I think I'm in trouble. You better go get Clint."

"Oh, the baby's coming!" Mrs. Gentry exclaimed. She hurried to the stairs.

"Mr. Clint! Mr. Clint!" she called at the top of her lungs. She was almost to his bedroom door when it flew open.

"Mr. Clint, come quick! Miss Mame. The baby. Hurry!"

Clint pulled on his pants and ran past Mrs. Gentry toward the scream coming from below in the kitchen. Buckling his belt, he took the steps two at a time. When he reached Mame, she was still sitting at the table, doubled over in agony.

It took Mame a few moments before she could speak. "Something's wrong. It's too early. The pain just came on so quickly. This can't be normal. Nothing should hurt this much."

Just then Paddy came through the door. "What's going on? What's all this racket so early in the morning?"

As soon as he scanned the room, he understood. "Quick, Mrs. Gentry, go get Doc Stuart. Clint, we've got to get her up to the bed."

Each man took a side and lifted under Mame's arms, bringing her to her feet. This was nearly impossible, for Paddy had to lean on his cane for support. But his adrenaline was flowing and Paddy took his place beside Mame, turning his weak side opposite her. He gritted his teeth so hard, he thought they'd crack, but he was determined to help. He had to.

Another pain stabbed through Mame, this time into her lower back. She stumbled, a sob catching in her throat. Clint immediately reached down put an arm under her knees and lifted her off the floor. Her belly might be huge, but the rest of her was still a small, precious handful to him. Paddy stepped away, sweat pouring from his forehead, glad to be relieved of his burden. Sorry, too, that he had not been man enough to give his son much help.

Clint rushed her up the stairs and took her to their bed, which was still slightly warm from his swift awakening just minutes ago.

Clint helped Mame strip off her wet gown, eased her onto the bed, and observed the large, red stain flowing from between her legs onto the bed. Alarmed, he grabbed some sheets left folded on the dresser and gently eased them under her. He tried to adjust the feather pillows under Mame's head to make her more comfortable, but she could not be still, thrashing her head back and forth in pain. Clint ran to the door and hollered out for Paddy to go see what was keeping Doc Stuart. Clint knew he could find the doctor faster, but he couldn't leave Mame.

He sat down on the bedside and took her hand in his. "I'm sorry, Mame. This is my fault. If only I'd left you alone at the falls, you wouldn't be going through this."

Mame lay flushed, with her hair tangled and wet with sweat.

"But if it hadn't happened, would we be together now?"

She looked at him lovingly and moaned as another wave of pain jolted through her. She couldn't help but wonder if this was her punishment for all her lying and deceiving these last eight months. She had been a dark, conniving child all on her own. Was there enough forgiveness in the world to save her?

"What will people think, Clint? I'm supposed to be only seven months along. Your father and Mrs. Gentry will think I'm a no-good trollop."

"It doesn't matter now. Who cares what anyone else thinks?"

Leaning down, Clint gently kissed her. Even with the situation grim as it was, a ripple of excitement went through him. They had not been able to be together in months because of her size and discomfort, so his need was great. This, mixed with the emotion of his first child coming into the world, made him edgy.

Mame felt him squeeze her hand a little too hard. They had become so close these past months together. As Mame looked up at Clint, she knew she had been in love with him for a long time, maybe even since their first spontaneous passion at the falls.

I pray this baby is Clint's. Please, God, don't let it be dark and evil like Jack Marsh. Knowing she would be almost full-term if the baby was Clint's, Mame shoved these bad thoughts away. It was Clint's. In her mind Mame begged and pleaded with God:

Please, Lord, let this baby's locks be light and golden like its father.

Doc Stuart arrived shortly, and Clint left the room so the doctor could examine Mame.

"Okay, Mame. I'll help you all I can, but the real work will come from you. Everything seems to be going normally as far as I can tell," he said as he checked her. "This could take all day. Sometimes first babies like to be difficult."

Difficult did not seem an extreme enough description when at eight o'clock that night—over twelve hours later—there was still no sign of a baby. Mame's pain was unrelenting.

Doc Stuart stepped out of the bedroom, leaving Mrs. Gentry to wipe Mame's forehead. In the hall, Clint waited, one foot propped up against the wall. Standing outside that door, Clint longed for the cry of a baby. This child seemed determined not to come into this world.

"Clint, things are not going exactly like they should be," Doc said in a low voice. "I'm going to have to try and hurry things along, and I need your help. Mame is losing too much blood. We need to get that baby born and the bleeding stopped."

"Okay, Doc." Clint stood up straight, ready for the task before him, or so he thought.

"What do I do?"

"Come with me. Follow my instructions, no matter how harsh they seem."

Nervous yet determined, Clint followed Doc into their bedroom where Mame lay, writhing and moaning. It was the worst thing Clint had ever seen, and oh, he had seen many harsh things having grown up with farm animals and cattle slaughtering. But Mame's anguish, the ghostly glow of her face, and the bloody, disheveled sheets made his heart pound. His defenses went astray. Clint could feel his own blood drain as his head swam, and he wobbled.

Doc glanced over, hoping that he was not gaining a second patient. There was no time to delay, so he was glad to see Clint's color return quickly.

"She's been in hard labor all day—pushing—and with the loss of blood, she's just worn out," said Doc, who was weary himself.

He directed Clint to wash up and dry his hands on a clean towel, which just so happened to be the treasured one with forget-me-not flowers embroidered by Clint's own mother's hand when she was no more than Mame's age. He glanced over at her photograph on the wall, and she gave him strength.

"Stand as close to her as you can, and when I tell you, place both hands high on her stomach and push down toward me," Doc said.

Clint was trying to talk to Mame and coax her to open her eyes, but she was too weak. He squeezed her hand and said, "I am right here with you, Mame."

He knew Doc was right. Something had to be done. Mame was deathly pale.

As he readied himself above Mame, Doc stood at the foot of the bed and placed his hands over Mame's abdomen trying to determine the exact position of the baby.

"I was afraid of that—it must be trying to come out feet-first. It's too late to turn it. It's going to have to come this way. Okay, Clint. When I say 'go,' push down. You ready? Go."

Clint forced himself to apply pressure to Mame's stomach, but he was afraid he was hurting her. The second he started pushing, her moans became fierce and much louder, reminding Clint of a mountain lion he once heard up on the ridge. Sounded just like a screaming woman.

"Harder, Clint. Harder. We've got to get this baby out."

Somehow, with one knee on the bed for leverage, Doc Stuart wrangled out both of the baby's feet.

"Now Clint, I've got the feet. One more hard push and we'll have a baby."

It was now ten o'clock at night. Sixteen hours of this incredible strain had just about gotten the best of Clint. He could not imagine how Mame felt, or how she could survive such torture. From the looks of the blood-stained sheets and the paleness of her face, she might not.

"Do it, Clint. Push—hard."

With all his might, Clint pushed while Doc steadily pulled the little baby's feet and torso out of Mame. An unrecognizable sound came from Mame; like that mountain lion had just got caught in a steel trap. It was too much for Clint to bear. It was just too much!

When the baby boy's little dark head popped out, Doc knew they were in real trouble, because right behind it, another head, this one light-haired, was crowning. The babies had been head-to-head. The same way the brothers would be for the rest of their lives.

With precision, he cut the cord and handed the first baby to Mrs. Gentry, who had worked with Doc Stuart all day.

"Wipe out the baby's mouth and nose."

As she took the little baby boy and worked on him, he began to cry. Clint shut his own teary eyes, let out a sigh of relief, then reached to hold his baby. Doc was still standing at the foot of the bed, working with Mame.

"Get back up there, Clint. We're not finished."

Clint turned around so fast he nearly lost his balance. "What now, Doc? Surely I don't have to mash on her any more."

"You do if you want your other child delivered."

Clint heard the words, but they didn't register until he bent and saw another head with a long lock of lighter hair straining against Mame's resisting body.

"Merciful heavens. Two babies?" Clint raked a hand through his rumpled hair.

None of them had suspected twins, but it certainly explained Mame's impressive size.

Clint had no time to think. This second baby took only one additional push from his powerful hands. It was in the head-first position, so out it came with no further problems.

This time, there was no moan from Mame, and she'd stopped stirring.

One dark. One light. Both babies were long, but neither was very plump since they'd come too early. Which was not uncommon for twins.

However, Doc wished he'd had a little more warning. How was he to know? Mame had only come to his office that one time early on in her pregnancy. But really, what could he have done different had he known there were two babies?

Doc passed the second boy to Mrs. Gentry. She repeated the cleanup, picked up the first baby, who appeared to be a might smaller than the light-haired one, and looked bewildered as she faced everyone, holding a crying baby in the crook of each arm.

Paddy had been waiting in the upstairs hall, sitting, and then pacing. It was harder to be still once Clint went inside with Mame, so he had retreated down the hall to his bedroom. He tried to distract himself with reading his Bible, but he couldn't remember what happened one line to the next.

When he heard the wails of his first grandchild, Paddy laughed with joy, dropped the Lord's book, and clapped his hands. Concern vanished from his face as he made his way back toward Clint and Mame's room as fast as he could. He was almost there when he heard another cry. At some level, he instinctively sensed that this cry sounded different. He knocked softly and then peeked through the cracked door just enough to see the results of all the commotion.

The scene was not a pleasant sight.

Blood seemed to be everywhere—the bed, the floor, all over Doc Stuart, Mame, Clint, and the *two* babies in Mrs. Gentry's blood-covered arms. Paddy's mouth dropped open and all he could think was: Mame's going to die. For a moment, Paddy was speechless. Then he knew he had to do something.

"I'm going to find more help."

The doctor looked up from working with Mame, nodded to him, and ordered Clint, who looked thunderstruck, to find cold water, ice if he had any, and more clean rags. Doc had to stop the bleeding.

As he gathered the supplies, Clint felt like he was moving in slow motion, as if he were out of his body, like this was happening to someone else.

"Is she going to be all right, Doc?"

"It's too soon to tell, Clint. She's in bad shape. Be quick about it now, get my supplies."

Clint hurried from the room, barely glancing in the direction of his new sons.

Thirty minutes passed before Paddy returned with two neighbor-hood ladies. They surveyed the grim situation, and then each one took a swaddled baby to carry to the kitchen.

Mrs. Gentry had sent Paddy over to her house early that morning to tell Amos what was going on and that she might be late getting home. Now she wasn't sure she'd ever get home.

The next morning showed no improvement. The situation was still grim. Doc Stuart worked diligently all night with Mame. The bleeding had slowed, but it hadn't stopped completely.

Mame had not moved since the babies' birth, not even a flutter of her eyes. That led to another problem; both babies were starving, wailing at the top of their lungs.

Mame was much too frail to nurse her babies, so the ladies filled makeshift bottles with warmed cow's milk and added a small amount of corn syrup. The foreignness of it all did not set well with the new-borns, but gradually the ladies got enough milk into them to satisfy them for brief stretches.

Mrs. Gentry and the two neighbors kept up the feeding vigil the first day, burping, holding, walking, and finally putting the babies down to sleep every closed-eye moment. Mrs. Gentry felt like the grandmother in charge, grateful though she was for the neighbors' help. All three women fretted over those babies something awful, all the while wondering what the chances were that their mother would ever wake up.

When would Mame rouse? Would she ever? Would the Paddington home ever recover from such chaos? Mame needed to wake soon and take some nourishment to build up her strength, or else she and the babies might not make it.

The late evening sun shone through the back kitchen window as Doc Stuart made his way to the door.

"Mrs. Gentry, I'm going home for a while to get some sleep. Just have someone change Mame's packing if it looks soaked, and try to keep waking her up. I believe the bleeding is normal now, so all we can do is pray she'll rouse soon."

As the old doctor walked out, he seemed a little more stooped than when he'd arrived over thirty-six hours earlier.

Mrs. Gentry trudged up the steps to check on things. She found Clint lying beside Mame on the bed, his arm woven tightly around her. The cook quietly closed the door and went to the next room, which now served as nursery to the two new Paddingtons.

"Land sakes, what a sight you are, Mr. Paddington, sitting there rocking that baby boy."

Paddy held one sleeping baby. Widow Montgomery had the other, feeding him with a hand-me-down bottle from the hurriedly gathered supplies. They'd had to bring in a second rocking chair from a spare guest room to accommodate the unexpected twin boy.

"Is Mame any better?" Paddy asked.

"No, she's still not moved, but Clint's finally getting some sleep. Poor fellow, ain't left her side. He's barely looked at his babies—God help us all if she don't make it." Mrs. Gentry straightened her apron. "I do know one thing, I'm sure way too old to be tending to one baby, much less two. So Miss Mame's just got to get well."

As she walked away, Mrs. Gentry wiped away a tear. What she lacked in delicacy, she made up for in generous concern. She returned to the kitchen, satisfied she'd done what she could. All was as well as it could be upstairs. She wondered if she'd ever be able to go home and rest.

The second morning after the childbirth, Clint was sitting by Mame's side when he heard a slight moan.

"Mame, can you hear me? Wake up. Please try to open your eyes."

Somewhere, as if down a dark tunnel, Mame could hear Clint's voice, but she felt too tired to answer him. He wouldn't stop calling her name. She willed her eyes to open long enough to see Clint's face. But trying to open them was like trying to wrestle the heavy lid off a rusty barrel.

What had happened? Was her baby born yet?

Everything was a blur, a nightmare more hideous than she could ever imagine. Was it a dream, or had someone been holding two screaming babies? And all that blood. Silently in her mind Mame screamed when she remembered that one of the babies had a jagged scar etched down its face, and its skin tone was dark, just like Jack Marsh's.

The recollection of that awful image came flooding over her like muddy rainwater into the barrel where she was hiding. Mame struggled against waking up. She never wanted to see that child's face. She'd just stay hidden in this barrel forever. Had there even been a second baby? For its face, she had not seen.

Clint continued calling her name.

"Mame, wake up! Please, Mame, you've got to wake up."

Yes—it is just a dream. There are no babies. It was hard for Mame to distinguish reality from nightmare.

Was she still asleep? Should she go back inside the barrel, or try and wake up?

Yes, she needed to open her eyes and end this wicked dream. But try as she might, Mame's eyes would not open. The barrel lid had slammed shut, and again there was darkness as she drifted off into a deep, murky, restless sleep for the remainder of the day.

Clint finally left Mame's side to check on the twins and found his father holding one as the other one slept. "Dad, what am I going to do? If Mame doesn't wake up soon and feed the babies, I'm afraid they won't make it. She's been unconscious for forty-eight hours."

"Son, Widow Montgomery said we ought to take the babies in to Mame. She said their presence might make her stir."

Clint rubbed his jaw and shook his head. "I don't know, Dad. She's so weak. I don't want her to move around and start bleeding again. But you're right. We've got to do something."

When Doc Stuart checked Mame that afternoon and said the bleeding was minimal, Clint knew they had to try doing something. Doc agreed the babies being near Mame might bring her around.

With the decision made, Paddy and Clint went down the stairs in search of Clint's twin sons. They found them in the kitchen. Mrs. Gentry had placed a pot of water on the stove to heat so she could scald the bottles' plastic nipples. She was becoming accustomed to juggling several chores at once. The neighborhood women had gone to their homes to prepare dinner, but they'd be back.

Paddy took the light-haired son and Clint the dark one from the one cradle they both shared. Carrying them carefully, they returned to Mame's room, approached the bed, and laid one baby on either side of Mame.

Immediately Mame felt someone's presence. Was it Clint? But what was that noise? The squeal of a wailing baby pounded in her head. It had to be her little one, and it sounded distressed. She had to wake up and get to her baby. With every ounce of strength she could muster, she strained to open her eyes.

The first thing she saw was a small, light-colored head lying in the crook of her right arm. A rush of relief flooded through Mame . . . blond hair, just like Clint's. But this baby was sound asleep. Where was the crying coming from? Searching for the sound, she turned her head to the left, and before she could stop herself, Mame screamed. It was just like in the nightmare. Two babies—one light like Clint, the other as dark as Jack Marsh's soul.

Was she still dreaming? No, the lid was off the barrel. This was not her imagination, but real. Before she could stop herself, Mame started panicking. "Someone, take this baby away! It's not mine. Take it away!"

Mame pulled her arm from under the dark-haired baby and tried to wiggle away from it, all the while gathering the fair one closer to her.

"Mame, it's all right. We've got two baby boys, and they need you. They're hungry."

As he spoke, the light-haired baby began to whimper, and automatically Mame pushed her gown away so the tiny mouth could find her milk-engorged breast. She paid not the least bit of attention to the other wailing bundle.

"Why is that baby here? Where is its mother? Get it out of here! Take it back to where it belongs."

Clint frowned. "Mame, I told you. Both babies are ours. You had twins."

"No, I didn't," she insisted. "This is my only son." She pulled the light one closer to her breast. "Take that one away." She glared at the dark one.

Clint reached down and took his son into his arms, trying to soothe his hungry screams. "Mame, you must feed him. He's starving."

Mame shook her head. "No, go find his real mother. Why are you trying to play this awful trick on me? Give that baby back to its mother."

Words bounced back and forth. Clint tried to make her understand, but he had no luck. Finally he handed the baby to Paddy and asked him to take the infant back to Mrs. Gentry so she could try and feed him.

"And Dad, send for Doc Stuart."

Leaving the room with the baby, Paddy wondered what could be wrong with Mame. It just wasn't natural for a woman to reject her own child.

Clint was thinking the same thing. When would this nightmare end?

Soon Paddy returned with Doc Stuart on his heels.

"Doc, I'm so glad you're here," Clint said just inside the bedroom door. "Mame's gone crazy. She won't take both babies. Says one of them is somebody else's. What are we going to do? We can't hold her down and make her nurse him."

The doctor gripped his shoulder. "Hold on now. Not so fast. Mame's still in shock from the trauma and blood loss. Give her time to get her head straight. Paddy said she took to the first baby she saw. That's perfectly normal. She'll bond with the other one in time."

Mame could hear them talking as if she wasn't even there. Lying in bed with her baby pulled close to her side, she knew she'd never bond with Jack Marsh's son. Every time she looked at it, it would remind her of that awful night, the evening she'd crossed paths with Scarface.

To her the baby looked just like Marsh. Except for the absence of the wicked scar, the child was Marsh's miniature double.

What was she to do? How could she explain not wanting her own child? She realized she'd have to force herself to mother both boys. Only the truth would explain her rejection. Mame had no choice but accept both babies, one a treasure, the other a curse.

Looking down at the boy in her arms, she believed he was the exact image of Clint. How could the other one be so different? She would just have to block out any possibility that Jack Marsh could be their father. Maybe as the twins grew older, she'd be able to tell for sure. But for now, she'd concentrate on believing that Clint was their father. That was what she'd believe. She'd have to or go insane for sure. The inside of the wooden barrel loomed before her.

As Mame looked down at the perfect likeness of Clint, she vowed that no one could ever know the truth. Only she and Marsh knew. She surely wasn't going to tell. Marsh—based on the outcome of his trial—was scheduled to be executed in a month for her brother's fatal wounding.

So her secret was safe. No one would ever know the truth. Mame would file away her secret in that "do not open" part of her brain.

"Go get my other son."

A sigh of relief escaped Clint. Mame wanted him to bring her second baby to her. As he watched her pull both sons close, one at either breast, he'd never felt more love for anyone or anything as he did for his new family right then.

They named the light-colored boy Henry Walter after Mame's father. Clint insisted they name the dark one Benjamin Jared after Mame's deceased brother. Mame argued, but since she couldn't rightly give a good explanation why she didn't want the baby named after her brother, she finally relented.

How awful it seemed to name a baby who looked so much like Jack Marsh after the brother he had killed. Another thing she'd have to learn to live with.

The boys' names were quickly shortened to Ben and Walt.

Mame's recovery was very slow. With all the blood loss, topped with nursing two babies, it was weeks before she started feeling like her old self.

The boys were very small, Ben weighing four-and-a-half pounds and Walt barely five, but everything else about them seemed perfect. Both were good eaters, and soon they were growing like the small tobacco seedlings Mame watched sprout so many times back home.

Clint wired Mame's mother soon after the babies were born. Mary wired back words of congratulations and happiness, but she had no plans to come and see the newborns. How could she? They were right in the middle of planting her tobacco. This was no surprise to Mame; she didn't expect her mother to ever put anything ahead of the farm.

Mame made a slow recovery, and the busy hours spent with the twins made the days and weeks speed by. Clint hired a nursemaid to help, and Mame found herself frequently handing Ben over to the helper. In reality, the only time Mame held Ben was when he suckled at her breast. No one seemed to notice, as they were all absorbed in the commotion the newborns had brought to the Paddington house.

CHAPTER TWENTY-TWO

Thou art my hiding place and my shield: I hope in thy word.

~ Psalm 119:114

JUNE 17, 1932: THE DAY Mame would never forget.

"Mame, sit down. I've got something you need to read." Clint handed Mame *The Charleston News* and stepped back to watch her. The front page headline read:

Convicted Killer Escapes

Jack Marsh on his way to be executed . . .

Mame dropped the newspaper on the floor, and her hands fell lifeless to her side. It was a good thing she wasn't holding one of the babies, for they would have surely been dropped.

"Mame, Mame, speak to me."

She couldn't. She sat in shock for almost half an hour. Then, deathly pale, she looked at Clint and asked, "Please bring me my boys."

Clint fetched them and laid one in each crook of her arm.

"You can leave us alone, I'm fine."

"Are you sure you want to be by yourself? I know how upset you are. I can't believe Jared's killer is loose. Let me sit with you and take one of the boys."

Clint reached for Walt, but Mame possessively drew him to her.

"No. I just need to be alone with them and my memories of Jared."

Clint understood and left the room, closing the door softly behind him.

Mame looked down first at Walt, then Ben, and a single tear slipped out of her eye. It rolled down her cheek and softly plunked on Baby Walt's forehead.

Oh, my precious baby boy. I thought it would all be over when Marsh died, but now he's as alive as ever, and he could be anywhere. He might even be looking in the window right now.

Gathering Walt closer to her breast, she let Ben slip further down in her lap. I'll never let him see you, Walt. I'll never let him get near you. Then she looked at Ben. I'll especially never let him see you, because if he does, he'll know the truth.

From that day forward, Mame made a fortress of the Paddington home. Keeping the doors locked and curtains drawn, she rarely left, guarding the boys' every move. She wouldn't even let Clint take them to church.

Mame stayed home with the boys. As they got older, she started teaching them Bible lessons that she remembered from her papa. Clint continued to grace the Paddington bench at the First Baptist Church of Charleston. After all, it was expected that someone of his social standing attend church.

More than once Clint had to bend the truth when asked where his family was. One boy or the other was sick, or Mame had taken them on a trip back home, or they stayed home to look after his father. Finally, the church members just quit asking.

Clint knew she was being an overprotective mother, but he understood that she was afraid since Jack Marsh escaped. On the other hand, Paddy thought it very strange. He couldn't say anything, because everything appeared different to him since his stroke. Maybe it was just his injured brain's way of thinking, but something was just not right. Mame was acting plain old ridiculous.

Paddy had come a long way since the onset of his illness. His leg and arm motion had been rehabilitated almost one hundred percent, but sometimes he lost his train of thought. A few times, he'd even found himself at a place without knowing how he got there. He wanted so badly to see Mary but was afraid to venture away from home that far. Maybe, just maybe, she'd soon come back to Charleston for a visit.

CHAPTER TWENTY-THREE

O death, where is thy sting? O grave, where is thy victory?

~ 1 Corinthians 15:55

THE YEARS SWIFTLY PASSED FOR the entire Paddington family. Soon it was 1940, and the boys were eight years old. For some reason, providence had not blessed Clint and Mame with more children. Clint believed it was because Mame had such a hard delivery with the twins, but deep down Mame wondered if it was another punishment for her sins.

Even though they'd not been blessed with more children, the years had been good to Clint and Mame. The love they shared was more solid than ever. It was a shame their lovemaking hadn't produced more offspring, but what did it matter? They were happy just as they were.

Paddy died that year, never to see Mary Blackwell again. Never fulfilling his need to confess. They had shared letters over the years, but Mary just could not bring herself to return to that wicked city where her baby Jared had been so brutally murdered.

Mentally, Paddy was never the same after the stroke and heart attack. He'd been prone to wander off. Someone in town always found him and brought him home safely.

The last time Paddy wandered down the road and couldn't find his way back home, the infamous Hobert Frost delivered him back to his doorstep.

Mrs. Gentry answered the knock at the door that day.

"Found him down by the creek. Don't even know his own name, worthless old fool. Done lost his marbles," Hobert told her.

Hobert smiled a wide, toothless grin. He was glad he'd lived to see the mighty Theodore Paddington brought down. What's he got to feel big about now? The old man can't even find his way home.

As Hobert stood there at Paddy's door laughing at him, a steady stream of yellow trickled out of Paddy's pant leg and puddled on the rock doorstep. When Hobert Frost saw that Paddy had peed himself, he slapped his leg in glee and laughed his way plumb out of sight. Mrs. Gentry took Paddy's hand and led him inside.

Paddy realized that he'd lost control. He instructed the entire household to never let him out of the house again. He was still a very proud man, and he didn't want anyone to see him like that ever again. To have to rely on someone like Hobert Frost for help was enough to make him consider killing himself. But his reverence for God held him back.

Besides, his last years enjoying his grandsons had been happy ones. Even though Mary had not returned to Charleston since Jared's death, his life had been good. If only he'd been able to shed himself of the guilt.

Mame had not seen her mother since she pulled out of Beckley the day after Jared was laid to rest up on the hill above the house. Mary wired them ever so often, and Paddy got an occasional letter, but as usual she showed no genuine interest in her daughter or her grandsons. Mary's tobacco business was thriving. She was the buyer.

Other farmers now brought their crops to her to sell. She had no need to go to Charleston and sell her leaf.

Clint had been running the family business since Paddy's illness, but Mary didn't need him now. She didn't need anyone.

Alone downstairs, Mame answered the ringing phone. It was her brother William.

"Hey, Mame, I've got something to tell you. Mother is very ill and asking for you. Will you come home?"

For a minute, Mame couldn't speak.

"Mame, are you there?"

Finding her voice, she asked, "How sick is she?"

"Deathly. The doctor says she's got no more than a few days at best."

For some reason unknown even to herself, Mame didn't hesitate. She knew she had to go.

"I'll be there as soon as possible."

Mame gripped the receiver in her hand so hard her knuckles turned white. Finally, she put it down and sat. She lost track of time as the afternoon sun slanted low through the open curtains in the west window of the parlor.

Clint found Mame in the same spot when he and the twins arrived home from riding.

"Hey, Mame," Clint called cheerfully as they came in the room. Knowing something was the matter when she didn't answer, he went to her.

"Mame, what's wrong? Are you sick? Why are you sitting here in the dark?"

After several moments of silence, Mame simply said, "Mother's dying. I've got to go back to Beckley."

She had never been close to her mother, not since she was a little girl before her papa died, but it was still a shock to know one's mother was near death. In disbelief, Mame looked up at Clint. He leaned over and touched her face with a gentleness he had only for her.

"She's always been so strong," Mame said. "I thought she was indestructible. I can't believe she's dying."

"Don't worry, Mame. I'll arrange for us to go to Beckley immediately."

Mame sighed heavily. "Clint, I haven't seen Mother in years. I can't imagine why she would be asking for me. But I feel drawn to her, as if she's pulling me back."

Walt and Ben stood at the doorway, listening to the talk about a grandmother they'd never met.

"I'll take the boys with me."

"We'll all go, Mame. I'll get Maurice at the office to do the buying while we're away."

For reasons Mame couldn't even explain to herself, she didn't want Clint to go. She felt a need to be alone with her mother, maybe to settle their differences, to square things before death swallowed Mary up.

"No, Clint. I've got to do this. The boys and I will leave first thing in the morning."

"Mame, you've driven very little out on the open road."

"I know. I'll just take the buggy. The boys will enjoy helping me drive."

"It's too far, Mame. That's silly of you not to let me drive you."

"No. I want it this way," she argued. "It will be a special trip for me and Walt . . . and Ben."

"Now you listen to me, Mame. No wife of mine is going to go that far in a buggy when there's an almost new '39 Ford out back in the shed. Besides, it will take you twice as long in the wagon, and what if you don't make it before she passes?"

Mame pondered a few minutes, knowing Clint was right.

"Okay. I'll take the car. We'll be fine. I know how to drive, and besides, you've been teaching the boys. They can help me watch for the right turns."

Walt ran into the parlor to stand before his mother. "But, Mom, I want to stay here with Lilly. Her calf is ready to come any day. I might miss it."

Lilly was his prize-winning cow, bringing home award after award from every exhibit at the fair. He had raised her on a bottle after her mother died birthing her, so she was very special to him, especially now that she was giving birth to her own calf.

Stepping into the gloomy room, Ben spoke, "I'll go, Mama. Walt can stay here with Lilly."

Despite their rocky start, Mame had formed a warm attachment to Ben, though her heart grew full of love merely looking at Walt. She really wanted Walt with her, but couldn't quickly come up with an excuse for him to go and Ben to stay. All of the twins' life, Mame had worked hard not to show favoritism, but she couldn't help but wonder sometimes if Ben sensed her detachment from him. It seemed to always make him try harder to win her approval.

"I really don't mind, Mama. I want to go and help you."

Ben felt he always had to beg for her attention, but that was okay. He was used to it.

CHAPTER TWENTY-FOUR

For where envying and strife is, there is confusion and every evil work.

~ James 3:16

THE NEXT MORNING DAWNED COOL and clear as Mame and Ben started out on the long trip to Beckley, one she had hoped never to make again. Something felt undone, unfinished, dark and foreboding but inevitable, and it was drawing her back.

The time passed fairly quickly as they traveled in the automobile. Mame felt sufficiently comfortable with her driving skills after the first twenty miles or so. It wasn't as if she couldn't drive. Ben read the road signs that would lead her home. She knew the way, but she let Ben think he was helping. Familiar landmarks took her back to that first trip to Charleston, to her destiny, to Clint.

Why must Jack Marsh's shadow forever loom over her? Why? Because he'd never been found. It was as if he'd fallen off the edge of the earth. Mame prayed it was so.

Along the way, Ben chattered happily, and Mame pointed out features of the rolling landscape and named road names she remembered. Both nibbled on food from the picnic basket that Clint and Walt helped pack for them.

Before she knew it, the homeplace came into sight. Mame felt a tightening in her chest. A gripping premonition of what was to come and what had been washed over her: Her mother—death—the grief she felt after her father was killed in the mine; all the resentment she felt for the long days and nights of hard labor running the house while her mother worked in the fields; the thanks and love she never received from her mother; all the love and tenderness that she so desperately needed as a young girl but never received; and all the ache of losing Jared at the hands of that wicked Jack Marsh, whom she'd entangled in her family's history.

It was the price she'd paid for her present happiness. In her head she heard the deafening roar of that leering crowd in the tavern that dreaded night as they cheered Marsh on.

Mame realized she was holding her breath so she couldn't smell the unforgettable stench of him. She was a haunted woman.

"What am I doing here?"

Ben looked at his mother, a mother who had always been there for him but who never went out of her way to show him special concern. How many times, when he was younger, did he awaken and see her cradling Walt in her arms, singing softly to him in the middle of the night? She had never nestled him that special way, not even when he had the chicken pox or croup. He wondered if for some reason she didn't see him sometimes, or if he was harder to hear than Walt. She felt far away, like Grandfather Paddy before he went to heaven.

"What, Mom?"

Snapping out of the daze of her disappointments, Mame looked at Ben. "Nothing, son. It's just so very strange to come home after all these years. So many memories . . . up on the hill . . . there past that grove of white pines behind the house is where your Uncle Jared, Great-Grandma Jane, and Great-Grandpa Thomas were laid to rest. You were named for my brother Jared. Did you know that?"

Mame didn't wait for Ben to answer. She just kept on reminiscing. "Your uncles and I were baptized down the hill from the house in the creek. I'll never forget the day I first began to feel the stirrings of the Holy Spirit. I began to understand Papa's Bible lessons . . ."

Suddenly the scarred face invaded Mame's thoughts. An overwhelming sense of guilt came over her. How could she preach about the Holy Spirit after what she'd done?

"Mama, are you all right?"

It took Mame some time to find words. "Yes, son, I'm fine. Just a lot to take in. Too many memories. My, how things have changed."

Where everything used to be weather-beaten and stained, it was now all clean and white-washed. There was a new addition to the side of the house. By the looks of the power poles lining the road and long drive to the homeplace, electricity had finally arrived in Beckley. And there were so many new buildings.

Pulling the Ford into the yard, all appeared quiet. Slowly Mame crawled from the coupe, and forgetting about Ben, she walked toward the house. Stepping upon the front porch, she paused. Images from the past rushed through her mind. There was Papa, coming home after a long day at the coal mine, his white teeth shining against the black dust on his face. That was the happiest memory Mame could conjure. All others, besides the rowdy times with her brothers, were of the sadness after her papa died. Smiles from anyone thereafter were few and far between. Other memories were of chores, feeding brothers, washing clothes, cooking, and falling into bed exhausted. And Will.

When Mame opened the front door, no one seemed to be around. She walked into the empty living room. Down the hall she saw a light shining through the slit under her mother's bedroom door. Hesitantly, she walked toward it and eased open the door. Inside the small space, the room was filled with extra chairs where all her brothers sat: Hank, James, Timothy, Thomas, and little William, now grown at nineteen years with a wife and baby of his own. Each gave her a smile or a nod, and William rose to give her a warm hug.

An overwhelming sadness enveloped Mame as little Will, who was now a foot taller than she was, swept her up in a big strong hug. She never had him come visit in Charleston like she'd promised, but they'd stayed in touch more than she had with any of the others. Wonder if he remembered her promise?

"Mame, it's been a long time. I remember the day you left. I thought I couldn't survive without you. But you know what? Mama was real good to me, always telling me how much like Jared I was."

Releasing each other, Mame moved closer to the bed where her mother lay. Mary stirred once she sensed Mame's closeness. Ben had followed Mame into the room and was eagerly surveying his unfamiliar family. Mary studied her daughter and then the young boy through half-closed eyes.

"Just as I thought," Mary said. Then louder, "Leave us alone. I want to talk to Mame."

"Mother, this is your grandson, Ben." Ben didn't move. This room didn't feel good, and it smelled funny. He edged his way toward Mame and stood behind her.

"I know who he is. Now everyone, leave us alone. I don't have much time. I've got important matters to discuss with Mame."

As the brothers filed out of the room, they all either spoke or patted her on the shoulder, but they felt like strangers. The years away had built a wall between them, yet Will gave her another hug before solemnly heading for the door.

"Ben, go with your Uncle William. I'll be out in a little while."

William put his hand on Ben's back, guiding him out the door, closing it behind them.

Since her papa's death, Mame had never known what to say to her mother, so she just stood beside her and studied how illness and age made a person look sunk-in like a hollowed out pumpkin that had sat in the sun too long. Mary's cheekbones protruded, and her once bright eyes were dark and clouded. Something had invaded her body, sucking the life right out of her, making a nearly sixty-year-old woman look like an ancient relic. When Mary spoke, Mame knew it was still the cold, hard mother she had so determinedly sought to get away from almost ten years before.

"Mame, I don't have much time left. I've got to go find your papa, but I can't leave this earth without trying to set things right . . . with you and you with the world.

"I won't go back as far as your papa's dying, but I will say I am sorry . . . for being jealous of your papa's love for you and yours for him."

In disbelief, Mame sank into a chair recently vacated by a brother.

"There was no excuse for it and especially no reason to let it carry over after he died. I resented you to the point of . . . not being able to show my feelings toward you." Mother closed her eyes. "I just loved your papa so much; I didn't want even you, his only daughter, to share any of that love." She opened her eyes and turned her head to meet Mame's gaze. "Now I know you could not help being your papa's little girl. I was selfish and wrong, selfish . . . trying to keep you tied down at the farm. I was an awful mother to you, and . . . I pray you will forgive me, but that's not my main concern. My main worry is . . . Jack Marsh."

Mame held her breath. She had not expected to hear her mother admit her jealousy or lack of love for her, but that was insignificant compared to hearing Jack Marsh's name fall from her lips. Had he been found? Or, was it just the hallucinations of a near-death woman?

Mame reached out and put what she hoped was a comforting hand on her mother's arm. "Don't think about these things now. It's not easy having a daughter. Jack Marsh is long gone, and we can't bring Jared back."

Mary seemed to take forever to find the strength to speak, but when she did, her voice was fierce and knowing.

"Mame, Jack Marsh is *not* long gone, nor dead. He is here, on this farm—has been ever since he escaped the execution he deserved." She paused as Mame gasped and pulled her hand away. "For the first few months, I didn't know who he was . . . but as time went by, tales of his past came to me through the other hired hands' gossip." Her gaze pierced Mame to her innermost being. "I know it *all*, Mame." Mary shook her head as it lay on her pillow. "You know, a man brags about such things as being with a pretty girl. It didn't take long for Marsh to find out that the pretty young lass . . . at the tavern that night . . . was the sister to the man he was about to be sent to the gallows for killing.

"After I figured it all out, I confronted him. I told him I was the mother of the man he had murdered. At first, he acted scared; after all, I was holding a gun to his head."

Mary drifted off for a short time, lost in her thoughts.

"I should have shot him that day. Ended it all. But I knew if I killed him, God might not let me go home . . . to heaven and be with my beloved Henry when it was my time to go. Now.

"I let Marsh sweat for a while, then lowered the gun. He sneered . . . roared with laughter, the situation all falling into place in his mind. He asked me, '*Where's your pretty little high-falutin' daughter? And why don't she come visit?*'

"Of course, I didn't answer him. I told him that if he ever tried to contact you, I'd pay to have him killed . . . maybe God would forgive me of that. But now with me about to die, I'm afraid of what Marsh might do. Your brothers know nothing about any of this, and . . . I pray they never have to."

Mame sat very still, trying to absorb all her mother had said. A moment of shame overtook her, but only for a second. She didn't have time for emotions and couldn't care less what her mother thought of her. She had a much bigger problem with which to deal. She'd always known deep down that he'd surface again, like a vulture forever hovering, looking to devour its next prey.

"Where is he now?"

"I sent him and a couple more men to bargain . . . on a shipment of tobacco. They'll be gone at least a week. By then, I will surely be buried and you'll be safe at home in Charleston. I don't want you to ever come back here again. You must never let Marsh see Ben. One glance and he'll know the boy is his, just as I was afraid when I learned the truth and did the calculations."

Mame straightened her back. "Walt is not Jack Marsh's son, Mother. He's fair and looks just like Clint."

"Mame, twins can't have two different fathers. You know as well as I do that Ben bears a close resemblance to Jack Marsh."

"I don't care. I know Clint is their father. He just has to be."

Mary shook her head, her eyes closed; a dry hacking cough shook her body. Mame stood and started to reach for a glass, thinking to offer her some water, but stopped. She could not.

Mary cleared her throat as best she could. "I hope you are right, Mame. I hope none of that no-good Marsh blood is running through my grandsons' veins. I'm sorry I drove you away and into Jack Marsh's bed. I hope someday you will understand and forgive me."

Mary squinted, her face full of pain. In a much weaker, softer voice, she gave Mame her last and final order.

"I will never mention this to you again, and you must also go to your grave with this shame. Just beware. Stay clear of anywhere Marsh might see you and the boys. He still rambles about the night he had his way with you and . . . how he's going to look you up one day."

Mary had said it all. She never spoke another word to her only daughter. She'd said all she intended to say. What else was there?

Mame sat near her mother well into the evening. Demons from the past danced in the shadows, laughing at her shame, her guilt, her unforgiving spirit. Would it never end?

Before she left the room, she held her mother's feverish head up off the pillow and gave her a drink of water.

That night, Mary slipped into a lifeless sleep that eased her off into eternity. If such things are possible, Mary Blackwell was resting in the arms of her beloved Henry.

CHAPTER TWENTY-FIVE

For the word of God is quick, and powerful, and sharper than any
twoedged sword, piercing even to the dividing asunder of soul
and spirit, and of the joints and marrow, and is a discerner of the
thoughts and intents of the heart.

~ Hebrews 4:12

MAME, HER BROTHERS AND THEIR families, and Mary's grandson Ben laid Mary Blackwell to rest on the hill behind the house right beside her beloved son Jared. Mary had made it clear she wanted to be buried as soon as possible after her death. She wanted no fancies, just a plain pine box like Jared's. She wanted it simple and to the point, just like her life had been, and she didn't want nosey do-gooders in her house snooping around, whispering about her. The Blackwells didn't need their burying food either—or their pity.

Mame didn't shed a tear. She stood in her funeral dress, feet lodged firm, fanning her face in the early July heat as she listened to the country preacher say his amens over the grave. She watched the tears roll down the faces of her brothers and their kin, but Mame found it impossible to conjure one single tear for her mother.

Suddenly, Mame missed her papa almost as much as she did the weeks right after he was buried in the mine. She longed for the affectionate hugs and unconditional love from him, a father who clearly adored and cherished his only daughter. Did a person ever get over losing that kind of love?

The funeral was over in short order. Only three elderly church ladies had heard in time to arrive, and one was still tying on her black bonnet as she labored up the hill panting. Neither do-gooder had had enough notice to cook covered dishes.

Didn't this private funeral match most of their dealings with that solitary Blackwell woman? She lived alone, inside her own head, and they reckoned she'd died the same way.

As the few guests, preacher, and family walked down the hill to the house, Mame heard a crack of thunder over the mountain and noticed a lone rider coming down the road. Before he was even in range, she knew. It was Marsh. Her heart pounded so loudly she could hear it in her ears.

Marsh wasn't due back for at least three or four more days.

"What am I going to do?" Mame said aloud.

"What, Mom?" Ben asked.

"Nothing, son. Hurry, we've got to get in the house and get ready to leave for home." Mame and Ben reached the back door before Jack Marsh saw them.

"Ben, get your things together right away."

"But Mom, it's after lunch already. Can't we stay until morning? I want to talk to my aunts and uncles and play with my cousins. I'm just now getting to know them. I like them."

"No, Ben, we can't stay another second. Gather your belongings while I get mine."

Mame wasn't too concerned that Jack would see Ben. The hired-hand quarters and larger barn were a good distance away from the main house and storage barn, but she couldn't take the chance.

"Get a move on now, Ben. Go."

He pouted but obeyed.

It took Mame only a few moments to gather up her belongings. Meanwhile, her brothers and sisters-in-law were busy with farewells to the preacher and neighbor women. The very ones Mary had not wanted in her house.

When the brothers saw Mame walk into the parlor with her suitcase, they were puzzled and a little more than annoyed. Hank and James excused themselves from the preacher, to try to talk Mame into staying a few more days.

"Why are you in such a hurry? There are things we need to talk about. Plans to be made," Hank said, touching Mame's arm.

"I've got to go. I can't stay here another night. And don't include me in any of your plans, that is, unless you're coming to Charleston. I don't intend on walking through the threshold of this house ever again."

James stepped into the dining room and went to the secretary that sat in the corner. Upon opening the top drawer, he pulled out an envelope. He then took Mame by the arm and pulled her around the corner into the bedroom. Hank followed and closed the door behind them.

"Mother said to give this to you after she was buried," James said.

Mame took the envelope from his outstretched hand, pulled the folded paper out, and opened it. The document inside was a deed for her mother's house and twenty acres of the land.

"What is this? Why in the world would I want this place?" Mame asked, becoming even more anxious to leave.

"Mama left us boys everything else, splitting it up equally. We've already got houses in Beckley and the business Mama started. We're satisfied and happy with our shares. Besides, Mama was intent upon your having this house," Hank said.

James sighed. "She said Papa would have wanted it that way." Taking a few steps back over to the dining room table, James reached and took their papa's Bible in his hands. "Mama also said that you should have this."

At that moment, a shadow passed by the window. Was Henry Blackwell there himself to make sure his wants were carried out?

The shadow was not the ghost of Mame's papa. It was a very much alive and breathing Jack Marsh. Mame had only caught a glimpse, but she knew. She didn't believe in spirits, but right now Mame was wishing for a spook instead of the dreaded devil himself.

A dead anything would be better than an alive Jack Marsh.

The Bible that James had laid in Mame's hands stung her skin. It felt alive with fire, scorching through to the bone. Quickly she threw her precious papa's Word of the Lord back down on the table. "No, I don't want it." In her mind she added, *I don't deserve it. I'm not worthy.*

CHAPTER TWENTY-SIX

Then shall he say also unto them on the left hand, Depart from me,
ye cursed, into everlasting fire, prepared for the devil and his angels.

~ Matthew 25:41

"I KNEW IT," JACK MARSH said out loud as he spit tobacco juice into the dust and kicked.

At first sight while he was riding up, he knew it was her. But he'd wanted a second look just to be sure. So he dropped his horse off at the corral and sneaked up to the house to look in the window. Marsh had then made his way to the barn for supplies as an excuse in case anybody had seen him. Most of the hired tobacco hands never went to the barn near the house. His usual job was to work at the warehouse, but sometimes he helped mend fences, and the fencing supplies were in the small barn here next to the house.

When he opened the double doors, Jack flinched. He was not alone. A young boy stood before him, and when their eyes met, it was as though they were looking into a magical mirror, seeing the past and future. They turned, taking each other in at different angles.

Jack kept his eyes on the boy as he walked slowly toward him. "Who are you, and what are you doing in here?"

"I'm Ben Paddington, Mary Blackwell's grandson. Who are you?"

"I work here, boy, and that's all you need to know. Why are you hiding out in here?"

"Mom and I are leaving for home today, and I don't want to go. I'm just buying some time. I didn't bother anything."

Jack took off his hat and wiped his greasy forehead with a soiled handkerchief. He had to get out of that barn so he could think.

"So you're Mame's boy, huh?"

"Yes, sir."

The boy seemed about eight or ten years old. Why didn't he look like that lily white, rich husband of hers?

Had it been that long since he bedded that girl? As Jack's mind reached back, he knew it had been close to ten years ago.

That boy was his. He knew he had bastards all over the country, and he didn't really care, but he felt peculiarly drawn to this boy.

Now what am I going to do about this? Miss High and Mighty still makes me want her. Now that Old Lady Blackwell is dead and buried, she's no threat to me. My worries are gone, buried six feet under with the old lady.

"Well, see you around, boy."

Marsh paced back and forth behind the barn, forming a plan.

Wiping his mouth with his tobacco-stained sleeve, a wide, devilish smile revealed broken, rotten teeth. He knew what he had to do, and the sooner the better.

Mame walked out to the front yard taking quick stock of the homeplace, her heart racing. Ben must be dallying with his cousins.

Marsh would have gone back to the bunkhouse where the workers stayed, wouldn't he? Everything was now uncertain.

She took a few more minutes to check out her surroundings. Things had changed a lot, but the main house structure was still the same as when she was a little girl: her mother and papa's bedroom—hers—the loft where her brothers had slept—the back porch that now housed a wringer washing machine—the new additions—a lavatory and toilet—a couple new bedrooms. For Beckley, it was fairly modernized. Mother had done well.

It really didn't matter to Mame if she owned the place or not. She had a home and was going back to Clint and Walt. She missed them desperately and hoped she would never see this place again. It could rot into the earth for all she cared. Or better yet, burn down.

Now that was a thought.

Hank met Mame on the back porch. "What will you do with it, Mame?"

"I don't know right now. When you get everything out of here that you and your wives want, just lock it up. I'll have to think about all of this."

Mame knew she would never do anything with this house. She would have to stay as far away from Beckley and Jack Marsh as possible.

Her sisters-in-law stopped working on the evening meal, wiped their hands on their aprons, and gave quick hugs to Mame and Ben, who'd finally made his way back to the house. Will carried her bag to the car, and one of the cousins gave Ben a little whistle to take home. Ben bid them a sorrowful good-bye, then kicked a rock that hit the hubcap of the car, making a loud dinging noise.

"Ben. Stop pouting and get in," Mame said.

"But I want to stay. Can we, Mama? Can we?"

Catching her sharp gaze, Ben knew there would be no persuading her to stay. He picked up his little satchel and threw it in the trunk.

Mame Blackwell Paddington knew she had to get away from there, and quick. She could almost feel the heated breath of the devil blowing down her neck. Mame's family knew it would be a long time before they saw her again. They also realized it might be never.

As she maneuvered out of the yard and down the road, Mame couldn't help glancing back over her shoulder, not at her family waving good-bye, but for the evil one, the jagged scar, the one who held her future in his hands. Sure enough, there he was, sitting on the porch at the bunkhouse in a straight-backed chair, reared back against the wall with a cap pulled down over his eyes. Thank goodness, Mame thought, he had not seen her. From her perspective, he seemed to be napping.

As Mame quickly drove out of town, she wondered when she'd see Will again. She hadn't felt guilty for leaving him behind this time. He had turned out just fine. At least Mother had done right by him.

CHAPTER TWENTY-SEVEN

And there was war in heaven: Michael and his angels fought against
the dragon; and the dragon fought and his angels.

~ Revelation 12:7

AFTER A FEW HOURS OF driving, Mame stopped so she and Ben could eat. Phoebe and Olivia had packed them a whole bag of leftover chicken, plus lemonade to sip on. Mame urged Ben to hurry, as she was anxious to get back on the road.

With his tummy full and lulled by the car's motion, Ben curled up in the backseat of the car and was soon sound asleep. Mame was worn out too but could not imagine going to sleep with so much on her mind. She was too anxious.

What if Marsh shows up in Charleston? What if he saw me? Will he come looking for me now that Mother isn't around to fend him off? My life with Clint will be ruined if he finds out how I tricked him and that Walt and Ben might not be his sons. Oh, God in heaven, please have mercy on me and never let Clint find out about that horrid night at the tavern.

Mame drove the Ford Coupe long into the evening. She wanted to get as far away from Jack Marsh as possible.

Eventually Mame felt the weight of the long day, and her eyelids began to droop. She needed to close them for a couple of hours. She was just on the outskirts of Cedar Grove. *It should be safe enough here,* she thought, pulling over at what looked to be a lane leading into a plowed field. Surely right here on the side of the road, no one would bother them. They were just weary travelers looking for a few hours of rest.

Mame woke immediately, jarred awake by the sound of a farm truck rumbling by. She glanced at her watch and saw she had been asleep for almost three hours. Looking in the back seat, she saw that Ben still slept soundly. Needing to relieve herself, she unlocked the car door and stepped out and into the woods a short distance away from the car.

Just as she stood, Mame heard a twig snap behind her. Had Ben woken and come to look for her? She spun around.

No!

The noisemaker was her worst-feared enemy.

He swaggered toward her. "Well, now, who do we have here? My long-lost sweetheart. Come looking for old Jack, did you? You want some more of me, don't you? After all these years, I can still remember the feel of you. You was the sweetest thing I ever been with, and believe me, I've been with a-plenty."

Marsh took a step closer to Mame. "Now, get on over here. Let's pick up where we left off. You run off and left me last time. Course, I did see you that one time after I took care of that puny brother of yours. Killing him weren't much harder than squishing a fly."

Mame's pulse raced as she backed away from Jack Marsh. She slid through tree branches walking backwards, then sideways, not wanting to take her eyes off Marsh. The sliver of moon didn't offer much light to guide her in the darkness. She couldn't see him clearly, but could hear his steps edging closer to her as they crunched the undergrowth. With each backward step she took, he took one forward. Mame had to get this good-for-nothing man as far away from Ben as possible.

Mame knew there was no use screaming. No one was around to help her, and she didn't want to wake Ben.

Mame had to stall, to outsmart Marsh.

"What do you want with me? Show a little mercy. I'm grieving my mother. Maybe we can hook up later when I feel better. My mother was a good woman—she helped you."

Marsh was quiet for a moment, and then he snorted. "Good woman, ha, she was a mean old hag. I never doubted for a minute she'd have me killed if I didn't do what she said."

Mame heard him rustling his clothes. He turned just enough in the slanting light so that she could see him. Mame's stomach rolled as the details of their previous encounter sickened her—his parading her before the other men, his sourness, his dead weight, his domineering movements, her torn clothing, and the scabs that took way too long to heal, not to mention the one inside her soul that never would.

Mame felt light-headed and grabbed onto a nearby tree branch. The stickers of an old-timey thorn tree pricked her. That was the first of the blood. She had to stay alert, to try to take charge. She bent her head slightly; willing the fear to go away so she could focus, and hopefully find a way out of this unpredictable predicament she was in.

Marsh had been rough and abusive in the tavern. She could only imagine how it would be here, alone, and now he was fueled by hatred and a murderous revenge. Mame could almost smell his need to hurt, to kill.

This could be worse than before. Mame had no idea what lay in store for her.

She continued to try and reason with him as he advanced toward her. "Leave me alone," she said sharply. "I've got to get home to my husband. If you hurt me, he'll kill you."

Marsh chuckled. "What about your boy back in the car? Why don't I just go and wake him up? It would be good for him to see how a real man loves on a woman. I'll teach him a thing or two. Let's wake him up."

Mame had been praying Marsh didn't know about Ben being in the car. Now her throat tightened.

"How do you know about him?"

"Old Jack knows all kinds of things. It's been a good while since he crawled in back of that fancy car. Probably sound asleep by now. Won't hear a thing if you hush. Or, I'll get him and let him watch. You pick."

"No, please don't do that. He's just a child." She felt a sob rising.

No matter that Mame didn't have the deepest love for Ben. He was still hers, and she didn't want him to be hurt, to know, or to see the awful things Jack Marsh could do. As repulsive as this was for her, it could be the ruin of a young child.

Apparently Marsh thought better of his teaching duty, and besides, he was getting excited. "Well, you come on now and be good to old Jack, and I'll leave the boy out. If you don't, he'll see things a boy ain't ready for. It's up to you."

Mame fought the dizziness as she continued stepping further away. She tripped over a tree stump, but at the last second, righted herself by grabbing a tree.

How else could she bargain? Was there any way to stop this nightmare?

Looking around the gray terrain, Mame frantically looked for some kind of weapon. There was nothing but brittle little sticks. If only there was a rock handy, or better yet a knife. *Maybe he's got one on him, and I can wrestle with him and find it?*

With each step Marsh took toward her, Mame retreated.

Then an idea came to mind. "Look, Jack, if you let us go, I'll give you money."

"Money? You got money on you?"

"No, but I can send it to you when I get back to Charleston. I can get it from my husband. How much do you want? A thousand, two?"

Marsh stopped walking and leaned toward her. Looming larger than she recalled, his scar glinted in the low light on his sweaty cheek, exactly like it had so many times in Mame's nightmares. He was so close that she could smell his dirty clothes and rank breath. But this time it was not whiskey running him. No, this time he was fully sober and not easily manipulated.

"How can you get me money without your fool husband knowing about it?"

He was close enough now to touch her. He reached out and glazed her cheek with the back of his hand. She didn't dare push him away, but took deep breaths to keep from passing out.

While he continued trailing his hand lower and lower, Marsh said, "I don't know of anything you can bargain with that would keep me from having you tonight."

Mame began to feel an icy detachment. Then she remembered the deed to her mother's house was still in her pocket. She pushed

Marsh's hand away, reached in her skirt pocket and pulled out the legal papers. Her hand shaking, she shoved it up toward his face.

"Here, take it! It's the deed to my mother's house and the twenty acres that goes with it. You can have it if you never cross my path again." Mame cleared her throat to calm herself. "That's the deal. Take it."

Marsh frowned but reached and took the paper. He squinted, barely able to make it out, and who knew if he could even read the words or not. But it did look official to him, like papers he'd had to X the times he'd been arrested.

"How do you think I would explain me having this to your brothers?" He snorted and threw the deed down at Mame's feet. "How long would it take them to figure out that I was the one killed your brother? Then I'd be dead. No, thank you, Lady. I ain't as dumb as you think."

"Then I'll sell it and give you the money."

Jack put his hands on his hips. All her pleading wasn't swaying him from what he intended to do.

"Right now," he said, "I don't give a crap about anything but having my way with you."

He reached out, grabbed Mame by the hair on her head, and dragged her fully resisting body further into the woods. Then he pushed her onto the ground.

The attack went on and on, as if Marsh was repaying Mame for every year he'd had to hide from the law, for all that had ever been done that crossed him, for every lesson he'd never learned, and for every ounce of love he'd never gotten and never would in this depraved life he'd lived.

His blows were relentless as his fists continued to pound into her. Mame went limp, disconnecting her mind from her body. Her spirit hovered above. A jagged line of coal mines exploded before her, collapsing, imploding. Shooting up from the ground were bloated, ghostly faces. Fine coal dust blew up into the air and into her lungs. She began to choke. The fine mist bled from the darkness of the night and settled all around her. She could not breathe. She was smothering in coal dust.

Mame had to find her father. He would help her. Then another explosion rumbled and shook the ground underneath her, plummeting pain throughout her slight body. She hacked and tried to sit up, but the falling dirt and rocks trapped her. She gasped and spit, trying to crawl out of the mine, squinting toward daylight, trying desperately to rid herself of the dreadful weight that was still upon her. She lay gasping, pleading for just enough of the invisible oxygen for one solitary breath.

Then suddenly the weight was gone and her lungs filled with air. Her eyes opened slightly, and she began to see shapes of trees in the blackness. Slowly she turned onto her side, where the brutal truth lay in the cold dirt beside her: the Great Red Dragon.

She was alive, but what a terribly penalty she'd paid. Once again she'd dueled with the devil, and once again she'd lost.

Mame lay motionless, trying to sense her bearings, and not about to move lest she irritate him further. Somehow a small consolation occurred to her that she could not have more children, thanks to her difficult birthing of the twins.

After several minutes, Jack stirred. He leaned on one elbow and stared at her. "Did you like that? I hope so, because there's plenty more where that came from."

The torture continued throughout most of the night. Mame's spirit traversed back and forth from the empty coal mines, helpless like the parrot that cries when the gas fumes seep in, too late, too late, too late.

At one point, she imagined Clint's face and pretended he had lifted her like an angel from this godforsaken forest.

There was nothing the Dragon did not do to her that night. As dawn was breaking, he stood up and looked down at what was left of the high and mighty Mary Margaret Blackwell Paddington. There was only one more thing left to do: He dragged her to a gulley and threw her in, kicking a few mounds of dirt and leaves onto her, then spit on her, leaving it to the animals to finish her off.

He walked slowly out of the woods, pulling on his clothes and boots. He got to Mame's car just as Ben began to stir.

CHAPTER TWENTY-EIGHT

But he was wounded for our transgressions, he was bruised for our iniquities: the chastisement of our peace was upon him; and with his stripes we are healed.

~ Isaiah 53:5

SPOTTING A DESERTED CAR ON the road wasn't too unlikely. Mountain men roamed these hills this time of year, searching for ginseng root. Noticing the car stayed on the side of the road all day did flare up old Franklin Pruitt's curiosity though. The second time he rode by it on his way home from the mill, it was late evening so he decided to check it out.

Everything seemed fine. Nothing was broken, and the keys were in the ignition. Didn't look like the kind of car a root hunter would be driving though, too fancy.

Franklin decided he'd wander around the area a bit and see what he could find. Maybe the owner would show up. About a quarter of a mile into the woods, old man Pruitt stopped dead in his tracks when up ahead he saw what looked like rags in a scattered pile. Reaching the trash, he saw it was ripped up garments, and he noticed impressions on the ground foliage, like something heavy had been dragged. It weren't deer season, what fool person kills a deer in the heat of summer?

Pruitt followed the trail until he came to the edge of an embankment. Expecting to see a deer carcass, Franklin searched over the edge. Looked like something was down there in the ditch. It could be large animal . . . or was it a person? Pruitt's eyesight wasn't what it used to be. He'd have to get a closer look.

He cautiously eased his way down into the steep ravine, grabbing onto roots and limbs. Scooting down toward the bottom, a noise stopped him. The sound led him to a crumpled up mound of flesh. Whatever it was, male or female, he was close enough now to see it was human. Surely this mangled form covered in dirt, leaves, and dried blood couldn't be alive.

It looked as though wild animals had been scratching and taking bites out of the body. From the length of the hair, it must have been a woman. Franklin was so taken aback that it was several seconds before he thought to remove his shirt and cover her with it. The thing on the ground moaned again.

"You hang on, little lady. I'm going for help." Pruitt pulled himself out of the ravine and ran as fast as an old man could to his buggy.

It took almost an hour to get back with his son-in-law. They carried Mame to their hay wagon, laid her in the back, and headed for town. The men knew they'd be lucky to reach the doctor in time for him to help what was left of this mangled woman.

"I've never seen anything like this. Do you think an animal did this to her? Could have been a rogue black bear."

"No son, I ain't never seen a bear strip a body down before it eats it. I think the devil himself got a hold of this woman."

The doctor had never witnessed anything so broken yet still alive. His patient was torn from the inside out, top to bottom, front to back, a splintered, shattered vessel of raw hide and mutilated flesh.

Word spread fast around town about the battered woman. A few men went out looking for clues. Someone found the pile of ripped clothes and gathered them up. Another man found the deed and drove Mame's car into town. They pieced together the information from the deed and phoned the home of Mary Blackwell down in Beckley.

Hank was at the homeplace gathering personal items before closing it up. The ringing phone startled him. He was lost in thoughts of his mother, the tobacco business, and what Mame would do with this place.

"Hello."

"Yes, is Mary Blackwell home?"

"No, I'm sorry, my mother passed away a few days ago."

"Sorry to hear that, mister. This is the sheriff down in Cedar Grove. We found a woman with a deed to Mary Blackwell's house in her possession. Do you know who she might be?"

"What do you mean? Why can't she tell you who she is? She's my sister, Mame Paddington."

"I'm sorry, sir, but she's not able to tell us anything. A local found her on the side of the road beat up pretty bad, and she ain't woke up to tell us anything."

Hank pulled a chair back from the table and dropped heavily into it. "Thank you for calling, Sheriff." He ran an unsteady hand through his hair. "I'll call her husband and let him know. Where's my nephew? Is he there with you?"

"No, sir, ain't seen nobody but that woman."

When Hank hung up, he immediately phoned Clint. "You need to go to the doctor's office in Cedar Grove. Mame's been in some kind of accident, and they said she's in pretty bad shape."

Clint felt as if his heart had stopped. "What about Ben? Was he hurt too? Is he okay?"

"I don't know. The sheriff said he hadn't seen anyone but Mame, no boy."

Clint slammed the phone down and ran into the kitchen to tell Mrs. Gentry the bad news.

"An accident—Mame and maybe Ben. They can't find Ben. Can you watch Walt for me? I'll be back as soon as I can."

"Why sure, Mr. Paddington. Anything you need done, you know I'll do it."

While Clint grabbed his keys and a few belongings, Mrs. Gentry watched Walt out the window, playing happily in the yard with a stray cat. How would she break the news to him? First she had to calm down herself.

Clint knew he should speak with Walt before he left, but what would he tell the boy? Your mama's hurt, and I don't know about your brother? No need to worry him, not yet anyway.

Clint spun out of the driveway, heading into the unknown.

Almost forty-eight hours had passed since Mame's attack. Clint rushed into the infirmary where Mame lay. What he saw made him run back outside and throw up. Barely able to pull himself back to the horror that was supposedly his wife, he knew he had to.

No, this person couldn't be his beautiful Mame. Her face was black from bruising, and both eyes were swollen shut. Her lips were cut and broken open from all the swelling.

"Her whole body looks like her face," the doctor said.

"Will she live?" Clint asked, looking for a chair to sit down in.

"Sorry, but my guess is no. I've never seen a body this broken up. Truly I don't see how she has survived this long."

Clint sat and put his face in his hands. Then he shook himself from his grief to ask, "Where is my son?"

The doctor looked puzzled. "Your son?"

"Yes, my son Ben was traveling with her."

"To my knowledge, no one was with her. There's been no mention of a boy."

"Who brought her in?"

"Old man Franklin Pruitt and his son-in-law."

Clint stood. "Where are they?"

"They live about a half-hour out of town."

"I need to find my son, he's just a boy." Clint paced the room, wringing his hands. "Is there anything I can do for Mame?"

"No. A broken body like this could stay in a coma for days or maybe weeks. All we can do is tend to her surface wounds. I shun to think what her insides might look like."

"Please keep her alive," Clint said, shaking the doctor's hand. "I've got to find my son. Please don't let her die."

He put on his hat, took one last look at Mame's unrecognizable face and bandaged body, and rushed toward the door, thinking of Ben and praying that whatever had happened to Mame had not also happened to him.

When Clint found the Pruitt house, Franklin told him the whole story. But he'd never seen a child. Even in the car, there was no sign of a boy or his belongings. All Clint could do was go back to the doctor's office and what was left of his wife.

Later that day, Hank arrived in Cedar Grove and filled Clint in on when Mame had left.

"Did Ben leave with her, or did he stay behind with you? Please tell me he's in Beckley."

"No Clint, Ben's not with us. He left with Mame."

So the search began. Clint, Hank, the sheriff, and several towns-people combed a five-mile area around where Mame was found. For a week, they searched from daylight to dark, but found nothing, no sign of Ben. Whoever had done this to Mame must have taken him, but why?

During the search, Mame slipped in and out of consciousness. After a few days, she was able to barely open her mouth to let Clint spoon in a little broth.

Clint sat with her all night, while the daylight hours were spent searching for Ben.

"Mame, please wake up," Clint begged. "I need for you to tell me what happened. Ben is missing. Can you tell me anything about who did this to you, and where Ben might be?"

In Mame's semiconscious state, her thoughts were swallowed up in a thick fog, but she could understand Clint enough to know that Ben was gone. She couldn't tell anyone that Jack Marsh must have kidnapped him. Her secret must stay hidden forever. With very little response, Mame lay for two solid weeks and one day. Finally, she regained consciousness and opened her eyes.

Clint came running when he arrived that night and heard the nurse hollering for him.

"Mame's awake. It's a miracle! She asked for water."

At her bedside Clint knelt, relief and weariness overcoming him as wet tears fell from his cheeks.

"Oh, Mame. You're going to be okay. Do you know who I am? Your head was beaten so badly the doctor said you might not remember some things."

Mame slowly lifted her bandaged hand up to Clint's face and touched his cheek. "Clint, I love you." Then she drifted off to sleep again. The next day she was more alert and told Clint all she could remember. She had walked into the woods to relieve herself and something, or someone, hit her in the head.

Thank goodness she couldn't remember, Clint thought. Her body looked as though an army had ravished it.

Mame sincerely cried when Clint told her Ben was missing. She didn't want anything to happen to her dark son, but she could not risk telling the truth. The sacrifice would be too great. She would just have to pray that Jack Marsh would not be as cruel to Ben as he had been to her. But for the life of her, she couldn't understand why Marsh would want to look after a child—unless he knew.

After a month of recuperation in the infirmary, Clint took Mame home. She'd been too beaten up to risk moving any sooner.

Clint was aware of World War II raging on the other side of the ocean and was glad that the USA was not involved. He was a father in a war of his own, trying his best to track down the enemy who had stolen his son.

There was a very sad and lonely homecoming to Charleston. For the next three months, Clint let others run his business while he stayed on the road searching for Ben. He went all over Virginia, West Virginia, and northern North Carolina, taking pictures of Ben to train stations, boat ports, and post offices, but no one had seen the boy. It was as if he'd dropped off the face of the earth.

Mame stayed home, trying to recuperate. Her outside body looked healed, but her insides would be scarred forever. The screams at night and constant tears were not altogether over the loss of her son. She was reliving that dark, smothering hole, the mine, dead bodies all around her, their eyes wide and staring: they saw, they knew. Why couldn't she have been one of the dead? She should be, that's exactly what she deserved.

Over time, Mame recovered, except for a few superficial scars that would probably fade with time. She still didn't have her full strength back and often felt faint. This too was not just from the trauma or the loss of her boy.

By the time the leaves had fallen, it was late October 1940, and Mame knew why she was not back to feeling like her old self: She was pregnant. It had been almost four months since Jack's attack, and there was no denying the roundness of her abdomen and the baby's first flutters. Up until now, Mame blamed her lack of the monthly on her injuries, but deep down, she knew. She was with child, and she knew that again it was the seed of Jack Marsh growing inside her.

Clint had not touched her since the attack. He was so grief-stricken about Ben that he'd made no effort to be intimate with her. Or, maybe he couldn't stand the thought of being with her after she'd been so violated.

It all made sense now. Clint must be sterile. That's probably why Mame hadn't gotten pregnant these past ten years. Walt and Ben were Jack Marsh's. No. It couldn't be; she wouldn't believe Walt was Marsh's son. He was growing into an exact replica of Clint.

At six months, there was no hiding the pregnancy. Even though Clint was not touching her, he could easily see her protruding belly. It made sense now why she was so tired, even after all these months of recovery. It was not just Ben's disappearance that kept Mame down-cast, quiet, and with little appetite. She was not looking healthy and robust like she had with the twins, either.

Clint knew that she carried her attacker or attackers' baby, be-cause he himself had failed to sire another child for a decade. Clint realized Mame knew the truth too, because she had not said a word to him about a baby.

Clint decided they had to talk.

Walt would also have to be told, and soon.

The light-haired son had behaved well for Mrs. Gentry while his parents were gone, but Walt had become nervous in his parents' ab-sence. He was very glad to see his mama and daddy back home, but where could his brother be? Walt couldn't believe his twin might be gone forever. While Clint and Mame were in Cedar Grove, he'd cried himself to sleep every night, clutching Ben's favorite toy, a wooden tomahawk with its handle wrapped in leather and an eagle feather glued to it.

He prayed that his brother's weapon would keep him safe and that he wouldn't have to use it, but he would if someone came after him too.

What was it like to be lost? How could Ben stand being away from home and Mama and Daddy? Would he ever be found? Would Ben ever get to see Lilly's new calf?

As the weeks turned to months, Walt overheard the talk about Ben. He was too afraid to ask anything. He didn't understand who could have taken him, but the deputies came around every few weeks, speaking in low voices with his parents.

Walt became agitated, wetting his bed, too afraid to get up and go to the bathroom. Most nights, he couldn't go to sleep unless Mame or Clint sat in his room. No one in the house was at peace. Even Mrs. Gentry was distracted and leaving ingredients out of certain recipes.

Coming down the wide staircase early one morning, Mame stopped midway, remembering her first morning in the Paddington house. Since then, all her hopes and dreams had turned into schemes, dark lies, and regrets. These sad thoughts were as sharp as her first smell of Jack Marsh.

Mame saw Clint sitting on the front porch.

"Clint, come inside; it's chilly. You'll be sick."

Clint looked up from his newspaper.

"Why don't you grab a wrap and come sit with me?"

Mame lifted her brown tweed jacket from the hall coat tree where it had not been touched in many long months because she had not left the house since returning from Cedar Grove. She pulled her arms through the sleeves and shook her head at how the coat barely fit across her protruding stomach. She shut the door quietly, so as not to wake Walt, whose nightmares had kept him up most of the night.

Clint patted the cushion of the white wicker settee beside him. She sat. He folded his paper and laid it aside. They both stayed silent until Clint finally spoke.

"I'm so sorry about what has happened to us, Mame. It's just . . . I miss Ben so much. He's always on my mind. I know I've not been much of a husband or comfort to you since the accident. At first, I didn't want to touch you for fear of hurting you." His feelings began to pour out. "Then I'd think of what it must have been like for you . . . I didn't want to . . . to scare you. I've not known what to do or say. You haven't even let me see you undressed. And you've got to tell me, I must hear it from you. Are you going to have a baby?"

Mame wanted with all her heart to reject his question, to expel it from her mind like she'd like to expel this thing growing inside her from her body. She waited but knew she could no longer delay the inevitable.

"Yes, Clint. You know I am. I know you're ashamed of me and of what happened, but I just don't know what to do or how to fix this. I want us to be like we were, so badly. Will you ever be able to love me again? What will we do with this—spawn of cruelty? Oh, Clint. I should have just died. I wish I'd never been carried out of the woods."

With a serious face, Clint turned to Mame. He placed his hands on her cheeks and lowered his lips to hers. Tenderly he kissed her, and then he took both her hands.

"Mame, I don't ever want to hear you talk like that again. We'll get through this. We'll take it one day at a time. When the baby comes, we'll take care of it. We can't blame the innocent for something he or she had no part in. And we'll love it because it is part of you."

He squeezed her hands, felt that they were cold, and rubbed them lightly.

"Tomorrow—we'll talk to Walt, and there will never be any mention of how his brother or sister was sired. Walt will just know that it's his sibling, because it will be, and that's the truth." Then he put his arm around her. "Are you ready to help me put our lives back together?"

Mame listened to Clint, but she knew things would never be the same. She was scarred in so many ways. The haunting memories and the menacing shadow of Jack Marsh would always be there. Mame realized that she had no alternative but to continue living with her lies. They were now her closest companions. She had no choice. Jack Marsh had put an end to all her dreams and aspirations. Mame pulled her coat tighter around her and answered Clint's question.

"Yes. I'm ready. I'll try as best I can to erase the memories. Walt needs us so badly, and maybe we'll find some joy again. Yes, maybe we just will." Mame forced herself to smile at Clint.

Sitting silently, Mame touched the spot on her belly where she felt movement. How would she handle another child of Jack Marsh's? The same way she had Ben. She'd do what had to be done, but nothing more.

CHAPTER TWENTY-NINE

And he is the propitiation for our sins: and not for ours only, but also
for the sins of the whole world.

~ 1 John 2:2

ON MARCH 8, 1941, DANIEL Madison Paddington came screaming into the world. Mame was twenty-nine years old, but she birthed this baby easily compared to having the twins nine years earlier.

At birth Daniel resembled Walt when he was born. Fair-skinned, blond, and—to anyone who didn't know better—they'd think Daniel looked just like Clint.

"How can it be, Mame? This baby looks so much like Walt and me. Could it be we were wrong, and Daniel is mine?"

Mame could not answer Clint. She must have counted back a hundred times: it had been exactly nine months to the day since Marsh had attacked her. It was as though that devil man still mocked her, abused her, and flaunted himself in front of her even in his absence.

Deep down, Clint knew the answer. He too had counted, but it was hard to bear. Mame had been gone only for few days to Mary's funeral before her attack. It was possible the baby was his. But as badly as he wanted it, Clint just could not for certain feel this baby was his blood. He sat studying the innocent child, but he felt numb.

It was not the infant's fault, but Clint knew he'd never be able to love it as his own. He would give him the Paddington name, but that was the best he could manage. For whoever sired this boy held his own son captive. Clint would never rest as long as Ben was missing.

Clint prayed for his heart to change. Not loving a baby just wasn't his nature. He wished he could hold, pace, and talk to this baby like he had with the twins, but he couldn't. Every time he looked at Daniel, he wondered what kind of awful animal his father must be.

The past nine months had taken its toll on Clint. He was beginning to look old, like his father. Worry wears ruts in a man's skin and takes away his joy. Some things you just can't fix.

A week after the birth, Mame still could not look directly at the child. Every time she glanced at Daniel to attend his needs, she saw Jack Marsh.

She didn't know if Clint would ever be able to touch her again, and without him, she had almost nothing.

Poor Walt was still clinging to her, scared of every shadow that moved. And now that the baby was here, he added it to his worries.

"Mama, why does he cry so much? Is he all right? Maybe he's wet again."

Mame was weary from it all. Walt was afraid Daniel would also disappear.

Would Walt's fears come true?

Around midnight on March 15, when Daniel was a week old, Mame finished nursing the hungry lad. With heavy arms and a weary heart, she walked with him across the hall to the nursery. In the icy moonlight she stood cold, tired, and numb. Laying the sleeping infant in his crib, she took the tip of her finger and lightly touched his warm head.

Why, he was no more than a rag doll to her.

She reached over and took the small feather pillow from the rocker. Hoping to make her dolly more comfortable, she placed it in the crib beside the babe.

"Hush little baby, don't you cry," she sang softly, humming the parts she couldn't remember.

Later that night she rose from the rocking chair, neatly folded the throw she had been covered up with, and laid it back in the chair. Picking up the doll, she wrapped him in a soft, warm blanket and went back to the rocker and lightly hummed to him until the morning dawn poked through the eyelet curtains. Without one tear, she laid him in his crib and went to Walt's bed, crawled in, and snuggled up next to him.

Mame fell sound asleep.

Mary Margaret Blackwell Paddington had truly stepped to the other side this time; the darkness of that night would follow her all the days of the rest of her life. She would never be the same. What little sanity she had left escaped her as the infant Daniel was laid to rest in a tiny grave in the Charleston town cemetery near their home. There was no thought of taking this body to the Blackwell family cemetery on the hill behind the homeplace. Jack Marsh's blood could never mire their sacred burial ground.

Neither parent shed a tear for the blameless baby boy. Walt thought it strange that his parents were not upset, but Mrs. Gentry assured him that they were in shock, that they were too hurt to cry.

The same could not be said for Walt. He felt reality weigh down on him full force. As he stood between his parents before the tiny casket and the small heap of dirt, sobs racked his young body. When he looked up at his mama and daddy's somber but dry faces, he knew they were trying to be strong for him. If only he could talk to Ben.

Mame felt only the sadness a stranger might feel upon seeing the black-dressed gathering out on the melting white graveyard snow. Such a shame the poor little thing had died in its sleep. He had been fine when she laid him down in the wee hours of morning the day before. She willed herself to cry but could not feel any connection to the pain she should feel. It was as if she didn't even know this child, the one that had kicked and squalled so much. The one who had pulled at her breast, the one she should have loved, but didn't . . . God help her. Was there enough forgiveness in the world to cover her sins?

No mourners joined them back at the Paddington house. Since Mame had barely left their house in nine months, or really years before that, they didn't have caring friends. No one, not even Doc Stuart, had known about her condition. Mrs. Gentry had easily helped with the birthing of the baby. Neighbors who heard about the funeral soon found out that she didn't want company, much less sympathy. Mame didn't even tell her family back in Beckley.

In a peculiar way, Clint was sad, yet relieved. What a shame that fate had thrown his family to the wolves. Maybe in time, they would recover, if only they could find Ben.

Fate had nothing to do with their misery; all by herself Mame had brought this darkness to the Paddington family.

CHAPTER THIRTY

Come now, and let us reason together, saith the Lord: though your
sins be as scarlet, they shall be as white as snow; though they be red
like crimson, they shall be as wool.

~ Isaiah 1:18

BEN PADDINGTON SAT AT THE same old, beaten-up wooden table he'd sat at for nearly a year, ever since that night by the roadside in early July. Now it was May 11, 1941, and tomorrow, May 12, Ben would be nine years old. He had seen much these past months and had learned early on to keep his mouth shut and obey. This past year had made him feel much older than his nine winters.

"We had a good day today, boy. Rounded up about twenty of them wild ponies. They'll bring some good money at the sale."

At first, Ben hadn't believed it when Jack told him that his mother had arranged for Jack to take care of him. Over the past ten months, he'd had plenty of time to think. His mother really had never loved him or cared for him like she did Walt. All of it really did make sense, except for his daddy. Daddy must have been told some big lie, because he would have come for him by now. He was never sure about his mother's love but knew his daddy cared deeply for him, just as much as he did for Walt.

Ben would never forget that morning when Jack Marsh took him from their car and threw him in the seat of his truck beside him. Jack had finally had to tie Ben's hands together to stop him from trying to get away. It wasn't until several days later, as he led Ben aboard a rickety old cargo ship in Charleston, South Carolina, that Jack told him that he had known his mother years ago.

"I was happy to hear from Miss Mame again when she came back through Beckley. She said she wanted me to take you and train you up. Said you'd had enough schooling. I always wanted me a boy of my own. She even paid me a hundred dollars."

Jack lied so easily; Ben thought it was the truth.

Jack had stolen money and supplies from the Blackwell ranch and managed to buy a small bit of acreage with a ramshackle house on it. An old drinking buddy had died and left him the cargo boat, which Jack used for his new scheme of catching wild ponies on the surrounding islands, breaking them to ride, then selling them.

As Jack Marsh kept spinning tales about his mother, Ben grew to believe beyond any doubt that his mother really had sold him. What he'd thought to be a kidnapping had really been a payoff to get him out of the picture so Mame could have her precious Walt all to herself. Ben eventually stopped crying and trying to run away. In the beginning he'd tried escaping and calling his father when they went into the bigger towns, but Jack kept him close.

He had actually been fairly good to the boy. This was a very different life than Jack was used to, and soon he realized he enjoyed having someone look up to him. He'd even let Ben sip whiskey with him. He was glad he'd taken the boy. It pleasured him to know he'd leave behind blood kin just like himself.

As time went on, Ben began to forget Charleston, and he stopped pining for his family. What choice did he have? Anyway, he loved the ocean and riding his horse along the coastline. The salty air was so thick he could lick it from his lips. Rounding up ponies came natural to him, and he felt at home with Jack. As the months turned to years, Ben seldom thought of his first family, but when he did, he pictured his mama. Then he would feel a burning hate in the pit of his belly . . . knowing one day they'd meet again.

The day Ben turned sixteen, Jack told him it was time he learned about women. Ben knew Jack had plenty of girlfriends over the years, for he'd brought them to the house each time, telling Ben to get lost for a couple of hours. But one time, Ben sneaked back in and watched it all. He knew a lot more than Jack thought he did. Ben was more than ready for some loving of his own. He knew where Jack was going to take him. It wasn't far; the house sat on a piece of land at the outskirts of town, and the front door was painted scarlet red.

A verse of Scripture rolled through Ben's mind, something his mama had taught him and Walt about their sins being scarlet, but Jesus would wash them as white as snow.

Mama teaching Bible verses . . . Jesus' saving power . . . yeah right, where is this Jesus, and where's Mama?

Thoughts of his mother left as quickly as they formed in his mind. He'd been forcing her out of his memory for years. She could rot in hell as far as he was concerned. Ben's heart had been hardened by all of Marsh's lies.

Oh yes, Jack Marsh was rearing Ben to be just like him.

CHAPTER THIRTY-ONE

Then goeth he, and taketh with himself seven other spirits more
wicked than himself, and they enter in and dwell there: and the last
state of that man is worse than the first. Even so shall it be also unto
this wicked generation.

~ Matthew 12:45

THE YEARS HAD NOT BEEN quite so good to Walt. Now at sixteen, he felt much older. Ever since his brother Ben went missing, his life kept getting worse and worse. Over the years, his mother and father had drifted farther apart.

It wasn't easy being the twin left behind. Sometimes Walt thought his dad didn't even see him. He felt as invisible as the spirit of Ben that floated through the house and might as well be dead himself. Everyone at the Paddington house was in his or her own private misery.

Mame wanted to tell Clint not to worry—Ben wasn't even his son—but she knew she couldn't. Overwrought with his failure to find Ben, Clint often came home late at night, drunk, passing out on the sofa. Even though Clint had never fully given up the pursuit of Ben, his hope paled. When a man loses hope, he loses himself.

Then one day, Clint disappeared for good. It wasn't unusual for Clint to be gone a week at a time, but this time it had been a month since he'd been home.

Mame and Walt didn't know if he was alive or dead, but one thing was for sure: every penny of the Paddington fortune and their savings had dwindled to nearly nothing. Thanks to Clint's obsession with searching for Ben, he neglected his business affairs. Not to mention the fact that when he was home, Clint was withdrawn, sucked up inside himself, gambling and drinking . . . a lot. He had to sell off his beloved cattle.

World War II had taken away many of the Paddington tobacco warehouse workers, and no one wanted to do business with a drunk anyway. So Clint shut down, stopped caring about all the details of life, and continued to drink away his nights . . . and then days.

The past seven years had left their mark on Mame as well. Deep frown lines etched her brow. Long ago, they'd had to let Mrs. Gentry go. Once again Mame carried the full brunt of household chores. As she sat looking over the Paddington financial records, she knew the turning point had come. Not only had Clint spent all their money, he had also accrued huge gambling debts. Every day, two or more men would knock on her door, demanding their money. Mame knew she should have been keeping tighter rein on things, but she just couldn't seem to stay focused. Often she drifted away into a fog of darkness, waking up humming the tune of some silly lullaby.

Mame felt the walls of the coal mine closing in on her, the blackened roof pushing her down farther and farther into the core of the mountain. If only she could slip into the darkness, or at least hide in the coal mine shadows. There where her papa lay, nothing left now but bones and teeth. In her imagination she pictured this often. Truly, at certain times she realized that she was growing more than a little insane. It was all she could do to keep the coal dust from completely clouding her head. She fought to keep her sanity, the household functioning, and be as good a mama to Walt as possible.

She could sell her mother's house in Beckley, but those proceeds would not bring them enough money to pay off all the debt and save the Paddington estate. So there was nothing to do but sell the house in Charleston and do what Mame vowed she would never do: move back to Beckley.

Walt showed no emotion when Mame told him that they were broke and moving back to her hometown. His father had been gone for a year now, and there had not been any happiness in their lives for many years, so Walt was glad for the change. He looked forward to it.

Walt had been the scorn of the schoolyard for quite some time. The boys called him "the loser's son with the crazy mama," and the girls didn't flirt or pay attention to him, even though he was a handsome young man like his daddy once was. Walt finally stopped going to school. Mame kept him busy running errands since she still rarely left the house. Hungry half the time, Walt took any odd job he could find just to buy food.

"It's okay, Mother. We'll make a new life." Walt was hopeful. How could life get any worse?

A new beginning was what had brought Mame to Charleston, but back to the former life in old Beckley she must go. This time she knew she'd be there to stay. It was what she deserved. The guilt over all she had done weighed her down a little more each day. She suffered from flashes from the past. When she went to bed, a baby's face floated into her mind. Who was this child, and why did he look like Clint? Mame would curl into a tight ball and hide her face in her pillow, burying herself in the darkness to avoid remembering.

"Yes, it's what I deserve," Mame said softly at their meager dinner of boiled potatoes the evening before they left for Beckley. It would be a few more years before Walt understood and felt the impact of what she meant.

That last night Mame walked the floors of the Paddington mansion. She went to every room and took in the smallest of every last detail. It was hard to find any remembrance of happiness there. With each thought of joy came a picture of pain . . . Ben, Jack Marsh, and that little baby that never seemed real to her.

Mame sat down at the top of the stairs and watched as images moved in the shadows. Swirling and twirling, dancing upon the walls and ceilings. Mame wondered if these ghosts would stay there at that house and entertain the new owners, or if they would follow her to Beckley. She knew the answer to that . . . they'd follow wherever she went, because they were her own personal demons.

Arriving in front of her mother's house in the same old '39 Ford she'd driven there when Mary was dying, Mame knew it was her destiny to die in Beckley too and be buried up on the hill.

Opening the front door to her old home, she walked in and headed toward the dining room. There it was, lying exactly where she had left it—her papa's Bible. She picked it up and gently thumbed through the pages, and then she hugged it close to her heart. The Word no longer held fire. Maybe God had forgiven her.

For weeks, Mame and Walt cleaned Mary's house and repaired things that had been neglected for the past eight years. Mame's brothers pitched in and were glad to see her, but they pitied the shape she was in and knew to keep their distance. Mame always kept things to herself, but James had found out about Clint's disappearance when he visited Mame during a business trip to Charleston.

Through the years afterwards, her siblings' invitation for Mame to visit was always turned down. All they could do was see her infrequently when their business brought them by the homeplace, and even then sometimes Mame wouldn't answer the door when they came to call.

Leaving Charleston nudged Mame into wanting to make up for her lies and—God help her—for letting Jack Marsh keep Ben . . . and she knew she was somehow responsible for the death of her own child Daniel. She should have checked on him more often that night. She was never exactly sure what happened, but deep down she knew it was something horrible. She couldn't get a clear picture of that night. The black coal dust clouded her memory and fogged up her mind. Each day became darker.

Mame always wore a sad, tortured look in her eyes. Her brothers thought she had never gotten over what that man had done to her on the road some years ago . . . Ben's kidnapping . . . her baby's death . . . and then Clint's disappearance. How could anyone find joy after all that?

Mame knew her sadness had nothing to do with what anyone had done to her, but what she had brought on herself.

Walt, on the other hand, settled right into life in Beckley. Being around all his uncles, aunts, and cousins for the first time was a lot to absorb, but he loved it and decided right away that a big family was what he wanted one day. He went back to school with his cousins. Afternoons he spent helping his uncles in the tobacco crops.

Mame took in people's washing and ironing and did any odd job that she could find. Her family and neighbors always found something she could do for income, for they felt sorry for her. Mame and Walt lived simple. Mame wished for no luxuries for herself, for she knew she was worthy of none. Her longings for riches had brought her nothing but emptiness. Mame wanted nothing for herself except the redemption of her tortured soul.

CHAPTER THIRTY-TWO

1950

*He that covereth his sins shall not prosper: but whoso confesseth and
forsaketh them shall have mercy.*

~ Proverbs 28:13

TWO YEARS HAD PASSED SINCE the move back to Beckley. Mame
was thirty-eight, and Walt had turned eighteen. It was three years since
they had last seen Clint. He must be dead, or he would surely have
contacted them. Every few months Mame would drive to Charleston
and visit with Mrs. Gentry, which she did on this day. Now eighty, Mrs.
Gentry used a cane, but she was still clear of mind and loved to see
Mame. Mrs. Gentry knew the real reason for her visits.

"Why, Miss Mame, come on in. I was just thinking it was about
time for you to shadow my door again. Strawberries have just come
in, and I put a cobbler in the oven. Come on in the kitchen and we'll
have some coffee."

Mame surveyed the modest room. It hadn't changed at all since
the first time she'd visited, shortly after she'd had to let Mrs. Gentry
go, and Clint had left. Somehow Mrs. Gentry made her feel closer to
Clint and the days when things were good.

"How have you been, Mrs. Gentry?"

"Fit as can be for an old, wore-out woman. My knees sure don't work like they used to, and they tell me my heart is weak. But considering everything, I am blessed, child. My house still gets full of my young'uns and all the grandbabies. I fill their bellies with my good cookin'. How could I be anything but satisfied? I am blessed."

Then she paused and dabbed at her eyes with the corner of her apron. "I have found peace with Amos going home to the Lord, and I'm looking forward to the day I can join up with him again."

As Mrs. Gentry spoke, a light breeze blew through the open kitchen window. The curtains fluttered, and the warmth of the late May afternoon filled the room.

Mrs. Gentry looked over at the flapping curtain. "Old Amos is still with me. His spirit comforts me through the day. Yes, ma'am, blessed I am. What about you, Miss Mame? Tell me how you're doing, and that fine boy Walt?"

Instead of answering, Mame got up and went to the stove where Mrs. Gentry always kept a full pot of coffee. She reached to the open shelf above and took down two cups, both chipped around the edges. After pouring their coffee, she returned with the steaming cups to the kitchen table covered with its familiar red and white checked tablecloth.

"Mame, how about checking that cobbler while you're up?"

Mame took the dishtowel, folded it, and opened the warm oven door. The sweetness of the sugared fruit wafted up Mame's nose, and a true smile broke across her face. She could always find a little bit of happiness here in the kitchen with Mrs. Gentry.

Mrs. Gentry had helped with the birthing of Mame's babies. She'd held her hand as she cried over the loss of Clint. Never had she ever once judged her, even when she knew Mame was far from perfect. Yes, Mrs. Gentry was more of a mother to her than she'd ever known.

Removing the hot dish from the oven, Mame set the bubbling dessert on the stove burner, got bowls, and spooned them each out a fair amount of cobbler. After a few bites of what the people of the Appalachians called sweet sonker, Mame finally answered her former maid and now friend.

"I'm the same as always. I get up each day. I breathe, work, eat, sleep, and get up and do it all over again. It's been over three years since Clint left. What could have happened to him? Why did he go?"

"Now, child, we don't know what's goin' on in the mind of another, or the why and why not's of each other's doings. All I know is that he must have gone mad over losing his boy Ben and then the baby. My lands, sometimes a body just can't take no more." She patted Mame's hand. "You always keep looking down that road. One of these days, that boy will find his head, and he'll be home. He was always a good young-un, and he'll find his way again. How'd you say Walt's doing?"

"He has blossomed into a fine young man since our move to Beckley. Walt is the only good thing that's ever come out of my life."

As always, Mame left her visit with Mrs. Gentry feeling a little better than she had when she'd arrived. She always reminded Mame that as long as she didn't know for sure Clint was dead, there was hope.

Pulling her car out of Mrs. Gentry's narrow driveway, Mame steered back to the main street. Soon she was at her usual destination, the old Paddington mansion. She parked opposite the house. It looked well kept, as usual. The Hutchinson family had bought it. Word was Mr. Hutchinson had made a fortune buying up property for next to nothing during the Depression and then selling it at ten times his cost when the country settled down.

Mame sat wondering what Clint would think if he ever did come home. Would he walk up to the door, try to put in his key, and find it would not fit? Would he understand that she'd had to sell? There were so many unanswered questions.

Where are you, Clint?

Mame's journey back to Beckley felt very long, for in her mind she traveled through many miles of winding dark tunnels before she reached her front door.

Right from the start, Walt loved his new life in Beckley and was the happiest he'd been since he was a small boy. He met a beautiful young girl named Emily Thompson the year he turned eighteen.

Walt was not but a few months into the courtship before he knew he'd met his future wife. In 1951, he and Emily were to be married. They were both barely nineteen years old.

Mame adjusted Walt's solid navy tie. She was so proud of him and loved his soon-to-be wife. It appeared they'd found the perfect match in each other.

"Merciful heavens, Mama. I'm scared to death to stand up in front of all those people," Walt confessed.

He and Emily both had big families. They'd all be there, as well as the usual well-wishers from around town.

"Oh, you'll do fine. Just repeat what the preacher tells you."

"What if I forget?"

"Then ask him to repeat it."

Walt was a quiet young man, maybe somewhat overly serious. But why wouldn't he be? He'd been through much in his fewer-than-twenty years. He and Mame rarely mentioned his father or Ben anymore, and never baby Daniel. It was just too painful. Walt could barely remember even having a baby brother. But today, they were all foremost on Walt and Mame's minds.

"Mama, I wish Daddy and Ben were here. I just know they're both all right. I can feel it. I dream sometimes that they are together, trying to get back to us. Something detains them, but they're always trying."

Mame looked away and wiped a single tear from her cheek.

"Walt, you're right. We just have to believe they'll be back and we'll be a family again one day. But for now, this is your day to be happy. You look so handsome, and your beautiful bride is waiting for you. Nothing should be in your thoughts right now but your happy future."

Walt put his arms around his mother and hugged her very tightly.

"I love you, Mama."

"I love you, too, Walt . . . very, very much."

Mame cried for many reasons at that simple church wedding. She thought about how Walt and Emily looked so much in love. Mame had taken fate into her own hands. Clint never had the opportunity to fall in love with her in his own good time. He was forced to marry her because she was pregnant.

And maybe Walt was not his son, but it didn't matter to Mame anymore. Walt still looked like Clint, and she knew that sometimes when he smiled, she saw Clint all over again. She loved Walt no matter who he was or where he had come from.

A surge of guilt overwhelmed Mame as she thought of Ben and where he might be, whether he was even alive, and of that baby who had fallen into a forever sleep.

Mame heard applause and snapped back into this welcomed occasion just in time to see Walt kiss his new bride. Mame's brothers all let out a loud whoop and tossed their hats into the air.

Maybe this wedding would be the beginning of good things. Although Mame knew there was no good coming to her, maybe Walt's life would be free of the shadows that plagued her. He deserved a good life.

Six months before, Jack Marsh lay dying from a stab wound. He wrestled with what to say to his son Ben, the son who still didn't know who he really was.

"Go find your ma, boy. Ask her who your real daddy is."

With that, Jack Marsh closed his eyes for eternity, and all the demons in hell applauded as they welcomed him into the lake of fire.

Unsure what to do, for a few months Ben stayed on the coast of North Carolina catching wild ponies, but Jack's last words haunted him.

Ask her who your real daddy is.

I don't want to see Mama, Ben thought. *She paid Jack to take me away. She didn't want me. Why should I ask her anything?*

But it kept eating at him until he decided to borrow a pal's old jalopy and make his way back to Charleston. When he stood in front of the big house where he'd spent the first eight years of his life, he knew his mother wasn't there. He could feel it. Still, he went up to the door and knocked anyway.

"Yes, may I help you, sir?" a servant asked.

"I'm looking for Clint and Mame Paddington. Do they still live here?"

"I'm afraid not. Mr. Paddington died, I believe, and his wife and son moved to a little town called Beckley up near the West Virginia border."

Back to her hometown, huh? Home again to the place she so hurriedly whisked him away from all those years ago. Now he understood her haste . . . she had a meeting set up with old Jack that she didn't want to miss. Now it all made sense. She couldn't give up the opportunity to get rid of the son she'd never wanted. *Well, I'll just have to look dear old mother up. It's high time my kin and me see each other again.* He reached his hand into his pant pocket and circled his fingers around the whistle his cousin had given him the day they left the farm. He'd carried it every dreaded day since.

The words the man at the door said suddenly registered in Ben's mind.

I believe Mr. Paddington is dead.

The devoted father of his childhood was dead. That would explain why he never tracked down Jack Marsh and got him back. The thought of his daddy gone only made Ben want to find his mother quicker. Mame Paddington had much to account for. A single tear traced its way down Ben's cheek.

Ben rolled into the town of Beckley at half past midnight. He had been out to the Blackwell farm only that one time as a boy, so in all honesty he didn't know which way to go. The map that had led him to town didn't disclose the location of the homeplace. Driving up and down the streets, he saw that the town was deserted, not a soul in sight, nor any sign of a light shining through a window. This town was locked up tight.

Ben pulled into Norman's Filling Station when he spotted the pop machine sitting out front. He put his dime in the slot and pulled the door open, grabbing a Dr Pepper. He sat down on a bench beside the pop machine and picked up a newspaper that had been left there by another patron earlier that day.

Simply by chance, as Ben was killing time by flipping through the pages of *The Beckley Miners Gazette,* a name jumped out at him. *Walt Paddington to wed Emily Thompson.* Walt's wedding announcement was there in the newspaper. The date was set for the day after tomorrow.

Ben closed the paper and smiled to himself. He was going to have a little fun. All he had to do was lay low for a couple of days.

The next day Ben spent riding the roads; eventually he stopped and asked an old farmer on a Massey Ferguson tractor for the needed directions to the farm. He crept by the driveway at least a dozen times. From the distance, he could tell that the farmhouse looked bigger than what he remembered as a boy, and there were many more sheds and a larger barn that had not been there before. That night he parked behind a rhododendron thicket down at the river and slept till the morning sun peeked over the mountaintop.

The celebrated day had arrived. Ben opened the truck door and went down to the river. He splashed water on his face, then took off his shirt and doused his upper body with the cold mountain water.

Strolling back to the truck, he took a clean shirt from the brown paper bag he'd brought with him and slipped it on. *I need to look good for Mommy,* he thought sarcastically.

He found a little diner on one end of town and reluctantly pulled in. He was tired of eating the junk he'd brought with him. When he saw they had curb service, he grinned. Not that he thought any of his precious family would recognize him after all this time, but he didn't want to take the chance. He wanted his arrival to be a complete surprise.

Through the church window, Ben found them all seated for the wedding. It had been almost ten years, but he would have recognized his mother and twin brother anywhere. His eyes didn't linger long on his mother; they fixed on his brother. Anger and hatred rose up in him until he was shaking all over.

Why did Mother keep him and give me away? I'll bet she still hugs and kisses on him.

Then Ben pried his attention away to the beautiful young girl at the altar. Her long, red curls trailed halfway down her back. Her skin was flawless against the whiteness of her wedding gown. When she turned, he could see the roundness of her bosom and the slight curve of her hips. *That could be me standing beside her if Mother had only kept me.*

That moment, Ben vowed to have this young woman for himself. He'd make his brother suffer like he had. Walt's bride would be his.

As the ceremony ended and they all left the church, no one noticed Ben lurking in the shadows behind the giant oak trees.

He sneered while the happy couple stood on the church steps, accepting congratulations. A long row of tables covered with white cloths held a two-tiered wedding cake, a huge punch bowl, and other refreshments such as homemade pickles, a celebration the likes of such Ben had not seen since he was young in Charleston. Everyone meandered around the perfectly clipped lawn where the smiling couple held court. Ben stayed carefully in the background the entire afternoon, scheming, lingering, and smirking as he recognized or could not recognize his various relatives.

Especially, he concentrated on Walt's luscious new bride—Emily Thompson Paddington.

Late that evening, Walt took his bride back to the little house he had rented for them.

While his brother loved the night away, Ben spent his night in town getting drunk. He no longer cared who saw him. All he could think about was how it would be to bed his brother's wife. Oh yes, revenge would be sweet.

For the next two days, Ben watched the rented house from afar, waiting for his chance. On the third day, Walt left early in the morning as if he were going to work. He carried what was probably his lunch in a brown poke, so Ben knew he'd be gone at least most of the day.

Emily heard a knock at the door. Everyone had respectfully left her and Walt alone for their honeymoon, but now Walt had returned to work with his uncles at the Blackwell Tobacco Warehouse, and Emily's first visitor had arrived. It was probably her mother. Emily opened the door. A strange yet familiar face looked in at her.

"Good morning. Is your husband home?"

"Not right now, he just left for work. May I help you? I'm his wife."

"Well, maybe you can. You see, I'm his brother Ben, and he owes me a few favors."

Emily recognized the name and certainly the similarity. Walt had told her about his twin brother who disappeared all those years ago.

"Oh, my goodness. Come in! Walt will be so shocked to know you're here! No wonder you look familiar—you're Walt's twin brother. Have you seen your mother yet? She will be so thrilled. I'm sorry for all these questions. Please sit down. May I get you anything?"

Ben followed Emily through the living room and sat down at the kitchen table. For a long time, he stared at her until she began to feel uneasy. Glancing down, Emily realized she still had on her night-clothes and began to fidget. Only a satin wrapper her mother had given her as a wedding present covered her gown underneath. The thin material did not leave much to the imagination.

She blushed. "Oh. I'm sorry. I thought it was my mother at the door. Let me get dressed. It won't take me but a minute." She rose to pass Ben, but he caught her by the arm.

"Like I said, my brother owes me something, and it won't take but a few minutes to collect."

"No. No. What are you doing?" she cried as she tried to pull free.

"I'm collecting. My brother owes me years of attention. He got all the love and affection from our mother, and now I'm going to get it back from you."

Ben rudely picked Emily up and carried her to the bedroom. The place where she had just lain with his brother. He could still smell their newly wedded passion. Emily fought him with all the strength she had, but he was too strong for her.

Walt had been very gentle with her during his lovemaking, so sweet and calm. But as his brother loomed over her, strange, conflicting feelings began to erupt inside her. As Emily claimed her prize, so did Ben. It was not his first trophy, but it was the most satisfying of his life.

Lying there on the same bed where Walt and she had lain only minutes before, reality dawned, and Emily pushed Ben away.

Emily asked. "Oh no, what have I done?" She spoke softly as she curled into a tight ball on her husband's side of the bed.

Ben lay there on his brother's bed, understanding what had just happened: Walt had made love to his wife for three days, but until a few minutes ago, she had not known the pleasure she was supposed to experience.

"I collected what was rightfully owed me. I showed you I'm better than my brother. I taught you how to be pleasured by a real man."

Emily crawled further away from the stranger who called himself Walt's twin.

"Get out of here. Leave me alone."

Ben threw his legs off the bed and stood before Emily. "Look at me, honey, because you'll never have me again. Night after night, year after year, when you're with my brother, you'll remember this morning and the pleasure that could have been yours—if fate had of saw fit to give you the best brother."

Ben rubbed his chin, thinking that justice had finally served him, but a threat was still in order.

"Take my advice. It wouldn't be wise for you to tell my brother you saw me today. No man wants a used woman for a wife." Pulling on his dingy clothes, Ben looked at her once more. "Don't worry, Mrs. Paddington. I won't bother you again. As long as you keep our little secret, you'll be safe."

Ben left that same day to return to South Carolina. But he didn't forget the sweet smell or the feel of his brother's wife. He knew she would never forget him. He had made sure Emily would never be the pure wife his brother thought her to be and expected. He felt satisfied with the revenge he'd taken on his brother. So sated, he decided to deal with his mother later. His vengeance toward his dear mommy might take longer than one afternoon.

When Walt got home from work that night, he couldn't tell anything was wrong. All he wanted was to bed his new bride again since he had missed her so much all day.

Emily had hardly recovered from the morning, but Walt didn't notice her hesitation. He wanted her, and he wanted her now. Emily tried to feel the pleasure she'd felt that morning, but it did not occur.

As time passed, Emily felt so guilty that she could hardly look at herself in the mirror. But neither could she forget. Sometimes when she was alone, she'd remember how Ben had made her feel and would know he was right. She would never tell Walt. He wouldn't believe it was all Ben's fault, and what was worse, it really wasn't.

Walt was so very happy those first few months that he didn't notice anything strange about his wife. Then when Emily announced the upcoming arrival of their first child, Walt was by far the happiest he'd ever been in his life. As the newlyweds prepared for the arrival of the new baby, time passed swiftly.

Very early on the morning of May 12, 1952, Mary Katherine Paddington screamed her way into the lives of Emily, Walt, and Grandma Mame Paddington. She was a beautiful little baby with eyes like her father's—clear, bright, and blue—and she was even born on his birthday.

Mame was there when her first grandchild was delivered. She could not help but remember the birth of her own babies and what had happened since. Would she ever be able to forgive herself? Or more importantly, would God ever forgive her? Would the dark shadows ever stop looming?

Maybe since Katherine was formed from love and truth, the darkness would end with her. *This child will bring sunshine to our lives,* Mame hoped.

She had no idea that Emily had started out her life as a wife the same way Mame had. Lies, all dreaded lies.

CHAPTER THIRTY-THREE

1953

A brother offended is harder to be won than a strong city: and their
contentions are like the bars of a castle.

~ Proverbs 18:19

BEN SETTLED HIS ELBOW ON the pillow and rested his head against his hand. He'd stayed busy this past year learning his new job. With some difficulty, he had kept away from Beckley . . . and Emily.

In his bedroom at the little beach house he rented at Folly Beach, he glanced at the young girl with whom he had just lain and who was now cuddled up next to him.

"How old are you anyway, Trudy? And why didn't you tell me you'd never been with a man?"

"I'll be sixteen next week. It was high time I became a woman."

Over time, Ben had become well known along the coast of South Carolina and at surrounding islands like Sullivan's, James, Kiawah, and Seabrook. After Jack Marsh died, Ben had gone to work for the county, patrolling the beaches and islands to make sure the wildlife was protected and their habitat preserved. He was not opposed to hard work and had turned what Jack Marsh had taught him about the wild ponies into a respectable living.

Trudy was not the only girl at the coast who had wrangled for the attention of the swarthy, muscular Ben Marsh. He was popular with the ladies, but none took his mind completely off Emily and that morning in his brother's house. She had been so full of passion. It was almost as if brother Walt had been fueling her flames just so Ben could extinguish them himself.

"Get up, Trudy."

Ben's attention returned to the young morsel at hand. "Put your clothes on. You'd better watch who you snuggle up to. Your next partner might not be as good to you."

"There won't be anybody else but you, Ben. I've known ever since I first saw you that I wanted you, and now I've got you."

"Oh no, little lady. No one has me. Just because you gave yourself to me doesn't mean I owe you one thing."

"Well, we'll see what my daddy says about that, Mr. Ben Marsh."

Trudy got up from the bed and slung on her clothes. Lazily Ben watched her.

"Yeah, go ahead, Trudy. Tell your daddy. I'll be sure to fill him in on how his little girl has been seducing me for months now, and all the dandy things she's been doing to me for weeks. I believe he'll understand I'd had all I could take."

"We'll just see who he believes, won't we?" Trudy said, flying out the door carrying her shoes, her hair a tangled mess.

Trudy was a wild thing, and Ben didn't know if she'd keep her mouth shut or not. Maybe this would be a good time to take a little trip back to Beckley and see how Mama was doing . . . and Emily.

Besides, he never did get around to asking his mama who his real daddy is.

If I leave right now, I can be there by dark.

Ben jerked his clothes on, and just like before, threw a couple of things in a brown paper bag, and out the door he went, destination Beckley, West Virginia.

Ben had sworn he would never bother Emily. In fact, he had told her she would never see him again. He'd taken his revenge on his brother, but he couldn't help himself. He had to see her. So here he stood at Walt's house in Beckley. He slipped around the corner, peeped in a bedroom window, and saw his mother sitting in a rocker—holding a baby.

However, there was no sign of Emily. Had she taken a job and left the baby with his mother? Where was Walt? Nowhere near, it seemed. Ben studied the room and the house a while longer. Since no one was around, it looked like an opportune moment to confront Mame.

Ben didn't bother to knock. He twisted the back door knob and walked straight in. Mame turned her head toward the noise. Footsteps were carrying someone closer and closer to the bedroom. She was not expecting Walt and Emily home quite yet.

It was a good thing that she was seated, for otherwise her legs would have buckled when she saw the man who unmistakably had to be her other son. It may have been over ten years since she'd last laid eyes on him, but those years had added to the confirmation that he was Jack Marsh's son . . . the resemblance was undeniable.

"Well, Mother. Don't you look cozy," Ben said as his powerful frame filled the doorway.

Mame gasped and impulsively pulled the baby tightly to her just as it began to cry. She yanked the light blanket up over her face almost as if to shield the baby from Jack Marsh's evil. There is no mistaking who this man's father is. The years had fashioned his face into an almost exact replica of his wicked daddy.

"Seems my brother has sired a brat of his own. I'd better warn him not to let you keep it though. You might decide you don't like it and pay someone to take it away, just like you did me."

Mame's heart was pounding. She stammered. "Ben, is that you?" Knowing it was, she didn't know what else to say. "You're back. Are you all right? Where have you been?"

"Where have I been? Like you don't know. Don't you remember that sorry night all those years ago when you paid Jack Marsh one hundred dollars to take me away?" His voice began to choke with rage. "Did I mean so little to you that you don't even remember?"

Mame rocked Mary Katherine, trying to soothe the baby's cries, as well as calm herself, but the rocker squeaked like an animal in a trap, and the baby wailed louder. She scowled up at Ben.

"What are you talking about? Jack Marsh attacked me that night. He left me for dead and kidnapped you. I swear I had nothing to do with him stealing you. Your daddy looked for you everywhere. He never rested a minute. For years he carried your picture with him, asking everyone he saw if they'd seen you. He plastered your photo in every place that would let him all over the state of West Virginia and even down into North Carolina. He drove himself mad with grief."

Ben hesitated for a few seconds wanting to believe his mother, but willing himself not to. "You would have a story, but you can't fool me. I know you never loved me or showed me any attention. It was always Walt you hugged and kissed, never me," Ben said, yelling over the baby's wailing. "I've already settled my score with Walt; me and his brand new wife got real close a few days after they were married. It suits me to know I pleased her when her puny husband didn't. And while we're at it, seems you strayed some too in your younger days. Just who is my real daddy?"

As soon as the question left his mouth, he and Mame heard a gasp from behind them. Ben turned just in time to see Walt's stunned face and Emily crumpling to the floor. With the turmoil and Ben's leaving the back door ajar, they had not heard the couple arrive.

How much had Walt heard? By the looks of Emily, they'd both heard it all.

"What in the world is going on here?" said Walt. "Mother, I thought you didn't know who attacked you. And what does he mean, *his real father?*" Walt glared at Ben. "It was supposed to be a happy day if I ever saw you again. And here you are talking about having your way with my wife. Why you lying son of a—" Walt jumped right up in Ben's face.

"Ain't no lie, dear brother. Wake her up and ask her."

Walt had not realized Emily had collapsed. When he turned to her, he was shocked to see a bright red stain soaking through her seersucker skirt.

Emily was expecting again. Not quite three months along, she'd been sick and spotting the entire time.

The baby in Mame's arms let out one last high-pitched howl before she spit up most of her milk on her grandmother's threadbare apron. One more mess Mame would have to clean up. As she sat in that rocking chair staring at her sons and at Emily lying on the floor in a pool of blood, she realized her sins were still following her. And now, obviously the shadows were swallowing up her boys too.

CHAPTER THIRTY-FOUR

1960

*Keeping mercy for thousands, forgiving iniquity and transgression
and sin, and that will by no means clear the guilty; visiting the
iniquity of the fathers upon the children, and upon the children's
children, unto the third and to the fourth generation.*

~ Exodus 34:7

"KATHERINE, I'M GOING DOWN TO the spring to get a bucket of water."

"Okay, Grandma."

Grandma Mame still insisted the spring water tasted much better than the piped-in well water.

Katherine stood at the sink peeling potatoes, humming softly to herself. She was looking forward to cutting the fresh apple cake Grandma Mame had baked for her birthday. The smell made her mouth water as she closed her eyes and breathed in the spicy aroma.

All of a sudden, the kitchen door burst open. In walked a man about six feet tall with long, shaggy, greasy brown hair. He was dressed in worn, dirty clothes.

Katherine's first instinct was to scream, but something inside her refused to be frightened by this man. All common sense told her to run, but she didn't. She just stood where she was and stared into the face of the man who would become her worst enemy.

He was the first to speak. "You must be Katie Girl. Come over here and give your Uncle Ben a big hug and kiss."

She didn't move an inch. Even at the young age of eight, Katherine sensed something very evil about this man. She had heard her grandmother ask God in her prayers every night to look after her son Ben, but Katherine had never seen a picture of him.

Katherine also remembered overhearing her grandmother ask God to forgive them for what they had done.

Once she had asked Grandma Mame about her prayers, but she had answered only with a long sigh, saying, "Some thing's you just don't need to know, child. Anyway, he's gone, never to return."

But Grandma was wrong. Here he was in full, living color, clouded with hues of black and gray shadows, shadows that would hover over their lives and inside their souls for many years to come. Those shadows held depths that young Katherine could not imagine.

That day, the day of her uncle's return, would be plastered in Katherine's mind forever.

Slowly Ben came toward Katherine. He was grinning, a smile that was not unpleasant to the eye.

"What's the matter, little girl? You're not afraid of your old Uncle Ben, are you?"

Katherine stood her ground as she watched him make his way to her. She gripped the potato-peeling knife tighter. A strange look came over his face. He reached down and tilted up her chin. Then he took a lock of her hair and twirled it in his fingers.

"You're the spitting' image of your mama . . . same golden-reddish hair . . . same bone structure in the face. But your eyes are different. No mistaking those eyes," he said. "They are just like Walt's. The same as when you were a baby."

As Ben talked, a fury built up in him. His eyes narrowed and he stepped back, as if Katherine were looming larger before him than any little girl ever could. He shook his head and stumbled a few more steps away from Katherine. Turning, he left the house as fast as he'd come in. Hands shaking, Katherine dropped her peeling knife onto the wooden floor, scarcely missing her bare big toe.

When Grandma Mame came back from getting the water, Katherine was sitting at the table with the knife in her hand. She was as pale as a late winter snow.

Mame could tell something had happened.

"What's wrong, Katherine? Are you sick?"

"A man was just here. He said he was my Uncle Ben."

The water bucket slid from Mame's hand as she began to mutter, "Oh, no, no, no—he wasn't ever to come back here . . . What will happen now? What will I do?"

Water was running all over the wooden kitchen floor, but Mame just stood there, clenching her hands at her sides like she was kneading dough. Her lips started moving, but no words came out. As the water flowed in all directions, so did Mame's mind. Thousands of thoughts and worries exploded in her head.

Katherine jumped up and ran to the back porch for the mop. When she returned to the kitchen, Grandma Mame was sitting right in the middle of the wet floor, crying. The only time Katherine had ever heard her grandma cry was late at night. Sometimes Katherine would wake up during the middle of the night and find her grand-mother sitting at the kitchen table, holding letters or photographs in her hands, and whimpering softly into her old handkerchief.

At these times, Katherine never approached her. She knew her grandmother loved her and took very good care of her, but there was a remoteness about Grandma Mame, as if she were in her own world where no one else was allowed to enter. Mame rarely showed any emotion, and never gave her granddaughter—or anyone else—hugs or kisses.

Katherine didn't know why Grandma Mame was this way, seem-ing afraid to love anything too much.

Mame knew the truth; all she had ever adored had been taken from her . . . gone, lost forever.

The sight of her grandmother acting this way frightened Katherine more than the stranger had. "Grandma, get up. You're get-ting all wet! Let me help you."

Katherine hooked her arm under her grandma's and helped her to her feet and then the few steps to the kitchen table.

Mame sat for a long time, wringing her hands and crying. What a pitiful story her life told, a saga of lies, deceit, and regret.

"Grandma, what is it? Are you sick?" Katherine asked.

Finally, Mame was able to speak. "Did the man say where he was going?"

Katherine shook her head. "No, he just walked out."

"He'll be back. I know he will. What kind of misery is he bringing with him this time?" Mame rubbed her eyes with her handkerchief. Ben had vowed he would never set foot in Beckley again. Why had he come back? He'd promised. All these thoughts and more ran through Mame's mind.

"Is he really my uncle, Grandma? The one I hear you praying for God to watch over?"

"Yes, Mary Katherine, he is your father's twin brother, my son."

"Where has he been? Why hasn't anyone ever talked about him?"

Mame dabbed her eyes with her apron and looked out the window toward the family cemetery on the hill. "Sometimes words are better left unsaid. There are some things you are better off not knowing."

That night after Katherine went to bed, she knew Uncle Ben had returned to the house. She could hear his and Grandma Mame's voices way into the night. The next morning, there he sat at the kitchen table.

"Good morning, Katie Girl. Come give your Uncle Ben a good morning kiss."

"Ben, leave her alone. She doesn't even know you," Mame said.

"Well, we've got plenty of time to get acquainted. I'm going to be living with you and your grandma," Ben said.

Katherine shuddered, knowing that the simple life that she and her grandmother led would never be the same. She already knew she didn't like this man.

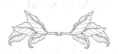

Over the next several years, Katherine learned to avoid Uncle Ben as much as possible. He was always telling her to sit on his lap, asking for a hug. At first she didn't think anything of it. Her other Blackwell uncles often hugged her. But it didn't take long for her to realize that

Ben was not like them. His pats and touches were not innocent but lewd, not at all endearing.

Katherine was developing into a beautiful, young woman with long, slender legs and an alluring face that seemed to capture everyone's attention. She was shy. Being raised by and living with her grandmother always made her feel a little different from her friends. There was no way she would ever ask any of her schoolmates to her home for a visit. She never knew when Uncle Ben might come home drunk. When he was drinking, he got mean. Katherine would lay in bed at night, listening to him scream all kinds of things at her grandmother, telling her she was the cause of all his troubles, and that he hoped she burned in hell.

Grandmother just sat and listened to him, never saying a harsh word. She probably knew he was out of his mind, drunk, and crazy. Everybody knows you can't reason with a fool, the Good Book even says so.

1968

It had been eight years since Uncle Ben had come to live with Mame and her granddaughter Katherine. His life before he came remained a mystery to Katherine. He told one story after another about his prior life, but they were so farfetched, who could believe them?

Throughout the years, one thing he often asked her grandma puzzled her. More than once she'd overheard Uncle Ben asking Grandma Mame if someone named Jack Marsh was his daddy. Katherine learned not to ask questions since the topic rapidly set off his anger. But she still couldn't figure things out since she knew her grandpa's name was Clint, not Jack.

For the first few years, Ben worked steadily on the farm, helping his uncles, but for the past year, he had slacked off his chores. Katherine's great uncles never said much to Ben. They mostly let him do what he wanted to do. They felt sorry for his kidnapping and his years away from family. Whatever he had survived had made him ornery and distant, and some things just can't be fixed.

Then the days came when her uncle started being at home every afternoon when Katherine returned from school. He stared at her all the time, never saying much, just watching her every move. A few times Katherine had even woke at night to find him standing beside her bed, and occasionally he'd call her Emily, her deceased mother's name.

"Just checking on you, Emily. *Emily*, I mean *Katie Girl*. Just checking." Then he would leave as quietly as he'd entered.

On May 12, 1968, Katherine's sixteenth birthday and Ben's thirty-sixth, she was having a wonderful day. Bobby Andrews, her first crush, had driven her home from school for the very first time, and her cousins had given her new curlers, white patent leather knee boots, and a blue mini skirt.

Katherine came in the front door, flushed with excitement and clutching her schoolbooks as she spun around the living room, for the moment lost in her own, normal teenage world.

"Welcome home, birthday girl," Ben said as he staggered toward her. Katherine smelled his drunken odor, and once again her guard went up. She had always stood her ground with Ben and never let him know she was scared of him. Today he had that evil, bleary-eyed look, the same as he did the first time she ever saw him.

"We should have a joint birthday party, just you and me. We're like twins, you know, like me and Walt." He reached out and lifted one of her curls. "That same golden-reddish hair, just like Emily's . . . I can still feel my hands running through it."

Katherine knew he was truly crazy, talking almost as if he knew her mother intimately. His eyes were closed, and he was swaying as if he were in a trance. Katherine stepped back, away from him, and went to her room. She brushed her hair so furiously that sparks flew into the air.

He makes me sick. I wish he would leave for good. It's so pleasant when he goes on his "trips." Grandma is so much happier. I don't know why or how she's put up with his abuse all these years.

Katherine remembered one time when he'd seemed more drugged than drunk. Suddenly, he'd grabbed and locked Katherine in a tight embrace and crushed his mouth over hers. His rough, unshaven face scratched her cheeks and lips. Frantically moving her head from side to side and wrestling against his bruising grip, Katherine broke free.

"Come on, Emily. You know you like it, remember?"

What was he talking about, calling her by her mother's name again?

Thankfully, the back door had slammed, breaking Ben's mood, and he had dropped his grip on her. Katherine had fled to her room before Grandma Mame could see the scratches on her face. She threw herself on her bed, sobbing.

I hate him. He's ruining my life. No one should have to live with such a nasty, vile person.

In his stupor, Ben had looked around and tumbled to a chair near the window. A warm spring breeze wafted in, fluttering the curtains, but he was oblivious to anything but his own cold, selfish need. Closing his eyes, he could still see Emily's look of passion, the same as he had that morning so many years ago.

CHAPTER THIRTY-FIVE

1970

*And the great dragon was cast out, that old serpent, called the Devil,
and Satan, which deceiveth the whole world: he was cast out into the
earth, and his angels were cast out with him.*

~ Revelation 12:9

ON DAYS WHEN UNCLE BEN was away, Katherine felt almost normal, like her life would be okay. But there were other problems.

Katherine returned home from school one day to find Grandma Mame in deep conversation, but no one was sitting at the table with her.

"Grandma. Who's there? Who are you talking to?"

Not noticing Katherine at all, Mame continued her discussion with the invisible companion. Katherine put her hand on her grandma's shoulder, and then she tapped the salt shaker against the table; nothing seemed to break the spell. Finally, after ten minutes of muttering, Mame stood up and walked outside. Katherine followed her as she walked near the river to the old springhouse they no longer used. Then she simply turned around and started walking back. Near the house, Mame stopped and turned to Katherine.

"Your Uncle Ben came home today. Stay away from him. He's evil, just like his daddy." Then Mame walked into the house as if nothing had happened. It was like she was actually reliving the day all those years ago when Ben had indeed come home.

Once Katherine dared to go back inside, her grandmother was her old self again. Over the next few months, Mame's slipping into the past happened at least once or twice a month. Katherine would find her grandmother talking to herself or crying. When she was like that, she never responded to anything Katherine said or did. When she was having these spells, nothing Grandma Mame said ever made any sense. Her ramblings were like a dog bringing in stray bones; a person could not piece together what the real animal had been or the true meaning of Mame's jumbled words. Worse, it seemed that at each episode, Mame stayed in the trance longer and longer.

Once, Katherine found her posed in the rocking chair as if she were rocking a baby. She was sobbing and begging an imaginary someone, "Don't let me kill my baby. Please don't let me." This sent shudders up Katherine's spine.

Each time when Mame would come back to herself, she remembered nothing. Katherine begged her to go to the doctor.

"Oh, you just caught me dreaming again, Katherine. You know I'm getting older and more than a little senile. I can't remember a thing."

Since Grandma Mame's eyes were open, Katherine knew she wasn't asleep. Something just wasn't right. Mame was not quite sixty years old, yet she'd started sleeping more, eating less, and doing fewer of her normal chores, or leaving them half-done.

Katherine resented having to take on more housework and keep up with her studies. What little social life she had fell by the wayside.

There was no denying that Katherine's grandmother was slipping away from her. She was sad watching the person who had raised her drift into this other world, a place where no one was ever invited, no one except her imaginary friends—or foes.

Katherine was doing the best she could to take care of things, but finally she knew she needed help.

"Uncle Ben, you're home most of the time during the day. You've got to keep an eye on Grandma while I'm at school."

"Yeah . . . yeah. Sure, Katie Girl. What's wrong with the old lady anyway? She hardly ever cooks a meal any more. She just sits and stares."

"I don't know. I've tried to get her to go to a doctor, but she refuses. Just watch her. I've found her wandering as far as a mile down the road."

The next week, Katherine came home to find Uncle Ben passed out on the couch and Grandma Mame nowhere to be found. Frantic, Katherine looked everywhere until she had no choice but to call her great uncles to help. They'd noticed changes in their sister too, but they saw very little of her, not enough to know how bad she was.

"Katherine, what in the world is this all about? What is wrong with Mame?" Uncle James asked as he met her at the house to continue the search.

She filled in James, Hank, and William, but Timothy and Thomas were away on business. They traveled widely and often for Blackwell Tobacco Company.

"I don't know. She's been talking to herself a lot, almost always distracted and nervous. She sleeps too much, and when she's not in bed, she's crying and saying crazy stuff. I've tried and tried to get her to go to the doctor, but she won't hear of it, says she's fine. I found her one day last week about halfway up the hill toward the cemetery. She couldn't remember how she got there."

"Let's go; we'll find her," Uncle William said, already walking toward the hill.

"Wait, we need to pray first," Uncle Hank said.

Katherine loved hearing her uncle preach the Word. He'd been picking her up and taking her to church since she was a toddler. They always tried to get Grandma Mame to go, but she declined every time, muttering something about not being worthy to step foot in a church.

About an hour into the search, a steady mist began to fall on the mountain. The early afternoon sun gave way to a foggy veil rising off the Elk River. The search continued into late evening, until finally they spotted Mame near the entrance to the old coal mine.

Running toward her, Katherine drew up short when she saw her grandmother had scratched at the dirt and pulled on the boards until blood seeped from her fingers.

Hank reached down and put a hand under Mame's arm to lift her. "Mame. Let's get you home where it's safe and dry. You know it's dangerous around these old mine pits. Don't you remember? Mother would whip us for coming out here."

But Mame jerked free and went back to digging at the boarded-up entrance.

Katherine couldn't believe what she was seeing. It was more than a little terrifying to witness the condition of her grandmother. Grandma Mame was dripping wet, covered in black coal dust, her hair was stringy and falling in her face. When she finally looked up and spoke, her words were clearly the words of a madwoman.

"Dry and safe. Why do I deserve to be dry or safe? How can I ever rest with him still in there? There will be no peace for me until I've undone my wrongs. I've got to fix things before Clint comes home.

He'll never forgive me if I don't." Turning back to the guarded hole, Mame dug with fury.

"Grandma. What are you doing? What's wrong with you?" Katherine screamed.

"He's in there! We've got to get him out. He's been in there too long."

"Who, Grandma? Who's in there?"

Uncle Hank spoke. "It's Papa. He was buried alive during an explosion in this mine fifty years ago."

Gradually Hank and the others wrenched Mame away from the haunting grave. Their destination was the hospital. As they were leaving with Katherine holding Grandma's stained hand, Mame stopped, looked back toward the mine, and whispered in a small, still voice.

"I know you're in there. I'll get you out. I'll set us free."

Grandma Mame was more than confused. She was promising to rescue her dead father Henry? Why, even his bones would be gone by now, or buried under tons of mountain soil.

"Come on, Mame. We've got to get you cleaned up," William said, putting his arm through hers.

"Will, I should have stayed with you. I'm sorry I deserted you. Can you forgive me?"

"Nothing to forgive, Mame. Everything turned out okay."

"No, it didn't. No, it didn't. No, it didn't." Mame continued to mutter those three words for most of the trip to the hospital.

Mame Blackwell Paddington stayed at the hospital for three days while the staff ran tests. Most of the stay, she was out of her mind, muttering those crazy things over and over:

"Jack Marsh is your real daddy. . . . Jared is dead because of me. . . . I didn't give you away, he stole you. . . . No, baby, don't be dead. I didn't mean to. . . . Clint. Forgive me." What did it all mean? It was as if her grandmother were being tortured, like demons were poking her brain with needles. The doctors told Katherine that Mame had all the symptoms of some new disease that was being researched, Alzheimer's. But there wasn't enough known about the mind-rending sickness to be positive. Mame was surely too young to have dementia. The way she carried on with her mutterings made the doctors suspect she was just a demented madwoman.

"No, you've got to help her," Katherine pleaded with new desperation. "She's not always been like this. She started getting confused only a few years ago, but it's getting worse every day now. Please help her."

The beady-eyed doctor in his white lab coat listened to Katherine's pleas. He felt sorry for this young lady who seemed to really care for her grandmother.

"I'm sorry, Miss Paddington. We'll do everything we can, but there is no cure that we know of for such an ailment. I'm afraid it will only get worse. She'll eventually forget who she is, as well as her family. What little we know about this disease has proven that over time, the patient wastes away and loses all life-sustaining skills. They simply revert back to a baby. Sometimes people like this hold on for years, and sometimes they go very quickly. Every case is unique unto itself."

Still believing that Mame was insane, the doctor made a suggestion.

"My advice is that you find a home that takes mental cases. She'll need someone to watch her around the clock."

Katherine listened to what the stupid doctor had to say. He didn't know what he was talking about. Her Grandma Mame was the smartest person she'd ever known. She wasn't a mental case.

"No. When it's time, I'll be taking Grandma Mame home."

She left the doctor standing in the hall with her uncles and slipped into her grandmother's room, crawled into bed, and curled up with her grandma. There in a tight ball, on the stiff white sheets of Mame's hospital bed, Katherine vowed never to put her Grandma Mame in a crazy house.

Her grandma was all she had. Katherine could not lose her, not yet. She wouldn't let her go, she'd hold onto her just as long as she could.

Grandma Mame had taken her in as a baby, and now Katherine would try to take care of her at home and continue going to school. Katherine had three more months until graduation. All she could do was try and handle it all.

The first few days back home in her own environment, Mame seemed like her old self. Katherine went on to school with a half-hearted promise from Uncle Ben to look after her. Mame's brothers and sisters-in-law also promised to look in on her from time to time each day.

With so much going on, Katherine had let her guard down concerning Uncle Ben. She was shocked back into reality late one night when she woke up cold. Reaching for her covers, she found them thrown off the bed. Standing over her was Uncle Ben. In the dim light, he appeared to be shirtless.

When he spoke, his breath reeked of alcohol. "The time has come. You've been asking for this."

Katherine began to tremble, and fear tied a hard knot in her throat as she spoke hoarsely. "Get out of here, or I'll scream."

"And who's going to hear you—that crazy old woman in the other room? You don't want your granny to know you've been teasing me all these years, do you?"

"Teasing? I've never teased you or anyone else. Now get out."

"Shut up, you little tramp. I'll bet you've had a dozen high school fellows. Now be good to Uncle Ben and he'll be good to you."

Lurching forward, he grabbed for Katherine. She had just enough time to reach under her pillow and roll to the far side of the bed.

"Touch me again, and I swear . . . I'll kill you."

"Oh, I'm shook up, but not from fear, little lady—from need. I will have you tonight."

As he lunged on top of her, Ben felt a sharp pain tear through his side.

"What the—?" He reached for his back, feeling the wet stickiness of blood as another searing pain shot up through his side.

"You'd better get off me, or the next jab will be through your heart!" Katherine's voice shook, but she meant every word.

Rolling off the bed with a groan, Ben hit the floor. There he lay until he could get to his knees. Then he stood up, weaving and unsteady.

"You little harlot. I'd kill you right now if I weren't bleeding to death. When I have you—and I *will* have you—I won't be easy on you. I'll make you wish you'd never been squirted out."

Then the half-naked drunk stumbled out and down the hall.

When she was sure he was around the corner, Katherine jumped up on shaky legs, locked her door, and switched on the lamp. She had been locking doors and hiding knives under her pillow since the first time she woke and found Ben standing over her. She must have been sleeping awfully hard not to hear him come into her room.

She was tired from all her new worries and responsibilities. She'd left her door cracked so she would hear Grandma Mame if she got up. Now she knew she couldn't take that risk again. She hoped she'd be able to hear her grandma through their adjoining bedroom wall. Though Katherine prayed that Grandma Mame had not heard anything through that wall tonight.

She had only nicked Ben's back, but his blood had splattered her sheets and the floor. She removed her soiled gown, wiped the floor stains with it, and threw the garment in the trashcan. She would never wear it again, tainted as it was by Uncle Ben's blood . . . and touch. She knew there would be stains on the hallway floor, but that could wait to be cleaned after Ben was gone. She hoped no one would visit and see the blood before she could get it up in the morning.

Katherine donned a fresh gown, stripped her sheets, and put clean ones on her bed. Breathing hard, she sat down on the edge of the bed. She couldn't even cry. What was she going to do?

Ben would never leave her alone. She could not run away—she had no money and no place to go—nor could she leave Grandma Mame with no one here to look out for her. Too upset to sleep, Katherine sat and worried until dawn.

Uncle Ben must truly be one of the devil's angels that God had cast out of heaven, Katherine thought.

CHAPTER THIRTY-SIX

And many of them said, He hath a devil, and is mad; why hear ye him?

~ John 10:20

STRANGELY, THE NEXT COUPLE OF months went rather smoothly. Uncle Ben had vanished. It wasn't unusual for him to stay gone for a few weeks at a time, but months were unusual. Katherine assumed he was off nursing his wound and his pride. Her great uncles quizzed her about his whereabouts, but Katherine assured them that she had no idea where he was. She knew better than to wish he was gone for good. Uncle Ben was like a mangy old dog, showing up every now and then to beg for a bone.

Grandma Mame barely noticed Ben's absence. Her blackouts and crazy talk continued daily now. One afternoon she said, "Clint will be here to get me any minute, and we'll go to the waterfall where we first made love."

Another time, she woke up screaming, "No! Stop! Please leave me alone!"

Then another time, Mame looked straight at Katherine and asked, "Do you know which one is your daddy? Your poor mother didn't, and it tormented her till her dying day. I didn't hate her for what she did.

I understood Emily. I know how sometimes people do things they shouldn't and then live to regret it."

"Grandma Mame, what are you talking about? Walt Paddington was your son and my father."

"Theodore Paddington killed my papa, you know. Blew him up in a mine. I hate him."

Then, as if by magic, she'd snap back to normal, not remembering or discussing any of the things she had revealed.

It was May 1970; Katherine was more excited about her upcoming graduation plans than worried about Ben showing up. What she'd do after she graduated, God only knew. Grandma Mame was losing her grip on reality more every day. Katherine knew she had to have help.

On Friday, Katherine came home to find Uncle Ben sitting on the living room sofa. Her heart sank. What might he have in store for her if he was home long and had his way?

"My sweet Katie Girl. You've grown much lovelier since I last saw you. How are you? Did you miss me?"

Katherine veered in a big circle around him to get through the room. She always checked on Grandma Mame first thing after school.

"Where you running off to? Ain't you even going to ask me if I recovered from your little knife accident?"

Katherine tensed and stopped in the hall. "Frankly," she said through gritted teeth, "I'm sorry I didn't kill you. If you force me to use it again, I promise you, I will go for your jugular."

In a flash, Ben jumped up and knocked over the table lamp. He leaped upon Katherine, grabbing her hair and jerking her off balance. Schoolbooks flew into the air. Ben spun her around and backhanded her hard across the mouth, sending her reeling onto the floor.

"I didn't know you liked it rough, but from now on, I can arrange that." Just as he reached down to slap her again, someone knocked at the front door.

"Who is that?" he said, seething.

A few weeks ago, Katherine's great uncles had arranged for someone from the county social service department to check on Mame while Katherine was at school. Ironically, they were a little late today.

"It's Stan from Social Services!" The knocking got louder. "Is everything all right in there? Can I come in?"

Ben was defeated for the moment. "Wipe that whiney face of yours and let him in. And keep your mouth shut."

Katherine picked herself up off the floor, barely able to stand for shaking. The attack had knocked her hair barrette off, so hair fell tousled over one eye. She adjusted her clothes and wiped tears off her cheeks. Rising as fast as she could gather herself, she ran to the front door and opened it quickly.

Stan could tell right away that something was very wrong. Katherine had never looked disheveled. Not once in the past month since he'd started meeting with her about her grandmother had she been unnerved. He also noticed her tear-streaked face and a bright red handprint on the left side of her cheek. A slight trace of blood was oozing from the corner of her mouth.

"Katherine, what's wrong? Is Mrs. Paddington okay?"

"No," Katherine said, confused. "I mean, she's okay, I guess. I just got home."

"Why is your lip bleeding?" Stan asked, just as a man came out of the kitchen. Stan grew edgy, trying to gauge the situation.

"Oh, the clumsy girl tripped over a kitchen chair and smacked the floor with her face," said Ben with a casual wave of his hand.

Stan frowned, looked at Katherine, then squinted past Ben and saw her books scattered across the floor.

"I'm Ben, Katie Girl's uncle. Who are you?"

"Stan Matthews." Stan reached out to shake Ben's hand. "I'm a social worker with the county. I work with homebound, terminal patients."

"Mama ain't terminal. She's too mean to die. She's just a little crazy." Ben ignored Stan's outstretched hand.

"Shut up," Katherine said. "You don't know what you're talking about. Grandma doesn't have a mean bone in her body."

"Yeah, right. One of these days, I might just fill you in on your granny's goodness." Ben nodded to Stan. "Good luck on your glory work." He left the house, slamming the back door.

Katherine took a deep breath, slumped onto the couch, and touched her sore lip.

"Are you sure you're all right?" Stan asked.

"Yes, I'm fine, for now."

"What do you mean, for now?"

Katherine didn't answer him. Stan decided he needed to mind his own business, but he knew something was not right here. Stan liked his job, except for some of the situations he saw happening in families.

"I'm going to check on Mrs. Paddington. I'm running a little behind today. I've got two more patients to see before I go home."

When Stan finished visiting with Mame, he came back into the living room to talk to Katherine. "You must try to get her to eat more. She's losing weight much too rapidly."

"I know. I can tell, but she just forgets when I'm not here during the day to remind her. I'll try to get Phoebe and Olivia, my great-aunts, to stop by more often. Everybody is so busy with their own families, I just hate for us to be such a burden."

"What about your uncle? Will he be staying long?" Stan hoped his questions would open the door for Katherine to talk about what just happened.

"Who knows? He comes and goes as he pleases." Katherine looked away. "He lives here, but he's out of town a lot. I can't depend on him."

Stan closed his medical bag. "Don't worry. I'll try to think of something. I'll come a little late tomorrow too, so I'll see you after school."

He wasn't a fool. He'd read Katherine's situation clearly: pretty young girl, totally unprotected from a mean and rough uncle. God only knew what she'd already been through and what lay ahead for her. Stan knew he'd be losing sleep worrying about Katherine. And, his concern was not totally professional.

The sun shone brightly on that late spring day, but there was a dark cloud hanging over the house where Katherine Paddington would lay her head that night.

Katherine went to bed before Ben returned home. Locking the door behind her, she finally fell asleep. The next morning before she was out of bed, she heard someone knock on the front door. Rubbing her eyes and putting on her worn robe, she unlocked her bedroom door. By the time she padded to the front door, Ben was already opening it.

"Good morning, I'm Nancy," said a cheerful voice.

Nancy Royall had been taking care of the sick and elderly for nigh on thirty years. She'd tended to her own granny and then both her mama and daddy before their passing. She was a short, stout woman who clearly knew her way around a situation. Her fondness for order was emphasized by her habit of squeezing and moving her hair pins to maintain the tight, high bun she wore at the top of her head.

"Stan Matthews arranged through the county for me to come every day and watch after Mrs. Paddington. Are you her son?" Nancy asked, patting her hair bun.

"Well, yeah, I am," said Ben, appearing flustered, "but we don't need anybody here. I can handle things just fine."

"No, you can't," Katherine said. "Grandma has gotten worse these past few weeks. She needs constant help, and you're never here anyway. Please come in, Nancy."

Nancy hesitated before stepping inside. She never knew what she was getting herself into, but whatever was going on, she felt sure she could handle it.

"Have you even seen her since you got home?" Katherine asked Ben.

"No, the old lady ain't been out of her room."

"And she won't be until I go in and help her get up and dressed," Katherine said.

She turned to Nancy, offering her hand to shake.

"I'm sorry. I'm Katherine, Mrs. Paddington's granddaughter. We are very grateful to have you. You're a godsend. I'm trying to finish high school, and now maybe I can!" Katherine was very excited and oblivious to her appearance. She had not looked in the mirror or dressed yet this morning. "Come with me. I'll introduce you to Grandma and show you where everything is."

"I'll be right back," Nancy said. "I've got some paperwork I need to leave with you. It tells you the times I'll be here. I'll take care of all your granny's needs, and I've been known to cook some fine suppers in my day." Nancy turned and strolled out to her ancient Chevy.

With the woman out of earshot, Ben grabbed Katherine's arm, "I hope you don't think that locked door's going to keep me out." Obviously, he had tried to come into her room last night.

Katherine jerked her arm free and just as quietly answered him, "Come on in and you'll get the same thing you got last time, just deeper and better aimed."

Nancy soon returned with the paperwork. "Read over it first chance you get," she told Katherine. "We should all be able to work together just fine." Nancy glanced pointedly toward Ben. Without one word of thanks, he walked past her and out on the porch.

Katherine led her down the hall and opened Mame's bedroom door. They heard her mumbling.

"Look at these marks all over me. I'm so dirty. How could I have let him touch me? I've got to wash him off me." Mame was standing in front of her mirror, completely naked and scrubbing herself with a dry washcloth. Over and over, she kept repeating herself.

"I've got to wash him off. I've got to get him off me. No one can ever know."

"Grandma, what are you doing? Come over here and sit on the bed. Let's get your clothes on. I want you to meet Nancy. She's going to help me take care of you."

Mame turned, her eyes narrowed. "He had the ugliest, most awful scar on his face." She reached up and touched her own face. "I've got ugly scars like that too, but you can't see mine. They're on the inside."

"Who's got a scar, Grandma?" Katherine said, shaking her head and looking at Nancy.

"Ben's daddy." Then Mame fell silent. Nancy and Katherine soon got her dressed and into the kitchen for breakfast.

"Poor child, come on now. Open up and eat a little more for old Miss Nancy. I've come to fatten you! Now open up."

It was a miracle; Mame opened her mouth and took the bite of scrambled eggs Nancy offered. Katherine felt tears run down her face as she watched. Maybe, just maybe, Nancy would be able to get through to her grandmother. Hope filled Katherine that Grandma would get better. She didn't see how she could get any worse.

Meanwhile, Ben had vanished again, which was a shame this time, because Katherine wanted to ask him how his father got an awful scar on his face. She had never heard a word about Grandpa Clint being scarred. She really wouldn't know though, because she had never met her grandfather. Katherine always assumed he was dead.

CHAPTER THIRTY-SEVEN

A prudent man foreseeth the evil, and hideth himself...

~ Proverbs 27:12

HE HEARD THE SOUND OF the waterfall long before he reached it. It had been over twenty years since he was last here. That day before he left Charleston for good, he had come here to think, as he always had.

His life with Mame Blackwell had been a lie.

How did it happen? How could I have been so deceived? I loved those boys like they were mine. How could Mame have done something so horrible? Bedding Jack Marsh?

Clint Paddington stood looking at the falls; he could not help but remember that day right here when it all began. She was so beautiful as she came up out of the water, drops glistening on her body.

Her loveliness was a deceiver.

Clint didn't love her at first, but not long after they married, he would have fought the devil himself to keep her. His love had grown strong through the years. That was one reason that he had left without a word. No matter what she had done, he had finally admitted to himself that he still loved her.

He'd come back because he still bore the Paddington family guilt. His father never got over being a part of Henry Blackwell's death in

Beckley's coal mine. What if his father had never risked opening the mine, knowing the explosive gases could still be churning inside? The old questions haunted Clint like the distant thunder he heard rumbling on that hot summer day.

The waterfall had changed as much as he had. His once-secluded spot was now a public park with people and picnic tables all around.

Why had he come back to Charleston after all this time?

The truth was he wanted to see Mame one more time before the sickness growing inside him smothered out his life. Despite the slow growing tumor, at sixty-eight he appeared to be the picture of health. Really there was little change in his looks, but his dark hair was now speckled with gray, and worry lines etched the corners of his eyes.

Roaming all over the country and drinking hard those first few years after he left Charleston had taken a toll on his body, but he'd got himself straightened out. He'd stopped running when he found work in a cloth factory in Elkin, North Carolina. Gradually he saved enough to buy a little farm. He led a simple life and made friends, but he never let another woman into his life. By law, he was still married to Mame, but in his heart, he had divorced her many years ago. However, divorce did not mean you stopped loving someone.

Clint left the falls and drove to the white house that had once been his family's home. He knew she had sold it. He'd stayed in touch with their old housekeeper, Mrs. Gentry, until she died a few years before. His whereabouts had been safe with her, thanks to her loyalty to the Paddingtons.

He wanted to see the house again. It really no longer bothered him that Mame sold it. It had been his fault anyway. Losing Ben had just about driven him insane. Drinking, gambling, and watching

Mame grow heavy with another man's child was unbearable. And then came the fateful day in the years after the baby's death when a letter arrived from Jack Marsh. It was long and detailed in a rough scrawl, with no return address.

The letter began:

Paddington,

I herd yur old lady got purdy ruffed up. Is a dern shame she sirvived. Sure werent what I meant to happen. I throwed her in that gulley for dead. The liar wench. She mite be alive but she shore aint goin to git happy. Let me tell you bout the night she came to the tavern. Gess she had a herd what old Jack had goin and wanted a piece of me. Never did make much sinse of it all till I saw her boy in the barn at his grandmaw's dyin. All it took was a little countin back to know he was my young-un. He looks jes like me.

Page after page, Marsh gave Clint unsavory descriptions of his and Mame's "times together." He didn't know how much Marsh made up, but he knew the basics were true. Mame had willingly given herself to that lowlife scum of the earth and then tricked Clint into marrying her.

In Paddy's old study, Clint had read the letter over and over, running his fingers through his hair, pacing the floor, and reading it again. He cursed. He cried.

Clint doubted that Marsh ever knew Mame birthed twins, since he didn't mention Walt in the letter. After all those childless years, Mame was pregnant twice by Jack Marsh, one of the sorriest, meanest men in all West Virginia and maybe the entire South.

Mame had known all along that Marsh kidnapped Ben. How could she be so cruel to let him go on searching until it broke him down? How could she let him lose everything dear to him—his wife, his family, his home, and his livelihood?

Oh, it wasn't entirely her fault. He had become his own version of the wandering Marsh, just barely a notch above him, with the scars and losses to match. But Marsh had never had anything to lose, unlike Clint.

How could I have been so stupid? How could a man be so in love that he could not see the truth right before him?

Every question mark in their marriage fell into place.

Clint thought and thought, until the only solution seemed to be to leave behind the life he knew. The only choice, surely, was to get away. He left without a word, for there were no words that would undo the tragedy that his life had become. It would just be his destiny to suffer until he died. He put behind him the Paddington legacy in Charleston, along with any hope of growing old with the beautiful girl from Beckley.

It was only by the grace of God that somebody hadn't killed him those first few years. Clint fought anybody who looked at him wrong and bedded any girl who'd lie with him. Yes, he became a sorry excuse for a human, just like Marsh.

If it hadn't been for Mrs. Gentry, he'd have been dead a long time ago. She stayed on him every time he got in touch with her. She told him that he wasn't the first man to be scorned by a woman, and he wouldn't be the last. He didn't know why he kept visiting Mrs. Gentry, for he knew she'd keep telling him Mame's sad stories. He had almost gone to Beckley when he heard about Walt's upcoming wedding. That boy still felt like his son. Either way, it seemed tragedy followed them all. Walt eventually disappeared the same way Clint had.

Clint missed Mrs. Gentry after she passed. He remembered that last time he'd sat at her table. She reached out and took his hands in hers, and she bowed her head and prayed with him. Lifting him up and asking God to guide his steps and give him the grace to forgive. That day Clint gave his whole heart to the Lord, and ever since God had been leading him home to Mame.

For the past two years, he'd had no information about Mame. He didn't know what he'd find. She might not even talk to him. But he knew this was his last chance to see her, to be able to look at Mame's beautiful face, one more chance to make things right. Over twenty years had passed since he'd seen her.

Tomorrow, he'd drive to Beckley. Tomorrow, he'd see her again. It was time the shadows from the past were brought to light.

CHAPTER THIRTY-EIGHT

Therefore whatsoever ye have spoken in darkness shall be heard in
the light; and that which ye have spoken in the ear in closets shall be
proclaimed upon the housetops.

~ Luke 12:3

"STAN, DON'T YOU THINK GRANDMA Mame is doing much better these last couple of weeks? Nancy has been so wonderful. And that new medicine is agreeing with her more than anything we've tried."

"Yes, Katherine, I believe your grandmother is doing much better. Her weight has stabilized. You said she's been her old self more lately too. Didn't you tell me she baked you a fresh apple cake today? I believe I can still smell it."

Katherine grinned. "Oh, you want me to offer you some, don't you?"

Stan returned her smile. "Don't mind if I do."

Stan and Katherine had become friends since the afternoon he'd found her with a bleeding lip and her lazy, foul-mouthed uncle's hand print on her cheek. Stan sensed the danger she was in even though she had never said a word to him about her problems with Uncle Ben. Stan's job didn't require it, but he began to drop by on Saturdays and Sundays to check on Katherine.

Ben hated these constant intrusions but didn't know any good way to stop them. After all, someone had to take care of the old woman. He sure wasn't going to. Too bad the county didn't send someone a little better looking than that Nancy woman though. She must weigh three hundred pounds.

And that Stan dude must be half girl. Whoever heard of a man nurse, or social worker, whatever that was?

Stan Matthews had just celebrated his twenty-ninth birthday. He could thank Vietnam for his nursing degree. He'd had a choice of medicine or communications when he was drafted. He chose medicine because it seemed more interesting and he'd always liked taking care of people. There were many times he thought he'd made a big mistake, especially when soldiers were brought in to the field hospital with arms and legs blown off, or their intestines held inside by a rag wrapped around their torso. Thankfully one year of active duty was all he had to pull of that useless war, a war that was still going on.

When Stan was five, his daddy had died. Several years later, his mother remarried and had two daughters, Annie and Rebecca, only a year apart in age. His stepfather, who Stan had never liked, ran off with another woman when the girls were very young. So Stan was not only a brother. He was a father figure as well. When his mother died, the army allowed Stan to return to Beckley to help raise his two half-sisters.

He was very glad the military had schooled him in a profession that paid good money. His nursing background had helped him land the head social worker job for the county. Raising two teenage sisters was not cheap. Now they were both away at college, but they came home almost every weekend. He was content with his lot in life—or so he thought until he met Katherine Paddington.

Stan first thought his growing attachment to Katherine was because she reminded him of his sisters. Time proved that theory wrong. He knew it was much more than infatuation.

He had not felt an attraction for a woman since he'd gotten that Dear John letter from Alice when he was in Vietnam. She just couldn't wait for him, she'd said. They had been engaged when he was drafted. She wanted him to marry her before he left for active duty, but somehow that just didn't seem right. Maybe deep down he knew Alice was not the right one for him. She was the wrong one, because by the time he got home, she was already married to someone else.

Katherine was different from anyone Stan had ever met. She had never known either of her parents. Raised by her grandmother on a very moderate income, she had done without much. Katherine said that her great uncles always tried to give them money and help fix up the house, but her grandmother always refused, saying they had all they needed, that she didn't deserve luxuries. Katherine never understood what Grandma Mame meant but did not question her.

Mame Blackwell Paddington was always unapproachable, but she took care of Katherine's needs and was never mean to her, so Katherine accepted their lives. She loved her grandmother. All was fine until Uncle Ben came home. Katherine said that then things became complicated, but that's all she would say.

To Stan, Katherine's commitment to her ailing grandmother went way beyond the call of family duty. He couldn't let her quit school to be the caretaker. She had only a month left until graduation. Then she needed to go to college in the fall. She was a very intelligent girl who made perfect grades. He couldn't understand how Mrs. Paddington's brothers weren't more involved in the care-taking, but Katherine didn't seem to expect anything from anyone. She and Grandma Mame were just used to taking care of themselves.

Katherine never suspected, but Stan was paying part of Nancy's wages out of his own pocket. The county would only pay for some-one every other day. He knew Katherine would not have accepted this arrangement. She was not the kind to take charity, so Nancy was sworn to secrecy.

Stan's affection for Katherine increased daily. Her willingness to sacrifice and her commitment to her grandmother matured her way beyond her eighteen years. The eleven years span in their ages didn't seem to be such a big gap at all.

While eating Grandma Mame's fresh apple cake in the kitchen to-gether, Katherine kept glancing at Stan. She didn't know what it was about him, but something drew her to him. He was so kind, always doing things for her grandmother. One day, she found him sitting beside Grandma Mame on the bed, reading her a story from a health magazine about a woman who was sick like she was. The story told of the woman's courage and how she fought every day to keep her sanity.

"Now, Miss Mame, you can be like the woman in this story. I know you are just as brave as she is. You have to try very hard to focus on each day. Live right now and don't let yourself slip into the past. We'll make you a to-do list each night for things you have to do the next day. Then we'll put it beside your bed, and you can read it first thing when you get up. Start out with even the simplest thing. Number one: get out of bed. Number two: go to the bathroom. Number three: get dressed, and so on. Then when you get confused during the day, just go to your list and see what is next. That will give you a starting point, even if you lose your place and have to start at the beginning again."

Stan did not know if he was getting through to Miss Mame or not, but he sure hoped so. She was not all that old yet, but her troubled years of heartache had spun webs on her face. She was very thin, and the long braid that ran down her back showed no sign of the yellow color it once was. Every once in a while Stan saw a little sparkle in her eye, and on the rare occasion when he would catch her smiling, Stan could see that she was once quite lovely.

Katherine listened as Stan softly encouraged her grandmother, trying to help her maintain some form of independence. He was the gentlest person Katherine had ever known, not to mention awfully handsome.

He still had his military physique. Not an ounce of fat was on him. He had a boyish charm about him. He didn't look at all to be twenty-nine. Stan had dark brown hair with a sun-bleached cowlick on the left side of his forehead. Standing not more than five-ten or eleven, he wasn't much taller than Katherine. When he smiled, he had a couple of teeth that weren't exactly straight, but this seemed to fit him. His dark, sincere eyes were almost as black as the coal-laden ground. She bet he had dozens of girlfriends.

Katherine had liked a couple of boys during high school, but her Uncle Ben soon put a stop to each friendship. Katherine remembered one night when a boy named Lance had come to pick her up. When she got into the living room, Uncle Ben was talking to him. His tone seemed charged with importance. She could not hear what was said, but Lance made a quick excuse as to why he could not take her out after all.

"What did you say to him?" she asked Ben, heartbroken.

"Oh, nothing much. Just a few family secrets. I wouldn't feel right not telling them poor, innocent boys about you stabbing your last lover."

"You didn't! Surely you are not that cruel."

"Oh, no. I'm not cruel at all. I'm just not going to let some prissy little brat get in your britches before I do."

Katherine knew there was no use arguing with Ben. She just went to her room and locked the door. Neither Lance nor any other boys from school ever called her again. One day, she overheard some girls in the cafeteria line saying that she was just as crazy as her grandma.

Katherine never hung her head or shied away from any of the rumors. In her short life, Katherine had survived much and believed that someday things would change and get better. At least she had kept Ben from molesting her, and that in itself was a major accomplishment.

As Katherine pondered all this, Stan walked out of Mame's room and found her sitting on the hall floor. She looked up and smiled. "Thank you so much for being so kind to her."

Stan blushed slightly. "It's not hard to be nice to someone as sweet as Miss Mame. I really think that with some organization and consistency in her life, she will be able to function for several years to come. But Katherine, there may come a day when she'll have to be moved to a home. Her condition may stabilize, but she will never be cured. Eventually, she will constantly have to have everything done for her."

Katherine understood. She had read a library book on this new disease called Alzheimer's, but hearing someone say it made it very real. Hot tears flooded her eyes at the prospect of not being with her grandma. Despite Mame's clouded condition, Katherine still talked to her about school and her dreams for a future. Truly, Grandma Mame was her best friend.

"Well, the day for Grandma to leave hasn't come yet," said Katherine. "Graduation is next week, and then I'll be home with her every day. Maybe if I work with her like you do, helping her make those lists, she'll be okay for a long time."

"It couldn't hurt, but you've got to do what's best for Miss Mame. Sometimes a special care home is the only answer. She hasn't wandered off in a while, has she?" Reaching for Katherine's hand, Stan pulled her to her feet. The opportunities to touch Katherine were few, but he relished each one.

"No, not since Nancy's been here with her. She really has been great. I'm so glad you were able to arrange for her to help. Her being here will make it possible for me to find a job. We could really use the income. Before Grandma got so sick, she sold part of her land back to her brothers and had my name put on her bank accounts. There's still a fair amount left for me to pay the bills, but it won't last forever. I need to work."

They walked into the living room and sat. "You do need to get out of the house. You are much too young and pretty to hole up here in this place like a hermit."

Katherine hardly knew what to say, so she blushed. This was the first time Stan had said anything about her personally. "I do get out," she protested. "I go to school and to church almost every Sunday."

"What about college this fall? Have you been accepted at any schools?"

"College," she repeated. "Are you trying to be funny? I haven't even applied. How would I afford college ... even if I could leave Grandma?"

Stan tilted his head with a frown. "Your great uncles seem pretty well off. Wouldn't they help you?"

"I'm sure they would, but Grandma would never hear of it." Katherine's gaze fell to her hands lying clasped in her lap. "She's adamant about us making our own way. She always said that we were just lucky her mother Mary had the foresight to leave her this house and farm. It was almost like she knew Grandma Mame would be coming back here."

"I don't think your grandma will even realize her brothers are helping you. That is, if you don't tell her. You know the old saying: what you don't know won't hurt you."

"I'm sorry, young man, but what you don't know *can* hurt you." Katherine and Stan had not heard Mame walk into the living room and turned, startled, toward her. "A lie is a lie, and lying can never do anything but mar you and cause you pain." After Mame said this, she went to the kitchen and very normally fixed herself a cup of coffee.

"Well, I guess she told me, didn't she?" Stan said.

Katherine laughed. "That sounds just like my old grandmother. And listen, she's puttering in the kitchen."

Stan laughed and shook his head. "Something snapped her back to reality for now, so go enjoy her. I'll see you tomorrow."

Stan rose to leave. "If I get Nancy to stay with Miss Mame one night, may I take you to the movies, or out to eat?"

Katherine was so taken by surprise that she didn't know how to answer.

"What do you say?" Stan asked, smiling. "Don't be afraid to hurt my feelings. If you're ashamed to be seen with an old man like me, just say so."

"No, no, that's not it. It's just—well—I don't get asked out. I'm a little surprised."

"Don't get asked out? Yeah, I'll bet. You just stay too busy with your grandmother. Well, will you go?"

Twirling her hair, which she always did when she was nervous, Katherine did look the schoolgirl part. Stan almost regretted asking her, for fear of a letdown. Maybe she really did think he was too old.

Delighted, Katherine finally replied. "Yes."

A wide grin stretched across Stan's face, and he quickly asked, "Does it matter which night?"

"No, I don't guess so—any time Nancy can stay with Grandma will be fine."

"All right then. I'll get back to you soon."

Stan left then, waving happily to Katherine as he got into his blue Ford. She watched it until the red brake lights were nothing but tiny spots before he turned the corner toward downtown Beckley. Katherine felt the happiest she'd ever felt in her life. Even Uncle Ben, when he popped into her head, could not dampen her spirits. Yes, things would get better. They already had.

An hour later, the phone rang. It was Stan. "I talked to Nancy. She said Monday would be good for her. Is that okay?"

"Yes," said Katherine. "That's fine."

"Great! I'll pick you up at six-thirty. I'll see you tomorrow too," he said. "It's okay if you change your mind and don't want to be seen with an old geezer like me. Just let me know." He hung up before she had time to answer and chuckled.

Katherine was not laughing. Her knees were so weak they were starting to quiver. Why was she so nervous? It was just like she was living in a movie. She was comfortable with Stan, so why was she being so silly? She felt giddy with excitement.

In the kitchen, Katherine's light mood was dampened when she saw Grandma Mame. There she sat at the kitchen table, her cup of coffee untouched, staring into space. Would she be able to hear Katherine? She needed to talk to her grandmother.

"Grandma, do you like Stan?"

Of course Mame did not answer, but she did turn and look at Katherine.

"I don't know what it is about him, but he makes me feel funny inside . . . kind of fluttery and weak in the knees. Does that mean I love him? He asked me out. We're going to the movies. Do you know how long it's been since I've been anywhere?"

Anticipation shone all over Katherine's face as she spun around in the kitchen, unable to sit still. She rattled on and on about what she would wear and how should she fix her hair.

"Grandma, do you think I should cut my hair? It's always been this long, tangled mess of curls. Uncle Ben has told me it's just like my mother's. Is that true? Am I like her?"

Katherine caught her reflection in the kitchen window. Night was coming on, and she had to start cooking supper.

"Grandma, are leftovers okay with you?"

Mame looked straight at Katherine. "Never deceive him, Katherine. Deceit will drive him away, and like my Clint, he'll be gone."

Katherine watched in surprise as big tears rolled down Grandma Mame's face. She ran and put her arms around her. It felt strange consoling her grandmother over a grandfather she had never known. The look in Grandma's eyes was enough to rip out Katherine's heart. She wondered if Grandpa Clint had loved Grandma as much as she loved him.

"Don't worry, Grandma. I won't deceive him. Why would I?"

"I don't know why we do the things we do, but don't fool yourself. Evil runs through your veins, and you'll have to fight it. Don't ever give into it like I did. If you do, you'll have the shadows following you the rest of your life." Mame got up and retreated to her room.

Grandma seemed normal, but she must be delusional again. She said so many strange things. Maybe she dreams things and then thinks they are real?

For several minutes, Katherine sat and puzzled over her grandmother, and then she rose to cook. Washing her hands at the sink and looking out the window, she saw Uncle Ben walking toward the house. Oh, she understood evil all right, and here it comes right now.

He won't like my going out with Stan. Should I cancel? No. I won't let Ben continue to ruin my life.

Katherine dried her hands and braced herself for another argument, or better yet, a clever way around one.

I won't tell him, and maybe he'll be away from the house on Monday when Stan picks me up.

CHAPTER THIRTY-NINE

But Abraham said, Son remember that thou in thy lifetime receivedst thy good things, and likewise Lazarus evil things: but now he is comforted, and thou art tormented.

~ Luke 16:25

MAME WALKED STRAIGHT TO HER dresser drawer and opened it to pull out a box. How long had it been since she had looked at her belongings? Lovingly, she opened the lid and touched the picture that lay on top.

"Clint," she said as her fingers lightly felt the yellowed image of her long-gone husband. She stood like that for many minutes and then reached beneath Clint's picture to one of the two young boys. One fair. One dark.

"Lord, please forgive me. Please let the evil end. How long will I be tormented? They were such sweet boys, especially Walt. Just like Clint, he was, the spitting image. Maybe a miracle happened: Maybe Clint was Walt and Ben's father."

No, she knew that was not possible, not after Daniel came, but why not believe it for a while? "What could it hurt?" she said aloud.

Mame knew most of the time her mind was spinning out of control. Sometimes she tried to stop it. Sometimes she just let it go. She knew she had said things about the past, but nobody knew what she was talking about.

I must stay in control. I must protect Ben. I know how mean he is, but that's my fault for letting Jack Marsh raise him all those years. I owe Ben.

Closing the box lid, Mame put it back into the drawer. Then she pleasantly slipped back to a sweeter time when life was better.

"Oh. Clint, you are so wonderful. You make me feel so good." Mame closed her eyes and remembered.

Clint remembered too. Every day an image formed in his mind too beautiful to comprehend . . . the way she moved, laughed, and smiled. That smile melted his heart and warmed him to the core of his very soul. That was long ago, when times were good, before the attack, before the baby, and before he knew about Jack Marsh.

Just like every time before, Clint pushed the bad memories away and tried to remember the sweet times. They had shared many wonderful moments. Mame Blackwell was the most spirited woman in the world. In the heat of their passion, she held nothing back from him. How would it be to see her again?

Clint had put off the trip to Beckley for three days. He wanted to go, but fear held him back. Would the anger he thought he had buried resurface? Would they even recognize each other? Would they even care any more?

Tomorrow, I'll go tomorrow. I can't put off any longer what I know I must do.

CHAPTER FORTY

A merry heart doeth good like a medicine: but a broken spirit drieth
the bones.

~ Proverbs 17:22

STAN LEFT THE BLACKWELL HOME Monday afternoon after reminding Katherine that he'd be back to pick her up at six-thirty. Nancy was to stay, prepare Miss Mame's supper, and then help her get ready for bed.

It was a blessing that Ben had left Saturday night and had not returned. He would probably be gone a week or more, as usual.

Right on time, Katherine heard the knock. Looking at herself one last time in the mirror, she decided she didn't look half-bad. She had left her hair out of the usual ponytail. Her mane had the softness that only naturally curly hair has. People sometimes commented that she was lucky to have the curls, but to Katherine it seemed a mess most of the time.

Stan had said to dress casually, that they would grab a bite to eat and then catch a movie.

Picking out her least worn-out pair of jeans, Katherine pulled them over her trim hips. She buttoned up a sweater that molded to her young figure. Katherine was old enough to know men stared at her sometimes and why they stared. But her modesty never encouraged them any further. Anyway, if a suitor ever were to come around, Uncle Ben would scare them off. What was the use in trying to look attractive? But tonight she wanted everything to be just right. With one last glance, she turned to go answer the door.

Nancy had already let in Stan. This was the first time Katherine had seen him in casual clothes. His jeans fit snugly and showed his slender physique. Western boots and a brown plaid shirt finished off his clothing selection.

When Katherine found her tongue, she said, "I didn't know you were a cowboy."

"There's a whole lot you don't know about me. You look great, by the way. Ready to go?"

"Yes, just let me tell Grandma good-bye."

Stan was the perfect gentleman. As they left, he opened the house door for Katherine and then the door to his '63 Ford Galaxy.

"I'm going to get myself a new car one of these days, if I ever get those sisters of mine through college."

Katherine saw nothing wrong with his car. At least he had one. Grandma hadn't owned one that would run in several years. If Katherine needed to go somewhere not within walking distance, she'd borrow one of her great-uncle's vehicles. Ben kept an almost new car all the time, but she would not dare borrow anything of his. She didn't know where he got his money. When she had asked, he said he had a business out of town that was doing well, but the rest was none of her business.

Stan drove to the only fast-food place in town. They ordered burgers and chocolate shakes and ate sitting outside at a picnic table. This

SARAH MARTIN BYRD 309

was not fancy, but it didn't matter to Katherine; in fact, it couldn't have been any better. She was having a ball.

At the Lyric Theatre on Main Street, they saw *Love Story*. Katherine was touched and cried during several parts. That's when Stan reached over and put his arm around her and pulled her close. When the movie ended, they remained in their seats while the other patrons filed out. After the last person exited, Stan turned to Katherine and gently kissed her on the lips.

Then they stood to leave. Neither of them spoke on the way home. Having parked in front of the Blackwell house, Stan got out and went around to open Katherine's door. Nancy had the front porch light on for them, but Stan clasped Katherine's hand and guided her around to the back door.

"Katherine, I had a wonderful time tonight. I hope we can do it again soon."

Katherine's lips still tingled from his earlier touch. She was hoping very much that he would kiss her again.

"Me too, Stan. Thank you for a great evening."

Stan stepped closer to her and took her in his arms. When his lips touched hers, they were as gentle as before. Pulling away, he turned to go. Then he hesitated, pulled Katherine back to him, and put his lips to hers a third time. He quickly pulled away.

"I've got to go." Stan smiled at her and touched her cheek with his hand. "Sweet dreams, Katherine. I'll see you tomorrow."

It took Katherine a few minutes to catch her breath. She was on fire, not just her lips, but also her entire body. She had never felt like this in her whole life. She waited until she heard Stan's car start, then she crept in the moonlight back to the front porch. Inside, all was well. Nancy was watching the late news on TV, and Grandma was sound asleep.

"Thank you so very much, Nancy, for staying with Grandma tonight."

"You're welcome. I don't have to ask if you had a good time. I can see it on your face." Nancy laughed and gathered her purse to leave. "Good night, Katherine. I'll see you in the morning."

"Good night, Nancy."

"Oh, I almost forgot. Some man called and asked to speak to Miss Mame. He said he was an old acquaintance. I told him she was already in bed. He was a very polite gentleman but wouldn't leave his name. He said he would call back."

"That's strange. No one ever calls Grandma. I wonder who it could have been?"

Katherine rolled and tumbled all night long. When she did drift off, she'd wake with the feeling of lips upon hers. She was very glad when her alarm clock went off and it was time to get up.

Tuesday was the last day of school. Graduation was not until the next night, and Katherine hoped Grandma would be having a good day so she could come. Stan had already said he'd bring Grandma if she were up for it.

That afternoon when Katherine got home, Stan was sitting with Grandma Mame. As Katherine entered her grandmother's bedroom, Stan looked up at her. Neither said anything, but their eyes locked and held. Something had changed between them.

Finally, Stan broke the silence. "How was your last day of school?"

"It was okay. I'm not sure why we even had to be there. All of our books were turned in a week ago. There wasn't anything for us to do today. After tomorrow night, there will be no more school worries. Really, I couldn't be happier. School has never been my favorite thing."

"Does that mean you're not going to at least enroll in community college?"

"I don't know." Katherine scowled. "I can't decide that now—there is too much going on."

"I see." Stan nodded thoughtfully. "How about I go grocery shopping and come back here and make us supper together? I make a mean dish of spaghetti."

Katherine was not expecting to spend another evening with Stan quite so soon, but the prospect surely did appeal to her.

"What do you say, Grandma? Should we let this guy make us supper?"

"Now wait a minute!" Stan put up his hands. "I'll need some help from both of you ladies."

Mame surprised them both by saying, "I think that it would be fine, Katherine. He seems like a sweet boy. Remember what I told you though, Katherine. Be careful."

Stan and Katherine left Mame's room in search of paper to make a grocery list.

"So, your grandmother has been warning you about me, huh?"

"No, actually she told me I had evil blood running through my veins, and for me not to deceive you. So I suppose you should be warned about me."

They both looked at each other and burst out laughing. Stan could not imagine one evil thing about Katherine. There was no predicting the things a patient like Miss Mame would do or say.

"Be right back," said Stan as he left with the shopping list.

That night was the happiest Katherine had ever spent in that house. She and Stan cooked and joked and laughed. Grandma Mame sat at the table, expressionless the whole time, but nevertheless with them. She even ate without constantly being told to take another bite. When she was finished, she got up and took her plate to the sink and started running dishwater.

"I believe all this laughter is good for Miss Mame," Stan said. "Is she humming?"

"Yes, I believe she is."

Then, right in the middle of washing a plate, she dropped it and completely shut down.

"Come on, Grandma. Let's get you ready for bed."

Katherine led her grandmother to the bathroom and then the bedroom, helping her change into her night clothes before helping her into bed. Then she tucked her in.

When Katherine got back to the kitchen, Stan was just finishing up the dishes.

He looked over his shoulder. "Do you towel dry them or just let them air dry?"

"Air dry usually, unless they won't all fit in the drainer."

"I believe they will. Here's the last pot."

Handing it to Katherine to rinse, their hands touched. Last night's kisses had been close to Katherine's mind all night. Just touching his hand made her heart flutter.

"Have you got it?" Stan asked.

"Yes, I've got it."

To break the tension, Stan asked, "What are your plans tomorrow?"

"Well, we have graduation rehearsal at ten a.m., and after that, I'll just come back here to be with Grandma until time to go to the real thing."

"What if I take you to lunch after rehearsal? Nancy will be here for Miss Mame."

"Okay, I guess. Where should I meet you?"

"Wait for me out front at school. I'll be there at noon."

When the dishes were done, Stan said he had to go. Katherine hoped the disappointment did not show on her face. She had wished for more samples of last night's kisses, but all she got was a peck on the cheek.

"See you at noon tomorrow. Bye, Katherine."

And, just like that, he was gone.

What did I do to run him off so quickly? Maybe he doesn't really like me after all. But, if he didn't, why did he ask me to lunch tomorrow?

Katherine shut and locked her bedroom door. It's just as well. Maybe I'll be able to get some sleep tonight. But again she rolled and tumbled.

Driving home, Stan was proud of himself. Sorry he had to leave, but knowing he just didn't trust himself to be alone with Katherine. If he didn't take it slow, he might scare her off.

Stan Matthews wanted anything but to take it slow with Katherine Paddington. He wanted her more than he had ever wanted anything in his whole life, but he respected her innocence.

CHAPTER FORTY-ONE

Therefore to him that knoweth to do good, and doeth it not, to him it is sin.

~ James 4:17

AT EXACTLY TWELVE O'CLOCK, STAN pulled up in front of Beckley High School. Katherine was watching for him just as they had planned.

"Hop in, kiddo. I've got a surprise for you."

"What kind of surprise?"

"I'm not telling you. You'll just have to wait and see," he said with a wink. "Just sit back and enjoy the ride."

Pulling out on the highway, Stan made several turns until finally he pulled into a narrow driveway. It curved through the woods a few hundred feet and then opened up into a field. There at the foot of the mountain stood a little yellow farmhouse. It was very small but immaculately kept. Katherine knew right away that this was Stan's house.

"You live here, don't you?"

"Now, how'd you ever guess that?"

"I don't know. It just looks like you."

"Looks like me? How can a house look like a person?"

"You know what I mean. Stop teasing me."

Katherine noticed that there were no other cars in front of the house. "Aren't your sisters home from college?"

"Yes, but they were going into town today, job hunting for summer work. They never have any trouble. They're each cute as a button, even if they are my sisters. They can waitress at any place in town and make loads of tips. They did last summer." Stan paused to get out of the car and come around to Katherine's door. "I told them they were going to have to help pay the bills, but of course I don't make them," he said as he helped her step out. "They're good kids, especially since they fixed us a picnic basket before they left."

They walked up to the porch with Stan still talking. "The girls' bedroom and bath are upstairs. Boy, how they fuss about not having their own rooms! Thank goodness I've got my own shower downstairs, or I'd never get a bath when they're home."

He held open the front door for Katherine. She saw that the inside of his house was just as clean and tidy as the outside. Inside the house didn't seem that small, especially with the partial second story. She noticed a photograph of a woman and picked it up.

"That's my mother," Stan said. "This was her family's home. She left each child equal shares in her will, and if any of us wants to sell the house, we have to sell to the others. . . . Mother loved this house . . . I do too."

Stan gazed around the room that was so full of happy memories. Katherine looked as well and noticed that the kitchen appliances were about as old as her grandmother's. The vinyl flooring was well worn but spotless. Sensing that Stan lived a similar, frugal life like hers, Katherine felt even more at ease with him. She knew he'd sacrificed much to keep his sisters in college.

"Come on. Let's go eat." From the hall table, Stan grabbed the loaded picnic basket, tossed Katherine a faded white and red log cabin quilt, and out they went. Not far from the house was a small meandering stream, and that's where Stan spread out the throw.

"Mother loved this place. After my stepfather left, she would come here and sit for hours. Sometimes she would read. Sometimes she would just stare. She said the sound of the water soothed her soul."

At that moment, a tiny hummingbird whizzed by. They saw it land on the bloom of a mountain laurel and start dipping its head up and down, drinking the sweet nectar. Then a rustling to the left drew their eyes to the edge of the woods from where the stream flowed. About the time they saw the young buck, antlers thick with velvet, he saw them. Unnerved by people being near his drinking hole, he made a blowing sound, stomped the ground, and quickly bounded away.

It certainly was a tranquil place, a beautiful hiding spot in the mountains. Katherine felt it was almost magical, as if a fairy might appear from behind a tree, or that a rock might speak. Katherine was giddy with happiness and the prospect of starting this new chapter of her life, one that might include a guy named Stan.

"Let's see what my darling sisters fixed for us."

Reaching into the basket, Stan pulled out a loaf of bread, a hunk of cheese, and some cold, leftover chicken from last night's dinner.

"It's a good thing I ate at your house last night, or there wouldn't have been any chicken left for today."

He must have a healthy appetite. Honestly, Katherine did not care what was in that basket. Just being here with Stan in this wonderful place was enough for her. She was almost too excited to eat, but eat she did. Between them, they drank a whole thermos of icy, sweet tea. They laughed and cut up until Stan reluctantly checked his watch.

"Oh, gosh. I've got to get going. I have another patient I've got to check on before I go see your grandmother." Katherine felt that the last thing Stan wanted to do was leave her company, but his responsibilities came first.

"Thank you for having lunch with me today," he said, kneeling and facing her.

"And thank you for having me."

Without even thinking, Katherine leaned forward and kissed Stan on the cheek. Her innocent action sent thrills through him. Before he could stop himself, he pulled Katherine toward him and kissed her soundly, just as he'd been wanting to all afternoon.

Suddenly Katherine stiffened as a flash back to the night Uncle Ben stood over her bed flooded her mind. She panicked and gasped.

"Oh, my goodness," Stan said, needing no explanation. "Katherine, I have scared you to death. I'm sorry. I'm so sorry for being so bold. Can you forgive me?"

He quickly moved aside. Katherine flushed with confusion. She scrambled to her feet. Hands shaking, she started picking up the leftovers.

Stan got up too. "I'm sorry I got carried away and kissed you. You are just so beautiful. Please, will you forgive me?"

Katherine slowly looked into his pleading eyes. "It's all right, Stan. You didn't scare me. I just remembered another situation that did. I—it's—oh, come on—you've got to get back to work."

Katherine helped Stan gather the picnic supplies. No, Stan had not totally scared her, but these new feelings did.

In front of Katherine's house, Stan got out and went to open the car door for her.

"Katherine, I really am sorry."

"It's okay. You don't have anything to be sorry for." She reached out and touched his hand. "I think I love you. Aren't you supposed to want to kiss the one you love?"

Stan was speechless. He was not expecting her confessions of love. Yet what did he expect? She was always direct and to the point. For a moment, all he could do was squeeze her hand.

"Yes, you are supposed to want to kiss the ones you love, but I'm afraid I've taken advantage of your innocence. I've moved much too quickly. Let's just slow down a bit. We've got the rest of our lives."

Leaning down, Stan kissed her lightly on the lips. "I'll pick you and your grandmother up at six o'clock."

Katherine went in the back door. Luckily, Nancy was in the living room watching television, so Katherine sat down at the kitchen table and put her head in her hands. She was almost shaking. Why did that awful vision of Ben pop into her mind? Stan was nothing like him. When she could find no answer, she decided that since she'd lost so much sleep the past few nights, she could use a nap. Yes, rest would surely do her a world of good.

Katherine walked into the living room. "Nancy, I can stay with Grandma today, so why don't you take the afternoon off?"

Nancy was concerned. "Are you sure you don't need me to help her get ready for your graduation?"

"No, thanks. I can manage. You probably could use a break."

After Nancy left, Katherine checked on Grandma Mame. She was sound asleep, snoring. Suddenly drained from all the emotion, Katherine went to her bedroom and closed the door. Falling in a heap on her soft bed. It was not long before she was sound asleep.

CHAPTER FORTY-TWO

Come, let us make our father drink wine, and we will lie with him . . .

~ Genesis 19:32

SHE KNEW HE WAS THERE before she opened her eyes. His evilness was palpable, even without his sour liquor odor. Quickly rolling over, Katherine reached for her knife. It was gone.

"Looking for this?" Uncle Ben laughed as he held up her blade. "Think I'm stupid enough to let you stab me again?"

He walked away from the bed, across the room, and laid the knife on top of the dresser. As he approached the bed, he pulled his shirttail out of his pants.

Katherine's gaze turned to every corner of her room, but she saw no escape. She had made no other plan, no other defense beyond her knife.

Oh, no. What can I do? I can't let him touch me.

She spoke through gritted teeth, "Get out of my room. Get out now."

"Now why would I do that? We've not had any fun yet. Old Uncle Ben's been waiting for this for a long while. Nothing's going to stop me this time. Besides, I hear you and Medicine Boy are getting pretty chummy. I saw him bring you home today. That sweet little kiss he gave you on the back porch steps made me realize if I was going to be your first, I'd better get a move on. I will be the first, won't I, Katie Girl? I better not be disappointed."

With swift, jerking motions Ben kicked his shoes off.

"What's wrong, little Katie Girl? Don't worry. I'll be gentle."

Katherine rolled as far away from him as she could. Her bed was positioned against the wall, so she was pinned into the corner.

"You better be good to me," he threatened, "or I'll just have to tell Mama about all our times together through the years."

"Together? Just times you've pawed at me like the dirty old man you are!" She sat up and clasped her arms around her knees, crouched tight against the wall. Her eyes scanned the room for a new weapon.

"Yeah, but she won't know who to believe, will she? Not in her state of mind. You know, I could tell her anything, and she wouldn't know any better."

Ben slowly approached the bed and put his knees on the edge, then reached for Katherine. First he pried her arms from around her knees. She wanted to scream, to cry out, but Grandma—sleeping or oblivious—would not hear her. Who would help her?

"Please. Don't do this," Katherine pleaded.

She slapped at him with both hands. Poking at his eyes . . . clawing with her nails, kicking him with her feet. But there was no stopping the crazed uncle. Ben reached for her again and again, yanking and turning her, tearing at her clothes.

Grunting from his efforts, Ben pulled Katherine to her feet. "Take your clothes off. All of them."

Katherine bolted for the bedroom door. Ben caught her by the leg, and she hit the floor with a loud thud.

"Where you going? We ain't done here, little lady." He bent down and ran his hand up her leg. Katherine tried to stand, kicking at the unwanted touch. She knew the knife lay right above her on the dresser. She had never been this scared in her life, but she was determined to get away.

"Okay, Uncle Ben, let me get back on the bed."

Calmly she rose, and then she grabbed for the stainless steel blade. As her fingers grazed the edge, a blow to her side sent her back to the floor.

"You're just a teasing little harlot."

One more time, Katherine pleaded. "Stop, leave me alone!" She struggled to get away from his assaulting hands.

"Be still, you little slut. You didn't push Medicine Boy away, did you?" he hissed.

Ben glared at the girl lying crumpled there at his feet. For a minute he went back in time . . . to Emily. Sweet, beautiful Emily, why was she fighting him now? Then another face came to mind, that silly young thing named Trudy.

Shaking his head to clear the visions from his mind, he hovered over Katherine. She swung her fists relentlessly, connecting them with any part of him they could find.

"Stop fighting me!" Trapping her wrists against the floor above her head, he had her pinned. With no other way to defend herself, she spit in his face. He stopped his assault for a second to wipe the saliva from his eye. Then without a word, he punched Katherine, the huge fist finding its mark at her temple.

Katherine swooned, but not before hearing the voice.

"Stop, Ben."

"Get out of here, old woman! We're busy."

Katherine tried to pull herself from the fog of the blow. Finally her vision cleared, and there she was . . . Grandma Mame. Then—in a tone neither of them had ever heard her use, she called to Ben.

"Benjamin Jared, stop it."

"I told you to get out of here."

"I'm not going anywhere. Don't you know? Can't you tell? Katherine is most likely your *daughter.*"

Katherine felt his grip loosen.

Uncle Ben jumped up. "Get out of here, you old hag. You don't know what you're talking about."

"I'm afraid I do. Remember, you told us what happened between you and Emily right after the honeymoon, the day Walt went back to work. The timing of Katherine's birth was perfect. Katherine could have come from Walt's seed, or yours."

"You stupid old woman, shut up!"

But the words of his mother had penetrated Ben's mind and made him wonder if what she said could be true. Barefooted, he grabbed his shirt and pushed past Mame, leaving the house with a loud slam of the back door.

Ben wondered why he had never considered this possibility. Katherine looked exactly like Walt, fair skin and all, but he was a twin, they had the same blood. One of his kids could easily look like his brother Walt. Ben's mind spun with the implications as he stumbled toward the barn. Why, he was no better than Lot from the Bible stories he remembered, sleeping with his own daughter. Bile rose in his throat.

For another icy moment, Mame stood watching Katherine. Then her eyes clouded, and she saw nothing but the past. She turned and deserted Katherine, who was huddled on the floor and near hysteria. As if from miles away, she heard Grandma Mame open and slam the front porch door.

Katherine pulled herself up to a sitting position and tried to control her shaking body. Finally she was able to stand. Noticing her shirt had been torn she lifted her robe from the nail on the back of her door. As she tugged it on, her grandmother's words tumbled over and over in her head: She could be your daughter—she could be—your daughter—your daughter.

What did it mean? Uncle Ben cannot be my father.

A loud knocking broke through her confusion. Dear God, please don't let it be him! Was he coming back?

Katherine had to hide. She tiptoed from her room, but not before picking up the knife. She stopped and listened at each corner, the blade positioned to strike. She kept going until she edged her way to the old kitchen pantry and stepped inside. She slumped to the floor, her thoughts running wild.

It's dark in here. I'm so scared. I know there are spiders in here. Still, I'd much rather face the biggest, blackest, scariest black widow in the world than to come out and face him again.

I'll never let Uncle Ben come near me again. Father or uncle, it doesn't matter! I'll kill him first.

The closet smelled bad, reminding Katherine of rotting vegetables and dried up spices. These aromas, mixed with the sooty smell of the old rock chimney that ran up one side of the closet, were almost more than she could stand. She swallowed the nausea rising in her throat.

Katherine leaned her head back on the wooden boards and closed her eyes. Her mind drifted back over her eighteen years, and some of her questions began to make sense.

Katherine's earliest memories were not of loving, cozy moments nestled in her mother's arms. In fact, she didn't remember her mother at all. She was told that her mother died when she was only six months old. Her father took her to Grandmother Mame's house only moments after the coffin was lowered into the hard West Virginia ground.

That day her father disappeared, never to be seen again.

Katherine seldom asked questions about her parents. The subject always upset Grandma Mame. She and her grandmother had led a good, simple life in the quiet coal mining town of Beckley.

But none of that mattered now. Katherine was never coming out of that pantry. A spider was nothing to face, compared to her Uncle Ben—or Daddy—which one was it?

CHAPTER FORTY-THREE

These things I have spoken unto you, that in me ye might have peace.
In the world ye shall have tribulation: but be of good cheer; I have
overcome the world.

~ John 16:33

CLINT PADDINGTON DROVE HIS CAR through the winding mountain roads through Beckley to the edge of Mary Blackwell's property, the place where Mame had grown up, that same house to which Mame had returned.

The house, outbuildings, and grounds looked nothing like he remembered, except for the acres of tobacco fields surrounding the house. The place had a deserted look about it, as if time or circumstance had mostly passed by this plot of land. He didn't know that most of the operation had been moved over to Mame's brothers' land where the new buying warehouse stood.

Up on the hill, Clint saw the family graveyard, and thoughts of Jared and Mary flooded his mind. They had all placed a mighty high wager when the Blackwells' destiny had crossed with the Paddingtons'. He couldn't blame all the wrongs on Mame. The Paddington family had started it with the mine explosion. How had things spiraled so out of control?

He opened his car door just in time to see a man run out from behind the house. This puzzled Clint and made him a little apprehensive, but undeterred from his goal, he walked toward the side of the house. Clint called out, but the man had disappeared into the barn. From this vantage point, Clint didn't see Mame leaving by the front door. Clint shook his head and went on toward the back of the house. With clammy hands, he took a deep breath before he knocked on the back door.

Katherine heard the continued knocking; she was still shut inside the pantry. Her heart pounded so fast she knew it would explode right out of her chest at any moment. She held her breath in the damp, tight space, willing the intrusion to stop. She had crouched in the corner so long her legs had begun to tingle, with pains shooting up and down her calves like she'd just run through a briar patch. She didn't dare move. She wanted to be invisible, to sink into the wood of the walls, to be nothing more than a remembered fragrance. What future could she ever dream to have under the constant threat of being molested by Uncle Ben? Daddy? Katherine shut down her thoughts, hugged her knees, and rocked.

Clint knocked and waited, knocked and waited. He had come a long way, and he would not easily give up. As he rounded the house to try the front door, he saw another man coming up the walkway. They saw each other at the same time, but Stan was the first to speak.

"May I help you?" Stan thought it was odd that a stranger should come from the back of the house.

"I don't know. I'm looking for Mary Margaret Paddington. Does she still live here?"

Stan recognized her proper name from Mame's medical records. "Yes, she does—she, her granddaughter, and son."

Clint felt his knees grow weak. The man he'd seen running must have been Ben, or could it have been Walt? No, this man had dark hair. After all this time of wondering if Ben had survived living with Jack Marsh, Ben was here, and Clint had seen him. Yet it did not sink in.

"Ben?" Clint asked.

"Yes, his name is Ben. He comes and goes around here." Stan wondered why he was talking to this stranger and telling him family information. For some reason he just felt comfortable with this kindly older gentleman.

"Miss Mame is inside," Stan continued. "I've come to pick up her and her granddaughter to take them to Katherine's high school graduation."

Clint's head throbbed. Granddaughter? All this time, wrong or not, he had thought of only his boys. Of course life had gone on, and it was only natural that he might have grandchildren. Just because Clint's family life ended for all practical purposes on the day he read Jack Marsh's letter, it did not mean everybody else's had.

Stan watched the older man and wondered if he was ill since he looked so pale. Kindly he said, "I hate to be rude, but why are you looking for Miss Mame?"

Clint was silent for a moment and then answered. "I'm Clint Paddington, her husband."

What awful timing. Stan was about to take Katherine to her high school graduation when, lo and behold, her long-lost grandpa shows up.

"Is she expecting you?"

"Well, no. I called the other night, but Mame had already retired. I didn't leave a message."

"I think you might want to talk to your granddaughter before you see Miss Mame. You see, she hasn't been well."

"What's wrong with her?"

"You'll have to talk to her family about that." Stan offered his hand. "I am Miss Mame's social worker, Stan Matthews."

They shook hands.

"Do you know where she is?" asked Clint.

"In the house. I'm supposed to pick them up at six o'clock."

"Nobody came to the door when I knocked."

"Katherine may have been getting ready, probably didn't hear you knock, and Miss Mame wouldn't have gone to the door even if she heard the knock."

Clint frowned at this news. "Why not? What's wrong with her?"

Stan avoided his question by walking to the door. "It would be best if you came back tomorrow. I don't think it would be wise to spring yourself on her tonight. She's got her granddaughter's graduation to attend."

Clint knew the young man was right. It was not fair to just pop in on her like he'd darted out all those years before.

Turning, he quietly called back, "thanks," and walked slowly toward his car. He could hear Stan knocking on the door, again with no one answering.

"Katherine. Katherine, are you in there? It's time to go!" Stan called.

Clint stood at his car, hoping to see his granddaughter appear, but she never came. He could feel the tension rising in the young man's voice as he called again. He even tried the doorknob, but it was locked. Stan then ran to the back door.

"Katherine, are you there? Open the door!" he said, pounding on the back door.

All kinds of thoughts went through Stan's mind. Some Alzheimer's patients got mean. What if? With that thought, he tried the doorknob, found it unlocked, and entered the kitchen.

"Katherine! Katherine, where are you?"

Stan looked in every room. There was no sign of her or Mame. Katherine's bedroom looked like a tornado had hit it; the lamp was on the floor, the bedding in disarray, and no blue graduation cap and gown in sight. Something was very wrong here.

Stan ran to the phone in the kitchen. Katherine could hear his movement all through the house. When she recognized Stan's voice, she felt relieved, but she still could not move. She was in shock. Not until she heard him on the phone could she make a move or a sound.

Weakly she said, "Stan?"

"Police station, may I help you?"

"Stan?" Katherine said.

He could have sworn he heard his name. Yes, there it was again.

"Stan?"

Stan slammed down the telephone and moved toward the sound of Katherine's muffled voice.

Again he heard her, but the sound seemed to come from behind a little door they used for a pantry. Baffled, he opened it. In the dark, Stan could not see her at first. Then his eyes focused toward the floor and he saw her huddled in a ball in the corner of the cabinet.

"Katherine! What in the world is wrong? Come out of there."

She shivered. "Is he gone?"

"Who?"

"Ben. Is he still here?"

"No, I haven't seen him."

Only when he had sworn that Ben was not there did she crawl out of the cramped pantry, head hung, trembling like a terrified puppy who'd just been pulled out of the river.

Katherine clutched fearfully at her robe with one hand while gripping the knife with the other; Stan knew something awful had happened.

"What happened? Are you hurt?"

She nodded. "Uncle Ben tried to force himself on me. He's tried before, but today he almost succeeded. Grandma Mame saved me."

Raising her head, Katherine looked straight into Stan's eyes. "Grandma said Ben might be my father. He can't be my father. He just can't!"

Concerned with all the commotion, Clint had walked back to the house and was waiting outside the back screen door, where he heard everything. He had no idea what was going on, except that Ben had tried to molest that young girl, his granddaughter.

Ben really is Jack Marsh's son? Like father, like son, Clint thought. Clint opened the screen door and stepped into the kitchen.

Katherine looked frantically from Stan to the familiar-looking stranger. Not taking the time to even ask who he was, Katherine started to panic.

"Grandma—where is Grandma?" She gripped Stan's sleeve. "I've got to find her. Is she in her bedroom? If she hadn't stopped him—oh it was awful."

Stan put his hands on her shoulders. "Katherine, your grandmother is not here. I've already searched every room while I was looking for you."

"What do you mean, she's not here? She can't be gone! She won't be able to find her way home. We've got to look for her."

Katherine looked down at her robe. She must find a new shirt.

"Mr. Paddington? I thought you were coming back tomorrow," Stan said growing impatient.

"What's wrong with Mame? Why won't she be able to find her way home?" Clint asked.

"Who are you anyway? What business do you have here?" Katherine said, agitated and anxious.

"I'm Clint Paddington, Mame's husband . . . and from what I've heard here today, your grandfather."

Katherine didn't look at all surprised as she stared at her grandfather.

"I thought I knew you. I'd recognize you anywhere. Grandma has described every detail of you to me a thousand times. Oh yes, you're my grandpa, all right. I don't know why you're here now, but I don't have time to get acquainted. I've got to find my grandma."

On unsteady legs, Katherine went to her room to shed the robe and find a shirt, the cold steel of the knife still clutched in her hand. She was in shock and now even more confused. Why in the world had Grandpa Clint shown up today? What about graduation? Where was her wicked uncle? She would have to think about all this later, no time now. Nothing was more important at this moment than finding Grandma Mame.

Glancing back at her disheveled room, Katherine shuddered at what had happened there just minutes before.

Clint called to Katherine as she moved toward the front door. "I'm going to help you find her. But, I'm puzzled. Why would she be lost? She's lived in this town almost all her life."

Katherine turned and snapped, "Listen, I don't know why you're here now, and I really don't care. All I know is you left Grandma many years ago and broke her heart, so it's none of your business what's wrong with her."

She flung open the back door and rushed out with Stan and Clint on her heels. Clint owed Katherine an explanation of what happened all those years ago, but now was not the time.

They separated and hunted the fields and riverbanks for almost an hour, meeting back at the driveway as agreed. No one had seen a trace of Mame.

"When Grandma first got sick, she went to the mine where her papa was killed. Maybe that's where she is," Katherine said.

Immediately all three jumped in Stan's old Galaxy. Katherine didn't question Clint going. Fate must have brought him there.

They pulled up in front of the mine gate. Kids had been sneaking up to the old mine to park, so a gate had been constructed to keep them out. Young people had no idea how dangerous an abandoned mine could be.

Katherine jumped out of the car and squeezed through an opening between the new gate and fence. Too large to pull themselves through, Stan and Clint had to climb over, dodging the barbed wire at the top. Katherine left them behind. In the distance, the men saw her kneeling at the mine entrance. Mame was lying beside her.

Again, Mame's fingers were bleeding from trying to dig her way into the boarded-up death pit.

Katherine dropped the knife she still held onto the black earth, and she lifted Mame's head into her lap and stroked her silver hair. "Grandma, it's all right. Let's go home."

Mame looked at her granddaughter.

"Katherine, are you all right? Ben didn't hurt you, did he?"

"No, Grandma. I'm okay. You came just in time. Thank you for saving me."

"I should have told you about him years ago, but I just couldn't let all those secrets out. I just couldn't. They are too awful. They need to be kept in the darkness. But I can't any more. It's time for them to be released so my tormented soul can be set free."

"Grandma, we've got to get you home and take care of those fingers."

"But I can't go and leave him here again. I've got to get him out and put him in a proper resting place." Then Mame twisted out of Katherine's lap and started digging, pulling at the boards like a madwoman.

Clint stood behind them. As he listened to Mame's voice, tears rolled down his cheeks. She was still mourning her dead father. It had finally driven her insane, and it was all his family's fault. His father's greed for money had caused all this. Everyone had paid the price. His father never forgave himself. *And then I took on his legacy. Look at me. I've lost everything—my love, my family, my life.*

Clint went to Mame and laid his hand on her shoulder. "Mame?"

She stopped her frantic pursuit to get into the mine but didn't move or turn around.

"Mame, it's me, Clint. Can you ever forgive me? I know my family caused your papa's death, but I had no idea it had affected you so badly. Let me help you, Mame. Let me help you forget. You can't get your father out of there. That terrible blast happened fifty years ago." Slowly Mame got to her knees and stood up. She faced her long ago husband. She did not say a word, but gently touched his cheek with her bloody hand. It was obvious to Clint that the years had etched rows of sorrow into Mame's face, but to him she was still the beautiful goddess from the waterfall. Time stopped.

Then she spoke. "Clint, I never thought I'd see you again. I don't deserve to see you again. You have nothing to be sorry for. It was all me. Everything has been my fault. I caused it all."

"No, Mame. My father gave the order all those years ago to open the mine back up. It was his fault."

"Clint, I know all of that. I've known it since before we were married. I heard you and Paddy talking one day. I have to admit I wanted revenge. I wanted you and Paddy to feel the pain I'd felt for all those years, knowing my papa was either blown up or had suffocated to death."

Mame swiped her forehead with the back of her hand, leaving a trail of black coal powder and blood.

"But that was no excuse for what I did with Jack Marsh. No excuse for the even worse things I've done since."

About that time, a huge army jet soared over their heads. Clint could see Mame's lips moving, but couldn't hear her words until the jet had passed.

"I deceived you so badly, I— "

"No. You don't have to tell me, Mame. I already know. Jack Marsh wrote me a letter. He told me everything. That was the day I left."

Katherine and Stan stood aside, listening and watching as some of the family mysteries unfolded in her grandparents' apologies. Her grandmother's crazy talk was beginning to make sense now to both of them.

"Let's get you back to the house, Mame. Your hands are hurt," Clint said.

"No, you don't understand. I've got to get him out. It must all be over today. This is the end."

"Listen to me, Mame. Henry Blackwell is in his final resting place. You wouldn't want to disturb him. After all, they searched for his body for days after the explosion. What makes you think you can find him?"

"I know exactly where he is. I helped Ben carry him here after he killed him."

Oh, dear heavens. She was worse than Clint thought. She had really lost her mind.

"No, Mame. That's impossible. Ben wasn't even born when Henry died in there."

"It's not my papa. Don't you understand? It's *Walt.*"

Katherine's knees began to buckle, but Stan braced her up. This day was just too much. What did her grandmother mean? Katherine had always been told her daddy "ran off" after her mother died. Grandma must be delusional again.

"Grandma, we've got to get you back to the house," Katherine said. "It's past time for your medicine. That's why you're saying all this crazy stuff."

Mame shook her head. "Katherine, the time has come for you to know the truth about what happened to your mama and daddy. You're old enough to understand, and I just pray to God you won't hate me."

So there in front of the old mine where the evil began, Mame slumped onto the coal-sodden ground. Clint squatted on the coal dust beside her. Stan pulled out a roll of gauze from his pocket, wrapped up Mame's torn fingers, and sat on her other side.

Katherine sank to her knees. Even Stan couldn't guard her any longer. Everything seemed to be happening in slow motion.

For some odd reason, Katherine asked Stan the time. Eight-fifteen. Right now she should be walking across the stage in the gym, getting her diploma. But instead, from her grandmother she was learning the greatest lesson she would ever learn: deceit, anger, and vengeance, and the way they destroy everyone and everything they touch.

Mame began her story. "Years ago, I was naïve. I put myself in a position to be molested by an evil man named Jack Marsh, not on purpose, but ultimately it was my fault. He was Walt and Ben's father. You see, I wanted out of Beckley. I wanted revenge and to live in the Paddington house with their money in Charleston. The only way my young mind could think to do that was to trap Clint into thinking he should marry me. Since his good manners prevented him from touching me again after our close day at the waterfall, I went looking for him at the tavern to try seducing him again." She pressed her thin lips together. "I got what I deserved that night. Marsh singled me out at the tavern. I prayed I'd never see him again after that. For years, I thought he was truly gone, but then one day, right here in Beckley on the day of my mother's funeral, I saw him. I didn't think he had seen me, but he had. Later that night, he attacked me on my way back to Charleston. He left me in the woods for dead, and he stole Ben.

"Walt was home with Clint, or Marsh would have probably taken him too. I don't believe he ever knew Walt existed, so Ben must not have talked about him. I couldn't tell Clint the truth, and that devil

Marsh raised Ben. So you see, Ben can't really be blamed for the way he turned out. It was all my fault."

Mame was unusually clear-headed, and her voice didn't falter as she continued. "One day when you were about six months old, Katherine, I was at your mama and daddy's house watching you while they were at the doctor. Your mother was pregnant again and having a real hard time. Ben walked into the house. I hadn't seen him in over ten years. He cussed and hollered at me for letting Jack Marsh take him, and for not loving him like I had loved Walt. Then he looked at you and saw those beautiful blue eyes of yours. Eyes that look exactly like Walt's. He started laughing like he was insane. He told me he bedded your mother Emily just days after she and Walt were married.

"We didn't know it, but Emily and Walt had returned home while Ben was carrying on. They had heard it all, and Emily's secret was out. She passed out cold, and when she fell, she hit her stomach. The doctor tried his best to control the bleeding and prevent the miscarriage of their second child, but the blood would not stop. Emily never regained consciousness and soon died. Walt never got to hear her side of the story, but Emily had confided in me, so I knew everything Ben had said was true. Lust is a very powerful need. Walt didn't believe Ben and never left your mother's side for those three days she lay bleeding to death. Thank goodness you were old enough to wean to a bottle."

Katherine's head was about to explode. Why did she have to know all this? But she couldn't stop listening now. She had to know the rest.

"Go on, Grandmother. What happened to Daddy—Walt?"

"That day after Ben had said those things, with the damage done to your mother—with Emily dying—Ben fled. We laid her to rest on the hill behind the house in the Blackwell cemetery. I can still hear Walt's words as we left the gravesite: *I'm going to find him and when I do, I'm going to kill him.*

"Walt did find Ben that same night at a bar in town. They had a terrible fight, but Ben fled. Walt went after him. They ended up in the backyard at my house. Just as I heard the commotion, I went to the door. I switched on the light just in time to see Ben hit Walt in the head with a shovel. I'll never forget that sound. Without going to him, I knew he was dead. The cold steel had split open his skull.

"What he'd done really didn't seem to affect Ben. Walt probably wasn't the first person he'd killed—or seen murdered by Jack Marsh. Just like Cain and Abel, that's what it was. Curse on us all.

"Ben said to me, *'what are you staring at old woman? Yeah, your precious boy is dead. That's what you both get for always leaving me high and dry. Now help me get rid of him. I'm not going to jail because of him. You know you owe me. Help me get rid of him, and we'll call it even. I'll leave, and you'll never have to see me again.'*

"Ben was right. I did owe him, but I didn't know if I could do what he was asking. If I helped him hide Walt's body, would it undo all the wrong I'd done to him? Would it even things out? I didn't know, but I went into the house and put you in the playpen, got some sheets to wrap Walt in, and locked the door behind me as I left you inside alone."

Mame continued to look at Katherine.

"I knew it wasn't safe to leave you, but I didn't have a choice. Folding Walt's crumpled body into the trunk of Ben's new Lincoln, we made our way to this very mine shaft. We threw him down a deep, dark hole. I know the exact spot.

"Ben drove me back to the house. I got out, went inside, and he drove away. I never saw or heard from him again until the day he walked into the kitchen on your birthday. You know the rest."

What a story, Stan thought. Miss Mame had really flipped. He stood and held a hand out to Katherine. "Come on, folks. We need to get back to the house and call the police so they can pick up Ben for attempted rape."

"No." Katherine put her hand in Stan's and let him pull her up from the ground. "No one can know about that. What would people think of me if they knew? I don't want anyone's pity. But we do need to call the police so they can get Ben for murdering my father."

Stan's eyebrows shot up. "You don't believe that story, do you, Katherine?"

"It's all true. I know it is." She crossed her arms and hugged herself "I've lived with Grandma all my life and seen all her strange moods— all those times I would find her crying at the table in the middle of the night. It all makes sense now."

Clint helped Mame to her feet and put his arms around her. She leaned back, looked up into his face, and spoke softly, "There's one more thing. Then everything will be out in the open. Right here in these coal mine shadows, all my secrets will be revealed. The shadows have won."

"What else, Mame?"

"I think I killed the baby. Sometimes it's all so fuzzy I can't determine the truth from the lies. I do know that I couldn't look at Daniel without seeing Jack Marsh. I know you'll leave me again after hearing this, but before you go, I just want you to know I have always loved you. I always will."

Mame expected Clint to push her away, but instead, he lowered his head to hers and gently kissed her.

"I love you too, Mame."

Looking over at his granddaughter, Clint saw tears streaming down her face. So much for her young mind to absorb. Then he noticed the dried blood in her hair. He reached out to push back the matted curl to look for the wound, realizing she must have struck her head when Ben was after her. Then he saw it—and gasped.

"No, it can't be. Surely my eyes deceive me."

"Mr. Paddington, what is it? What's wrong?" Stan said, trying to see Katherine's injury.

Memories from long ago came rushing back. Clint sat in his mother's lap while she rocked and stroked his head. Tracing her finger over the purple spot behind his right ear, somewhere from far away, Clint could hear her voice, saying, "You've got the Carter mark, just like my daddy, and his daddy before him."

"The Carter birthmark. Why didn't I think of that before?" He turned the young woman to face him. "Katherine, you are my granddaughter! You have the same mark as all my mother's ancestors. I guess since Walt and Ben were born with full heads of hair, I never thought of checking for a birthmark, and I never looked close enough at Daniel to even know what color his eyes were, and now it's too late." He shook his head sorrowfully. "How could I have forgotten about the Carter brand?"

Mame lowered herself to sit in silence on the ground. Then she raised her head and looked up into Clint's face. "You never told me. Let me see yours."

Clint knelt down and pushed his hair back, remembering well the spot his mother stroked.

Mame reached out to touch it. "Walt and Daniel had the same mark . . . Ben doesn't. If only I had known. Twins can have two different fathers!"

Mary Margaret Blackwell Paddington never spoke another word. She slipped away, far off somewhere beyond the mines, the tobacco, the birth marks, and the rolling hills. But this time, she was not tormented.

Her mind drifted back to her childhood, to the creek behind the homeplace. She could feel the cool water as it washed over her. She could see her papa's face as she came up out of the water. She felt the power of forgiveness. Mame was finally at peace.

CHAPTER FORTY-FOUR

And the dragon was wroth with the woman, and went to make war
with the remnant of her seed, which keep the commandments of God,
and have the testimony of Jesus Christ.

~ Revelation 12:17

AFTER TWO DAYS OF SEARCHING the mine, the Beckley Fire and
Rescue found Walt Paddington's bones. Dental records proved it to
be him. Clint arranged for Walt's remains to be transferred up on the
hill to a plot in the Blackwell family cemetery.

The Blackwell name was plastered all over the *Beckley Weekly News*.
It would be a long time before their secrets were not the main topic
of every nearby household. The public never knew the half of it, only
a few truths, and the rest was exaggerated.

Mame's medical history spoke for itself. She was so demented
that the detectives gave up trying to get a statement from her after
a few tries. A silent tongue and faraway look were all they ever got
from Mame Blackwell Paddington.

Katherine, Stan, and Clint never told the police about Mame's
involvement in Walt's death. No evidence existed to incriminate her.

Clint never told anyone about the presumed truth of how baby
Daniel might have died. Whether Mame was responsible or not, the

deed was done, and Mame had punished herself enough. No sentence could have been as cruel as the torment she placed on herself.

The police tracked down Ben Paddington in South Carolina. Not only was he arrested for Walt's murder but he was also found to be a major drug runner, thus explaining to Katherine why he was always gone for weeks at a time, kept a new car, and had plenty of money.

Stan held Katherine's hand as they walked back to the house after a much belated graveside service for Walt.

"Deep down, I knew Ben could not be my daddy." Katherine glanced back over her shoulder. "My real father never left me, and now he rests up on that hill."

Katherine received her diploma in person from the high school principal. She never once complained about anything she had missed or the things that might have been.

Clint stayed in Beckley. He patiently helped take care of Mame until he succumbed to his disease a year later. After he died, Mame refused to eat another bite.

In the short time they had together, Katherine grew to love her grandfather. So much had happened to him and her grandmother. She couldn't hate either one of them.

Clint was so good to Grandma Mame. To pass the time, he would sit and read to her for hours, or they would just hold hands in silence. It didn't seem to matter that Mame never spoke to Clint. They didn't need words.

The sweet bond of love they had for one another was good for Katherine to witness. She saw that true love could weather any kind of torture. Murder, deceit, lies, the devil . . .

Two weeks after Clint passed away, Mame was laid to rest beside him up on the hill behind the Blackwell house. Rain threatened while the preacher prayed, and the thunder and lightning cracked and streaked over the mountain as it quickly approached the mourners who huddled under their black umbrellas.

Was the God of good fighting the god of evil for Mame's soul? Did she deserve to be saved? Do any of us?

Tobacco fields set in new seedlings surrounded the funeral party. Mary Blackwell and her determination to survive paid off in monetary value, but had the sacrifices been worth it?

A few weeks later, up on that craggy hillside, Katherine stood reflecting on the Blackwells' good and bad fortune. She embraced her life, reeling but not faint. She would not forget the secrets that shaped and formed her family for so many years. Looking up over the great mountain range, she saw a lone bolt of lightning flash above the treetops. A few seconds later, the thunder rumbled yet again.

Stan stepped forward to take Katherine's hand, and together they ran back to the house just as the clouds opened, bringing nourishment to the tobacco fields.

From somewhere farther away, deep down in the core of the mountain, Mame's never-ending prayer echoed:

God, please bless Katherine. All my lies are now out in the open. Forgiveness has been asked, forgiveness given. There are no more shadows to follow Katherine. I now rest in peace, knowing my sins have been cast as far as the east is from the west.

The rain poured down harder, and the lightning struck more fiercely. God knew better. He knew who was coming.

"Be sober, be vigilant; because your adversary the devil, as a roaring lion, walketh about, seeking whom he may devour" (1 Peter 5:8).

CHAPTER FORTY-FIVE

For we wrestle not against flesh and blood, but against principalities, against powers, against the rulers of the darkness of this world, against spiritual wickedness in high places.

~ Ephesians 6:12

BEN PADDINGTON'S TRIAL FOR THE murder of his twin made national news.

In Charleston, Trudy Bauguess sat in front of her television. Her eyes widened in recognition even before his name popped up on the screen.

"Benny! Hurry! Come look at this. I've finally found him."

A younger image of Ben Paddington entered the room.

"Look, Benny. There's your daddy. They said his last name is Paddington. He told me it was Marsh. That's why I couldn't find him."

Benny Bauguess looked at the TV screen as the camera zoomed in on the man's face. No doubt it was his father. They looked almost alike—same rugged darkness, same hard eyes. It was like looking into a mirror and seeing his future self.

"So, that's the buzzard who knocked you up when you were fifteen?" He had heard the story a million times.

"Almost sixteen. Yeah, that's him. He's to blame for the awful way our lives have turned out."

Trudy's father had kicked her out the day she told him she was pregnant. For the past twenty years, she had struggled, doing whatever was necessary to feed herself and her son.

Looking for Ben became her obsession. Every extra dime she made was spent on the search. Her need to find him had overflowed on to and fully pricked Benny. He scoured the South for his father, never settling down. His only goal in life was to find his sorry excuse for a daddy. And there he was: Benjamin Jared Paddington.

"Where do you think he's been all these years? Reckon he's got a wife and more young'uns? I guess I'll just have to pay him a visit at that prison."

The newscaster went on to say that Ben Paddington was related to the Blackwells who owned and operated Blackwell Tobacco Company in West Virginia.

Benny laughed, his eyes dancing with the same fiery evil that rousted and bent his father and grandfather. His mind began forming and plotting a plan. Surely these fine Blackwells would want to take care of their poor deserted nephew.

Benny felt a confidence he'd never felt before. He let out a whoop and stomped his scuffed boots on the creaky floor.

"We're headed to Beckley, West Virginia, Mama."

Benny picked his mama up and swung her around till they both fell down laughing.

"But should we go to the prison and meet your daddy first?" Trudy asked.

Cocking his head in thought, Benny then said, "Let's go see dear old Dad. I want to thank him in person for showing us where our rich relatives live."

At that moment, on the final resting grounds of the Blackwell homestead, a barely noticeable tremor shook the headstone of Mame Blackwell Paddington. It was as if her spirit heard the threats of Benny Bauguess, and her dead bones began to rattle.

Thoroughly pleased with his plan, Benny let out a loud cackle, setting off a quiver beneath the hill behind the Blackwell house. The mountain swelled and shuddered; the quake would be felt for many miles around.

It was as though Mame might try to escape the mound of West Virginia soil and stop the evil. Another of Jack Marsh's descendants' seed was about to make its ill-suited entrance into the Blackwells' future.

Some might say it was just the fault line making a natural fine-tuning, or some would say that children do inherit the sins of their fathers. Would Mame's sin follow her even beyond the grave?

"The fathers shall not be put to death for the children, neither shall the children be put to death for the fathers: every man shall be put to death for his own sin" (Deuteronomy 24:16).

The mountain lets forth another tremor; a violent shift of the earth pushed forth mounds of earth. Was the mountain trying to spit up every single coal miner who had ever surrendered his life to the depths?

All the souls who had been swallowed up by the dark pits moaned and wailed, begging for release. The mountain continued to shudder, tottering from the quake. A dark, dismal shroud fell over Mary Blackwell's old house. Katherine, sitting inside, didn't notice as the coal mine shadows engulfed her in a faint mist of gray.

Cousin Benny is coming.

Heteropaternal superfecundation: The ability to produce fraternal twins by different fathers. Dr. John Archer recorded the first medical case study in 1910. Since 1978, sophisticated human leukocyte antigen testing made this condition easier to prove.

For more information about

Sarah Martin Byrd
and
In the Coal Mine Shadows
please visit:

www.sarahmartinbyrd.com
www.facebook.com/SarahMartinByrd
www.twitter.com/SarahMartinByrd
www.SarahMartinByrd.com/blog

For more information about
AMBASSADOR INTERNATIONAL
please visit:

www.ambassador-international.com
@AmbassadorIntl
www.facebook.com/AmbassadorIntl

*If you enjoyed this book, please consider leaving us a review on
Amazon, Goodreads, or our website.*